ON THESE
SILKEN SHEETS

ON THESE SILKEN SHEETS

Sabrina Darby

AVON

An Imprint of HarperCollins*Publishers*

ON THESE SILKEN SHEETS. Copyright © 2009 by Sabrina Darby. All rights reserved. Printed in the United States of America. No part of this book may be used or reproduced in any manner whatsoever without written permission except in the case of brief quotations embodied in critical articles and reviews. For information address HarperCollins Publishers, 10 East 53rd Street, New York, NY 10022.

HarperCollins books may be purchased for educational, business, or sales promotional use. For information please write: Special Markets Department, HarperCollins Publishers, 10 East 53rd Street, New York, NY 10022

FIRST AVON PAPERBACK EDITION PUBLISHED 2009.

Designed by Rhea Braunstein

Library of Congress Cataloging-in-Publication Data
Darby, Sabrina.
    On these silken sheets / Sabrina Darby. — 1st Avon pbk. ed.
        p. cm.
    ISBN 978-0-06-178028-8
    I. Title.
    PS3604.A7245O6   2009
    813'.6—dc22

                                                          2009012861

09 10 11 12 13 OV/RRD   10 9 8 7 6 5 4 3 2 1

To my amazing beta-reader sister . . .
and to my husband. I never wrote erotic romance before you.

ON THESE
SILKEN SHEETS

PART I

Against the Wall

Chapter One

Some things never change, Carolina thought as she pressed up against the wall of the library, obscured by shadows and long, voluminous draperies. She might be eighteen, in London, and at her first ball ever, but she was still stuck in the ignoble position of watching Henry Bosworth make love to another woman merely ten feet from where she hid.

He was older, of course. The mouth that now kissed the unknown woman's neck was that of a man and no longer a youth. And just as she had six years ago, watching his well-formed hands clutching a round bottom through layers of clothing, she imagined those hands on her.

A pause in the lady's moans drew Carolina's gaze upward. With a silent gasp, she flattened herself further against the unyielding wall.

Bosworth stared straight at her, a small smile curving his lips. Though the light in the room was dim, she knew his eyes would be green, that murky green that reminded her of marshes and ancient deities.

He murmured something to the woman in his arms and the lady laughed, her bejeweled fingers *tsk*ing at him, even as she broke away. He followed her to the door, kissing her yet again, and then closed it behind her.

Carolina heard the faint but clear click of the lock.

Dear Lord, why had she decided to find a moment of privacy?

That thought fled as she wondered if he would recognize her. She must look vastly different, all those awkward angles having given way to a fuller, more proportionate body.

She didn't, couldn't, move as Bosworth approached. She merely watched in appreciation, with baited breath, as this taller, more muscular version of him prowled across the room, peeling his gloves off as he came. His black hair glinted in the dim light. His breeches fit him as if molded to his frame, and she could see the distinct outline of his male part.

Would that part, too, have grown with age? she wondered, unconsciously licking her lips.

Now he was inches from her. She could smell him. She remembered that scent, of sandalwood and other spices—the sort of spices that permeated one's skin and lingered in one's mind long after the source was gone.

He extended one arm, resting his hand against the wall, close to her head. His other hand touched her cheek, one long finger running along her jaw.

She knew she should be frightened. She knew she should protest and run away, and indeed, she was terrified. Because his hand felt too good on her skin.

She stared at his sleeve, at the display of sartorial skill so close to her face.

"You like to watch," Bosworth stated, his voice low, gravelly, as if he had spent the last six years smoking cigars. And maybe he had. She knew nothing of him but that he'd been a friend of her father's back then—a guest stopping at their country house for the night.

She didn't answer, couldn't. But she dragged her eyes to his. She shivered as he trailed his finger down her neck, across the bare skin of her chest and finally dipped down into the ruffles of her dress, skimming the hollow between her breasts.

Abruptly his hand left her.

"I'd wager you're dripping wet," he murmured.

As if his words were magic, she felt the hot rush between her legs, the familiar aching heaviness.

In her single bed at night, it had always been him she had seen and imagined while her hands explored her body and brought her to ecstasy. In fact, the night six years ago that she had watched him between the downstairs maid's plump white thighs, arcing into her again and again, was the first night Carolina had thought about her own body that way—the first night her fingers had experimented.

His hand grasped her dress, lifting layers of cloth to bunch up between them. She opened her mouth to speak, to tell him to stop, but his bare hand was already above her stockings, on the naked flesh of her thigh, and moving upward.

He cupped her in his palm, his thumb brushing over the slight protrusion where all the sensations seemed to clump. Then he slid one long finger through the slick folds and entered her.

She moaned, her head turning toward his outstretched arm, even as her knees buckled.

His hand felt so much better than hers ever had.

"Molten velvet," Bosworth rasped, his hot, open mouth meeting the tender flesh of her ear, nibbling, his tongue creating pinpoints of acute pleasure.

He started to withdraw the hand between her legs and suddenly Carolina found her voice.

"Wait, I'm almost there," she begged, feeling the tight spiral of pleasure nearing its peak.

He laughed against her.

"I like a woman who knows what she wants," he said, keeping his hand between her legs. His fingers stroked, working their magic until she finally exploded against him, shivering and bucking on his hand.

Henry shifted, reaching down to hold her up beneath her derriere. He hiked one of her silken legs around his waist and finally freed himself from the constraints of his breeches. The woman in his hands was still shivering with her own climax and his cock pulsed in empathy. He wanted nothing more in the world than to bury himself in her hot, wet depths.

His cock knew its way, unerringly finding the exquisitely

yielding entrance. He thrust upward into her, reveling in the tightness.

God, she was small—a hot, wet glove stretching to fit him. The friction felt incredible. He groaned against her neck and grasped her buttocks with both hands. He pulled her down, even as he made a powerful thrust upward.

She cried out, stiffening against him in a way that had little to do with pleasure. For a moment, caught between the delicious feel of being buried to the hilt in her tight sheath and the shock of his discovery, he stilled.

"Please," she whispered, her breath ragged. He didn't know whether she begged him to stop or to continue.

He would never have guessed, never have imagined, that the stranger in his arms, who so passionately and willingly accepted his caresses in a library that belonged to neither of them, was a virgin.

Had been a virgin.

But that didn't matter anymore. What was done was done, and his body yearned for its own completion.

"It won't hurt the next time," he whispered, even as he retreated and then thrust again, following the instincts of his body. Letting go.

She smelled like honeysuckle, like lush, verdant summer, and he lost himself in the feel of her clenched around him. Tight as he thrust in. Tight and clinging as he pulled back and then sunk in once more. His mouth open in a guttural cry against her neck, he released himself inside her, his mind completely empty of anything but the overwhelming pleasure of the moment.

The storm passed. With a final shudder, Henry eased out of her body. He slowly released her leg and then took a half step back. She slumped against the wall, a look of shock on her face, and he laughed.

She might well be shocked. She'd just given a girl's most precious commodity to a stranger up against a wall.

"Who are you?" he wondered aloud. "No, wait," he said, when she parted her lips, "I don't want to know."

No, he thought, taking another step back. He would keep this as he had intended, a momentary affair. He had no wish for a wife, especially one he had only vetted sexually.

He looked down to button up the falls of his breeches, and even in the dim light, the reddish tint of her blood caught his eye. He extracted his handkerchief from its pocket and tidied himself up.

She hadn't moved. Still stood there, frozen.

He sighed and lifted her skirts once more. Her hand fluttered down to protest and he laughed again at that futile gesture.

There wasn't much blood on her thighs but what was there, he wiped away gently, unable to resist a few soft caresses, enjoying her shivering response.

"I recommend a trip to the retiring room to further clean yourself up," Henry suggested, dropping her skirts and coming to his feet.

The woman nodded but she still didn't move.

"I'll leave first," Henry said into the silence. "Wait a few and then you can follow."

The door closed behind him and Carolina finally shifted, her hand stealing down to the juncture of her thighs, pressing through the layers of cloth to the still pulsing mound. Inside, she was sore.

Henry Bosworth had just . . . had just had *relations* with her. And dear Lord, he didn't even know who she was!

Chapter Two

Henry stepped into the noise of the ballroom in a bit of a drunken stupor. Not that he'd had a drink, but he was fully sated and enjoying the post-coital languor. When he'd entered the library with Lady Islington, the assignation had been a bit of friendly flirtation—a momentary passion. He'd wanted a woman and that woman was willing.

But the lady he'd had instead—just thinking of the feel of her thighs in his hands stiffened his cock.

He almost turned around, thinking to stop her before she left the library, to have another go at her. But that was foolish. If he was caught with that erstwhile virgin he'd have to marry her. He'd done enough damage for one night.

What lovely damage.

The ballroom was cramped, crowded with people, many of whom he knew well. Since he'd inherited the title, most of them wanted to know him better.

The goddamned title.

As if reading the direction of his thoughts he heard a voice out of his past.

"Bosworth!" Nobody called him Bosworth anymore. Society much preferred Stanton, Viscount Stanton. It had taken Henry four years to get used to thinking of himself—not his older brother, James—as Stanton. James had been the viscount for most of Henry's life.

And now Henry was.

He swung around to meet the man who greeted him, recognizing him instantly. He hadn't seen Lord Hargreaves in four years. Not since Henry had retreated to his country seat to put his brother's affairs in order. Though Hargreaves was a good decade older, much of Henry's misspent youth had been in his company. In fact, his misspent youth was in a great part *due* to Hargreaves's influence.

"I haven't seen you in ages, boy!" Alistair Hargreaves appeared pleased to see him. The old satyr still looked strong and virile, despite his dissipation. His blond hair had started to turn gray, but only just. "But you're not Bosworth anymore. Congratulations on your inheritance."

Henry knew why Alistair congratulated him, because it meant Henry had money. When Henry had followed Alistair around

London in the past, he had ridden the man's coattails. His own brother, James, had refused to finance his town life. Henry, himself, felt ambivalent about his brother's death.

"It's fortuitous to see you. I'm stuck attending these events for the season."

Henry arched an eyebrow up in inquiry but his eyes drifted toward the hallway door. He wanted another glimpse of the woman he'd fucked. He wanted to see what she looked like under the brighter lights of the illuminated ballroom.

"Did you ever meet my daughter, Carolina?"

Carolina. The name conjured up a vague image of a young girl, small for her age. He'd thought she was much younger than the twelve her father insisted on. And then, a memory he'd forced out of his mind from sheer embarrassment came crashing back.

Twenty-two and always randy, he'd been stopping with Alistair at the man's country house on the way to a house party. He'd plowed a receptive maid in the library, on a large leather-topped desk. Just as he released himself into her, arching back, he'd opened his eyes and looked up.

From the shadows of the carved wooden landing, the large, curious blue eyes of Alistair's twelve-year-old daughter looked down at him. She'd watched the whole episode.

Just like what had happened this evening. Eerily similar. A shiver of apprehension ran down Henry's back.

He nodded slowly.

"Well, she's eighteen now, so I had to bring her to London for her season. This is her first ball."

Henry heard the words, but he'd caught sight of a pale face under the archway. In the soft glow of the candlelight, she was even lovelier. He could also see just how young she was. Clearly not the experienced woman he'd first imagined.

Across the room, her eyes met his and widened. She grew even paler, and Henry felt the blood leave his own face.

Alistair followed his gaze.

"I see you recognize her." The baron's words chilled Henry's heart, confirming his worst suspicion. "She's grown up quite well. But she looks ill." An angry note entered Alistair's voice. "I do hope she isn't one of these frail girls. That won't do for marrying her off."

"She looks lovely, Hargreaves," Henry murmured, watching Carolina hesitantly approach them.

Something in Henry's voice must have alerted Alistair, because the baron glanced at him sharply.

"Stay away from her, Stanton," Alistair warned. "She's my daughter and an innocent."

"But of course," Henry agreed, laughing. And he thought once more of the feel of her wrapped around him, pulsing and wet.

Carolina reached them, a fluttering butterfly, her eyes darting from him to her father and then back to him. She'd managed to freshen her appearance and he imagined that only he would see the slight creases he'd created in her skirt when he'd bunched the fabric tightly in his hand.

"My dear, this is Lord Stanton." Henry watched surprise flicker in her blue eyes. "You've met before. Of course, he was merely Bosworth then."

"It is a delight to renew our acquaintance, Miss Hargreaves," Henry said, smiling and bowing over her hand.

"A pleasure," Carolina managed. "Father, I'm feeling a bit—"

"I would love nothing more than the pleasure of this dance," Henry cut her off, ignoring Alistair's frown and Carolina's slight shake of her head.

He didn't wait for an answer from either of them, just took her arm in his own and navigated her toward the dance floor.

"You *do* like to watch," he whispered, escorting her through the crowd.

He felt, more than saw, her flush.

"I didn't." Her protestation faltered as she took her place in the dance.

He saved his conversation for when the steps brought them close together.

"For the last twenty minutes, I've done nothing but think

about you, about how it felt to thrust into you and feel you clench me tight."

They broke away again, and he had the benefit of seeing the effect his words had on her.

"I want you again."

Chapter Three

Carolina was grateful that her governess had forced her to repeat the dance steps incessantly. If the moves had not been ingrained in her body, she was certain she would have stumbled and ruined the dance.

Bosworth's words resonated through her body.

"I want you again."

Hadn't he said it wouldn't hurt the next time? She wanted to know the pleasure. She shook her head slightly, trying to banish the thoughts. This was absolutely ridiculous. She'd already compromised herself completely and now she was thinking of continuing to act wantonly, disregarding all society's mores.

Who would want to marry her now?

That thought fled as quickly as it had come for she didn't really care. She knew that no matter what she wanted, she was only in town to be shown off, that her father would make the negotiations, pick a husband without any consultation.

And here, dancing with her, was the man who had captured her imagination all those years ago, who had actually possessed her just minutes ago.

She wanted him, too.

Six years ago, after he'd spotted her watching, he'd slid off the maid and dismissed the woman with a sensual pat on the rump.

Carolina had looked curiously at the then much smaller man-hood he hid away in his breeches. The mystery of the biology had fascinated her.

But then he'd hooked his finger and beckoned for her to come down and she had. There in the library, after the most fascinating visual lesson she'd ever had, in a room that smelled of sex, she got to know and fall in love with Henry Bosworth.

Stanton, she reminded herself firmly. She must call him Stanton now.

The dance ended.

He took her arm in his and even that slight contact made her dizzy.

"Meet me . . ."

He didn't finish his sentence. Her father had come forward to join them, his arm extended to take Carolina away.

"She looks a bit overwrought for her first night," Alistair said firmly. "But later I'll be at that club we used to frequent, if you're of the mind for it."

That club. More of a house of sin, where every hour of the night was an exercise in excess. Not a bad way to spend an evening, or a thousand evenings as Henry had. As Henry and Alistair had together.

He'd shared more women with the man than he could count. Now he'd had the man's daughter, too.

The baron had warned him off a good half hour too late. Alistair should have hung a sign around the girl's neck proclaiming her identity.

Or maybe even that wouldn't have stopped Henry from stalking her across the room and ascertaining if indeed she was as aroused by watching as he'd guessed.

He studied their figures disappearing into the crowd in the direction of the entryway. Carolina's skirt swayed with each step, clinging ever so subtly now to the left side of her derriere and now to the right. Henry was as hard as a rock.

He thought briefly about finding Lady Islington and finishing off where they had started. *No.* The club would do well enough.

Chapter Four

An hour later, Henry stepped into the dimly lit warren of rooms that made up Harridan House. The name itself was a joke, enticing a man to leave his harridan of a wife at home to find comfort in other arms.

It was upscale in its clientele but low in its tastes. Anything could be found here for a price and everything was.

He stopped at the doorway of one red silk-lined room and watched the naked writing figures within.

The man and the woman, both vaguely familiar, curved around each other on the floor. Just like most of the visitors to this house, they forwent the optional masks, not caring who watched, and the more the merrier.

His own words echoed in his head. *You like to watch.* He wanted Carolina. But she was home, safe in her bed, in her father's house.

Her father. Alistair.

Henry backed out of the room and prowled through the club now with a purpose. His senses overloaded with naked bodies, musky scents and primal moans, he scanned first one room and then the next, brushing away hands and sexual advances.

Then Henry saw him, Alistair, sunk into a deep chair, his breeches around his ankles, a plump, naked woman, her white skin golden in the candlelight, straddling him, rocking back and forth.

Alistair's hands grasped her hips, guiding her movements. His intermittent *smacks* resounded off her generous flesh.

Henry came close, ran a hand down the woman's shoulder,

gaining both her attention and Alistair's. He reached around to cup one breast, which overflowed even his large hands.

"I'm glad to see you join us," Alistair gasped, his movements slower now. "I just got here myself. A long night ahead." The woman giggled, playfully reaching back to grasp at the front of Henry's breeches.

He let go of her breast and stepped back slightly, just out of reach.

"Take a seat, Stanton," Alistair said crudely, spreading the woman's buttocks with his hands to reveal the puckered hole within. "She can handle it."

Henry smiled slightly. That rarely interested him, though he'd had his fair share of filling a woman that way.

"Not tonight, Hargreaves," he said apologetically. "I'm afraid I have other arrangements. I merely came by to whet my appetite. But I'll call on you. At the townhouse?"

"Yes, yes," Alistair said, his eyes closing as he turned his attention away from Henry. Hips thrusting up.

Henry left the club quickly after that. He knew his destination now and he didn't have much time. Alistair may just be getting going, but surely, in four years even that insatiable man's appetites had slowed down. Henry likely only had three hours for his purpose.

Chapter Five

The Hargreaves townhouse in Berkeley Square had been the home of many of Henry's sexual revels. Of course, then, Hargreaves's daughter had not been in residence.

But if he was in luck and the staff had not changed, then they would be amenable to a bribe and let him in.

He went around the back to the servant's entrance and rapped firmly on the door. It was well after midnight and a few minutes passed before a familiar footman sleepily opened the door.

"Mr. Bosworth!" Jack, the footman, cried after a moment of stunned surprise. "What are you doing at this entrance? The baron's not in now."

"I know that, Jack." Henry pushed his way in, not wishing to stand so conspicuously out on the side path where servants from the house next door might see him. "I'm up to no good, as usual."

Jack laughed. "Well, it's been an age. If I remember, it was always the scullery maid you liked."

"That and every other maid," Henry agreed. "But I'm here to see Miss Carolina."

Jack's eyes opened like saucers. "I don't think—"

"Shh, Jack, she's expecting me, but her father isn't, and if we can keep this between us . . ." He extracted three sovereign from his purse. It was a large sum but Henry had paid far more for a night with a woman he desired.

"Right you are, Mr. Bosworth."

"Now if you'll just show me to her room . . ."

Bemused, Jack did as Henry asked, leading him soundlessly through the house, up the main staircase so as not to awaken the other servants.

They stopped in front of the third door on the second floor.

He'd been in this bedchamber before, years ago. It had been rather bare then. He wondered if it was still the same, if Carolina now slept on the same mattress where he'd fucked any number of women. He and Alistair both.

Henry waved Jack away and then looked at the white painted barrier. His cock had become uncomfortably tight in his breeches and he shifted the weight with his hand.

The same hand then reached forward and slowly, so slowly, turned the doorknob. The well-oiled hinges opened without a creak and he slipped inside. He stood still in the pitch-dark room, letting his eyes adjust until he could make out the bed.

He took off his shoes. He shrugged out of his coat, his breeches next, and so on until he wore only his shirt and stockings. Then, he came to stand just by her.

She lay on her back, her arms stretched over her head, tangled in hair that he knew to be a rich chestnut brown. Her face lay tilted to the side, sumptuously exposing the long column of her neck. The top three buttons of her night rail were undone, offering him just the slightest glimpse of the upper curve of her breasts. He remembered the feel of that flesh in his hand, through the layers of her evening gown, filling his palm perfectly.

The counterpane and sheets beneath had been pushed down to her waist, and he reached forward to pull them back completely.

Carefully, he climbed onto the bed, watching her for signs of wakefulness, but she didn't move as he settled his weight next to her.

Experimentally, he ran a hand up her leg, from behind her knee and up the silken skin, feeling the heat rising as he neared her center.

She moved now, shying away from his hand, her arms bending. He waited until she stilled before moving above her, between her legs.

He parted the swollen nether lips with his fingers, which fluttered against him like a heartbeat. He saw her eyelashes flutter as well, and before she fully woke, he guided himself in.

Her eyes opened sharply and she struggled against him.

"Shh, love, I couldn't stay away," Henry whispered into her ear, pushing deeper into her. She was hot and yielding, her thighs spreading further as she welcomed his cock into her.

"Henry?" she said disbelievingly, his name on her lips sounding like an erotic caress, as if she'd been saying it forever, as if they'd been lovers for longer than a few hours.

"Come, put your legs around me," he urged. She did, wrapping her thighs around his hips, gasping as she felt the long, thick length of him slide all the way in, filling her completely.

"Why are you here?" she managed to ask and he laughed.

"You need to ask?" He pulled back and thrust in deep again,

starting a rhythm, his left hand snaking under her buttocks to encourage her own movements. "I have thought of nothing but you since I was inside you earlier. I could not rest until I'd tasted you again."

"But how?"

"Shh." He kissed his way from her ear to her mouth. "I'll answer your questions later."

Then he placed his mouth on hers, nibbling on the plump flesh, and realized with a jolt that this was the first time he had kissed her lips.

He feasted on them now.

Her hands ran down his back, moving under his shirt, burning his skin with her tentative strokes.

He shifted the rhythm, pulling out almost completely, teasing her. With short strokes he pushed the head of his cock in and out, until she lifted her hips, trying to bring him deeper inside.

A soft mewling cry escaped her lips and she finally grasped his buttocks in her hand and forced him to do what she wanted. He sank back into her and gave himself up to the animal within. After all, it was what he wanted too.

Chapter Six

Much later, Henry reluctantly withdrew from her body. She was facedown on the bed, collapsed under him in climax. Her breathing was deep and even as it had been for the last few minutes.

He was tempted to have at her again, but it was late now and the servants would soon be awake. He needed to make his way from the house unnoticed.

As if reading his mind, a faint scratching sounded at the door, the signal Jack had said he'd give.

Henry managed to find his clothing and put it on in some semblance of order before he reached the door. He looked back at Carolina but she slept on, deeply.

He smiled with satisfaction. He'd used her well; she'd likely sleep late into the day.

Henry followed Jack out of the still-silent house. At the door, he thanked the footman.

"If you don't mind me asking, Mr. Bosworth, how was she?"

"It's Lord Stanton, now, Jack," Henry said, by way of chiding him. "But I'll tell you this. I'll be back, so watch for me if you want to line your pockets a bit more."

"Yes, my lord."

Chapter Seven

Sometime in the morning, her maid entered the room and Carolina waved her away. When she finally awoke much later in the day, early afternoon, she stretched like a cat among the cool sheets.

If her body didn't feel so . . . stretched, aching in all the right places, she would have thought it a dream. But no, she knew that Henry had been there, had somehow, beneath her father's nose, snuck into the house.

He'd been so certain of himself, of his reception, that he'd been inside her before she even woke. And how had she received him? Like a cat in heat.

She wanted him again.

To think that just twenty-four hours earlier she'd been petri-

fied about entering society! Carolina had sat in the drawing room
of her aunt, who had agreed to act as a companion for the season,
and watched that lady sneeze in succession until she apologized
that she would not be able to attend the ball that night. Alistair
would simply have to go.

Carolina had wanted to feign a cold herself. But no longer.
Now the season stretched forward before her as a buffet of carnal
delight. The man of her most secret dreams desired her, pleasured
her, and she knew he would again.

She breathed in deeply and smiled at the scent—the scent of
Henry on her body. She almost didn't want to bathe. She wanted
to savor the aroma, to lie abed all day until he came to see her
again.

He would come! He *must* come.

But she knew, too, that he'd look for her at the Emerson ball,
because she'd said that was where she would be this evening.

So she rang for her maid.

Chapter Eight

The Emerson house glittered like the crown jewels. And as
Carolina moved across the dance floor, the rainbow of shiny
colors blurred around her. She struggled, as she had all evening,
passed from one unwanted partner to the next, for a glimpse of
Stanton. She wasn't entirely certain he'd even arrived yet.

The dance ended and her partner, a Mr. Farthingdale, led her
back across the room to her aunt Agathe. Agathe had assured her
that Mr. Farthingdale, the son of her friend, was a good catch for
all his not having a title just yet. As his uncle's heir, he stood to be a
viscount soon if that man continued to have no sons of his own.

Title or not, the slight, blond Farthingdale would never be the sort of man to impress Carolina. No. She had been ruined six years earlier when Bosworth's image had become her ideal of manly perfection—black hair, a wicked gleam in murky green eyes, and long, muscular limbs.

Despite her partiality, Carolina knew better than to expect Stanton to ever ask for her hand. He'd told her in that library at Hargreaves House so many years ago that he would never marry. He loved a variety of women too much to ever imagine settling down with just one.

Perhaps he shouldn't have said as much to an impressionable twelve-year-old, but considering what she'd just witnessed, Carolina hadn't uttered a word of protest. Rather, she had imagined being one of that succession of women.

And now she was.

Aunt Agathe stood just before her, her silk gown a vibrant rose that reflected back upon her round face, making her look younger than her forty-some years. She had no gray, unlike her younger brother, and she took great pride in the fact.

"I can see you don't care much for that one," Agathe said irritably, after Farthingdale had left. "But you really shouldn't make it so obvious to your partner. There is not an infinite number of eligible gentlemen. Beware, lest your father choose an old toothless lecher for your husband, as your grandfather did for me."

"He'll choose whom he wishes," Carolina said frankly. She didn't know her aunt very well. She'd grown up at Hargreaves House in virtual isolation. Even her father had rarely visited. Yet in the two weeks she'd been in town, she'd come to find that Agathe was someone with whom she could speak honestly.

"True, but if you find yourself partial to someone, I might be able to sway your father's mind," Agathe revealed, smiling conspiratorially now.

Carolina struggled to keep her face an impassive mask, but she had to look away as well to cover the hot flush that filled her face at the thought of Henry.

"Hmmm, Lord Stanton is approaching."

Carolina looked up sharply, certain her decadent thoughts must have conjured him, and followed her aunt's gaze to where Henry now walked, with that familiar erotic prowl, directly toward them.

"He's a pretty man," Agathe said, appreciatively. "A tasty piece as well."

From those few words, Carolina knew that her aunt had bedded Bosworth. She looked at her curiously. Agathe had given up her widow's weeds and remarried only a few years earlier.

"Don't look at me like that, girl, it was before Mr. Mustle-whaithe!" But her aunt's voice lowered quickly when Henry came to stand before them.

"Mrs. Mustlewhaithe," Stanton greeted Agathe, bending low over her hand.

He straightened and turned his attention to Carolina.

"I had the pleasure of meeting your lovely niece last night," he said, his sensuous smile nearly turning Carolina's legs to puddles of flesh rather than anything sturdy enough to keep her upright.

"Did you, Lord Stanton?" Agathe said archly. "I'm not certain I like the sound of that."

"Never fear, Agathe," Stanton said, "your brother warned me away, at least until she's safely married."

Agathe laughed richly, her peals growing when she caught sight of Carolina's flush.

"Did he warn you away from me as well?"

"No, but your husband did," Henry lamented. "So I'll console myself with a dance with your niece."

"You hear that, Carolina?" Agathe prodded her when she didn't move. "He's asking you to dance."

Carolina didn't need any further encouragement. She took Henry's arm and walked away with him.

"How are you?" he inquired in a low, more serious tone, when they'd passed earshot of her aunt.

"I'm very well," she replied.

"Good." He flashed that wicked smile again and they took their places in the dance.

She stood five feet away from him. His eyes, so dark and intent, surveyed her body. She felt the trail in a shiver down her spine and a sharp longing in her belly.

She'd never given much thought to how she looked, knowing that fine feathers made the lady and a dowry sold her to the highest bidder. Tonight, underneath his hot gaze, she knew she was beautiful, like Helen of Troy. Like Lady Godiva in all her nakedness.

She had the power to make Henry desire her, perhaps to make many men desire her, and the thought made Carolina feel dangerously wicked.

They were surrounded on either side by other dancers, but that hardly mattered. As she stepped forward to meet Stanton, to take his hand and switch sides, she tilted her head just so, watched him out of the corners of her eyes and offered up a coy little smile.

His left eyebrow rose sharply.

"Temptress," he managed, in a low whisper, before the dance took him away from her, to take the hand of a lady nearby.

"Am I?" Carolina asked archly, when he met her once more. As their hands met, he ran a finger along the underside of her palm. The jolt of fire to the junction of her legs startled her and her lips parted, her eyes glazing.

It was an answer of sorts, she realized, but *she* was the one tempted.

"And how do I compare to my Aunt Agathe?" she teased, after another interval.

"You're quite greedy tonight," Henry answered. "But there is no comparison."

Carolina stepped away from him, fiercely satisfied. She stared at him hungrily, forgetting to be subtle. The skin of his jaw, just above his cravat, begged to be kissed. She wanted to run her tongue along it, to suck on his neck, to lick his lips, to undress him and see his full body.

He met her gaze with a scorching, heavy-lidded one of his own.

The dance continued tortuously until Carolina, her nipples

taut against the low bodice of her dress, and her legs moist with overflowing desire, took Henry's arm to leave the floor.

"Beg off the next dance," Henry instructed. "From the ladies' retiring room there is a hallway; follow it to the end and take a right. The second door. Meet me there in ten minutes. Or sooner."

She agreed with a look, her fingers playing with the soft underside of his wrist, understanding now just how sensitive that region was.

"Ten minutes will be an age," she admitted.

Chapter Nine

Henry left her with Agathe, grateful that her aunt was engaged in conversation with Lord Weyburn and had missed the sexual undercurrents between him and her niece. Or perhaps she was merely ignoring them. It didn't signify.

What did matter was how incredibly lucky he was. Somehow he had managed to stumble upon a woman who was quite obviously eager for everything he could offer her. Carolina didn't even seem to mind that he'd fucked her aunt as well.

The second door down the hallway was a large linen closet used by the servants. With a handful of coins, Henry had commandeered the use of it for a few minutes. Not nearly enough time for his desires, but it would ease the tension until he came to her that night.

He pulled his gloves off, carefully folding them and placing the pair on a shelf behind him. He caressed himself through the cloth of his breeches as he waited, thinking of her breasts and what they would look like bouncing above him.

Tentatively, Carolina opened the door. He saw her in the dim light of the hallway and pulled her into the lightless closet, closing the door behind her.

His lips found her cheek and made their way to her open, waiting mouth, his tongue touching hers, dancing, thrusting.

She moaned into his mouth. Then he felt her gloved hands running down his body, searching under his coat, down further and playing with the outline of his cock.

He growled low in his throat.

"Unbutton my pants, take me in your hands," he ordered and she followed his directions, pausing only to pull off her own gloves. The first touch of her bare fingers on him nearly made him come.

This would not be a long seduction with prolonged foreplay, but as he gathered her skirts up and reached for her hot folds, he knew it didn't matter. She was wet and ready, dripping even, panting with desire.

"Yes, now, please!" she cried.

He lifted her by her buttocks, his hands gripping the yielding flesh. With one of her feet, encased in its delicate dancing slipper, finding purchase on a shelf, and her other leg wrapped tightly around his waist, he entered her.

The feel of him inside her, pushing upward through the tight, muscular canal was a delicious shock, a pause in the building desire. It felt right, perfect, as if he should always be joined in such a way. And then he kept moving: pulling out and thrusting back in, relentlessly, though she wouldn't have it any other way.

He shifted, supporting her weight with his left arm, his right hand coming up to cup her left breast. He tugged on the cloth of her dress, freeing the flesh. His bare hand on her breast, his thumb circling her nipple, made her move her hips more urgently against him.

"You're perfect," Henry said into her ear, his breath hot and ragged. "Perfectly made."

He said more but she didn't hear him because the blood was roaring in her ears and her body was convulsing around him, exploding, shooting fire in every direction. Her toes tingled. Her nipples as well.

She collapsed in his arms, but he kept her up, pinned against the wall as he thrust harder and faster and finally released himself inside her with a hoarse cry.

As her breathing evened out, she laughed with the sheer pleasure of it.

"You'll come to me tonight?" she asked. He was pulling out of her and she winced at the absence.

"Greedy girl." She felt his smile against her lips. "Nothing could keep me away."

Chapter Ten

Agathe examined her critically when Carolina finally returned to the ballroom.

"There was a line," she offered, by way of explanation for her long disappearance.

"I was beginning to think I'd have to come fish you out," Agathe said rather crudely.

"And there was so much gossip to listen to, I wasn't really in a hurry," Carolina added, hoping to distract her aunt's attention. As much as she liked the woman, she didn't think she could confess her newfound sexual escapades.

"What gossip?" Agathe took the bait, her placidly indulgent expression assuming a predatorial caste.

"Well, I don't know any of the people mentioned, but perhaps it will have some meaning to you," Carolina began. "I believe I heard that Lady Emma is now engaged to Lord Stanley Broughton, and that it is the first engagement of the season."

"Hmm, that is news," Agathe mulled over this. "But Broughton isn't much of a loss, all things considered. He may have considerable wealth and be the brother to a marquess, but he'll never make a good husband. I wonder if Lady Emma knows."

"Why won't he make a good husband?" Carolina asked, thinking of Bosworth. "Is he a rake?"

Agathe laughed. "I suppose he might be, but there aren't many men in the ton with his proclivities. He likes other men." After a pause where Carolina stared at her blankly, waiting for more, Agathe added, "sexually."

Carolina's jaw dropped.

"That's possible?" Then she thought about the unknown Lady Emma. "Well, he must be attracted to women as well, don't you think?"

"He'll make do enough to get an heir off of her," Agathe agreed. "Actually, in the scheme of things, it isn't such a bad way to go with a husband. He'll leave her alone and she'll have the freedom to dally where she desires." Her aunt grinned wickedly. "If you wish, my dear girl, I'll find you a husband of the sort. I believe Lord Sedgwick is of that persuasion."

Carolina had danced with Lord Sedgwick early on in the evening.

"No!" she gasped. "But he was staring at my bosom quite lasciviously. Are you certain?"

Agathe shrugged. "I have no personal knowledge of the matter. Perhaps your father would know."

The matter of her aunt's "personal knowledge" caught Carolina's attention. She thought again of Henry.

"Auntie," she asked, "when were you and Stanton lovers?"

Agathe shot her a knowing smile. "No use looking in that direction, no matter how delicious he is. That's a man who will never marry, and no need considering. His cousin is his heir, and a more upstanding young man you'll never meet, with four sons already!"

Carolina waited.

"It was years ago, maybe five or six, when he was riding your father's coattails. Poor Thomas was on his deathbed and I needed the comforting. Just two or three nights we shared over the course of the year, but I remember clearly how well formed Bosworth is."

Carolina blushed, thinking of just how that well-formed part had felt inside her minutes ago.

"No need to be missish, Carolina. I can see you are lusting after him," Agathe chided her. "And what young girl wouldn't be? But wait until after you've given your husband an heir. Then you may follow your desires."

Carolina nodded at this advice, as if she agreed, as if she'd stay away from Stanton. But her aunt Agathe didn't know two important things: one, that Carolina, like Henry, would not dishonor her wedding vows, and two, that the damage had already been done.

What lovely damage.

Chapter Eleven

Y ou never came," Lady Islington complained, rapping her fan on Henry's arm.

A lush woman, she was quite skilled with her tongue, he knew, but her delightful rosebud mouth was not the one he wanted on his cock this evening. No, he looked forward to that new pleasure with Carolina.

Tonight, or the next night, or any that the long stretch of the season had to offer. He didn't think he'd tire of her soon. And she was so eager for it.

"Ah, but you want me now," Lady Islington purred, staring as he grew hard in his breeches.

Henry sighed. It was the one problem with the damned new tailored fashion for men. There was no privacy.

"But of course, my lady," Henry agreed. "Anticipation has its own pleasure." He kissed her hand and backed away before she could cling to him.

It was just after two. The ball would continue for a while longer, but Henry was no longer interested. Unless he could get Carolina away again, and even then, he wanted her in her bed.

No, he wanted her in his bed.

That he couldn't have, not just yet, until he learned the habits of the Hargreaves townhouse better. Until he had Carolina's full cooperation.

But he wanted her in his bed with every candle lit and all the luxury of time to peruse her body, to savor each sweet curve.

Chapter Twelve

When he came to her that night, Carolina was waiting for him. She helped him undress, rolling his stockings down with the aid of her teeth, lifting his shirt over his head, her breasts pressed against his back.

"No more torture," Henry said gruffly. "I want to fuck you now."

Carolina paused at the harsh word. *Fuck.* Was that the word for what they did?

"I've never heard that word before," she whispered in the dark and then tried it on her lips. "*Fuck*." It rolled off her tongue with a satisfying strength. "Yes, Henry, I want you to *fuck* me."

"You're a naughty girl," Henry said, grasping her hips as she moved onto her hands and knees on the bed. "Wonderfully naughty," he enthused, sinking into her, pumping her with long, rhythmic strokes.

He reached his hands up to grasp her swinging breasts, lifting their weight, kneading the flesh.

"Fuck me, Henry," she whispered again, a smile on her lips as she buried her moans into the pillow.

The effect of her words almost had him losing control, but he caught himself, evening his breath, and he lowered his hand to speed up her climax. This first round would be quick.

But they had many hours yet and he had no regrets.

Chapter Thirteen

At the Huxley ball they met in the conservatory, and with her knees pressed into the thick Aubusson carpet, Carolina learned how it felt to have him fill her mouth, his fingers massaging the back of her neck as he slowly eased in and out of her. When the rhythm changed and grew more urgent, he held her head in place and she gave herself over to his passion.

He'd spent himself within her mouth and she'd held his buttocks, her own juices flowing, the knot of tension begging for release.

But noises in the hallway alerted them that they were out of time, and instead, behind the screen in the ladies' retiring room, Carolina's fingers had brought her own climax.

When he asked her to dance a half hour later, she told him about it, describing how she'd thrust her fingers up into herself, imitating his, how she'd stifled her cries into her fist.

That night, despite all sanity, he lit a candle in her room and urged her to show him. His eyes, intent with passion, had watched her from under those heavy lids, as her hands ran down her own body, tugging on her nipples until they stood at attention, making circles down the curve of her hips, the taut flat expanse of her belly, until she reached the triangle of dark curls.

He touched himself as he watched her, stroking the hard length that she knew to be velvety soft. Even as her own passion rose, she licked her lips in appreciation. Now that she had his taste, she craved it like water.

So, just as she felt the quickening in her, before it rose to too high a crescendo, she bent over and gently moved his hand away. Keeping her eyes on his, she took first one heavy sac into her mouth and then the other. Then with the hard point of her tongue licked from base to tip.

Henry never let her finish. He growled deep in his throat, pulling her up, urging her astride him. And when she was positioned to his liking, he pulled her down hard, even as his own hips thrust upward.

Chapter Fourteen

Carolina's days and nights developed a pattern. Sometime in the evening, at whatever event she attended, he would arrive, whisper to her the location, and she would meet him for a quick, scorching embrace. Then, just hours later, he would come to her room.

The evenings when assignations were not possible made the nights even hotter and more urgent.

In the pitch darkness of her bed, she learned every taste of his body, from that appealing curve under his jaw to the salty effusion of what she'd learned to call his cock.

The footman, Jack, had become quite cheeky, winking at her when he opened the door of her carriage in the afternoons. And after her first appalled shock, she'd understood that he approved, and she winked back.

Carolina's mornings and afternoons passed in a haze of anticipated passion. She went for drives in the park, teas and calls, picnics and other outings.

Now, recognizing the glimmer of attraction in other men's eyes, she flirted shamelessly to relieve the boredom until night came and Henry.

There were other handsome men, other intelligent men, and indeed Carolina realized she knew nothing of Henry but his body and his sexual skill.

Over the weeks, two men became her regular companions: Anderson, Earl of Oakley, and Sir Robert George. They both had been vetted by her father, and Lord Hargreaves made it clear that if she chose between these two men he would be pleased with his daughter.

Neither man was the toothless old codger of whom Agathe had warned, a fact that had its own detractions, for a younger man might take offense if one soon sought a lover. If she too quickly craved Henry's touch and too quickly threw away all her morality.

Oakley was young, just finished with his studies, but he had a mature demeanor and was actively looking for a wife. Tall and dark haired, he reminded Carolina of Henry six years ago, when he might very well have still been called a youth, though past his majority. That alone made Oakley appeal to her, even if his touch on her gloved hand was exceedingly polite and gentle, and her pulse remained even in his presence. His love of poetry also appealed, as well as the fact that he'd taken his place in the House of Lords with passion and dedication.

His attraction was entirely different from Bosworth's. In Oakley she would find a safe, attentive, responsible mate. Agathe had assured her that he was a man who would never take a mistress. Her childhood self, before Stanton, would have longed for such a man to ride up and free her from her isolation.

Sir Robert George was older, older than Henry and nearer to her father's age. Though not much taller than she, he had a straight nose, full lips and eyes that she couldn't help but think pretty. He was also exceedingly wealthy.

He whispered naughty jokes in her ear as if he knew she was ripe for the plucking. She laughed nervously, but his breath was sweet against her ear and she thought he would not be hideous in the marriage bed—might even be skilled enough to get past her apathy. But aside from the naughty jokes, she found little of his conversation appealing, and she rather suspected that with this man it would be much harder to conceal her lack of virginity.

When the time came, Carolina knew she would have to confide in Agathe and ask her how to attend to that small task. Her aunt would surely know.

Chapter Fifteen

One afternoon, Carolina went for a drive in the park with Sir Robert and her aunt. The lane was full of carriages and the horses marched along sedately.

"Do you ride, Miss Hargreaves?" Sir Robert asked, leaning in closer than necessary. Aunt Agathe coughed discreetly but he ignored her hint.

"I do ride," Carolina answered. "It is one of the great pleasures of the country."

"But always sidesaddle?" Sir Robert pressed. Agathe coughed harder and Carolina patted her on the back, but at the woman's rolling eyes she realized just what Sir Robert was suggesting. The man was a walking bag of double entendres!

She flushed hotly, though she knew she should pretend no

knowledge of what the man meant, but the vision of her above Henry, her thighs clutching his hips, setting the pace, had her wet and pulsing.

Sir Robert smiled and she realized that he thought her blushing was in reaction to him.

"I think it would be nice to walk," Carolina said abruptly.

"A stretch across the grass would be lovely," Agathe agreed, and Sir Robert pulled on the reins accommodatingly.

He handed the reins to his tiger and came around to help first Agathe, and then Carolina, down. His hands lingered on her hips.

"Perhaps you'll ride with me," he suggested as she slid down to the ground. His hands slid up as well, coming to rest just under her breasts.

"Perhaps," Carolina said calmly, schooling her features into the picture of innocence.

She looked past his shoulder to where Agathe waited impatiently and then saw Henry, not so very far away, astride his own sleek mount, his lips thinned into an angry line as he watched them. It was the first time she had seen him in bright light since she'd arrived in London, and she thought him magnificent.

She wanted to run to him, but she settled with moving past Sir Robert and joining her aunt. Together, they watched Henry incline his head slightly in greeting and then turn his horse around.

"I'm surprised to see him," Agathe drawled. "I've always rather thought of Stanton like a vampire, appearing only at night, shunning the sunlight."

Carolina realized with a jolt that she never saw Henry during the day, only at night, though she'd always mentioned her daytime agenda, just in case.

"There are any number of places a man may spend his days," Carolina returned, affecting an idle tone. "I'd say it's simply coincidental that we chance to see him on this one."

Secretly, she thought differently. He knew very well that she had other beaus, that her father sought a husband for her.

But maybe seeing was different from hearsay, Carolina thought, puzzling over his harsh expression. Was it possible that seeing Sir Robert holding her so familiarly had made Henry jealous?

She longed to confide in Agathe and ask what the older woman thought, but that would mean admitting to her nighttime activities, and she didn't want to just yet. Not until she was ready to give them up.

In any event, how could it matter if he was jealous? Henry had said quite clearly, so many years ago—his words influencing her own views on the matter—that he would never marry, not unless he could be faithful to the vows before God, and as that was impossible, so would be marriage.

Chapter Sixteen

D o you want him?" Henry asked, one long finger engulfed in Carolina's heat.

She found it hard to think as he added another finger. She marveled at how different the feel of his fingers was from his cock. Where one instrument incited pinpricks of excruciating pleasure in her belly, the other filled her, stretched her, made her feel as if she and Henry were one melded person. Joined with him, she forgot where he began and she ended. And movement— sometimes it felt as though they were underwater, as if she were swimming in the lake back home and he was everywhere around her and in her.

"Do you want him?" he persisted.

There were three of his fingers in her now and his thumb traced magical circles. She didn't think her legs would hold her up much longer. She turned her face to the arm he had stretched out and licked the underside of his wrist hungrily.

"Carolina."

There was a pleading note in his voice and it caught her attention. With glazed eyes she looked into his eyes. They were so dark. *Dear Lord, how could green eyes ever be so dark?*

She glanced away, to the pale yellow of the fabric-lined walls. This was somebody's bedchamber, someone in the Allyns family, but she didn't know whose.

She swung her gaze back to his.

"I want only you, Henry."

The tension in his face eased. His hand retreated and she heard him fumbling with the falls of his breeches.

"But I may have to marry him if my father insists." She wasn't quite sure why she added that last, but it served to infuriate Stanton. He pulled her hard against him, kissing her, and then lifting her up.

Dizzy, she felt him cross the room. Then the edge of the bed was beneath her and he thrust into her, claiming her, the force of his actions pushing her deep into the counterpane and feather mattress beneath.

She held him tight in her arms and hugged him tighter inside as she'd learned to do, her muscles clenching. She understood his possessiveness and she reveled in it.

She wanted to scream when she came, hard, arcing up against him, but she bit his hand instead.

He grabbed both her arms then, lifted them up over her head and held them there as he kept thrusting until he too climaxed and collapsed over her.

Their ragged breaths sounded like thunder in the quiet room.

Then Carolina laughed. After a moment, Henry's low rumble joined her. He leaned up on his elbows and stared down into her smiling face.

"So, whom do you drive out with tomorrow?" Henry asked, before dipping back down for another kiss.

Chapter Seventeen

Something changed between them that night, and they were both aware of it. The halcyon days were coming to an end, so they played games and teased each other more than before. Every look was a seduction, every moment a secret shared. And in between the sexual explosions, Carolina began to learn about her lover.

He'd spent the last four years since his brother's death up in Yorkshire, putting the ancestral estate to rights, because even though his brother had disparaged Henry's town ways, James himself had slowly been bleeding the land dry.

Henry didn't care for politics but he did care about the people on his land, the people who relied on the Bosworths for their livelihood.

"It's the very least I can do," Henry said, his arms bent behind his head, Carolina's head on his chest. "Those men and women make my way of life possible."

Silently, Carolina traced circles on his bare skin, enjoying the texture of his hair on her fingers.

"That's why my father . . ." she said, after a while, ". . . that's why he wants to marry me off so quickly. Because we're short of funds." She finished the last in an embarrassed, barely audible whisper.

Henry let out a breath of a laugh, still aware that they were in her father's house, that he couldn't make too much noise.

"When I was younger, I used to live off your father half the time, as I never had funds of my own," Henry explained. "I never imagined Alistair couldn't afford the life."

He slid out from under her and turned onto his side. The drapes were open and he could just make out her face in the moonlight.

"You're all the currency he has left," Henry mused, running his hands over her curves. "And I took the priceless virginity."

"Thief," she teased, spreading her legs for him.

"Greedy girl."

Chapter Eighteen

Henry told himself he didn't feel guilty. He did feel, however, the same desperation that Carolina felt, the sense that things couldn't go on this way much longer. And the thought made him wild and reckless in his need.

Carolina was his but she wasn't, and in his need to possess her, he felt he had to show the world he possessed her as well.

Under the smirking gaze of Jack the footman, Henry secreted her out of the house. Once in the privacy of his closed carriage, he handed her a plain black cloak and a silk mask, as if she were going to a masquerade.

"But where are we going?" Carolina asked yet again, laughing.

"Someplace where we can indulge your desire to watch."

She stopped laughing. Her blue eyes, under the mask, widened.

"You may see people you recognize while there, but with your disguise they won't recognize you. Do not acknowledge anyone," Henry instructed.

She nodded, taking it all in.

"But what is this place?" she asked for the fifth time.

"Harridan House," Henry revealed as the carriage drew up to the curb. "A place of decadent sin, where I spent much of my youth. This, my greedy girl, I share with you."

The carriage door opened.

Henry ran a teasing finger along the lower half of her cheek and then climbed out. Firmly on the ground, he turned back, reaching up to assist her. She held his hand tightly, looking all around her as she stepped down.

The stone building was in a respectable part of town, if not entirely fashionable, and looked just like every other building on the street. If it weren't for what Henry had said, she would never have guessed that it was a house of sexual indulgence. Henry made it sound impossibly wicked, as if what happened inside went beyond the passionate acts they did together. She couldn't even imagine.

The entryway was dim, lit by infrequent candles, and Carolina thought a great many of the guests must stumble over themselves.

Two young women and a young man greeted them in strange costumes reminiscent of ancient Greece but hardly covering any skin at all. Henry waved them away and led Carolina deeper into the house.

They entered a room to their right, where a dining room might normally be situated, and Carolina found that, indeed, a long dining table took prominence in the room.

Laid out upon the table were two women, head to head, as if they were that night's meal. One of the women looked rather bored, but at the sight of Henry and Carolina she began running her hands down her body with growing enthusiasm, seducing them, urging them to touch her.

To touch her, perhaps like the woman behind her was being touched, with a man's head nestled between her legs and an ardent tongue feasting on her folds.

Carolina found herself stepping forward to get a better view. Henry followed, his hand resting possessively on her hip.

She watched the stranger's tongue disappear inside the woman.

"Henry?" Carolina whispered, questioningly, leaning back against him, slightly dizzy.

"There's much more, love," he whispered back, "come."

As they left the room, she looked back over her shoulder. The woman who was alone brought her hand back up to her mouth, her gaze locking with Carolina's as she licked her finger.

Completely, utterly shocking, Carolina thought, swiveling her head back. *And utterly arousing.*

Chapter Nineteen

They climbed a staircase and entered what in a respectable house would have been the drawing room, but in this house was a melee of decadence.

There were sofas and chaises, all occupied, but Carolina was most startled by the appearance of three beds out of their normal habitat, the canopies and gauzy draperies offering the only privacy. Henry led her toward one where the gauze was pulled back. Writhing on the bed was a face she recognized.

She pulled Henry back and leaned close to his ear to whisper. "That's Lord Sedgwick!"

She thought of what Agathe had told her of the man's proclivities.

He was buried to the balls in a woman, his movements only curtailed by the man behind him, who thrust into his backside as if Sedgwick were a woman and that hole meant for such a thing.

"Yes, and his companion is Lord Stanley Broughton," Henry revealed and Carolina giggled.

"I've heard the man's name before, but it's different to suddenly be able to put a . . . a body to the name."

"Yes, I imagine when you do finally meet the man, you'll look at him quite differently." Henry smiled, sharing in her amusement. But then he pulled her away from that bed as well.

"Have you ever done that?" Carolina asked, hesitantly.

"Used an ass as a cunt?" Henry said crudely, and she blinked at the words.

"*Cunt* is another word for . . . for my . . ." she stopped, realizing she had no good word for that area.

"Yes." Henry grinned, wickedly. "It is. *Quim* is another, but it has such a different sound to it. Wetter, don't you think?" Her eyes glazed over and Henry knew just what effect his words had on her. "Next time you beg me to fuck you, ask me to fill your cunt as well."

"All right," she agreed, looking forward to it.

"But to answer your question, only with a woman, and it is not my preference."

She nodded and he was suddenly glad that he was truthfully able to say that because he thought she looked a bit relieved.

Out of the corner of his eye he spied Alistair in one of the other beds and Henry carefully guided Carolina out of the room. *That* was something she didn't need to see.

He led her up another set of stairs, to the smaller, more private bedrooms. The first door on his left was open and the room occupied.

It was a much simpler scenario, a man flat on his back, a woman sucking his cock into her mouth. Both man and woman glanced at the new arrivals but with lazy smiles returned to their business.

Henry stood just behind Carolina, listening as her breathing quickened. *This* she liked. He encircled her with his arms, opening the cloak, tugging on the bodice of her dress until her breasts eased free of their constraints and filled his hands.

She startled at first at the exhibitionism of it and then relaxed against him, pushing her breasts against his palms. He rolled her nipples between his thumb and forefinger, bringing them to their full extension, pleased with her response.

"You like watching this?" he asked quietly as he licked the sensitive skin behind her ear.

"Yes," Carolina breathed. "And I like your tongue and your fingers."

He ran his hands down her sides till they came to rest on her hips, then he turned her around and leaned her against the open door.

He lowered his head to her right breast, ran his tongue across the nipple, then lightly grazed the sensitive flesh with his teeth.

He knelt down before her and inched her dress up, past her knees, past where her stockings began, up to her waist.

She took the material in her hands as if he had instructed it. She parted her legs unconsciously. Wanting. Needing.

He kissed a trail up the naked flesh of her thighs. He heard the climaxing groans of the man on the bed and knew Carolina was watching that man. Her thighs glistened and he breathed deeply the scent of her arousal.

Henry licked the thin skin where her thigh met the triangle of dark curls.

And then he drew back.

"Tell me what you want," Henry demanded.

"Your tongue on my cunt," she said without hesitation, now that she had the vocabulary for her desires.

And he gave it to her.

He licked her, ran his tongue up the wet slit, delving inside, enjoying her panting cries. He moved his mouth up to her clit and brought his fingers up to fill her while he concentrated on the nub.

Her hands found purchase in his hair, playing with the thick waves, and he echoed the massaging circles of her fingers with the movement of his tongue.

"The man on the bed," Carolina said with difficulty. "He's watching us, and he's doing to that woman what you're doing to me. He's *imitating* us!"

The fresh gush of hot juices filling his tongue let Henry know just how aroused she was. His own cock was painfully hard, his balls tight and begging for release.

He focused his movements into small hard circles over her clit and used his hand like his cock, three long fingers filling her. The rippled muscle clenched him hard and he stroked her gently, separating his fingers slightly, changing the sensation.

Her moans came faster, sharper, louder. Her hands gripped his head almost painfully and she screamed, clenching tight around him again and again as she climaxed.

He kept his hot, open mouth on her, his tongue now stilled. Slowly, he slid his fingers out and then back in again to pull more tremors from her. Finally, he took his hand away, released his hold on her hips, and she slid down the door to join him on the floor, her skirts falling down around them.

She looked at him through dazed, sated eyes, lips parted, and he brought his wet hand up to her mouth.

"Taste yourself," he instructed, and slid one long finger into her mouth like he had her cunt only moments before. She sucked on it slowly, her eyes widening at the taste of her own arousal and then her tongue licked the sensitive length of his skin.

He slid his finger out and cupped her cheek in his palm.

"You're so beautiful," he whispered.

Her lips quirked up in a small smile. "I feel that way when you look at me."

The other couple squeezed past them, stepping over Henry's legs as they left the room.

The room was silent in their wake. Carolina could hear laughter, moans and low conversation. But all distant, all far away.

Henry's green eyes were yielding, open, saying things that she wasn't certain he meant, that she so desperately wanted to believe.

"What are we doing, Henry?" she asked. Then those beautiful eyes shuttered, grew dark, and he moved his hand away, wiping it idly on his pants.

"There's still more to see here," he answered, his tone devoid of emotion.

Henry stood up and offered her his hand. She put hers in his and stood as well. Then pulled her dress back up over her naked breasts.

They left the room and found the hallway further down crowded with people, all peering into another room. Henry led her that way and she followed, wishing she had said nothing.

They moved to the edge of the raucous crowd, gaining a sliver of a view into the room where on the bed, Sir Robert George, naked, sat astride a rather large woman with very large breasts. He straddled her abdomen, her breasts wrapped around his cock and he pumped back and forth.

There were all sorts of ribald jests about how the woman was bigger than he was. Carolina looked away. She thought of Sir Robert asking her if she rode. She would never be able to look at the man without thinking of this. If she had any say, she would accept Oakley as a husband over him.

A hand touched her breast through the dress and instantly, Carolina knew it wasn't Henry's. She shied away, looking back at the man who'd touched her.

She didn't know him, had never seen him before, but he reached his hand out again as if he thought she wouldn't mind.

"Don't touch her again," Henry said suddenly in a low, dangerous voice.

"I've never known you to be possessive, Stanton," the stranger said.

"She's mine for now," Henry responded simply and led Carolina away.

They moved quickly through the house, down the stairs and waited in the entry hall while the carriage was brought around.

Side by side, they stood, the silence palpable until finally, Henry took her hand in his.

Later, as Henry walked her to the service door of her father's townhouse, he pressed up close behind her and whispered harshly in her ear, "Until you marry, you are mine only. No other man will touch you."

"But I'm not yours," Carolina returned, looking straight forward, struggling to not tremble. "I'm not your mistress. We're lovers and my body belongs to me. And when I marry, my body will be my husband's."

She knew her words infuriated him but he said nothing else and walked away.

Chapter Twenty

S he wasn't at any of the balls the following evening. Henry knew this because, after spending much of the night at the soiree she had mentioned attending without so much as a glimpse of her, he had made an appearance at almost every event in town.

So she was angry with him. What of it? Henry thought. *So she wanted to make some sort of point.*

He tried to stay away but he knew very well his days with her were numbered. Early in the morning, when the servants would be waking and he shouldn't be sneaking into the Hargreaveses' house, he did.

He furtively crept into her room, locking the door behind him.

"Henry?" she called out. There was no anger in her voice. Relief swept over him, stunning him by its very presence. He moved quickly to her side, his hands reaching for her. She flung herself into his arms. "I'm so sorry, I had no way to let you know."

"What's wrong?" he asked slowly, feeling the clammy skin of her forehead against his chin.

"I feel as though I've been turned inside out. I was so violently ill when I woke up yesterday." After a pause she added in a pitiful little voice, "I thought you weren't coming."

"If you ever need to reach me, send Jack. I pay him well," Henry said.

Carolina laughed. "And I'm certain my father doesn't, or his loyalty wouldn't be so cheap."

She fell away from him, back onto the covers, and curled up in a ball, moaning.

She looked so small—small and frail. His chest aching, he lay down beside her, drew the hair back from her neck, and slowly massaged the tight muscles of her shoulders.

A soft sigh escaped her lips. He worked his way down her spine, kneading the muscles, caressing the tension away until he heard her deep, even breathing and knew that she slept.

A bemused smile on his lips, Henry pulled her close. He rested his arm on the curve of her hip, breathed in the honeysuckle scent of her hair and listened to the sounds of her sleep.

Chapter Twenty-One

When Carolina woke up, hours later, Henry was gone. She sighed deeply, touching the still warm imprint of his body.

It wasn't fair. As a child she'd thought she'd loved him, thought that lust was love and confused the two until when the man stood before her, she let him take whatever liberties he wished.

Now, Carolina knew that her childhood self had known nothing. In fact, two months ago in that library she *had* known nothing. If she'd known that love could be as painful as this, she would have run away.

Last night when he'd tried to claim her as his own it had made her angry because all she wanted to be was his!

She'd thought stupidly that she could be mature and adult about this affair. Enjoy this time for herself with the man she lusted after and then go contentedly to whatever marriage her father dictated.

She would never be content.

The thought was underscored by the pain of her stomach clenching, and Carolina stumbled out of the bed in search of the chamber pot.

Chapter Twenty-Two

Carolina clutched at the teacup. The delicate brew had managed to calm her stomach, but her father's pacing did nothing to help the dizziness.

"I am proud of you, Carolina," Hargreaves said, pausing by the fireplace. His long, chiseled face looked almost jovial. "Both men have come to me quite adamant that they want you as their wife. Sir Robert is wealthy enough to make up for the discrepancy in rank, so I'll let you have your choice. Whom do you prefer?"

Sir Robert, with his compact, wiry body, pushing his cock between the fat woman's breasts, stuck in her mind. Despite herself she was somewhat aroused by the sexual image. She was realizing that some configurations of humans engaged in sexual acts she found more titillating in her mind, distant from reality, than she did actually seeing them in action. When she had thought again about Lord Stanley Broughton and Lord Sedgwick, their bodies moving so fluidly, muscles flexing, her quim had grown heavy and moist at that image too.

But she didn't want Sir Robert. She didn't want the man inside her or to wake up to him beside her every day. Beyond that, she knew that he would not be faithful.

Carolina had come to realize that that mattered to her.

"I believe I would be happiest with the earl," she answered softly.

Hargreaves was silent a moment, studying her face. Then he clapped his hands and smiled.

"The earl it will be then. And you shall be a countess."

Chapter Twenty-Three

That evening, watching Carolina dance with Oakley twice in a row and then again an hour later, Henry knew what she hadn't yet told him. The man had proposed and she had accepted.

It rankled him, though he knew it shouldn't. She wouldn't marry the man for months, and even when she did, despite what she had said, he could convince her to forget her morality. He had already, hadn't he?

It still bothered him. He hated the idea of another man's hands on her, another man's lips on her, of her doing anything to please any other man.

And she would try to please her husband. Despite her attraction to Henry, he knew that much about her: she would do everything she could to make the marriage work. He felt ill at the very thought.

He *was* uncharacteristically possessive of her.

He should have forced himself away the minute Carolina had become a habit, something, someone, he depended on. But Henry had never been good at denying himself anything.

The song was almost over. There was maybe a minute more

of the country dance. Henry made his way across the ballroom to where Agathe stood. The next dance would be his.

"Stanton!" Agathe cried, turning from her female friend and taking his arm, leading him a few steps away as if it were his idea to walk. "It's always such a delight to talk to you!" In a much quieter voice she added, "and thank you for getting me away from Mrs. Abernathy!"

"I am always happy to be of service, Mrs. Mustlewhaithe," Henry said, indulgently.

"Don't I know it?" she responded coyly. "But of course, those days are past."

"A pity," Henry agreed, playing the game, though any attraction he'd harbored for Agathe had run its course years ago, swiftly, as his passions always did. "How is your husband?"

"Missing me dreadfully, naturally," she said, batting her eyelashes. "But he will see me soon, as I have succeeded in my service to my brother. Carolina is engaged." She paused and he knew clearly that he was supposed to inquire to whom.

"Lord Oakley, I presume, is the lucky man?"

"You've been watching closely," Agathe's eyebrows arched up in surprise. "But then, I suppose, we have seen a great deal of you this season."

"Such charming company," Henry said simply.

"Yes, well." Agathe studied the dance floor where Carolina and Oakley were just performing their final bow and curtsey. "I had wondered at one point if you were thinking of taking a wife. Your admiration for Carolina has been quite clear."

Henry laughed, but even to his ears, the sound was hollow. "I would think my admiration of a beautiful young woman would always be clear."

He too watched as the couple grew nearer. Carolina's arm rested lightly on Oakley's sleeve. Her head was inclined slightly, as if she listened intently to whatever the earl was saying. And Henry knew the very moment when she saw him standing by her aunt. Her eyes widened, brightening, her face lighting up just before she schooled her expression into a more placid look.

That light had been for him and a strange joy Henry had never before felt unfurled in his chest. What would it be like to always be greeted with that look? Despite his tumultuous emotions, he managed to do the pretty.

"Congratulations, Oakley, on your very good luck."

"Thank you, Stanton." Oakley grinned. "I'm quite delighted."

"Do you mind if I dance with your affianced bride?" It rankled Henry to have to ask, to give precedence to this pup in his overly perfect clothes.

"I would be delighted, Lord Stanton," Carolina said quickly but looked to Oakley for approval. Henry's jaw clenched tightly.

Oakley nodded.

"I don't know how anyone could dance in here anymore," Agathe complained. "It's so terribly hot."

Henry held out his arm and Carolina glided toward him. The moment the slight weight of her hand rested on his sleeve, all the tension left him. The world had righted itself and Carolina was where she belonged.

He escorted her to the dance, away from Oakley. And the moment the crowd separated them from view, he led her out onto the terrace.

"Henry, what are you doing?" Carolina asked, startled. "We can't be seen out here, not now."

"We're hardly alone," Henry returned, though he was scouring the deep shadows, looking for a place where they could be. It wasn't safe, he knew, but he couldn't explain what possessed him. He needed her. He needed to be inside her.

Then he saw what he wanted, on the side closest to the ballroom doors, a set of stairs half obscured by a potted plant. Service stairs, leading down to the kitchens and cellars but not in use tonight. Slowly he inched her toward them. Luck was with him. No one was watching and he gestured for Carolina to precede him, sliding past the plant, down into the darkness.

The uneven brick at the bottom was further obscured by an ivy-covered trellis, and here Henry gently pushed Carolina down.

"We shouldn't do this, Henry, I'm engaged," she protested.

"You're not married yet," he said gruffly. "Take your gloves off and place your hands on the fourth step." He slid her skirts up even as she did what he said.

He stared at her round bottom for a moment, bare above her silk stockings. He ran his hands down the heart shaped curve and at the juncture where her thighs met, the gleaming slit with its thatch of curls. He cupped her moist heat in his hand, enjoying her muffled cry.

With his other hand he fumbled with his buttons, impatient to free himself, to be inside her. Finally the cloth fell, and his cock stood free, pulsing and painfully hard.

He leaned close to her, guiding his cock forward, until the head rested at her folds. Closing his eyes and savoring the sensation, he slid home.

He groaned at the pleasure and held her hips firmly, staying still deep inside of her.

"Thank you, Oakley," Agathe's voice wafted down to them from the overhead terrace. "It was getting so dreadfully hot in there, I just needed a breath of air."

Carolina stiffened in Henry's arms and she looked back at him over her shoulder, her eyes wide with fright.

Henry smiled, that wicked smile, and a fierce triumph filled him. If it was possible, his cock grew even larger inside her. The thought of him fucking her with her fiancé a mere ten feet away was a powerfully erotic one. She was his.

He slowly pulled out till just the tip of his cock was inside her. Then swiftly, he thrust back in, hard, making her gasp.

"These affairs can get tediously crowded," Oakley agreed. "May I get you anything else? A lemonade?"

Henry pumped in and out smoothly, working her cunt. He reached under her hips to play with her clit, to draw fast, firm circles over the little nub. The sound of his balls slapping against her seemed deafening.

"No, no, I'm quite all right," Agathe said.

Carolina let out a soft little moan, and he felt her near her peak. She looked back at him helplessly, biting her lips. He swiveled his hips, moving his fingers faster.

Carolina shuddered, her eyes rolling up and then her head flopping back forward as she started pulsing uncontrollably, clenching his cock with her climax, drawing his own out of him.

He pumped hard—one, two, three times—and then released himself inside her, throwing his head back with a soundless roar.

"So, what is this speech I hear you are going to give in the House tomorrow?" Agathe asked.

"The reformers are trying to ruin our countryside," Oakley said irritably. "But come, surely that's not what you wish to speak of on such a lovely night?"

Leaning over Carolina's back, Henry kissed her neck and felt himself slip out of her hot sheath. He pushed up to keep himself in as long as possible, pistoning his hips in small thrusts.

The stone staircase was cold and hard under Carolina's bare palms but she stayed where she was, her breathing coming back to normal. She was afraid to move, afraid to make any noise with her fiancé still on the terrace.

She felt Henry move against her, stimulating the still sensitive area. She swallowed. He was already semi-hard within her and she knew if they stayed there just a moment more, he'd be fully extended and rock hard.

Dear Lord, he already was! But this hard length of him felt delicious. It felt so good to be filled up and stretched like that. His movements were slower now—long, languorous thrusts and retreats.

She was so wet, filled with his first release and her own lubrications, that each movement created squishing sounds and she feared being discovered.

"Shall we go back inside?" she heard her aunt say.

As their footsteps retreated, Carolina let out a little moan.

"Close, wasn't it?" Henry teased, his hips doing little circles now.

She tilted her head back just enough to look at him from the corner of her eye.

"You're wicked," she chided, but the scolding was undermined by the soft, pleased curve of her lips.

"Yes." Henry breathed against her ear. "I'm very wicked. And I'll show you just how when I come to you tonight."

Chapter Twenty-Four

When the bright white light of morning burned across Henry's eyes, he buried his head in the pillows and cursed his valet, Thompson. Was it too much to ask that the man draw the draperies at night?

Of course, Henry knew it was his own fault that his situation was so slipshod. Living in rented rooms with a maid who came for a few hours a day when he had a perfectly good townhouse he could open up was his own fault.

But he still thought of that place as James's, and he didn't have enough interest to do the entire overhaul the house would need in order to rid it of his brother's hideous taste.

From the position of the sun, Henry knew that it was past noon. He'd only made it into his bed at five that morning, having left Carolina's bed dangerously late.

He moved his hips against the bed, enjoying the feel of his cock filling with blood, rising up.

He just couldn't get enough of her. He was tempted to call on her, find a way to have her even in the middle of the afternoon, in the bright light of day.

That would be a novelty. He smiled at the thought of how she would look, naked and laid out before him on the grass of his country estate. He imagined having her to himself for the entire day, being able to take his time about every detail of their encounter.

He rolled on his back, flinging one arm over his eyes to block the sun, and grasping his cock with the other. He rubbed the dripping pre-cum over the entire length and then massaged the head.

There was a small folly on the Yorkshire estate, faux ruins of a Norman castle. He imagined Carolina there, her creamy thighs spread before him, the sun gleaming on her glistening pussy. He could almost taste her on his tongue.

He groaned, his hand moving faster—long, firm strokes.

He'd part her plump lips, reveal the hard, pink little nub within, and the folds which would be slick with her pearly juices.

His balls tightened, the blood roared in his cock and in his head. He cried out as he let loose, his semen spurting from him as he arched his back into the orgasm.

He sunk back into the bed, his sticky hand flopping down onto the sheets.

He may have come, but it wasn't enough. He wanted to taste her.

Chapter Twenty-Five

"Congratulations, Hargreaves," Henry greeted Alistair an hour later at White's. "I heard of Carolina's coup."

Alistair raised his eyebrows and Henry realized he'd slipped and used her Christian name.

He shrugged. "More alliterative, don't you think? Carolina's coup rather than Miss Hargreaves's?"

"True," Alistair agreed. "I'm proud of her. Oakley's around here somewhere. Have a drink with us."

Which, of course, was the last thing Henry wanted.

"I'm surprised he's not with your daughter today."

"Agathe has taken Carolina on a shopping expedition. I believe I'll be receiving a rather large bill from Madame Bellerosse this week," Alistair said with a wry smile.

Henry laughed with him but his mind worked quickly. He knew exactly where Madame Bellerosse was located. He also knew the location of her back door and had successfully executed little assignations there in the past.

He thought of his morning's fantasy and licked his lips.

"You know, Alistair, I'd love to join you, but we'll just have to do it later."

Henry made his exit as quickly as possible, before he ran into Lord Claddogh and Mr. Haverstock, with whom he had engaged for a drink. He stopped only to leave an apologetic note with one of the servants for those two men.

Chapter Twenty-Six

If the devil was on his shoulder, the devil wanted him to have his way. After picking his way through the filthy mews, Henry slipped into the dressmaker's workroom, startling the three seamstresses who sat there among sumptuous fabrics, sewing industriously.

"I was never here." He winked and flashed his smile, that one Carolina called wicked.

The women tittered.

"But, can you tell me, is Miss Hargreaves in the sitting room?"

Arch, knowing looks all around, but one of the women spoke up, putting down her work.

"I believe, sir, that she's here with Mrs. Mustlewhaithe. I'll just check and see where she is right now."

As the seamstress passed him, Henry slid a guinea into her hand and she bobbed a quick curtsey.

After she left, Henry looked around the room, waiting impatiently. The other two women had returned to their work, but he felt their curious sidelong glances.

Just when he was about ready to charge through the thick curtains separating them from the rest of the shop, the seamstress returned with a sly smile.

"Miss Hargreaves is currently in the changing room. Alone," she revealed. "I asked Lily the shop assistant to make sure Mrs. Mustlewhaithe was amply occupied for a good, um, ten minutes?"

"Excellent work, ma'am," Henry said admiringly. "I'm in your debt."

The seamstress blushed and led him through the break in the curtains. On the other side was another small room with two smaller curtained-off areas and a large, well-made mirror in between.

The seamstress indicated the area to the left and then, giving a saucy wink, left him to his own devices.

The curtain parted slightly, revealing the welcome sight of Carolina's blue eyes. They widened upon seeing him, and then she opened the curtains more and he slipped through.

The room was crowded with silks and muslins. Two dresses hung on a hook against the wall and another lay in a heap on a bench.

"You shouldn't be here!" she whispered fiercely. "My aunt is just in the other room."

"That hasn't stopped us before," Henry returned, taking in the lovely view before him. She stood there in only her chemise and stockings. The fine linen covered her from shoulders to knees but it clung to her lush curves. "I woke up with the taste of you in my mouth."

Carolina's lips parted and she closed her eyes.

Henry took advantage of her silence and drew her into his arms. She pressed herself against him, fitting perfectly, and he bent his head, bringing his mouth to hers.

"Sweet," he breathed against her lips, "so sweet."

Then he broke away. He looked around the small space. The only place to sit was the bench, so he pushed her dress to the side, ignoring her protests.

"Sit, love," he whispered.

"Henry," she started, but he rested his forefinger to her lips.

"Let me, Carolina, please."

Their eyes locked. After a long moment, she ran the pink point of her tongue down the length of his finger and then took the whole into her mouth, sucking.

Henry swallowed hard. He supposed that was as good an answer as any. He slid his finger from her mouth and she backed up and slowly sat down on the bench.

Henry knelt down on the floor in front of her, keeping his eyes on her face. He parted her smooth knees with the palms of his hands. Her breath was coming faster, anticipating.

He looked down. Her chemise had ridden up, revealing the expanse of her thighs, more delectable than he had envisioned just that morning. He leaned down and kissed her at the place just above her stockings. He worked his way up her thigh, alternating long licks with hot, open-mouthed kisses until he was near enough to smell her musky scent.

He pushed her chemise further up so that she was completely open to his view. Under the thatch of tight curls, the slit was wet with her arousal. Pearly juices already visible.

Just as in his fantasy, he parted her plump lips, revealing the hard, pink little nub within. He blew hot air over her clit. When she writhed under him, he held her thighs more firmly. Finally, he lowered his tongue to her.

She moaned—a long sound of yearning.

He knew exactly how she felt. Her pretty flesh pulsed and creamed under his ministrations and he lapped the sweetness up as if he'd never eat again.

He looked at her face. Her eyes were closed and her neck arched back. Her hands massaged her own breasts through the chemise.

He slid his tongue up into her, twisting it inside her, enjoying Carolina's ragged gasp. Then he changed his tactics, bringing his fingers to take his tongue's place, and as he thrust his fingers, he sucked her clit into his mouth, flicking his tongue across it in short, hard strokes.

It didn't take very long. Carolina's body went rigid, her hands dropping to her sides, her thighs clenching around his face as her legs stretched out. And as she did, he felt her inner muscles convulsing around him, her juices dripping from her and onto his waiting tongue, onto his hand.

She let out a soft keening sound and he knew she was struggling not to scream.

Finally, she bucked against his mouth again and again, and then fell back against the wall.

He scrambled quickly up, taking her face in his hands, plunging his tongue into her mouth, kissing her deeply.

He kissed her until her breathing evened out and then he moved away, smiling at the sated glaze of her eyes.

"Thank you," Henry whispered and then he stood. He peeked through the curtains. The room was clear. With a final hot look at Carolina, he slipped back through the curtains.

He stopped for a moment to look at himself in the mirror. He straightened his coat and attempted to fix the limp frill of his cravat.

"No, girl, I don't want to see another one, I want to see how my niece looks in that blue silk." Agathe's voice rang clearly from the other side of the thin door that led to the shop. "Let me by."

He stared as the knob of the door began to turn. He was tempted to stay there. Hell, he was tempted to go back to Carolina and give Agathe something to find.

Instead, he pushed his way into the second curtained changing area, which he found, thankfully, empty. He made his way halfway through before Agathe entered the room.

"Stanton!" she cried, "You naughty man! Whom do you have in there?"

Reluctantly, Henry came back out, keeping the curtains tightly closed behind him.

"A gentleman never tells, ma'am." He managed a smirk. "I must protect her identity."

Agathe laughed.

Henry didn't wait for her to grow more curious. He bolted from the room through the other draperies that led into the workroom. From there he made a rapid escape into the street.

Agathe stood there a moment, eyeing the tightly drawn curtains. She loved gossip and it would be delicious to know who Stanton's latest paramour was.

She stripped off one glove and then let it fall to the floor.

With a heavy, exaggerated sigh, she bent down to pick it up. And while down on the floor, she picked up a tiny bit of the curtain to look under. And then she raised it more. And then she stood up and yanked the curtains open.

The area was completely empty. No blushingly guilty woman. No woman, period.

Agathe turned around with an angry, growing suspicion. She threw open the other set of drapes to the room in which Carolina was changing.

Carolina, in the middle of the room struggling with her dress, stopped and stared at her. A startled fear was caught on her face—a revealingly flushed face, above a revealingly rumpled dress.

"He was with *you*, wasn't he?" Agathe accused, and Carolina couldn't find the strength to deny it. A lazy smile curved her lips and her aunt gaped.

"Finish getting dressed, we're leaving," Agathe ordered, and then yanked the curtains open again.

Carolina watched her leave with a sigh. The game was finally up.

Chapter Twenty-Seven

The day was hot for early June, but as the open carriage rumbled along the London streets, Carolina was covered in a cold sweat.

"I don't know how it escaped my notice." Agathe curled her lip in disgust. "I suppose the fact that Stanton has paid you particular attention, dancing with you frequently, should have triggered my suspicions, but I thought he was merely lusting after something he couldn't have."

Carolina said nothing, staring out the side of the barouche.

"Don't hide your face from me," Agathe complained, pulling on Carolina's bonnet, forcing her to turn her head. "I'm not the one who has ruined herself. And with Stanton!"

Then Agathe fell silent. A moment later she sighed lustily.

"Well, I suppose if it would be with anyone, it would be Henry." Agathe's full lips finally relaxed into an amused smile. "It was worth it, wasn't it?"

Relieved at the change in her aunt's demeanor and eager to share after months of holding back her secret, Carolina nodded, grinning wickedly.

"He was worth every minute, Auntie," she admitted. "He's the most magnificent man I've ever met."

"Come, dear, you haven't met many men," Agathe chided. "But that's not far off from the truth. And at least he knows what he's about. He was always meticulous about protection."

At Carolina's blank look, Agathe's jaw dropped and her eyes narrowed.

"Protection, dear," she prodded, "you know, vinegar-soaked sponges or those clever little sheaths?"

Carolina bit her lip and then slowly shook her head. "We never used any of that."

Agathe's small, gloved hand flew to her chest and she let out a deep, shuddering sigh. "All right, I won't get hysterical. Tell me, dear, does he pull out before he . . ." She made a small gesture with her other hand.

Carolina shook her head.

"Are you a complete idiot?" Agathe gaped at her. "You do know how babies are made, do you not?"

Carolina nodded again, and then the blood fled from her face. "I do know, but I never! I never thought about it. I was entirely caught up."

"Clearly," Agathe said reprovingly, cutting her off.

They rode in uncomfortable silence for a few moments before Agathe reached out and took Carolina's shaking hand.

"I suppose that is what comes of not having a mother." She sighed again. "Tell me, when did you last have your courses?"

Carolina thought about it. She'd been in town just over two months. Henry had been to her bed almost every night. She hadn't considered, had never wondered why her courses didn't come.

"Just before London," Carolina admitted, understanding now just what situation she was in.

"And you are normally irregular?" Agathe pressed.

"No," Carolina shook her head. "I'm like a well-wound clock."

"All right then," Agathe clapped her hands together, serious and determined. "We'll just have to move the wedding up. We won't tell your father, or the young man, we'll simply say . . . we'll say that you wish to be married while everyone is still in town for the season, so they may see your triumph."

"We won't tell?" Carolina whispered.

"That should appeal to the men's vanities as well," Agathe continued. "No, of course we can't tell! You'd be ruined. Just like you would never say you weren't a virgin. And we'll take care of that as well with a little trick." Her lips settled into a determined line as she nodded. "Yes, this is the course we'll take. Leave it to me, dear. And by all means, Carolina, do not tell Stanton."

Don't tell Stanton? How could she not tell Henry that he was going to be a father? That she was going to be a mother?

Agathe must have seen something on her face because, much more gently and with a sad smile, she addressed her niece.

"You *must* not tell him, dear. It was his carelessness that has put you in this situation and his intentions were never honorable. You owe him nothing!" Agathe emphasized. "Nothing."

Then Agathe turned away, muttering to herself. Carolina thought she could just make out the words.

"Even I was never so stupid . . ."

Chapter Twenty-Eight

Agathe insisted on still attending the ball at the Vadebakers' home that evening. Carolina protested. She didn't want to see anyone, but she especially didn't want to see Henry. She didn't think she could face him after realizing that she was carrying his child.

But when Agathe arrived a few minutes before Oakley, Carolina was waiting in the sitting room, dressed in the pale blue silk gown she had originally planned to wear. She couldn't quite believe that she was actually with child as the dress fit as perfectly as always.

"Well, child, you may thank your aunt for her hard work this afternoon on your behalf," Agathe whispered, perched far too close to Carolina on the blue sofa.

Carolina looked at her blankly.

"I have wrought magic, my dear," Agathe explained. "I have convinced both your father and Oakley that the sooner a wedding can be had, the better. At the very height of the season, before it begins to wane and all society leaves for the summer. The wedding will be next week." Agathe stared at her expectantly, a pleased smile on her lips.

Carolina found it difficult to breathe. She knew she should be grateful, but it was all too much. The pressure on her chest increased and she struggled to take deep, calming breaths.

"Thank you, Auntie," she managed, finally.

Agathe nodded in acknowledgment and then continued on, "I will take care of all the details, of course. It won't be easy to pull such an affair together, but I will manage."

Her aunt continued to ramble on about all the arrangements that needed to be made, but Carolina heard none of it. In just a week, she would be a wife. But she would be wife to the wrong man—to Oakley.

She should be marrying the father of her child.

Oakley arrived, in all his gentlemanly perfection and she didn't have to fake the blush that filled her cheeks. She felt like a fraud, committing such a hideous deception on this man. It was no way to begin a life together.

The Vadebakers' large house was set back from the street in a small park, and and even from outside, the windows glowed with the light of myriad candles.

Her family and soon to be family were there in their entirety that night, a united front. Everyone except for Mr. Mustlewhaithe, and he was expected to arrive in town in a few days.

Carolina felt smothered by the attention. Her father had never been so kind to her. Oakley was overly attentive, whispering in her ear that he was so very glad she had wanted to move the wedding up, that he was eager as well.

Agathe had obviously said a few other things to the man to get him to expedite the wedding.

Oakley's mother, as well, clung to her side, introducing her to all her matronly friends. Carolina smiled till her cheeks hurt.

Chapter Twenty-Nine

Henry circled the ballroom. There was never a moment when Carolina was alone, she was always surrounded by people, and there was Oakley, by her side or just a step away.

He could ask for a dance but that wasn't what he wanted.

A firm hand touched his arm and Henry looked to his side to find Agathe staring daggers at him, her small hand like a claw.

"You'll stay away from her from now on," Agathe hissed through a plastered smile.

So she knew. He carefully extracted his arm from her grip, studiously fixing the now wrinkled sleeve. He'd wondered, it was why he'd stayed away so far this evening, waiting for some sign from Carolina.

"No, I don't think so," Henry drawled. Nobody told him what to do.

"You will, Stanton," Agathe persisted. "We've moved the wedding up to next week. And Alistair has worked far too hard for you to mess this up now. You've already done too much damage."

Next week? Henry struggled not to show how shocked he was by the expedited wedding.

"She's not married yet, Agathe. I'll do as I like," he murmured, pulling his hand away.

"Not unless you intend to marry her and we both know how likely that is," Agathe said scathingly. "You have no trouble stealing other men's wives, but when it comes to your own vows you're quite a romantic: you believe a man and woman should honor the words they speak."

"True," Henry admitted, "but as you said, I have no trouble stealing other men's wives."

He walked away from her, continuing his perambulation of the dance floor, always keeping a clear view of Carolina. Aggressively, he put himself in her line of sight.

Her gaze flew to him and her eyes widened as they met his. She shook her head just slightly but he ignored the warning.

With a slow smile and a subtle jut of his chin, he indicated for her to follow him. He left the room then, unsure if she would actually come to him.

He chose a room down the hallway at random. The room was lit as if in expectation for later entertainment, but it was currently empty. He paced anxiously, counting the seconds, placing bets against himself. Calling himself a fool for caring.

Chapter Thirty

As she slipped from the ballroom, Carolina told herself she was only meeting him in order to tell him she could no longer do this.

She would say good-bye. That was all.

She strolled down the hallway, aware that there were others near her. She had no idea where Henry had gone, but by now she knew his habits.

She headed to the rear of the house, away from the sound of the orchestra and the signs of other guests. She turned a corner. There was one door in this hallway slightly ajar. She pushed it open further.

It wasn't a large room, and the wood paneling and forest-green upholstery made it seem even smaller. The large billiard table in the center of the room took up the most space.

And Henry was bent over that table, a long wooden cue between his hands, setting up a shot.

"Close the door and lock it," he said, though he didn't look up.

She did as he said, hearing the clink of wood against wood and the rolling sound of the ball across the table. She turned around and leaned against the door.

Henry had straightened.

Dear Lord, the fashions fit him so well and he wore them with the perfect level of insouciance.

All her best intentions fled.

She wanted to taste him. She wanted to taste him the way just hours ago he'd tasted her. She wanted to see his face grow boyish with pleasure and hear his low moans.

She would tell him that it was over. But not yet.

Carolina closed the short distance between them and slowly descended to her knees before him, her eyes trained on his.

She ran her hands over the front of his breeches and found him already hard. She unbuttoned the flap of cloth and took him in her gloved hands.

A small drop of pearly liquid rested at the tip of his cock; she licked at it with her tongue, moaning at the salty taste of him. She took him hungrily in her mouth, savoring his hot, velvet skin, swirling her tongue around him. Her hands came up to hold his buttocks, pulling him further into her mouth.

He stopped her, pushed her away and lifted her up from the floor. Her mouth felt empty, but as he laid her on the billiard table, pushing her dress up to her waist, she was eager for what he had to give.

He parted her thighs as he had hours ago, but now he leaned over her, sliding his tongue into her mouth just as he slid his cock inside her.

Exquisite, she thought. Her inner walls were stretched to their limit, but she wanted him in her even deeper, even harder.

Then he pushed her down to the table, tugged at her dress to free her breasts. He ran his hands over the soft globes and then moved on to her hips. He leaned back, pulling her down toward him.

She felt him pressed up into the very center of her, balls deep, and she sighed with the pure pleasure of it.

"Touch yourself," he whispered. She did as he said, one hand stealing down to her clit, hard and stretched above the pumping column of his cock.

With two fingers she rubbed little circles over the small muscle. Her flesh was slick and her fingers kept slipping, but she kept them there, the sensation building too quickly.

He felt impossibly hard within her and the little swivels he made with his hips hit her in places inside that shot straight to her nipples.

Suddenly she tensed and arched her back, coming up off the table in her climax as her cries filled the room.

He slid out and turned her over. Still shaking from her orgasm, she rested on her forearms, her hips pressed against the wood of the table, and Henry thrust back into her.

She felt him everywhere inside her, as if there was nothing left of Carolina and she was only the relentless thrusting of his cock. Each movement pushed her overstimulated clit hard against the table and kept her convulsing around him with pleasure.

His cock grew harder, larger within her as he neared his climax, and the feel of him triggered her own. She exploded even as she felt him release himself into her, pumping hard, again and again, until he had nothing left to give.

Chapter Thirty-One

"Agathe is right. We can't do this again," Carolina whispered, struggling to hold back the tears. "You aren't the only one who believes their word should mean something. I'm pledging myself to Oakley."

"But not yet, not till next week," Henry said firmly. He wouldn't let her go just yet. Not until *he* was ready. Not because Agathe manipulated them.

"No, Henry," Carolina shook her head, disengaging from his embrace, studiously rearranging her dress. "Starting now. *We* will never happen again."

She didn't look at him, not the whole time she walked toward the door. He watched her swaying stride in disbelief. She was leaving him there without a backward glance.

She opened the door and paused there. He started toward her. Maybe this was a game, maybe she wanted him to stop her. He'd play that game.

But then she spoke, and the words hit him as she slipped out the door.

"It was lovely while it lasted."

Henry held himself back from striding after her. He took a deep breath in and let it out in a long exhale. For good measure he repeated the process until he was certain that even if he chose to look for her now, she'd have made her way to the safe bosom of her family.

It really was just as well. He would have started to tire of her soon in any event. A man could fuck just one woman for only so long. Variety was a necessity of life. Especially for a man like Henry.

Yes? And just what sort of man was he? Henry ridiculed himself. He was the sort who now looked at every woman's form hoping to see Carolina's shapely body, her chestnut hair, the soft curve of her cheek, the gentle slope of her nose—the way a little crease formed between her eyes when she was frustrated or the way she seemed to light up from inside when he came to her.

Henry wiped his hand down his face in disgust. He should be institutionalized for such thoughts.

One woman was exchangeable for another. Simply because he'd wanted to own Carolina for a little while, because he'd given in to the easy jealousy of knowing he could not just discard her when *he* was ready, was no reason to rhapsodize about the sheen of her goddamned gleaming curls!

Alistair had warned him that one day he'd be taken in. One day he would fall in love, or think he had, and marry some very fuckable woman, and then he'd learn that marriage vows meant nothing. They were simply an archaic way for the church to ensure that children were fed.

But the woman who'd claimed his heart was marrying some-one else, so Henry didn't have to worry about fulfilling Alistair's prophesy. Especially not with the man's own daughter!

Wait—who'd claimed his heart? Henry looked around the room wildly. The billiards table upon which he'd just had Caro-lina filled his vision.

All right, a billiards table—there would be something to drink around here somewhere. He scanned the walls till he found the cabinet.

Blessedly, behind the marquetry was a half-filled decanter of amber liquid. And beside the decanter, four crystal glasses.

He poured himself a taste and sipped it experimentally. It was a fine Scotch, something he'd had before but couldn't place. He filled the glass, ignoring all rules of etiquette. Who would see him regardless?

Then he took a large, foolhardy gulp, enjoying the harsh fire as it burned through his throat and his thoughts.

Goddammit, he loved her! He couldn't even make the mistake of marrying her because she was marrying Oakley.

He hadn't thought about it consciously, but he hadn't had another woman since he'd first fucked Carolina that night in the library. He hadn't wanted anyone else.

Henry downed the Scotch and poured himself another glass. It was a fine Scotch whisky, meant to be savored. He sipped at the drink, rolling the liquid over his tongue. He'd have to find out where Vadebaker got his stuff.

If he really wanted to, he could still marry her himself. Henry brushed the insidious thought away as quickly as it had come. Stealing another man's fiancée was completely dishonorable. He took another sip as he paced the room.

And fucking another man's fiancée wasn't? Henry laughed, thinking his morality ridiculously twisted.

He was well on his way to a delightful drunk. He could feel the liquid just beginning to tickle at his balls. His cock stirred a bit.

The familiar sexual stirrings comforted him. He knew just where to spend this sort of feeling, and he wouldn't have to sneak into Hargreaves's townhouse to get there.

Chapter Thirty-Two

It was still early when he arrived at the club. Many of the usual members wouldn't have even left their balls or routs yet. Which meant Henry had the pick of the luscious beauties who lined up before him in the foyer.

He scanned the women in their flimsy Grecian outfits. A brunette, her pert breasts clearly outlined by the thin cloth, caught his eye. Until he realized that she reminded him of Carolina. He directed his attention instead to a voluptuous little blond.

"You." He gestured to her with a curved finger and she came to his side quickly.

"Gina, my Lord," she said, curtseying. "Just me?"

"Yes, just you," Henry said, frowning.

"It was me and Cynthia the last time I had the pleasure." She offered a sexy little pout. "I remember how insatiable you are."

"Just you tonight, Gina."

She curtseyed again and then led him upstairs. To that same third-floor bedroom where he'd had his mouth on Carolina.

"Not this room," he said brusquely and they moved further down the hallway.

He felt clearly that this place was becoming too familiar, too full of actual memories and not merely those hazy, lust-filled encounters of the past. He would have to find another venue for his entertainments.

The room they finally entered was cool in its blueness. From the blue fabric-lined walls to the tapestry behind the bed and the fresco painted on the ceiling, it was an underwater paradise with the intention to drown the inhabitants with pleasure and dissipation.

He stood by the door of the room, taking the whole atmosphere in. Little Gina stared at him.

Finally, she came near and put one small hand on his chest, tugging lightly on his cravat until the whole thing disassembled. Henry watched her hand trail down his clothing, brushing over his pants as if searching for his cock. The cock he knew to be still soft and hidden.

"Strip for me, slowly," Henry commanded, stilling her hand. "And then lie on the bed on your hands and knees."

Gina smiled, obviously pleased to have a task.

"Whatever you desire, my Lord."

Chapter Thirty-Three

Walking away from Henry was the hardest thing she had ever done, and Carolina was not proud of it. She knew she should be. She should be thrilled that her latent sense of responsibility had finally awakened.

She wasn't. As she walked slowly away from the billiard room toward the rooms set aside for women's private needs, she could feel Henry's seed dripping down her thigh. She knew now what that viscous liquid meant. The effects of two months' plowing had taken root inside her.

His scent was all around her, inside of her. Knowing that it was for the last time was killing her.

And in this child, she would always have a reminder of him. A reminder to both torment and comfort her.

She felt the trail of semen hit her stockings, and that thin fabric soaked up the excess. Abruptly she veered, changing her course. She stopped in front of a large silver decorative plate, which offered her a view of herself. She looked sad, slightly rumpled but not overly so. She reached up to tuck one errant curl back into place and then returned to the ballroom.

Agathe was waiting for her, disapproval etched clearly in her ever-so-slightly down-turned mouth.

"You let him fuck you again, didn't you?" Agathe said, an odd note in her voice.

"It's over," Carolina said, simply.

"Good." Agathe pursed her lips together. "If Oakley were any other sort of man, I'd recommend you seduce him before the wedding, so he isn't suspicious when the babe is born two months early. But he's a true gentleman." She said the word *gentleman* as if she held no respect for the idea.

"He has kissed me," Carolina managed a smile. "A quick, close-mouthed kiss on the cheek."

As if she had conjured him up, the earl appeared before her, admiration in his eyes.

"You missed our dance, my dear," he said, smiling, "but I forgive you—how could I not?"

"You're too good, my lord," Carolina looked down at her hands.

"It's not too late to join, however." He offered her his arm and with a frozen heart, she took it.

Chapter Thirty-Four

Gina's naked buttocks faced him like two halves of a very ripe melon. Henry was pleased to find himself stirred at the sight.

"Touch yourself," he directed and she shifted her weight. One lithe arm reached underneath and he could see her fingertips massaging the folds of her cunt.

Yes, that's what he needed to see, Henry thought as he massaged his cock to a full erection.

He reached into his coat for the ready supply of the expensive French sheaths he always had.

And came up empty.

His hand stilled.

Where were the little envelopes? No, not just where, but *when* had he last even thought of them? When had he last used them?

The answer he came up with caught in his throat. He strode

quickly to the windows, fumbling with the draperies and latch and flinging them open to let the cool night breeze in.

"M'lord?"

Panicked, he turned around to find Gina still fondling herself, but staring at him in confusion.

"Do you want me to continue?"

Henry shook his head to clear the myriad thoughts—the one pervasive thought—from clouding his head.

"No, Gina." He swallowed hard, waving with his hand. "Would you mind leaving, please?"

With a frown, she slid from the bed and Henry stopped watching her. He turned back to the open window and breathed in deeply of the cool air. The wind tickled his genitals and he pulled the falls of his breeches back up, refastening the buttons.

He was always careful. Always.

But he hadn't been with Carolina. Not from the first moment he'd released himself inside her up against the wall. If ever a man wished to get a woman with child, he would have acted the way Henry had and continued to do.

And now she was.

It all came together in his mind: her retching sickness, the months of uninterrupted sex, the ridiculously short engagement.

Bloody hell, they were going to pass his child off as Oakley's!

A hot fury the like of which Henry had never felt before filled him. Didn't he even have a say in this? Carolina didn't even think it appropriate to tell him he was going to be a father?

Propelled by his anger, he was outside the club and in his carriage before he realized his own actions.

It was not that late. There was a very good chance that Carolina was still at the ball, but there was also the chance that she'd already have returned home.

Chapter Thirty-Five

Jack had not wanted to let him in. But ten quid had eased the man's sudden qualms.

She wasn't home yet, so Henry cooled his feet in her room, nursing a glass of brandy that another tip to Jack had procured.

He was going to be a father! The thought didn't scare him as much as he would have thought. When he wasn't furious, thinking of the deception, he imagined Carolina, her belly naked and swollen. It was a surprisingly arousing thought.

He'd just finished his drink when he heard footsteps in the hall, and Carolina bidding good night to her father.

Henry hid himself behind the dressing screen just as Carolina entered, followed by her maid.

He watched her undress, the maid helping her, her body illuminated by candlelight. Her body was curved in all the right places but her belly remained flat and taut. For a moment he doubted the conclusion he'd come to.

Finally, the maid left. Carolina, in her voluminous nightgown, stood before her mirror.

Henry stepped out from behind the screen. She let out a little shriek before catching herself, her hand pressed to her mouth.

He walked to her, coming to stand behind her and he splayed the palm of his hand over her stomach.

"I told you, Henry." Carolina finally found her voice, meeting his gaze in the mirror. "It's over, you shouldn't be here."

"Are you carrying my child, Carolina?" he asked.

Her eyes widened but she didn't speak.

"Tell me the truth," Henry said, his voice low and intent. "By God, tell me the truth."

Finally, she nodded, her face pale, her eyes glistening.

"I believe that I am," she admitted. "I am with child. Yours."

It was too much. He buried his face in her neck and pulled her close to him, nearly crushing her in his embrace.

"Henry," she gasped, "I can't. I need air."

He loosened his grip and spun her around to face him, his hands on her arms.

"You will not marry Oakley," Henry stated gruffly. "Not with my child in your belly. You're mine, Carolina. You will always be mine."

Chapter Thirty-Six

When he crushed his lips to hers, Carolina let him. When he carried her to the bed and tore her nightgown from her body, she let him do that as well. And when he thrust into her, claiming her as his own, saying that she was his and no one else's, she met his passion with her own.

It was a relief that he knew, that she didn't have to keep such a hideous secret. And if he wanted her, she didn't care anymore if she betrayed her duty to her family. She would go with Henry wherever he wanted her, however he wanted her. It was enough.

So she was deliciously surprised when, spent inside her, their sweaty bodies panting with exhaustion, he murmured against her ear, "In the morning, I'll tell your father that you are marrying *me*."

Then he fell asleep and stayed with her through the night, her body curved against his, within his arms.

Epilogue

The library in Henry's Yorkshire estate was not particularly large, and books were crammed everywhere into the tight space in a way that made Carolina think they were just about to topple down. But in all the nine months she'd lived in this house, the piles and stacks always managed to remain where they were.

The only object in the room in any danger of falling down was Carolina.

She was shaking. Of course, that was due to Henry, who had just carelessly ripped the bodice of her morning dress and liberated her breasts from their constraints. Her full, plump breasts, which now overflowed in his hands.

In the mirror on the far wall, she watched his dark head, bent, licking his way down toward the soft globes. A rush of wet heat flooded her thighs at the sight of his mouth on her body. Then he took one rosy oversensitive nipple in his mouth and she felt the not completely pleasant twinge of her milk seeping out.

"Careful, love," she murmured, and he quickly released the tender bud, coming back up to kiss her mouth.

"I'm a jealous man," Henry breathed, circling his hips against hers till she could feel the hard heat of his cock despite all the layers of cloth between them. "I think we should rethink the wet nurse."

"Little Gemma is quite greedy," she teased. "You'd have to hire two."

He thrust himself against her as if he could make the offending fabric disappear from sheer force.

"Which reminds me, Agathe wrote that my father has run up another stack of debts . . ."

"Shh, not now." Henry tugged on her earlobe with his teeth. "But I've already heard from his solicitor. No more about your father."

Carolina laughed and reached down to gather her own dress in her hands, tugging up on it.

He followed her lead and undid the buttons that held up the falls of his pantaloons.

It was hardly elegant, but a desperate man could not be choosy. It had been eight weeks since he'd sunk himself into her heat. And seven months since he'd been able to press himself flat against her. He'd enjoyed all the myriad ways they'd loved each other between then, but he was ready for this. More than ready. He was rock hard and dripping.

She was dripping as well. He could smell the musky scent of her arousal and it was almost too much—he almost came against her thigh.

He guided the tip of his cock into her and the first exquisite touch of her hot, wet folds was like a welcome home. The sweetness of the sensation surprised him with its domesticity.

Then he needed more. He thrust upward, plunging deeply into her, pulling her down so that he filled her fully.

She cried out, and the sound of her pleasure made him wild. He shifted her weight in his hands, pressing her into the wall as he thrust—short, rapid thrusts that stimulated the already throbbing muscle of her clit.

She was as ready for her climax as he was. He knew the sounds of her rising by heart. He'd even heard it in his dreams all those times he'd reached for her in the night.

He pulled her close against him, supporting all her weight in his arms. With a gutteral cry, he released himself into her, claiming her mouth with his own.

She looked again at their reflection in the mirror—the surging movement of his hips against hers.

Some things never change, she thought, pushed over the edge by the view and riding the crest of her own climax, *but some things change in just the right way.*

PART II

The Education of Lord Oakley

Prologue

A magical spring night on which all the stars aligned.

*A*ll of London, or at least the ton, has descended on the Vadebakers' *house this evening,* Oakley thought. Or perhaps it was simply that most of his family, cadet branches and all, had come out to show support for his engagement. Not that he needed any social or moral support. Carolina Hargreaves might be the daughter of a debauched and spendthrift baron, but the family was still old and well connected. Carolina, herself, was as lovely and innocent as young debutantes came.

She embodied every poetic womanly ideal Oakley had imagined in his school days, which admittedly were not far behind him. Additionally, she would make the perfect decoration for his arm as he moved his way up the political ladder. With her natural reticence and classic English beauty, she could only be an asset to him in his secret march toward a future post as prime minister.

Had she not shown an instinct for public life by requesting that they move up their wedding in order to take advantage of the full swing of the social season? There was one more detail that intrigued him: her surprising impatience. Her aunt, Mrs. Mustlewhaithe, had hinted that Carolina was modestly eager for the wedding night.

A good omen. He'd heard many stories of men saddled with a frigid wife and forced to seek companionship from other sources.

That was not the life Oakley wished for himself. He desired a life without scandal, without mistresses.

He looked around for his fiancée. She was nowhere to be seen and his searching gaze fell on Mrs. Mustlewhaithe's face. The older woman, still beautiful for her some forty years, looked uncharacteristically dour. Her expression eased into a pleasant smile when she noticed Oakley's attention.

"She'll be back momentarily," Mrs. Mustlewhaithe explained, "she went to the retiring room."

Oakley frowned. That was the only negative he had found in Miss Hargreaves's character; she spent far too much time in the ladies' retiring room. But what could one say to that? It was a trifle, a mild peculiarity.

"I'll see what's keeping her," her aunt said with a tight smile before forging ahead into the crowd.

Chapter One

One day later

> **Love is swift of foot.**
> **Love's a man of war,**
> **And can shoot,**
> **And can hit from far.**

An atypical sneer curling his lips, Oakley recalled the stanza from George Herbert's poem *Discipline*. Just as well that he hadn't actually been in love. The only thing shot and wounded in this whole affair was his pride. A man never wished to be jilted by his fiancée.

A man never wished to be a public laughingstock.

Especially when that man was the Earl of Oakley and had spent the whole of his twenty-four years struggling to live up to the responsibility the title demanded, shying away from anything remotely scandalous.

He should have seen the hints. Her retiring nature was due to disinterest; her long disappearances at the balls, secret trysts.

He'd been engaged to Miss Carolina Hargreaves for little more than forty-eight hours when this morning, her father, vastly apologetic, revealed that his daughter had run away.

With the notorious rake, Viscount Stanton.

Oakley had stood by and watched them dance without the slightest idea that Stanton would steal the girl from right under his nose.

Having spent the greater part of the afternoon at White's, drinking himself under the table, he knew well that his name now spotted a number of bets on the books.

"Bad luck, Oakley."

He looked up from the Scotch he was nursing.

"Mind if I join you for a drink?" Sir Robert George didn't wait for Oakley's answer before he settled himself into one of the comfortable leather chairs. Only a week earlier this man had been his rival for Carolina's affections.

"Not at all," Oakley said archly. He would have invited the man even if Sir Robert were not already sitting. After all, he was nothing if not polite.

"I'm surprised you didn't call him out," Sir Robert mused.

"I'd rather put the whole ordeal out of my mind."

"Impossible. It's on everyone's tongue. Why, it's even likely she'd been tupping Stanton before she agreed to marry you."

Of course, it was likely, Oakley thought. The situation kept getting worse and worse.

"Marchmont saw Stanton at Harridan House with an incognito lady . . ." Sir Robert trailed off suggestively. "I wish I'd known. I'd have had a chance to sample her charms. A very tasty armful, I would imagine."

"Harridan House?" Oakley ignored the other part. He had no idea if Miss Hargreaves—Lady Stanton now—was a tasty bit or not. He'd not so much as kissed her lips.

Sir Robert looked at him incredulously. "Don't you know? You've been missing out, my friend." *Friend. Now that word was a stretch.* "It's just as well. An innocent like you should never have Hargreaves as a father-in-law. His daughter clearly follows in his footsteps." The older man shook his head regretfully. "I only wish I'd known sooner."

Oakley knew that Sir Robert had also offered for Carolina but the deceiving miss had decided to ruin Oakley's life instead.

"What is this Harridan House?" Oakley asked again.

Chapter Two

W hat exactly is Harridan House?" Maggie Coswell asked in a discreet whisper behind her fan.

The laughter that met her question was the exact opposite of discreet, and the rich, throaty sound drew many curious glances their way. It felt to Maggie as if the whole of the theater had decided the little scene in Diana Blount's box was the true play. Doubtless Diana had intended that very effect. The voluptuous redhead required men's admiration and attention for her daily sustenance.

Maggie sighed and tried to make herself invisible behind her fan. Not that she really had to worry, with Diana sitting next to her. Her own mousy brown curls and muddy brown eyes were enough to cast her invisible to most men. Which was exactly as she'd liked it the past three years since her husband's death. *It was only lately she'd begun to . . .*

"It's a private club, my dear," Diana confided, leaning forward so that the expanse of generous and well-formed flesh rounded above her neckline was better exposed to view. "Open to men officially and women unofficially. Within its walls, any fantasy you desire might be had. One lover, two . . . a woman, man . . . whatever you wish. The dress code is a mask, a cloak and little else, though many forgo the mask and the cloak."

"And you are suggesting that I . . . ?"

"A lover so often comes with as many strings as a husband. I've been having the devil of a time shaking my latest. Allow yourself one night at least to taste the pleasures as freely as you like," Diana suggested. "Tonight, in fact."

"How do you know about this place?" Maggie ventured, ignoring for the moment the frightening idea of doing just as her friend suggested. *This very night.* "Have you?"

Again, Diana let out that rippling, sensuous laugh and the echoes of it played on Maggie's skin.

"My dear, I am going to tell you a secret that very few people know. As my dearest and oldest friend, I require that you hold it in the strictest confidence."

They *were* old friends, second cousins even. They'd both grown up in the farmlands around Exeter; Maggie, the daughter of a merchant, had married a wealthy lawyer, and Diana, the daughter of a doctor, had married a wealthy baronet. A *very* wealthy baronet, who'd left her a very wealthy widow. Despite the longevity of their friendship, Maggie was suddenly certain that there were a great many secrets Diana had gained since moving to London seven years earlier.

"Roger, that old roué, founded the place years ago. He owned it under a corporation to keep his name clean, but I've inherited it, you see." Diana grinned, catlike. "I could tell you quite a bit about the men of the ton . . ."

"No!" Maggie gasped in shock. She'd imagined scores of lovers, but not this. This was wicked, depraved and absolutely intriguing. "Was your husband satisfying?" she managed to ask delicately, wondering at the idea that Diana's ancient husband had any sexual capability. The poor man, seventy-two on their wedding day, had not been in good health.

Maggie's own husband had been three times her age, but as she had married at a very young fifteen years of age, his forty-five had been remarkably lusty and virile. She may not have particularly cared for her husband, but she had learned much from him and she still longed for his touch.

"Roger had his own proclivities." Diana shrugged, her expression uncharacteristically shadowed.

More secrets, Maggie realized. Yet secrets were the natural result of seven years' absence.

"I would like to see this place," Maggie admitted. "But perhaps tonight might simply be exploratory? I don't think . . ."

"Ah, Maggie-doll." Diana grinned, breaking whatever heavy thoughts she'd had. "Let this evening be *exploratory*!"

Chapter Three

Through the window of the unmarked carriage, Maggie observed the bustle of activity in front of the otherwise inconspicuous house. Located in a respectable part of town, if not entirely fashionable, it looked just like every other building on the street. If Diana had not revealed to her the truth, Maggie would never have guessed what lay behind the stone walls.

Diana's carriage did not stop at the front. Rather, it turned the corner and entered the mews. At the last possible moment, Diana handed Maggie a pink silk half-mask, which covered the eyes and nose. Then she tied a red one over her own eyes and pulled the hood of her cloak up over her betrayingly auburn locks.

"The servants know me only as Madame Rouge," Diana explained, "otherwise I could never enter society as I do."

Maggie wondered if anyone was fooled by these flimsy disguises. As she knew no one in London and her looks were utterly forgettable, Maggie had no fears on her own accord. Diana was a different story.

Masks in place, they entered at the rear of the house, through the small walled garden, and climbed the stairs to the private suite on the first floor, which the baronet had always retained for his use and Diana continued to keep.

The maid who awaited them, dressed soberly in gray, looked no different from any other lady's maid. The contrast of her plain outfit served to heighten the opulent effect of Diana's apartment.

All of China's silkworms must have been put to use to create the furnishings. And all those furnishings had been created with only one thought in mind—the facilitation of intercourse.

The high bed was lush with scarlet draperies and sheets. The chaise longue was upholstered in burgundy velvet, an impractical fabric unless one wanted the softest feel under bare skin.

Maggie imagined herself spread out on that seat, her late husband running long lengths of red silk over her body. Thomas would have known what to do with every nook, cranny and instrument in the room. There were quite a few objects about which she could only speculate.

Had Thomas ever visited this house on his many trips to London?

"Whom would you like to be tonight?" Diana asked when the maid opened the large wardrobe and revealed an astonishing collection of skimpy costumes.

"Whom?" Maggie stepped toward the magical shimmering closet, her hand outstretched.

"You can be anyone tonight, Maggie-doll," Diana urged, "Venus, pearls dripping from your body like waves, or Hippolyta, the Amazon queen."

Diana, herself, had changed into a simple red sheath and was wrapping a length of gold tissue around her hair to create a concealing turban.

Maggie had to admit, in the dim light, under the glamour of the unusual dress, Diana looked very unlike the Lady Blount who had just attended the opera.

"Tonight this room is yours, my dear, if you should desire its use."

Maggie hardly heard the offer. She was too busy imagining the possibilities of pretending to be someone she was not.

"And here, coz, step behind the screen and put this in." Diana pressed a small damp sponge in Maggie's hand. "It's better to be prepared."

Maggie closed her fist around the contraceptive, still staring at the array of costumes. She could be anyone—someone more graceful, more beautiful, better born, divine even.

She sighed lustily and pointed at a length of fabric in varying shades of blue. The effect shimmered like the ocean.

"Excellent choice," Diana agreed, with a sultry laugh. "Excellent."

Chapter Four

Oakley had never in his life imagined such decadence. Within the inconspicuous stone walls of the stately house were three floors dedicated to nothing but sex, with every effort made to accommodate the voyeur.

It was ridiculous to see grown men with masks over their eyes but their bodies as bare as the day they were born.

Oakley didn't think he could perform for show. Nor did he desire to do so. As he kept pace with Sir Robert George, touring room after room of shockingly erotic tableaux, he wanted nothing more than to leave the house and retreat to the arms of the courtesan he'd visited less than a dozen times over the last year when need overwhelmed. There the decor was stately, the doors closed and locked.

The dining room was a play on the very idea of a meal, two women spread out on the table length-wise, their naked bodies offered up as succulent dishes. Sir Robert assured him this was the usual fare in the ground-floor room, a tempting morsel for those who didn't care to venture deeper within the club.

What should have been the formal drawing room on the first floor was now a room taken over by three large, canopied beds and many smaller sitting areas.

Oakley was astounded to see men conversing and enjoying their brandy as if they were at White's, while only a foot away an orgy of human flesh writhed. He was further shocked to recognize a number of men he knew from Parliament, men he had thought faithful to their wives or at least discreet.

He wondered, despite the mask that concealed a good third of his face, how much damage he did to his reputation simply by standing in this room.

Then he imagined Carolina there with Stanton and recalled that he was already the butt of society's jokes.

"So this, Sir Robert, is where you spend your time," Oakley drawled, sparing a glance for his companion. He could not imagine enjoying himself in such an atmosphere. No matter how hurt his pride, he didn't wish to compound the pain by developing a venereal disease.

"It's a much livelier club than Brooks's," Sir Robert grinned, stopping a woman dressed in a short, diaphanous imitation of a Grecian toga and pulling her toward him.

The woman giggled and ran her hands down Sir Robert's chest.

"I can sponsor you as a member, if you like. No better way to get over a broken heart."

"If your heart is broken, I'm certain I can repair it," the

woman said saucily, reaching out toward Oakley's crotch. Her fingers barely feathered over the cloth of his breeches before he stepped away.

"Ah, I see," the woman purred, "you would prefer a man."

Sir Robert laughed and Oakley flushed, his anger rising to cover his embarrassment. But such a comment didn't deserve a response.

"Shall I leave you here and continue the tour on my own?" Oakley asked, stiffly.

Sir Robert sighed and pushed the woman away.

"No, no, my poor man, I shall keep you company till we find you the proper companion for the night."

They left the drawing room. The hallway was larger than most London homes, and two more fenestrations led to other rooms; one set of ornate double doors appeared to lead to what in a normal house might have been the master bedroom.

"Closed doors?" Oakley wondered aloud.

Just then the gilded wood parted and two female visions entered the hallway.

Oakley sucked in his breath at the sight. The taller one, dressed in a scarlet gown and matching mask, her hair concealed entirely by a gold turban, was magnificent. Her lush body pushed against the luxurious cloth and begged to be touched.

"Ah, you are a lucky man to see Madame Rouge," Sir Robert breathed. "Her appearances are rare. She is a goddess."

"She is?"

"The proprietor of the club. She took over two years ago, but no one knows her true identity. Not that it matters. I've been wanting to bed her since I first laid eyes on her."

"Who is her companion?"

"That, Oakley, I do not know."

The lady in question floated in a sea of gauze and silk, her brown curls obscured by a fine net woven with pearls and seashells. A blue mask concealed the upper portion of her face but revealed a set of perfect pink lips, curved just slightly upward toward well-defined cheeks. Her slim body was as delicate as an opera dancer's; her small, pert breasts, outlined by the silk, offered a different eroticism than that of her companion's more overt sexuality.

A goddess in truth.

Her sweeping gaze settled on him. From this distance, and with the obfuscating mask, he could not discern the color of her eyes, but the intensity of her gaze jolted him.

He felt her hot glance in every fiber of his body, down to his cock, which hardened instantly and lay uncomfortably against his lower abdomen.

Sir Robert's swagger disappeared and he strode with purpose across the room. Oakley followed him, unaccountably nervous.

Chapter Five

He wore one of those silly masks, merely a swath of black silk over the eyes, but from the glossy black of his hair, the piercing blueness of his eyes, to the straight nose and strong jaw, she knew she'd know him even when the mask was gone.

If she ever saw him again.

How could she not recognize him? He was beautiful. Tall, well built. Maggie's appraising gaze flittered down his body to where his breeches lay tight against his hips, revealing just how well built he was.

"Who is he?" she managed to ask, watching the two men approach. In a moment the stranger would be before her and she would have to decide how far she wished to explore.

"Sir Robert George," Diana answered, "please don't tell me

you desire him. I've seen him in action. Skilled, well-endowed, yes, but—"

"No, the one behind him."

"Ah." Diana let out an appreciative sigh. "I don't know. He looks familiar, but I don't believe I've seen him here before."

Maggie laughed nervously.

"Oh, my sweet cousin, it only took a moment in my house to tempt you beyond repair." Diana grinned wickedly. "Take the key." She pressed the metal into Maggie's hand.

"Tell me, Madame Rouge, if tonight I might fulfill your fantasies."

Maggie dragged her attention back to Sir Robert George. The man reminded her of her late husband: mid-forties, blond, hawkish features, still in his looks and lusty. She'd had enough of a man like him. Four years, in fact.

"No, my dear." Diana allowed him to kiss her hand before drawing it back from his grasp. "But I believe I have many women who may fulfill *your* fantasies."

"You are my only fantasy," Sir Robert insisted.

Maggie giggled, rolling her eyes. The man was too much.

"Present your friend, sir."

Sir Robert's expression darkened, as if suddenly he saw his companion as a threat to his own plans.

"Madame Rouge, may I present to you a young man of town and nobility who has never before graced these rooms," Sir Robert said finally. "He comes as my guest."

"And what may we call you," Diana asked, "while you are here in disguise?"

The man cleared his throat.

"Tonight, I wish only to be Poseidon."

A hot flush reddened Maggie's cheeks, even as she heard Diana's surprised laugh.

"Poseidon?" Sir Robert looked at his companion as if the man had sprouted horns or acquired a trident at the very least.

"I see that my own dear friend needs no introduction," Diana interrupted, taking Sir Robert's arm. "Come, we shall stroll through this garden of earthly delights together."

Maggie struggled to collect herself in Diana's absence. She had thought it would be difficult to actually seduce an unknown man and engage in acts she had heretofore only experienced with her husband, but tonight, standing in this strange club, Maggie was aware of nothing but the present.

It was her move, she knew. By introducing himself as the god of the sea, he had announced his interest in her. Now Maggie had only to let him know the interest was returned.

How did one say, *I find you attractive, and for this one night, I might choose you to end my loneliness?*

She wet her suddenly dry lips with the tip of her tongue. His lovely eyes widened and she stilled, stricken by memories. *Yes, this was how seduction was done: the little touches, the coy glances.* It had just been too long since she had practiced the art.

She stepped toward him, closing the distance, and laid her arm on his sleeve.

"Sir, I've only just arrived. Would you care to stroll with me throughout the house?"

"Fair Amphitrite, most divinely faire, I am yours to command." So, he was a man who not only clearly knew his Greek mythology, correctly identifying her costume as that of the sea god's wife, but also quoted poetry.

"I take that as a promise," Maggie said with a slow smile, thinking of how she would like to command him, to request that he bring her to the edge of ecstasy and hold her there for hours until finally neither could hold back any longer.

"Please, do," Poseidon said. She shivered at the sound of his low, even voice tinged with desire. She knew without doubt that this man, this stranger, wanted her as much as she wanted him. She had never before experienced such pure, unadulterated lust.

Maggie let the man escort her up the dim staircase.

They didn't speak and the silence allowed for all of Maggie's other senses to take over. Where her hand touched his arm, heat radiated from him. Dizzy from a sharp pang of desire, she swayed closer and caught his clean male scent, overlaid with a spicy cologne.

She tilted her head back and found him looking down at her. As if by mutual accord they stopped their ascent, halfway up the stairs. He took a step down, so that he only needed to lower his head to reach her lips.

She was drunk. Overwhelmed. Everything about this man aroused her. His lips searched hers and she fell into the heat of the kiss.

Her husband had skillfully played her body like an instrument and taught her to please him, but she had never felt this before, this all-encompassing need that had nothing to do with finesse and everything to do with the part of her that was simply a female animal eager to mate.

He broke away first. She wondered if her expression appeared as stunned as his.

"Let's forgo all this," Maggie managed to whisper. "Come with me."

She led him back down the stairs, racing nearly, down the hallway, to the large double doors. For only a moment, she fumbled with the key Diana had given her and then they were inside.

Chapter Six

For the first time in years, Oakley felt ruled by his cock. His wits had surely gone lacking, because all he wanted was to bury himself deep inside this whore, who looked more like a sea goddess than a prostitute.

All the prudence of twenty-four years fell away at her touch—her soft, velvety touch that even now stripped him of his evening clothes.

She'd brought him into Madame Rouge's private room with its locked door. With its surfeit of rich materials and bold, lurid colors, the decor was both more opulent and more vulgar than any townhouse he had ever seen.

This woman had taken charge and Oakley was finding that there was something to be said for letting a woman lead, for losing oneself in the intensity of passion.

All sensation focused on where their bodies joined—their open, searching mouths, her teeth tugging at his lip, her hands running over the bare flesh of his chest. The palms of his hands and pads of his fingers tingled as he slid them over her lithe body, across the flimsy silk of the garment to the more luxurious silken skin of her buttocks.

Through the cloth of his breeches, her hand found his straining cock and he twitched against her fingers.

He reached around the curved flesh of her bottom to between her legs and skimmed his finger over the moist folds.

His sea goddess shivered.

Oakley felt like an untried boy. It had been months since he had touched a woman, delved into the velvet folds as his index finger now did, into her hot, wet, mysterious depths.

She unfastened his breeches. The cloth fell away and her soft hand grasped him. He shuddered at her touch, his eyes closing briefly, enjoying the exquisite pleasure of her fingers stroking the hard, pulsing length of him.

It was all he could do to not embarrass himself completely and spill into her hand.

He slid his finger out of her and clutched her buttocks in his hands, lifting her, fitting her tight against him. She snaked her hand out from between them and linked both behind his neck, her legs swinging around to grasp his hips. The center of her pressed flat against him—

Torture.

He ducked his head back down to possess her mouth, to lose himself in the sweet heat. Through the dizziness of passion, he staggered across the room and laid her down on the bed.

The back of his hands met the sensuous red silk counterpane even as he poised the tip of his cock against her nether lips. He slid into her moist heat in one smooth thrust, her muscles clenching around him.

He groaned into her mouth as his hands ran up her body, one coming to rest on her breast, the other rising up to entangle itself in her soft hair.

"You feel . . . wonderful," she whispered, even as he pulled back till just the head of his cock remained buried in her folds.

"*You* feel wonderful," he managed to respond. Her legs pressed against his buttocks insistently, and he followed her lead, thrusting back in, pushing her deeper into the feather bed.

She gasped, "You fill me up so completely."

She knew exactly what to say, Oakley thought briefly, finding it hard to hold on to what little control he had. It had been far too long and her hot canal gripped him exquisitely. He set a hard, fast rhythm, pumping into her continuously until his vision blurred and his climax overtook him.

Arching away from her with a hoarse cry, his arms extended on either side of her, pushing into the bed, he thrust deep into her a final time.

His seed came out in convulsive bursts, till finally, shaking, he lowered himself on top of her, his lips finding her neck.

The sound of his own panting was deafening, but beneath, he could make out her ragged breath. Reluctantly, he slid himself out of her. Her legs dropped away and she propped herself up on her elbows, looking up at him.

He pulled his breeches up and refastened them. It was still early. He could easily further prepare for the speech he was supposed to give in the morning.

"You were delightful," he said, reaching for his usual words after a sexual encounter, knowing they were inadequate for the passion he had felt.

She simply stared at him with an odd expression. Hard to tell under that mask, but he didn't like the set of her jaw or the slight downturn of her mouth. Was that *disappointment?*

A twinge of anxiety chilled his spine, a sensation he hadn't felt since his first sexual experience at eighteen.

In that heavy silence he simply stared at her. She stared back, assessing him.

Finally, she sighed and sat up, bringing her legs onto the bed, tucking them under her.

"You aren't really going to leave yet, are you?" she asked plaintively. "Here I am trembling at the edge of desire and you wish only to leave?"

"Uh," Oakley began but stopped. He had no idea what to say to that. Clearly some other part of him did, for his cock, so recently sated, began to stir at her words.

She moved in a cloud of silk, the scent of cloves and citrus filling the air.

Suddenly she was in front of him, her knees pressed into the thick rug. He half expected to feel her hands at his crotch, hot on his burgeoning erection. Instead, her soft touch caressed his ankle, encouraging him to lift his leg, and in surprise, he did. He looked down, to where she sat on her heels, slipping first one of his evening slippers off and then the other.

She glanced up. Candlelight caught the glint in her eyes—brown, with hints of amber—despite the surrounding mask. The baubles in her hair shimmered. Her perfect lips, that he now wished only to have wrapped around him, lifted in a seductive smile.

"You'll stay awhile, my powerful god of the ocean." She shifted, kneeling now, her hands finally coming to the buttons on his breeches. Her forearm brushed against him even as her fingers worked on the fastenings.

She let out a soft sigh and for a moment he thought the sound was his.

"A man with a form such as yours should be naked, should be admired," she whispered, as she undressed him.

She wrapped a spell around them, filled the air with sensual magic. All that seemed to matter was the present.

His clothes fell, a puddle of unnecessary fabric at his feet.

She stood and stepped into the circle of his arms. The feel of her silken costume teasing his naked skin struck him just as his mouth met hers.

You can be anyone tonight. Diana's words echoed through Maggie again as she closed her eyes, let her head fall back into the cradle of his hands and savored the mark of his lips on her neck. She had chosen to be Amphitrite, and here she was, with her husband Poseidon. That made it safe, perfect and right.

In the wake of their first bout of passion, unreleased energy had remained as a tight knot in her belly. While she had undressed him, the sensation had eased slightly; she'd fallen back from the edge. Now, as he kissed her, it built again.

Tonight she was Amphitrite—a goddess, powerful—and desire made her uninhibited.

"Touch me," she whispered. "I need . . ."

Her words drifted away as he slid the shoulder of her dress down and kissed the soft flesh of her breasts.

His tongue found one of her already taut nipples and swirled around the small mound. Pleasure dizzied her. She drifted back, losing her balance. His strong arms caught her, lifted her and then he carried her back to the bed.

This time, he placed her in the center and when she fell into the soft, silken bedcovers, she was certain that they had descended into the ocean's depths, made red with passion.

The bed shifted subtly as he joined her, his warm, naked body covering hers, his lips meeting hers. He suckled, licked, and delved; his teeth tugged and nibbled. She met each hungry action with her own, wrapping her legs around his thighs in imitation of what they had earlier done. His cock was hard against her once again and for a moment she wanted only to have him fill her.

He pulled away, looking down at her. His mask was slightly askew and his eyes were dark shadows.

"What would please you?"

Maggie's breath caught in her chest as his words sunk in. Thomas had never asked, never given her the choice. He'd told her what to say. He'd known unerringly what to do and how to manipulate her body to completion. This, this felt . . . powerful, open and full of possibility.

"I want you to kiss every inch of me, my neck, my breasts, my hands, my thighs, my . . . cunt," Maggie breathed. "To lick me at the center of my being until I explode, and then I want you to fill me up and take me there again."

"Sweet Amphitrite," he whispered and lowered his lips to hers.

Later, his head nestled in the junction of her thighs, he reminded her that Poseidon was the god of earthquakes as well as the sea.

Chapter Seven

Maggie didn't want to move. Her body ached in every imaginable way, most especially her rather sore nether region. It had been too long since she'd engaged in such vigorous sexual activity, any sexual activity. And her Poseidon was a most well-endowed man.

She giggled into the silken sheets. *She* had been a most instructive teacher!

She turned slowly in the bed until she faced him. He still slept heavily, his dark curls matted against his head, his eyelashes long and dark against the pale skin of his eyelids.

She knew very well she had tired him out. Three years of celibacy had made her rather insatiable. It was clear that he had never worked so hard in the bedroom in his life.

She lifted her hand and touched the soft pink of his lips with her finger. As he stirred, she traced a line along his jaw to his ear, toying with the bottom of the black silk mask, which, although rumpled and creased, remained in place.

For a moment she was tempted to pull the distracting, silly fabric away.

In sleep, he was young and beautiful, boyish. The memories from the night before crested over her: his blue eyes, so sweet, gazing up at her, wanting so much to please once he realized he hadn't.

Despite her protesting muscles, Maggie wanted him again.

She moved her hands lower, skimming his neck, down his chest, delving underneath the covers. When she reached the most tender part of him, already semi-hard, she smiled. Her fingers closed around him.

His cock stirred in her hand, rising, growing. She found a leisurely, firm rhythm and then, to that gentle touch, added her mouth on his shoulder, her tongue licking. She willed him to wake up to this pleasure.

Gutturally, he uttered something. His lips parted, his brow furrowed, but his eyes remained closed. The sound had merely been the confused garble of dreams.

Wondering how far she could take this before he woke up, Maggie slid under the covers, lifted her leg and straddled him.

She eased herself down on his cock, at first watching his expression carefully, enjoying the small signs of pleasure that shifted across his face as he slept. Then, as she knelt down, her buttocks almost touching her heels, the muscular walls of her wet slit stretched to their limit and the length of him pressed against the deepest part of her, she let her head fall back.

She shivered at the slight, sweet breeze her hair created as it passed over her shoulder. She savored the novel sensation of being completely in control, of being able to use his body to pleasure herself exactly as she wished.

She cupped her breasts in her hands, flicking her thumbs over her sensitive nipples. She pulled, tugged, massaged and kneaded the flesh even as her hips moved, up and down, slowly at first.

Too quick, the sensations built. She moved faster on him, her hands falling down to the bed to offer balance, her eyes closing in order to concentrate more fully on the exquisite feeling.

But it was his hands on her breasts—warm, welcome and perfectly timed—that sent her over the edge. She cried out as her body convulsed with ripples of sensation.

His hands moved to her hips. She opened her eyes and found him staring at her as if he wanted to devour her. Another shudder racked her body and she clenched around him.

His eyes closed for a moment. Then he lifted her up, sliding her off his cock. He pulled her down next to him and rolled over until he was on top of her, his strong thighs between hers.

He slid back inside smoothly, filling her deeply again. Maggie sighed, her back arching, her lips curling in satisfaction.

He pulled out and thrust back in, hard, relentless, pushing her overstimulated body to its limit.

She opened herself up to him, to his passion. She was an empty vessel, a worshipper in his glory. The waves of the sea they inhabited swept over them both, again and again.

In their sweaty, sated embrace, she fell asleep again. When Maggie next woke, Poseidon was gone.

Chapter Eight

"Where were you, Mama?" the young voice demanded accusingly. In all of Emma's six years she had never spent more than a day without her mother. Now, for one night of passion, Maggie had practically forgotten her child even existed.

The pleasant afterglow disappeared in an instant.

"Really, Margaret, if you plan to be out all night and half the day, you might at least write a note so we know you haven't met your death!"

Emma's half-sister, Olivia, stood by, her mouth pressed into a thin line, but Maggie did her best to ignore her. What mattered was not her stepdaughter's judgmental eye, but Emma's hurt feelings.

"We were so scared," Emma agreed. "Livvie couldn't sleep at all!"

Maggie took another look at her stepdaughter and finally noticed the shadowed eyes and the fragile composure. Though Olivia was only four years younger than Maggie, she was practically just a child herself, barely out of the schoolroom. With all their difficulties, it was sometimes hard to remember the younger girl had her own feelings, her own hopes and expectations of this sojourn to London.

"I am so sorry, Emma, Olivia. I should have sent a note. I stayed at Lady Blount's," Maggie said, consoling herself that it was not really a lie as Harridan House belonged to her friend.

Olivia nodded mutely.

Maggie sighed. What was done was done. She couldn't fix the past, but she could ensure that she never made such a mistake again. Nothing, not even one amazing night of passion, was worth her family's discomfort.

Her traitorous pussy clenched in remembrance and Maggie closed her eyes for a moment to erase the wave of dizzying need.

"Ask Betty to bring some tea, will you, dear?"

When Emma ran off to find the maid, Maggie sat down, a bit indelicately, on the sofa.

Dear Lord, she was bone tired. Delightfully so.

"Aunt Grace asked, as her husband's mother is going back to Bath, if I'd like to stay with her for a fortnight. Next week, that is," Olivia said, sitting down opposite.

"What did you say?" Maggie asked with a sigh. Her sister-in-law, Grace Malwerk, was convinced she knew how to take care of Thomas's eldest daughter better than Maggie did. The woman thought her higher pedigree and marriage to the great-nephew of an earl put her leaps and bounds above Maggie.

Perhaps it did. She sighed again. Admittedly, at fifty, Grace could be more of an authority figure for Olivia. It had been very odd at fifteen to become mother to an eleven-year-old. Especially one who had been taught to look down upon a country girl.

"I said I'd have to ask you, naturally. She sent a note for you today. It's in the entry."

That, at least, was a relief. No need to worry about Grace showing up and ringing a peal over her head for staying out all night. Maggie studied her stepdaughter. She was a pretty girl, blond hair like her father, a rounded, well-proportioned form. She danced gracefully, sang beautifully, had all the other usual household accomplishments and a lovely dowry to top it all off. She should have her pick of any number of men.

"What would you like to do?"

"I think it would be fun. She has so many other connections, you know. Not that Lady Blount isn't a fine woman, but she hasn't actually invited me to anything."

"Darling, you *were* invited to the play." However, Maggie was very grateful Livvie had chosen to attend a soiree with her aunt instead. She would never have had such a night otherwise.

"I want to go to the theater!" Emma came running back into the room. She threw herself on the sofa beside Maggie and laid her head on her lap.

As Maggie ran a hand over her daughter's braided hair, she was doubly grateful. After all, last night was likely the only decadent night she *would* have.

Chapter Nine

All the way home, a thought nagged at Oakley that he had forgotten something. Still woolly-headed from the night of passion, he checked his pockets for all his belongings: pocket watch, purse, cards, handkerchief. Nothing was missing.

When he arrived at his townhouse, his always-stoic butler, Davis, gaped at him, dumbfounded by Oakley's rumpled appearance.

"Have a bath drawn," Oakley ordered, even as he climbed the stairs.

Only once he was within his own bedroom did he remember. "The speech!"

"Did it go well, sir?" Justin Thorpe, his valet, inquired as he helped Oakley to undress.

"No," Oakley said with disgust, biting out the words. "It did not go well as I did not give it."

Thorpe's eyebrows rose in surprise.

"Don't look at me like that!" Naked, Oakley strode across the room and through the door to the bathing room, where the tub had been filled with steaming water. As the chill air raised gooseflesh on his body, he realized that only two days ago, he would have pulled on his robe to make even such a short journey. "I'm a fool," he declared, stepping into the tub.

"No one would ever call you a fool, my lord."

"Hah!" Oakley sank down into the bath, enjoying the lightly scented water that washed away her scent. *His sea goddess, Amphitrite.*

Hah! Oakley echoed again, silently. She was hardly a sea goddess, simply a very skilled whore who had woven an impressive spell around him.

His cock stiffened as he thought of all those impressive skills, her pointed, unerring tongue, her engulfing heat . . . Unconsciously, he arched back in the tub.

A small cough from the corner reminded him of Thorpe's presence, and Oakley dragged his thoughts away from the witch.

"Have you ever heard of Harridan House, Thorpe?" Oakley asked, reaching for the bar of soap.

"Harridan House, my lord?"

"It's a club, a private club I believe, practically a brothel." His voice was laced with derision, but Oakley knew the ridicule was aimed solely at himself, at his own lack of discretion and responsibility. Against his better judgment he had engaged in activities that had compromised his position in society.

"I see, my lord." Thorpe sounded intrigued. "Is it only for Quality, sir?"

"I'm not certain," Oakley mused. "There are gentry there as well. I recognized an MP from the lower house. But there is some level of exclusivity, I believe."

"Did you enjoy your visit, my lord?"

Oakley turned to his valet and caught the smirk before the other man wiped the amused expression away.

Actually, I did, Oakley thought. *I enjoyed it so much that I forgot myself and my duties completely.*

"More hot water, Thorpe," he said instead, standing in the deep porcelain tub. As the water ran down his body, he imagined it took with it all the residue of his encounter, leaving him clean and free to return to his normal life.

But no amount of water could erase the thought of her small, lovely breasts in his hands, the pink nipples hard under his thumbs.

Chapter Ten

"Tell me all," Diana insisted. Maggie shied away from her friend's lascivious curiosity, out of place here in her modest sitting room, in the bright light of day. "I've already had a report from my maid, Lucy."

The encounter had faded in Maggie's mind to some erotic dream that she couldn't shake. Hard to believe it had actually happened.

"She said the two of you wanted a bath, and a late supper, and then breakfast. You didn't leave the club till well after noon."

Maggie flushed.

"Yes, and I forgot completely to send Emma and Olivia a note that I'd be away," she complained. "I don't know what came over me."

Diana laughed. "Abstinence my dear, that's what came over you. Three years of abstinence and you were starving for some cock."

"Di!" Maggie gaped at the vulgar word. It was one thing entirely to use those words in the bedchamber, but here in the sitting room?

"I do own a sex club, Maggie-doll," Diana chided, "I won't pretend to any false modesty, at least not around you. In any event, Lucy said you screamed with the best of them."

This time Maggie turned beet red. The thought of Diana's maid eavesdropping on her activities was mortifying.

"Is her account true?"

A quick flash of her own cries, of the man's mouth on her clitoris, his tongue licking delicate circles around her sensitive flesh sent an exquisitely sharp pang of longing right through her core. He was a fast learner, her Poseidon.

"Yes," Maggie managed, fighting against the memory. "The man was . . . very accommodating."

Diana laughed again. "You have a rather droll habit of understatement, my dear cousin."

"Yes, well . . ." Maggie trailed off, playing with her dress, "I was completely irresponsible. If you had seen the look on Emma's face."

"You are entirely too hard on yourself," Diana interrupted quickly. "You are a young woman who has been locked up for three years in Exeter. One night is hardly a reason to flagellate yourself. Unless, of course, you do it for pleasure."

"Di!" Maggie gaped, wondering if such a thing could be pleasurable.

"Next time you'll send a note," Diana continued, not fazed by Maggie's shocked outcry.

"Next time."

"There will be a next time, darling," Diana insisted. "Perhaps not with the handsome Poseidon but with the man you choose to make your lover . . . or your next husband."

"Di," Maggie asked hesitantly, "do you truly sleep with all those different men? When you are Madame Rouge?"

Diana shook her head, with a small, almost embarrassed smile.

"When I am Madame Rouge, I prefer to maintain my distance. Once in a while, very rarely, I take a man to my bed at Harridan House. But mostly, I enjoy what I learn about all these society fops when they are at their most animalistic. It does help me to choose my lovers. It's how I chose Lord Shelby."

Maggie nodded. Diana had pointed out her current lover at the theater.

"Madame Rouge, you see, is my way of keeping an eye on the proceedings. Ensuring the quality of the establishment." Diana laughed again, and then leaned closer to her. "Sometimes, when I am away, or indisposed, I have Lucy dress up in one of my costumes and pretend to be me. Her bust is much the same as mine. In a turban, mask and dim light, that is all it takes to confuse these poor men."

Maggie nodded again, hoping that was true. It meant there was less chance of anyone recognizing either of them through their flimsy disguises.

Chapter Eleven

Later that night, at a soiree in the respectable home of Mr. and Mrs. Arthur Cartwright, Esq., Maggie sat on the sidelines with the other wives and widows. Ostensibly, she was listening to their chatter while keeping an eye on Olivia, who danced an impromptu country set with one of the young men. However, Maggie's thoughts were far away. As still as her body was, her blood was boiling, overheated from images that would not leave her mind.

His chest had been beautiful, broad and muscular, covered with a fine smattering of hair that had rubbed against her breasts erotically. The same fine hair covered his arms, tapering down to his hands—those well-defined, strong hands that had lifted her effortlessly, touched her everywhere and entered her.

Her pussy grew hot and full as she thought of those fingers, slipping in and out like she had asked, his tongue joining.

Maggie caught herself just as she started to lean back in her chair, her eyes closing. Dear Lord, at the rate she was going she'd have an orgasm right there in Mrs. Cartwright's drawing room without even lifting a finger.

She pressed her legs together tightly. As if that could ease the warm fullness between her legs!

She sighed heavily. It was too bad that she couldn't afford to see that man again. The one night had only whetted her appetite for more.

For more of him. He had been perfect for her, perfect for experimentation, for the first foray. Some time in the future, after she settled Olivia with some respectable young man, she'd find herself a lover and be far more discreet and careful than to ever let little Emma suspect.

As they drove home, Olivia was chatty with excitement.

"Do you think Mr. Smith will call on me?"

"It would only be polite after dancing with you twice to give some sort of indication of his admiration."

"His admiration," Olivia sighed. Maggie smiled, for once in charity with her stepdaughter. It wasn't often the younger girl asked her opinion in any sort of serious way. She usually just gave polite lip service to the idea that Maggie was in any way her mother.

"And just when I've decided to stop with Aunt Grace for a while." Olivia sighed again.

"You aren't going for another week," Maggie reminded her. "If he doesn't call before then, he isn't a man you'll wish to worry about."

"True." Olivia studied her. "Margaret, are you ever going to remarry? Are you looking for a husband while we're here as well?"

Maggie stared at her in shock. Did the girl know, somehow suspect? She shook her head. Impossible. Livvie's mind was simply on men and marriage. It was natural for her to wonder.

"I might someday," Maggie admitted. "But I wasn't thinking this year. This season is yours, dear."

Olivia seemed pleased by that.

"I agree," she said. "It just wouldn't seem right if my *mother* were trying to marry before me."

Chapter Twelve

I *want you to kiss every inch of me, my neck, my breasts, my hands, my thighs, my cunt."*

It was all very well and good to castigate himself for missing his speech, to vow never to step foot in that club again or lose himself like that. It would have been an easy task, if he didn't have Amphitrite's insidiously erotic words running through his head and the impossible image of her naked body spread across the scarlet sheets.

At least the voluminous ceremonial robe conveniently hid his rather rampant erection. He'd received enough ridicule from his peers for missing his speech the other day. Ridicule from some and censure from others. Due to his carelessness, the motion at hand would be postponed unless the House unanimously decided to allow it to be put forth.

Not likely. Not in this political climate, with Sweden as Britain's only ally and all this hullabaloo in the Iberian Peninsula.

The unyielding red bench had never felt so hard and the debate had never sounded so cacophonous to Oakley's ears.

He found himself fidgeting, tapping his fingers, looking up to where the light shone through the high windows, the angle of the sun indicating it was almost time for lunch. A sidelong look at his pocket watch revealed it was three quarters of an hour until noon.

He knew exactly what he wanted for lunch. Or rather, whom. Rather than accompany his mentor, Lord Marsdon, to a meal at their usual tavern, he wanted to play hooky and hie across town to that very odd Harridan House. He wanted to find his sea goddess. He wanted to thrust his cock into her ocean.

Bah! That was a horrible piece of metaphor. Oakley grimaced. *His cock into her ocean?* Certainly, he could find a more romantic way to describe these very carnal desires. He was hardly the long-dead, debauched Lord Rochester, peddling smut through verse.

Why should his thoughts of this woman be romantic? he chided himself. She was a whore and it was all about fucking.

Apparently he had been, and still was, in great need of fucking. That word had never entered his mind so frequently or so satisfactorily before.

All around him, the Lords stood up. A final vote before breaking. But on what? What had he missed? He had been sitting here daydreaming about poetry and fucking, for what must be the thousandth time this hour, and he had completely missed something obviously important.

He shook the thoughts from his head. He didn't need distractions. Being jilted gave him the excuse to visit that infamous club for one night. It did not give him license to completely throw away his duty.

He stood up. Two chambers for the Scottish courts of session, that was what they voted on now.

Two, the numbers of times he had brought her to climax that following morning.

He passed through the door, indicating he was content with the bill as it was.

She had tasted so sweet. And her kisses had been sharp, the desire nearly piercing his gut with the intensity.

"To lick me at the center of my being until I explode, and then I want you to fill me up and take me there again." He had taken her there. Further than he had ever imagined, his own stamina increased tenfold. Riding her, he had felt like a stallion.

And he had also felt like a young lad, first learning the mysteries of a woman.

He would get her out of his mind. There was too much to do; the country was at war.

The short hand on his watch read twelve more minutes till noon.

Chapter Thirteen

This was ridiculous, Oakley thought as he stroked himself to orgasm. It had been five days since he'd fucked the whore—he deliberately used the word to remind himself—and he could concentrate on nothing but her silken body, her passionate cries, the feel of her under his tongue and around his cock.

He stared at the underside of the bed's canopy, his eyes following the thin, designed lines of the fabric.

He gave in to thoughts of her as the sensations rose.

What he should do, he mused in the momentary satiation, was find the woman and have her again, get her out of his blood.

It was a sensible-enough idea. If he had her a few more times, the novelty would wear off and his mind would be free to concentrate on his duties.

A few hours later, for the first time in his life, Oakley deliberately sought out Sir Robert George. He found the man eating lunch at their club.

"Come, Lord Oakley, have a seat. You know Lord Percy and Mr. Molineaux?" Younger than Sir Robert, Lord Percy had just inherited the family title but had yet to take his seat in the Lords.

"Afternoon, gentlemen." Oakley pretended to nonchalance. "Actually, Sir Robert, I'm in a bit of a hurry, must get back to Committee. I beg a moment of your time."

"Certainly." The baronet raised his brows in curiosity, but excused himself and followed Oakley a few steps away. "How can I help you, Lord Oakley?"

"If you don't mind, I was hoping you'd invite me as your guest again to that club."

"Ha ha!"

Oakley winced as the other man clapped him on the back. "It's an insidious place, isn't it? I must assume your night went well!"

"Yes, rather." Oakley nodded.

"Mine was titillating if not satisfying," Sir Robert confided. "I had the pleasure of Madame Rouge's company while I had three different women, none of whom was her. She's a teasing witch, she is."

Oakley nodded again. If he had to listen to the man's exploits in order to see his little sea goddess again, he would.

"I was thinking of a visit tonight, as it happens," Sir Robert said.

"Excellent."

"If you wish, I'll sponsor you for a membership," Sir Robert reminded him.

As he made his way back to Parliament, Oakley didn't think it would come to that. One more night with the woman was all he needed. He simply had a few oats in his system he needed to sow.

Chapter Fourteen

"Come, my lord," Sir Robert chided him. "Surely one of these two lovely ladies will satisfy you as much as your mystery lady, your *Amphitrite*."

The room smelled of sex and if Oakley turned his head in any one direction, he could see any number of interesting sexual combinations.

Oakley didn't bother to look at the two women in their diaphanous Grecian robes that revealed more of the rounded globes of their breasts than it concealed. Just as the other night, they didn't interest him.

He knew exactly what he wanted. Entirely his luck that this was the night that she did not work. Perhaps it was a sign. Divine intervention.

"No, I'll leave you to your pleasures, George," —Oakley frowned in regret— "and I'll seek mine elsewhere."

As he walked home, he ripped the slim mask from his eyes irritably and stuffed it in his pocket. He knew very well that the only pleasures awaiting him this night were a stiff drink and a volume of Donne's poetry. Perhaps later, he might even have the feeble company of his imagination and his own hand.

Chapter Fifteen

Maggie studied the Etruscan vase. She had never seen so many interesting antiquities. Well, she amended silently, the statues and urns at Harridan House were extremely *interesting,* but they could hardly be shown in a public venue such as the British Museum. Then she and many mothers like her would be unable to bring their children.

A few steps ahead, little Emma examined a pottery fragment with great curiosity.

"Good, she's finally occupied." Diana slid her arm through Maggie's and drew her close. "I've been wanting to tell you this the last hour, but the little darling has always been in earshot."

Maggie laughed. "She does have very big ears."

"Then I'll say this quietly and quickly. He was looking for

you," Diana revealed, with her amused smile. "Your Poseidon. Lucy saw him and he asked after you, after the fair *Amphitrite*."

"Hmphh," Maggie sniffed, trying to keep her overactive imagination at bay.

"She also said he left immediately upon hearing you were not there, nor planned to be," Diana pressed on.

"Oh."

He had come back for her. *For her alone.* Somehow that made all the difference, and from Diana's sly grin, she knew her friend understood.

"What do I do?" She dropped Diana's arm and turned to face her.

"Well, you could make him your lover in truth," Diana suggested. "You did mention you were interested in acquiring one . . ."

"But then he would see me as I am." As plain as I am, Maggie amended silently, rejecting the idea.

"You're lovely, darling."

Diana's rolling her eyes and being kind would never change the truth.

"What I mean is, perhaps, in the way we women look at such things, you are not . . . the most classically beautiful, but men view these things differently. He will be unable to resist you."

"Men are no different than we." Maggie shook her head. "They are human creatures."

Despite her best intentions, the thought of him looking for her, wanting only her, intrigued her. She thought about meeting him again. She considered the idea for three long days and three overheated nights.

With Olivia leaving for her aunt's, Maggie's evenings would be more at her disposal. Surely, if she was responsible this time, if she warned Emma that she would not be back until late, she could be discreet and no one the wiser, no one adversely affected.

On the fourth day, Maggie sent Diana a note: *Let the games begin.*

Chapter Sixteen

So silly to be nervous, Maggie thought as she waited in Diana's room for her masked lover, her mysterious Poseidon, to arrive. Once more, she dressed as Amphitrite, adorning her hair with seashells and pearls and her body with the blue silks. Once more, she tied a mask around her eyes.

She'd already seen every inch of his body . . .

There was no clock in this room, indeed in any of the rooms of Harridan House, as the intent was to have members lose themselves in the sensuality, but she guessed the hour to be near midnight.

Soon, soon.

How would she greet him? Elegantly? As if they were in a stately drawing room? Seductively, as if she were a courtesan only wishing to please her lover?

That brought a wide catlike smile to her face. She did want to please him. She wanted to hear him cry out his pleasure uncontrollably, to feel his responsive body beneath her hands and mouth. Inside her already wet, pulsing flesh.

"Ma'am." Diana's maid interrupted her thoughts, approaching with a small bowl. The scent of vinegar wafted through the air, wrinkling Maggie's nose.

Maggie sighed. It was hardly romantic to have to insert the damned thing so high within herself. But then again, she knew it would be even less romantic to have a child of a man she knew only as *Poseidon*.

"Thank you, Lucy," Maggie said, and plucked the sponge from the liquid.

When the maid had retreated from the room, back to wherever it was she spent her time eavesdropping, Maggie stretched one leg out on the bed and lifted the hem of her dress.

With one hand she touched the folds of her cleft experimentally. Her hot cream was already seeping between the tight lips. She ran the back of her finger across the surface, savoring the light touch, the first physical hints of pleasure.

She remembered the way his long fingers had felt, slipping inside of her, pushing up. Desire had stabbed into the very center of her at the touch, to her nipples, to the tips of her own fingers.

She pushed up deeper, as he had, her thumb flicking the hard nub of her clitoris. Her breath came out in a fast rush of air. She stayed there, making little thrusts upward, her thumb circling.

Too good.

She slid her fingers out and then readjusted her position, both feet flat on the floor, leaning against the bed, arching her head back.

She cupped her own breasts in her hands, marveling at the extra sensation the thin layer of silk offered.

She slid a hand back down, back to her pussy, to play in the hot, wet slit.

She imagined him kissing her there, his mouth closing over the sensitive flesh, teeth grazing, bringing her to her peak. His thick, hard cock would fill her up, even as he still touched her.

She moaned, feeling the first tremors of an orgasm build. Her fingers moved with urgency now, pulling the building climax. Her breaths grew more labored, her moans more fervent. Then, the crest came, before she was ready, washing over her, bucking her hips up and then back against the bed.

Her cries subsided and as she quieted, the room sounded different. With effort, Maggie opened her eyes, lifted her head.

He stood by the rear door of the room. He'd come from home or some other place of casual entertainment, wearing trousers instead of the more formal breeches.

Why had Lucy led him to that entrance? Let him sneak up on her . . . .

He watched her through the slits in his black silk mask, his eyes heavy lidded with desire.

How long had he stood there watching her?

Long enough.

Languorously, she lifted her right arm, fingers still damp with her juices, and beckoned to him. Then, she ran that same hand up her thigh, up her hip, pulling the silk of her costume with it, all the way up to her breasts.

He was at the bed in an instant, his coat shed, his cravat untied and discarded.

He gathered her to him, half lifting her up from the bed. He dragged her mouth to his and she lost herself in his heat.

The hard ridge of his erection pressed between her thighs, heat radiating through his trousers.

Hungrily, her fingers worked the ties of his waistcoat, stripping him layer by layer of each cloth barrier. His hands moved swiftly as well, running over her body, slipping the straps from her shoulders and the fabric down her body to pool on the floor.

A moment later, she pressed her naked body against his and reveled in the contact. To feel another human's bare skin against hers was heaven. Heaven, comfort and all the delights of the world.

He stepped back. Her eyes raked over him. He was a beautiful mixture of young, lean maleness and strength. His broad chest tapered down to slim hips. His muscular thighs were those of a sportsman, an equestrian. Even his feet were well formed and beautiful. Her gaze returned to his cock, which jutted out from him, straight and erect, the rounded head gleaming with its first pearly drops.

The desire to taste him was overwhelming.

"I've thought of nothing but you for these last eight days. I can't get you out of my thoughts, my dreams," he murmured, and she realized he had been perusing her body with as much detail as she studied his. "I even see your legs spread open before me—open, wet, pulsing—when I sit in Lords."

She laughed. "Well, sir, my sweet Poseidon, I've thought of you endlessly as well."

Maggie pressed her naked body against his and then slid down to the floor. She caressed his cock with her cheek. His low groan pleased her. She wanted to hear those sounds from him all night.

"I was so pleased that you'd asked after me."

She couldn't be as pleased as he was, Oakley thought as Amphitrite ran her clever tongue up the length of his cock. He had been delightfully surprised when Sir Robert had sent him a note indicating that if Oakley accompanied him this night, the woman would be waiting.

Her tongue swirled around the head of his cock, teasing the sensitive area just before the hot, wet cavern of her mouth closed around him.

She had been worth the wait. Worth the wait and worth risking his reputation. The angels themselves could hardly resist that tongue of hers, he thought, moaning. He gripped a bedpost for support.

His other hand tangled in her hair. His thumb found the cool, smooth surface of a pearl, his index finger, the rougher edge of a seashell, and all around was the silken mass of curls. There were so many sensations, melding and separating, coming and going, even as her mouth slid down further, taking in more of him, inch by blessed inch.

Her soft hands ran up his thighs, his buttocks, and she pulled him toward her so that he felt her lips against his groin, and his cock fully engulfed in her. She lessened the pressure, pulling off of him. A sweet breeze tickled his cock as she moved back till only the tip of him was in her. He wanted to bring her back but he kept the touch of his hand on her head light and waited with held breath for her next move.

She swirled her tongue over him again and then slid back down, tantalizingly slowly.

He didn't want to come this way, but she gripped his buttocks, cupped his balls and took him in fully, smoothly, her lips tight around his cock. The touch undid him.

His hips jerked against her mouth as his semen spurt from him, into her, again and again. When he thought he had no more to give, she swirled her tongue around him and he twitched again.

Slowly, she released her hold, easing off of him. She pressed her check against his now soft penis. In the quiet of their ragged, calming breaths, he played idly with her hair.

"Welcome back," she whispered, glancing up at him through the slits of her blue mask, a devilish little smile on her lips.

Welcome, indeed.

Chapter Seventeen

Hours later, Oakley slid from the nestled heat of her body. It was leave now or risk sleeping late into the morning, missing the 11 A.M. Committee meeting and breaking the fragile pact that he had made with himself. He could have this pleasure as long as he kept it in its place.

"I want to see you again," he stated, pulling up his trousers. He had known from the moment he'd walked in this room again and seen her pleasuring herself, that he wouldn't be satisfied with just one more night. This was a phase he needed to pass through. There seemed no sense in fighting his inclinations.

"Then we are in agreement." She stretched like a cat on the bed, still gloriously naked, her back arching, pushing her breasts out to attention. "I wish to see *you*."

"Tomorrow."

"Yes," she agreed, sliding off the bed. She padded toward him and wrapped herself around his body, arms about his neck, lips meeting his.

Chapter Eighteen

When he arrived the next evening, earlier than their arranged time, Amphitrite did not await him in Madame Rouge's suite. Rather, the maid explained that she had decided to take a stroll through the house.

He found her on the third floor, leaning against the frame of one of the many bedroom doors kept open with sculpted bronze doorstops depicting different sexual positions.

She shimmered in the dimly lit corridor, drawing him in more powerfully than any siren song. He came behind her and pulled her against him, his hand resting over her flat belly, his lips finding the bare skin of her shoulder.

"My lord, Poseidon," she breathed, resting her head against his chest. "It has been an age waiting for you."

"And how have you kept yourself entertained?" He dragged his gaze away from her and into the room. So intent and attuned he was to Amphitrite—her heat, her scent, the way her perfect derriere fit against him—that he was almost stunned to see and hear that anything other than her existed in this house.

A woman, nude, her hands tied with silk rope that was fastened to a hook in the wall, writhed on the bed. Her legs were spread, revealing every inch of her lovely pink flesh, which grew pinker under the lash. She was moaning. And the moans were tinged with the sound of pleasure, not pain.

"Ask for more," demanded the masked man who, fully dressed, administered the whipping to such tender flesh.

Oakley didn't recognize him. He wanted to pull Amphitrite away, to take her somewhere private and do all the things he had imagined doing to her all day, but she was watching the scene before them intently.

"No." The woman on the bed shook her head. Her companion looked briefly at Oakley, his expression fierce, almost challenging, then he turned his attention fully back to the woman on the bed. The whip slid across her cunt, the length of it teasing her flesh till just the tip of the harsh device still stroked the swollen lips.

"No," the woman said again, but this time, it sounded different.

"Ask."

The tension in the room was high. This was a play of power between these two. Who would hold out longer? Who would get their way?

"D . . . Rouge . . . mentioned that people enjoy such a thing, but I've never seen it before," Amphitrite whispered, her hands reaching back to run down Oakley's thighs. She pressed herself tight against him, wakening his cock to instant hardness.

He found it hard to think about what she had said when her soft, silk-clad buttocks formed such a nice pillow for his now erect length.

But Oakley had never seen such an exhibition before either, and he found it vaguely appalling; a man should never raise a hand to a woman. He found it hard to believe that working in such a house, this was the first time Amphitrite had witnessed such actions. Perhaps she was a different level of courtesan here. He should ask at some point, but he couldn't think of how to phrase such a thing. Perhaps he would ask Sir Robert.

"Is this . . ." he hesitated, doubt flooding him, unsure that he could fulfill her desires, "something that would please you?"

Even as he spoke, the woman on the bed cried out, begging, pleading for anything the man would give, and the whip descended again.

Amphitrite inhaled sharply. Then the sound relaxed into a laugh, nervous to his ears. Or was he attributing his own thoughts to her?

"I think that to let myself be bound in such a way . . . would require enormous trust," she said. "And even then, I don't believe I would ever like, or find it pleasurable, to be struck."

Oakley relaxed. He wanted to give her pleasure. He *needed* to give them both pleasure.

"But watching," she continued, "is terribly arousing."

He stepped away from the room, pulling her with him.

"*You* are arousing, my little goddess," he whispered, bending down to kiss her.

The man could kiss. The first teasing feather of his lips brought all the heavy heat that had settled in her pussy swirling up around her dizzyingly. His arms held her up; she could feel their strength across her back.

Then the wall was behind her and she was pinned between this man, his burning, open, searching mouth, and the cool plaster. Now the wall kept her steady so his hands could move: his fingers on the bare flesh of her arm, then bunching up the silk of her dress to touch the flesh of her inner thigh. There was nothing for her in the world but his lips, his breath, his touch—his heat.

The world swirled around her once more, his arms replacing the wall again, lifting her up like she was a bride, like they were crossing the threshold.

And she was—she was Amphitrite, Poseidon's bride, entering the depths of their underwater retreat, where passion colored everything: red, scarlet, burgundy, indigo.

He'd brought her to Rouge's room and locked the door behind them.

In the center of the bed, she watched him undress: yank off his boots, shrug out of his jacket, undo his waistcoat, loosen his cravat. He stopped then, holding the wrinkled length of fabric in his hand.

He looked up and his blue eyes shocked her, reached her deep inside. Somehow she knew exactly what he was thinking.

She shook her head slowly, thinking of the woman upstairs, her body bound and straining, her breasts raised, round and lovely.

"Do you trust me?" he asked, coming closer.

Did she? She didn't know this man but she'd already entrusted him twice with her body. Well, more times than that if one counted effusions rather than nights . . . What would he do if she let him, if she gave him this power over her?

"I don't know," she said, but she knelt on the bed and let her dress slide from her shoulders.

He walked toward her, his gaze lingering over her body.

"Lie back."

Curious, she pushed aside the flimsy dress and did as he said. He reached the side of the bed.

He sat beside her, studying her body as if she were a delicacy he wasn't quite sure how to eat. The tension of wondering, waiting, was killing her.

Finally he moved. He slowly teased the length of the cravat across her body, from her ankle, up her calf, up her thigh. Tantalizing her.

She shivered, wanting and needing his touch.

The cravat still moved, over her hip, across her rib cage, over her left breast, leaving the nipple puckered and aching in its wake. He slid the fabric across her chest, to the underside of her jaw, and Maggie arched her head back to take more.

Back down her body the teasing cloth went, over her right breast, to her hip, across her thigh. She parted her legs, welcoming him to touch her however and wherever he liked.

The fabric swept across her overheated flesh, drawing pearly fluid from her folds, and she clenched her thighs tightly together, trapping the cravat, rubbing herself against it.

She heard his low groan like it was water in the desert. Her lips parted, willing him to kiss her. Willing him to cover her with his body and fill her aching, empty cunt with every inch of him.

"No, not yet," he whispered and pulled the cloth away from her. "Lift your arms over your head."

She did as he asked, watching him, even as her thighs pressed together again and again, seeking relief for her throbbing cunt.

He took her wrists gently in his hands and wound the length of cloth around them. Immediately, instinctively, she tested the knot. It gave a tiny bit then stopped, the binding secure but not painful.

Again he paused, studying her.

"Touch me," she demanded, thinking of their first night, of how he had pleased her.

"Shh," he brushed away her words.

But he did touch her, he had to touch her. It was what he'd wanted since he had first seen her in the hallway upstairs. It was what he had wanted since he had left her last night and all through his working day.

He followed the well-defined path of the cravat and kissed her ankle, the sensitive hollow by the bone. He kissed his way up her calf, and licked the tender place behind her knee till she writhed under him in agony and he could smell the sweet scent of her arousal.

Her soft, supple skin yielded to his tongue as he worked his way up her leg, over the mixture of curves and firm muscles that met each kiss and caress.

He knew what she liked. She had told in explicit terms, guided him, taught him. He wondered if he could use that knowledge to tease her, bring her to the edge of ecstasy and hold her there.

His lips on her hip, his senses overwhelmed with her body, he understood completely now John Donne's words: "O my America, my new-found-land." He explored, claimed the territory of her body for his own, and branded his seal on her with each touch.

"It's too much," she cried out, twisting her head away, when he teased overlong the delicate skin of her neck. He held her still and kissed her again, but he pressed his palm against the damp, aroused flesh between her legs to ease the tension.

The feel of her heat was too tempting and Oakley slid his third finger between the folds, pushing deep inside.

She bucked against him, trembling, close to the edge. He knew she wanted more, wanted him filling her. He wanted that too, but not so soon.

"Now," Maggie urged. He moved his hand away.

She held her breath, knowing she'd feel him, the head of his cock pushing the walls of her pussy apart.

He moved away.

The absence of his body hardly eased the fever between her legs. She watched him now, as he undressed, wondering what he would do next, how he would tease her, taunt her with unfulfilled pleasure.

Finally he stood nude by the bed, wearing only the strip of silk around his eyes.

He straddled her. He knelt above her, his knees on either side and she stared at his body, at the beautiful muscles and firm skin. Her fingers itched to touch him and she twisted her wrists help-lessly within the knot of the cravat.

He rubbed his cock over her breasts, settling in the valley and squeezing them just slightly together, pillowing him.

Then he moved upward, the musky scent of him intoxicating. The heat of his balls touched her neck as he touched the head of his cock to her lips. She opened her mouth eagerly to take him in. Her tongue swirled over the glistening drops at the tip, savoring the tangy taste.

He pushed his hips forward so that he slid hard and full into her mouth. She welcomed him in, sucking, licking. Her thighs writhed, trying to ease the almost painful tension in her now dripping pussy.

He pulled away and moved back down her body, rubbing his wet cock over her skin, then running the head up and down the slit of her nether lips. She strained to watch him, the sight of his cock against her pussy unbearably arousing.

Fill me! She wanted to yell, but she held back. The rules of this night's game were different and she was afraid he wouldn't give it to her if she asked for it.

He moved down yet again, till his breath was hot on her cunt. The silk of his mask teased her skin even as his tongue swirled around the nub of her clitoris.

She was rising. She knew that sensation, that almost cold, sur-prising build. She closed her eyes in anticipation.

But apparently, he knew too, for Poseidon's mouth left her. She shuddered in frustration.

Then his hands pushed her legs apart, wider, and the heat of his body covered hers.

"Come for me," he whispered.

The sudden, hard thrust of his cock took her over the edge and she wrapped herself around him even as she bucked and trembled against him.

He was relentless now, pushing her past her orgasm, till her body was one mass of tingling movement, and starbursts overlapped behind her closed eyes.

Only when he finally released himself inside her did she find the afterglow, the soft, drunken comedown, more intense than anything she had ever experienced before.

Chapter Nineteen

Oakley's days split in two: the respectable, conscientious lord by day, fulfilling his civic duty, and the passionate adventurer at night, exploring the new lands of an exotic woman.

It took Sunday, a day of church and rest, to keep Oakley from Amphitrite's arms.

"We haven't seen much of you," Lady Oakley stated, assessing him over the long dining table as they took dinner. "Not since that *incident.*" The aborted betrothal—but his mother could hardly know that he didn't care about Miss Hargreaves anymore.

Charles snickered and Oakley skewered his youngest brother with a look. The nineteen-year-old rolled his eyes and Oakley felt very much like being as childish as his sibling.

"You're never home, dear," his mother continued. Charles snickered again.

"What?" Emily demanded.

Oakley belatedly realized what his little sister had discovered before him: Charles had some small bit of information he found vastly amusing that he thought no one else knew.

Which could only be . . .

"Charlie, I hope you don't expect me to advance your quarterly allowance. If you aren't going to go to university or join the army like our brother, the least you could do is be responsible." It was a sad excuse for obfuscation and Oakley knew it. Unfortunately, so did everyone else. Or, at least, all but his youngest sister, Isabel. At six, she was still more concerned with her make-believe world than with any society gossip.

"You're young, darling," Lady Oakley said after a moment, as if there hadn't been any interruption. "You don't have to get married so soon."

"You do have two younger brothers," Charles added, grinning. "And if you cock up your toes, I know Philip will be kinder with the purse strings than you are."

"It should suit both your purposes that marriage is the last thing on my mind," Oakley stated with a sigh. In fact he was grateful to Stanton for winning Carolina away. How had he ever thought he could have been happy with her?

But then, he hadn't known anything about passion a week before. Oakley now knew that when he did marry, the woman would have to be someone who stoked his ardor as greatly as Amphitrite. Otherwise, if he married simply for duty, the temptation to be a philanderer would be too great.

Chapter Twenty

B ut who would ever arouse him as Amphitrite did?
Two days later, in the thin, early morning light that crept between the folds of the heavy velvet indigo curtains, Oakley studied the woman beside him. She lay on her stomach, her face pressed into the pillow and one hand curled under. The mask had shifted in the night and lay twisted around her neck so that if he lifted the heavy mass of curls he would see her face.

She had been so careful to keep the mask on all night, to insist he keep his.

His fingers itched. He lifted his hand to her head, ran it over the curls, down to the dip of her neck. There he parted the silken strands and stroked the soft skin beneath.

He'd keep her mystery. There was an erotic fascination with making love to a woman one knew so intimately but did not really know at all.

He slid his fingers over the corded tie of the mask, down her spine, down to the curve of her buttocks and thighs. One knee was bent, her leg pulled up. He delved in between to the hot slit beneath and stroked the tight curls that blanketed her mound of Venus.

Her legs shifted, allowing him greater access. The tenor of her breath changed and he knew she was awake.

His index finger slid into the tight, wet passage. *Awake and aroused.*

He leaned over and kissed her neck, even as his fingers continued to play. He knew now what she liked, what elicited those surprised, high-pitched cries of delight.

Oakley licked a path to her earlobe and then caught the tender flesh between his teeth, nibbling, licking.

Her body trembled under his ministrations, her hips pushed against the bed and his hands, circling.

Her movements quickened and he matched her pace with the quick strokes of his tongue and the motion of his hand.

Suddenly she arched up, crying out, her muscles griping his fingers convulsively, drenching them in her juices.

He slid his fingers out, grasped her hips with both hands and covered her with his body. He raised her hips to meet the first thrust of his cock and smoothly slid home.

He wasn't certain if the sigh was hers or his. Perhaps it belonged to both of them. She fit him like the tightest, warmest glove, tailored perfectly for his body.

He kissed her neck again, even as he slowly thrust in and out, finding the morning's languid rhythm, stoking the embers of her climax.

He stretched his arms out and threaded his fingers through hers, savoring the tension of pulling away even as she pushed back up against his thrusts.

They made love slowly and languorously, as if they had all the time in the world. And indeed, they did. If he could stay right there, buried in her velvet heat forever, he hardly cared if he made it to his morning appointments at all.

Chapter Twenty-One

There he was. Across the room, standing amongst a group of men, his tall, lean form, elegant within his evening attire. Though the broad expanse of his back faced her, no doubt about his identity existed in her mind. When he turned slightly, his profile revealed, Maggie stared hungrily at the mouth that, only hours ago, she had suckled on as if in a dream.

Within a moment's inquiry she discovered he was Lord Oakley. The woman, a Mrs. Frampton, filled her in on all the recent gossip: his failed engagement, the rumors about the famously stuffy earl suddenly engaging in much less stuffy activities.

Maggie flushed at that, knowing she had been his companion in those activities.

She looked around wildly for Diana, for some center within the swirling world she had suddenly entered. She located her first by her laugh, then she saw her friend standing near the buffet, not seven feet from Lord Oakley.

She made her way toward Diana carefully, unable to tear her gaze from Oakley. She had almost reached her friend when he and another gentleman broke away from their small cluster and headed in the direction of the refreshment tables, directly in front of Maggie.

She held her breath, horrified, excited. Perhaps in just a moment he would see her, know her, and perhaps embarrass her completely.

But he walked right past her without recognition. Why would he recognize her? Lacking the glamour of candlelight, costume and face paint, Maggie was plain. Utterly forgettable.

He was an earl. She was nothing but the widow of a lawyer. Her presence at this ball was an oddity in itself; they should never be frequenting the same social circles. Were this not the home of Earnestina Ashburton, Diana's close friend, Maggie would never have obtained an invitation. Lady Ashburton had received her cordially but with distance, and as much as it rankled, Maggie could not fault the woman for her discretion. After all, what mattered was that the invitation had been proffered.

But here she was, inches from the man she knew so intimately, with whom she had even shared her darkest fears, and yet she could not touch him the way she wished.

"Maggie, dear," Diana whispered, joining her where she stood, still rooted in place. "You look ill. Don't tell me the crab cakes are off. I had four of them already, but they did taste—"

"No," Maggie interrupted. "It's not that. It's . . . he's here."

Diana didn't need to be told which "he" she referred to. She scanned the room.

"Are you certain?" she said finally.

"Quite," Maggie assured her, with a tight smile. "I'd know him anywhere."

"Well, where is he then? Who is he?" Diana pressed.

"You mustn't tell anyone," Maggie said, quickly.

Diana shot her a quelling look and Maggie smiled sheepishly. "Yes, I'm sorry, Di. You are the *great* keeper of secrets."

"And don't you forget it." Diana accepted the apology. "Well?"

"Lord Oakley."

"Oakley!"

"Shh." Maggie pulled Diana toward the far end of the room. From their new position, they both observed him as he stood with two other men whom Maggie did not recognize, drinking his newly acquired punch.

"Handsome he may be, but I would never have taken him for a man who could make a woman scream," Diana remarked, admiringly. "It's always the quiet ones, isn't it?"

"He hasn't recognized me," Maggie said, hating the plaintive note in her voice.

"Now I understand why the man's name came up on the list of member applicants," Diana mused. "He's completely besotted with you."

"With my body, perhaps," Maggie said, blushing, "as I am with his."

"You know, my dear, I've never actually met the man before. Shall we endeavor to get ourselves introduced?"

Oakley viewed the small group of females bearing down on him with a small, silent groan. Ever since his failed betrothal, women had been throwing themselves at him, thinking he was either eager for a marriage or needed to be consoled.

His hostess, Lady Ashburton, was dragging two women of similar age with her. They weren't much older than the current crop of debutantes, but the bold colors of their dresses and their more confident strides signified they were wives or widows rather then fresh-out-of-the-schoolroom misses.

He sighed. He wouldn't have even come tonight, but he'd wanted a chance to speak with Lord Westley in a more social setting, where he could feel out the man's thoughts on the upcoming vote in the Lords.

"Lord Oakley!" Lady Ashburton said, warmly. "I'd like you to meet a very good friend of mine. Lady Blount, Mrs. Coswell, may I present Lord Oakley?"

He bowed.

He had seen Lady Blount before. With her striking auburn hair, overflowing bosom and husky laugh, she was hard to miss. The slender Mrs. Coswell also looked familiar—intense brown eyes, pale fine skin, brown curls.

"A pleasure, ladies." Oakley smiled, polite as always. Inside, he was not feeling so polite. He hadn't been feeling particularly polite ever since that first night he had stepped inside Harridan House and lost himself there.

Lady Blount started a conversation about something; Oakley couldn't hold on to the thread of the discussion. He nodded his head in what seemed the appropriate spots, his eyes focused away, on the ground. He barely noticed when Lady Ashburton excused herself.

The hem of Mrs. Coswell's gown was decorated with a rectilinear, neoclassical stripe.

He sighed. Everything reminded him of Amphitrite. His body had clearly decided that it craved more and more carnal delights. He wanted nothing more than to leave this tiresome ball and head straight to the club. But she had said she would not be there before one.

Until now he had not stopped to wonder how her time would be occupied before then.

"Do forgive me, Lord Oakley, we'll have to continue this

scintillating conversation at some other time," Lady Blount said, grabbing his attention. "I must say hello to Lady Burke."

He watched her go, the sarcasm of her pointed words sinking in. He certainly had not been holding up his end of the conversation. He decided to go in search of a drink.

Then he realized that the quiet Mrs. Coswell was still by his side, waiting expectantly.

How he swallowed his impatient groan, he never knew, but he held out his arm and inquired if she would like some refreshment.

She rested her gloved arm on his and smiled up at him. For a moment he was struck by the familiarity of her sweet smile, the way the pink lips curved up so easily. He knew now just how lips shaped as hers would feel on his cock, on any part of his body.

With effort, Oakley pulled his thoughts away before his body betrayed his imagination and embarrassed Mrs. Coswell. He had to stop thinking of his little sea goddess and imposing her image and skills on any woman who crossed his path.

"Where is Mr. Coswell tonight?" Oakley asked, as they made their way across the crowded room. He had no idea if she had already addressed the question during the portion of the conversation to which he had not been attending, but he hardly cared.

"My husband, God rest his soul, died three years ago," the widow answered. For a moment, he thought her hand clutched his arm tighter. It wasn't an unpleasant sensation, rather it made him more aware of the heat emanating from her. He found himself holding his arm closer to his side, drawing her nearer to him. He almost thought he could smell citrus and cloves.

Horny goat, he chided himself.

They found themselves standing on the balcony, breathing the cooler air as they sipped their champagne.

"He was a barrister," Mrs. Coswell said, and Oakley wondered briefly how the wife of a barrister had gotten herself invited to Lady Ashburton's house. As if she read his mind, she added, "He was very well known in London, although we lived in Exeter. My cousin, Lady Blount, has been so kind in showing me around. It was rather . . . *lonely* in Exeter these past three years." She met his eyes boldly as she emphasized the word.

Was she suggesting that she was amenable to an affair? Over the rim of his champagne flute, Oakley studied the woman. She had a lovely, slender figure. Not one he would have thought himself attracted to prior to three weeks ago. Indeed, she was vastly different from Carolina Hargreaves's lush beauty. But ever since he had met his Amphitrite, he had found himself interested in women who resembled her physically.

Mrs. Coswell stepped forward to the rail of the terrace and into a fall of moonlight that illuminated the subtle amber specks in her brown eyes.

"Perhaps you met him," she started, her head tilted back so she could better look at him. "At some political dinner or event. I hear you are very engaged in politics."

"I don't recall," he said apologetically, "however, if you had been by his side, I am certain I would always remember."

Her eyes widened briefly and then her lashes fell. Her lips curved upward into a pleased smile.

Rather pleased himself, Oakley returned the smile. He hadn't known, before a fortnight ago, just how to elicit such a look. He was fairly certain he had started to crack the mystery that was woman.

Chapter Twenty-Two

His ardor stoked to a boiling point, Oakley left the Ashburton house and headed directly for Harridan House. He needed Amphitrite in a way he'd never needed another woman before, and that little widow's resemblance had made it worse.

It was a few minutes before one, before their appointed meeting time, but Oakley hoped to find her there. The insidious thought tugged once again that perhaps he shouldn't arrive so early—he might find her engaged in activities of which he'd rather be ignorant.

Hell, he didn't want to be ignorant. What Oakley wanted was to have her entirely to himself. As long as she worked at a place like Harridan House, he was fooling himself if he thought he was the only one.

By the time he climbed the staircase to the first floor and knocked on the beautifully carved and gilded wooden doors, jealousy held Oakley firmly in its clutch. It hardly mattered that she was there, opening the door to him, reaching for him with her soft hands.

He couldn't stop the torrent of questions.

"Who were you with? How many men have you fucked today?" He heard the vulgarity leave his mouth as if he were two men, the rational and the insane.

She backed away from him till she stood pressed against the bedpost, one hand fisted against her chest.

For a long moment she didn't answer and he tried to scry her expression from under the mask and the curtain of hair that hid her downturned face.

Then, out of the corners of her eyes, she peered at him.

"None, only you," she said, lifting her chin.

"I'll give you everything, love," he said, thinking quickly now, following instinct. "Everything if you'll just be mine, alone. A house, more jewels than even the glitter in this room, clothes fit for a countess."

"There has been no one but you. What would I do with another man, when you leave me so utterly satisfied?"

"Carte blanche," he continued.

The curtain of curls returned and he waited in agony for her response. He had not felt this sort of anxious tension even when asking for Miss Hargreaves's hand in marriage.

"I don't work here," Amphitrite whispered, finally.

"That doesn't matter, I can provide for you . . ." His voice trailed off. The import of her words sank in. Slack-jawed, Oakley stared at her. *Don't work here?*

"Like you, I came seeking something not in my life."

She was some woman he might know in society. A widow, a wife . . . And that last thought became all important, because what if she wasn't even free to be his?

"Are you married?"

"I never intended to use this place this way, but I found you," she continued. "For now."

"Are you married?" he repeated insistently. *This* he needed to know. Had he been unwittingly cuckolding some man? Worse, did she share a marriage bed with this unknown competitor?

"No." She sounded surprised. "Just as you are not, but I never thought to ask . . ." Her words fell away as she seemed to contemplate that failing.

Though he couldn't quite settle it all in his mind, he knew what he wanted: Amphitrite in his bed and his bed only.

"Then will you?" Oakley pressed, taking her hand in his, pressing his lips to her wrist. He'd get to the matter of her identity later, after she'd agreed, after she was his by contract. He knew enough about her. He knew that he desired her as he had never before desired a woman.

"Will I what?" she asked, as if he had not said *carte blanche*, had not offered jewels, a house, the love of his body.

"Be my mistress."

Ice-cold reality flooded Maggie. The hazy, drunken dream of their love nest fled.

If he had said lover—if he had simply suggested they get to know each other outside of Harridan House. If only . . .

She slid her hand out of his.

What they had been doing, had engaged in, was an affair of equals. At least, that was how Maggie had seen it. But he had thought she worked here, thought that with his newly obtained membership he was paying for her time.

That alone rankled.

Mistress . . . He knew nothing of her, except her body, their few conversations here in this room.

If he knew her as herself—well, he did, and see how well that had gone. He'd hardly noticed her at first.

Even if he had, a man such as he, an earl, would never see her as an equal, the way he might the widow of a member of the nobility.

The woman he had asked to be his wife had been the daughter of a baron, not the daughter of a merchant. Not a widow and mother of little social standing.

Wife. Maggie almost laughed at the word but it helped to clear her mind. It was time to end this . . . affair.

She lifted her head, drawing herself up to her full height.

"I think you'd better leave."

It was time to put Amphitrite to sea.

Chapter Twenty-Three

She'd refused him. No explanation, nothing. She merely asked him to leave and then promptly retreated into another room. He'd waited for five long minutes for her to return, trying to bring his thoughts into some semblance of order. Then he walked out the door, down the staircase and out the rear door into the mews where his carriage waited.

Later that night, Oakley still wondered what had gone wrong. He had been jealous, yes. He had asked her to be his mistress, yes. The mistress to an earl was not such a mean thing; he would be generous. If she simply didn't want to tie herself to just one man . . .

Oakley had to admit that he no longer was interested in sharing her. He would either make her his alone, as he had somehow deluded himself into thinking he had been doing, or find some other woman with whom to slake his renaissanced lust.

He clearly was attracted to other women; there had been that intriguing widow just earlier in the evening.

The following morning, he fidgeted impatiently through the endless debates. At the luncheon break, he returned to Harridan House and found she was not there.

Hardly a surprise. She seemed to be there only when they made an appointment to meet.

He walked through the many rooms, thinking to find some other woman, some other situation, but he knew that nothing here would interest him now. His membership to this *exclusive* club was useless.

Chapter Twenty-Four

New undergarments will not cure my *mood*," Maggie warned direly, even as she plucked up a flimsy lace nothing between her gloved fingers.

The dressmaker's shop was nearly empty, but not entirely so. In fact, the one other customer, busy selecting among three patterns, was one person too many. Maggie wanted to be alone. So she could cry. In frustration.

"Darling, listen," Diana whispered. "If I had thought you'd get this attached to the man I would have warned you off of him a week ago. It is simply sex, love. There are plenty of men for *that*."

It had been just sex, Maggie knew. That wasn't the problem, wasn't the reason she was having trouble making it through the days, giving Emma her proper attention, or keeping up her end of conversation at social engagements.

The problem was that Maggie was simply not ready to stop having *his* particular body, and his particular voice, his particular expression when he reached his climax, or gave her hers. She had felt safe with him. Safe and unfurling, like a rose that had been kept in the dark too long and could now open without shame of its delight in the sun.

"I want him," she said stubbornly.

"Then you shouldn't have given in to your pride," Diana said scornfully. "You didn't *need* to end it. You still don't need to. He came looking for you two days ago and left quite frustrated when he couldn't find you."

Maggie gaped at her. "How could I possibly become his mistress? I am a respectable woman!"

Diana's laugh was galling. Her friend pulled the flimsy chemise from her hand and dropped it on the rosewood counter.

"I don't mean that you must stay in a house he pays for and sit in his opera box like some well-feathered bird. But it would be possible to reveal who you are and simply have an affair."

"He wouldn't want *me*," Maggie insisted. "He wanted the mysterious Greek goddess who met him in lust and revealed nothing of her mortal form."

Diana remained silent. Maggie took that for assent, because even her cousin had to admit that was true.

Chapter Twenty-Five

When Maggie ran into Lord Oakley again, at an even more unlikely, more intimate, venue, she began to believe that

God had a rather twisted sense of humor. She had been crying for the last three nights, her eyes were still red, and though she had evened her blotchy skin with a light powder, just seeing him standing across the small room caused a flush to redden her cheeks.

The conversation at the Gordons' home was always political. Mr. Gordon and Maggie's late husband had been good friends, and the couple had often visited them in Exeter.

When Oakley approached her after dinner, Maggie found herself trembling. That would never do. She steadied herself and offered him the sort of sultry, confident smile she imagined Diana would give.

"Mrs. Coswell, it's fortuitous that I should meet you again," he said. The warm expression in his eyes reinstated the trembling.

"Is it?" Maggie was a bit shocked that he had thought of her at all—at least as herself and not the mysterious Amphitrite. Perhaps he had been wondering if he knew her. Perhaps he had finally figured out that she and Amphitrite were the same? Considering the ugly way they had last parted, would he then be smiling at her so seductively?

"I've been thinking about what you said when we last had the pleasure of conversing." He let his hand brush against hers, long enough that she could feel the hot pressure of his thumb under her wrist. *She had taught him how sensitive that area was!* "I think we should take the opportunity to get to know each other better."

Maggie nearly choked on her sherry. *Dear Lord, he was propositioning her!*

Pride made her want to slap him, and anger at the way he seemed to so easily forget Maggie-as-Amphitrite made her want to throw her sherry on his smug face. But her stupid little heart and her traitorously aching loins wanted only to say yes.

Yes, let's have an assignation. Yes, I want to know what it feels like to have your body fill mine again, your hard, long cock thrusting inside me and your tongue licking its way up my neck. Yes, let's go away now.

She knew something of her passionate, desirous thoughts must have been written on her face, because Oakley's smile widened and he dipped his head down close to hers.

"I am so pleased," he murmured.

As he walked away, she wondered how he had ever fooled society into thinking he was a dull man. There was nothing in the long, lithe lines of his body, or the wicked twist of his smile that suggested anything other than a red-blooded man entitled by his birth to whatever he should desire.

And right now, clearly, what he desired was plain, ordinary Maggie Coswell.

Chapter Twenty-Six

He'd planned well. The small flat was in an out-of-the-way part of town where she knew no one and no one knew her. It would be easy to meet there and avoid prying eyes.

What was she doing?

Maggie Coswell, widow of a respected lawyer, mother, stepmother . . . in broad daylight, engaging in an affair? With an earl? Never mind that she had already slept with this man, slept with him when she didn't even know his name, if he was married, or if he had slept with half of London. Never mind that she had left her morals at the door of Harridan House three weeks earlier.

None of that mattered, because it was almost as if it hadn't been her. That had been a dream, a voyage of drunken desire that took nothing of herself, of Maggie.

Daylight flooded the room.

"Margaret." He pulled her into his arms.

"Maggie," she managed to say, twisting away from him. Everything felt wrong. "Margaret sounds too much like my grandmother."

She looked around, nervously, seeking something to make herself comfortable, something that would reassure her she was not making an irreversible mistake.

"Maggie." Oakley stepped near her again. He cupped her cheek with his palm and turned her to face him. His hand, warm against her skin, held a measure of safety. She met his eyes with her own hesitant gaze.

There. She sighed. In the depths of his startlingly blue eyes was the comfort, the reassurance she had been needing.

Lord Oakley might be a stranger to her, the room might be unfamiliar, but she *knew* this man.

"My lord," she breathed. She turned her face so that her lips met his wrist.

His breath sucked in. She glanced up and found his eyes closed, his expression pained.

He took a step back, freeing his hand.

"Perhaps, a glass of wine?" he suggested.

All her awkward nervousness flooded back. She nodded mutely. Perhaps a glass of wine would help. *Dear Lord, what was she doing? And why did he now seem as rattled as she?*

"Is something the matter, my lord?" she ventured.

"Oakley," he muttered, pouring a glass for each of them from the decanter on the side table. Finally, he turned, but he left the glasses where they were. "Nothing is the matter . . . it's just . . ."

He was next to her in three steps, his arms crushing her to him, his lips claiming hers. For a brief moment, Maggie wondered at the sudden change. Then she was caught up in the rapture.

His lips were everywhere, on her cheek, her earlobe, her neck. He pushed at the collar of her gown to kiss her chest. His hands ran down her back and came to rest, clutching her buttocks. She met his fervor with her own.

They undressed almost shyly. Maggie stood in her new lace-trimmed chemise and waited for Oakley to finish unfastening his waistcoat.

Then she started again, rolling one stocking down at a time, growing more confident under the heated light of his eyes.

He was naked before she. Catching sight of him, she stilled.

She marveled at his body, illuminated by sunlight, the broad shoulders, the well-defined arms, the hair that tapered down to his hands.

And his chest, muscular but not overly so, his stomach young and taut. The hollow at his hip begged to be kissed but she held back, taking in all of him, from the jutting erection whose call her body weeped to answer, to his long legs, ankles and feet.

He had been beautiful by candlelight, but a man such as this deserved to be admired in his full masculine glory.

Suddenly shyness and doubt filled her again. The same light that revealed him so wonderfully would make her vulnerable. He would see clearly every flaw.

Had he noticed by candlelight the faint marks on her belly that came from carrying a child?

He stepped forward.

Taking a deep breath, she forcefully shrugged the emotions away and raised her hands, letting him lift the chemise over her head.

There was her body and his, both nude, both alive and warm. Tentatively, he cupped one breast in his hand, running his thumb over the nipple.

The glamour of Harridan House, its myriad silks, disguises and dimly lit rooms was far away. What was here was this woman, like any other that he might pass on the street.

So like the woman who had unleashed a passion in him Oakley had never even suspected, who had made him truly understand the sensual nature of John Donne's poetry.

But yet so unlike.

Maggie was shy; he could feel her hesitation even as he skimmed his fingers over her skin. She seemed new to this, new in the way Oakley had felt just weeks ago.

Her body in his hands was a mass of contradictions: delicate but firm, small but strong. Every inch of her glowing and lovely in the afternoon light.

He needed to possess her, to make her his the way he had thought to make Amphitrite his. He drew her toward him, his lips finding hers, and she came alive in his arms.

They melded together in a hard, fierce branding. He took her to the bed, his hips nestling between her thighs even as he moved from her mouth to the arching column of her neck.

His cock parted the damp flesh. He thrust into her, groaning at the sensation of her hot, tight muscles spreading to accept him and then hugging him tight.

He withdrew only to thrust again, deeply, till there was nothing between their bodies, and the heavy weight of his balls fell flush against her.

He found his pace—long, hard strokes. Her hips rose to meet each thrust.

Her thighs clenched his hips, her hands ran over his back, kneading the muscles till he thought he would melt inside her, enveloped by her body in every way possible.

He tugged at her earlobe with his teeth and ran the pointed tip of his tongue over the skin.

Her body tensed. He circled his hips, using his cock to find the places that made her cry out.

When she finally came, arching against him, her whole body clutched him. Her climax pulsed around him, milking him, and dragging him to the peak of his own orgasm.

He released himself into her in hot spurts, his hips bucking into hers, pressing her deeper into the bed, his cries guttural and delirious against her neck.

The fire dampened, the red haze receded. In that sated moment, Oakley knew clearly, this earthly woman was a goddess too.

Chapter Twenty-Seven

"Your brother won't be sent to Venezuela, then?" Maggie asked, her head nestled on his shoulder.

The sun had risen an hour before but despite the rules and boundaries they had laid out on their first night together, neither Oakley nor Maggie made any effort to move from the embrace.

"No. More likely the Peninsula, but who knows? For now, he's in Cork."

The difference in his situation amazed Oakley. Though the mysterious edge that had tinged his encounters with Amphitrite was absent, this affair with Maggie Coswell satisfied him in every way. Simply knowing that he could find her, communicate with her easily, made it more possible for him to concentrate on other matters.

And he found he could talk to her about anything, from the brewing storm in the Peninsula to his political ambitions. She slipped from lover to advisor easily, listening carefully to everything he said.

He found he liked the simple domesticity of these post-coital moments.

Although he sometimes still wondered who Amphitrite was and why she'd ordered him to leave so abruptly, he found her increasingly absent from his thoughts, relegated to the fringes—a woman with whom he'd shared a playful interlude but nothing deeper and lasting.

"I've never been to Ireland. I've heard it's lovely," Maggie said. "Green, blue and wet."

"That sounds like England," he pointed out, laughing, caressing her breasts with an idleness fast gaining purpose.

"You're right," she agreed. "I should have said greener, bluer and wetter . . ."

As wet as she was, beneath the tight, damp curls, under his searching fingers.

Maggie came to know that flat the way she had known the bedroom at Harridan House—the scents, colors, pattern of light on fabric as the hours of the day changed. This time, however, she wore no mask. The difference was infinite.

Without the need to conceal identities, Maggie found the peaceful moments between bouts of lovemaking filled with conversation. She'd known already he loved poetry and despised hunting, claiming there was no sport in torturing an animal. He now spoke of his ambitions, his ideas for their country. He spoke of his family and the responsibility he'd had for his younger siblings since his father's death.

She found herself sharing un-loverlike stories of her life in Exeter, stories of her daughter, her late husband even.

Maggie thought that this intimacy, this sharing, had grown deeper in two weeks than four years of marriage had forged with her husband. She never wanted the halcyon days to end.

Chapter Twenty-Eight

I'm having a dinner party," Diana announced the moment she flounced into Maggie's sitting room in a new straw bonnet that made her look like a girl fresh out of the schoolroom. "I'm giving Lord Shelby his congé."

Maggie laughed. "And here I was thinking that you look much

more like my cousin from the country than Lady Blount, secret purveyor of all things illicit."

"Not all things, darling." Diana winked, untying her bonnet. "Does this silly hat really make me look so unsophisticated?"

"Very much so," Maggie admitted apologetically.

"Wonderful!" Diana smirked with a devilish glint in her eye. "Then it will be just right for my purpose."

"I'm not certain I want to know." Maggie grinned back. But of course she wanted to know. Her own thoughts weren't far from the gutter. It had been three days since Olivia had returned, and Maggie hadn't found a moment to get away to see Oakley.

She'd grown rather spoiled in the previous fortnight, finding it easy to leave Emma to her studies or the nanny for a few hours here and there.

She was extremely frustrated, and from the letter he had sent, she was quite certain he was as well. "So is that the reason for the party?"

"A small one, yes." Diana grinned. "I'm inviting two lovely young men whom I've had my eye on. I thought perhaps I should invite your Lord Oakley as well?"

The very thought skewered Maggie with its brazenness. Oakley and she together in public?

"Is that wise?"

"No one will know the two of you are having an affair," Diana reminded her. "Really, it isn't as though you haven't been to the same private events. It will be vastly fun. Although the last time I talked to the man he didn't listen to a word I said. If he wasn't so sweetly handsome, I'd ask what you see in him."

Maggie considered the idea. She couldn't find any real reason not to go. Except for one . . .

"Are you inviting Olivia? She'll be devastated if you don't."

"And I should care?" Diana raised her eyebrow, but then she grinned again. "I did invite her to that play. *She* chose not to attend."

"Not that she'll see it that way." Maggie sighed.

"True," Diana conceded. "Don't worry, I was merely teasing. I would never think of not extending the invitation."

Chapter Twenty-Nine

From the street, Diana's townhouse glowed with candlelight, and for a moment Maggie had the sensation that when she crossed the threshold she would be met with a decadence equal to Harridan House.

Then she climbed the stairs, the butler opened the door, and she saw instead the same elegantly decorated house she had visited numerous times before.

"Thank you for the use of your carriage," Maggie said as they embraced. "I simply didn't feel comfortable sending Livvie off to her aunt's house in a hired hack."

"Of course." Diana waved her hand dismissively and then took Maggie by the arm. "I'm so glad you are here first. I have been trying to decide for the last hour whether I want to seat Lord Donavan to my right or Mr. Travistock."

She dragged Maggie with her into the dining room. The long table had been beautifully laid out with the best china, crystal and linens. It was a far cry from the small house Diana had lived in near Exeter.

"You do realize that after all of that, with Olivia not attending, I *had* to invite Jane Cooke to even the numbers," Diana whispered as if they weren't alone, looking a bit put out despite the smile that curved her lips. "You have not had the fortune of meeting her yet, but I shall make certain after dinner that you do."

Maggie was willing to meet whomever Diana wished. Nothing seemed to dampen the excitement brimming within her. Soon, Oakley would arrive.

Torture.

Oakley shifted uncomfortably in his chair once more. His cock was hard, had been hard from the moment he'd caught a whiff of Maggie's perfume.

He should never have agreed to attend Lady Blount's dinner party.

But starved for the sight of Maggie, for her scent, he'd jumped at the invitation. And here she was, standing just a foot away, her hair caught up in a Psyche knot, a few tendrils left to graze her neck, to tease him and make him want to place his mouth where the silken strands touched silken skin.

He'd forgotten how the strictures of society would keep them apart even when they sat merely five feet away from each other.

Society, and more specifically, Jane Cooke. Why Maggie had chosen to sit by the woman was beyond him. The lady was horse mad and had no other conversation. Not that he couldn't hold his own in a conversation about Arabians or Thoroughbreds, but too much was rather tedious.

"You aren't listening again, Lord Oakley." Lady Blount chided him and he forced himself to look at her. "I'm not certain if it's my company or simply that you'd rather have another's."

His gaze flitted back toward Maggie.

She looked delicious in her ochre dress, the clever undergarments and low neckline revealing the creamy swell of her breasts.

"Yes, I suppose you're right," Lady Blount continued, and for a moment Oakley wondered what he had said that she agreed with. "You'll simply have to give Mrs. Coswell a ride home. I can't part with my carriage again tonight."

Oakley glanced back at Lady Blount in surprise. Comprehension dawned.

"You're very astute, my lady," he said, appreciatively. "And I am extremely grateful."

"Or you will be." He heard Lady Blount murmur as he turned his attention back to Maggie.

She looked like a ripe fruit he wanted to pluck from the tree and eat.

Now, Oakley had plans for that fruit.

Chapter Thirty

The following day, Oakley called on her as if his intentions were honorable, in full daylight of every respectable matron staring out her window. Maggie kissed her daughter on the cheek and left her in the care of the nanny before she went downstairs to greet him.

When she entered the room she found him standing by the mantel, a bouquet of tulips in his hand.

Tulips that reminded her of his tongue, opening her up to him like a flower, while the carriage moved and rocked across the London streets.

She'd hardly placed one of her lavender slippered toes into the room, when his head turned and his eyes met hers, the piercing blue shaking her to her bones.

"You shouldn't be here."

It was a breach of every rule they'd set in this affair.

"I missed you," he said simply.

She perched on the blue settee. He sat beside her. Close, closer than any man should. Then again, she had agreed to an affair. *She'd held him deep inside her last night, even as the carriage slowed before her house. She hadn't wanted to let him go, to see him leave.*

But she had not agreed to bring the affair here. Not in her house.

He took her left hand, and raised it to his lips. He wore gloves, the leather soft on her bare skin.

His lips felt even softer. And aroused memories that pulled up all the deep, dark desires of their two sinful weeks.

At a sound in the hallway, she quickly pulled her hand away, inching away from him.

A moment later Olivia walked in. She stopped, startled, at the threshold. Oakley stood immediately.

"Forgive me, I didn't realize we had company," Olivia said, politely. But the younger girl didn't move, staring instead at Oakley with blatant curiosity.

"Not at all. Come in, darling, and allow me to present to you, Lord Oakley. Lord Oakley, my stepdaughter, Olivia Coswell."

Olivia strode into the room, smiling pleasantly, and Maggie wished her stepdaughter was still staying with Grace.

"Miss Coswell, a pleasure." Oakley bowed, perfectly correct, as befitting a man of his station and reputation. Maggie realized that she knew so little of that side of him. The Oakley she knew was passionate, roguish and reckless. The Oakley she knew had no problem offering to take her home in his carriage in order to fuck her to exhaustion.

"I didn't know we had such lofty acquaintances," Olivia said flirtatiously. Maggie thought she would drop dead right then and there from embarrassment. That was all she needed!

"It was so kind of you to call," Maggie interjected, anxious for the awkward situation to end. She stood as well.

"Right, yes, well." Oakley seemed to pick up on the hint. How wouldn't he, when she was being so obvious? He walked toward the door with two sets of female eyes trained on him and then stopped, turning abruptly.

"Mrs. Coswell," he said apologetically, "I don't know how I could be so forgetful, but I came here today with the intention of inviting you to the opera this evening."

For a moment, Maggie didn't know what to say. The invitation was clearly a breach of the secrecy of their affair, but then so was Diana's dinner party and even this visit.

Olivia's eagle eyes were taking everything in. Maggie reminded herself that it was perfectly acceptable to attend the opera with a man. After all, she was a widow and not some impressionable young girl.

"And certainly, you must bring Miss Coswell." Maggie's gaze sharpened on Oakley's bland expression. For the briefest moment she was struck with a piercing jealousy, before she reminded herself that the extended invitation was the only polite thing to do with the girl standing there in the room.

"You're too kind, Lord Oakley," Maggie managed to say. "We accept your invitation."

The moment he was out the door, Olivia turned on her and began an inquisition.

"Who is he? How do you know him? Where did you meet him? Why didn't you tell me we had company?"

Maggie held her hand up tiredly. "Lord Oakley and I met at Lady . . ."

She didn't get to finish before Olivia started on another rant.

"Oh, I see you've been having quite a time with me out of the house. Consorting with earls!"

"I suppose you don't wish to attend the opera tonight, then?" That seemed to work, for Olivia immediately backed down and mustered up a rather contrite look.

"Of course I wish to!" Olivia cried. "But what shall I wear?"

Chapter Thirty-One

Oakley stopped thinking and simply followed his instincts. He knew that if he, even for a moment, questioned himself, he would have to ask what he thought he was doing.

It was one thing to take a lover, especially a lover of inferior birth. It was entirely another thing to chaperone that lady to social events. And beyond that, to escort the lady *and her stepdaughter*!

So he didn't think. He simply did what felt right. Unfortunately, he couldn't completely shut out the judgments of the world.

First there was Sir Robert, at White's, who approached him slyly.

"I haven't seen you at Harridan House. I've heard you've been seen about town with a certain widow. A bit low for an earl, but then, a man's choice of mistress is often suspect."

Then Lord Marsden, his mentor, remarked in a studiously nonchalant way that a man of ambition should always be discreet.

Finally, there was his mother.

She stopped him in the hallway outside of his bedroom just as he headed out for the afternoon.

"Darling, there's been talk. You have been seen squiring that plain Mrs. Coswell around town. *And* her daughter. I know the girl is lovely and has an enormous dowry, but you can't be thinking of marrying such a common girl."

"Marry Miss Coswell?" Oakley laughed. The girl was the furthest thing from his mind. Well, except for the fact that he cursed her presence daily for getting in the way of his desire.

His mother's expression grew more stern and Oakley stopped laughing.

"I am relieved on that account, but that can only mean you are having an affair with her mother. Oakley, tell me this is not the case."

"Why ever must I tell you that?" Oakley said defensively. "I'm a grown man. Men have lovers."

"They do not appear with their very common mistresses at society events!" Lady Oakley insisted, drawing herself up to her full impressive height, almost as tall as her son.

"She is not my mistress," Oakley said truthfully. After all, Maggie had made their relationship very clear. Another one of the rules they had set that first night at the flat. They owed each other nothing.

Chapter Thirty-Two

It was perverse, Oakley knew, but his mother's words made it impossible to think of anything but Maggie. She was supposed to meet him much later that night, after they'd each been to their separate social engagements, but he had the overpowering urge to see her immediately, to prove that he could, no matter what anyone or his mother thought.

He found her at home, looking lovely in a blue afternoon dress. More importantly, she was alone when she greeted him in the sitting room.

She was surprised but her face glowed as if she was happy to see him and he felt an answering swell in his chest. It was in her company that he now felt most alive.

He kissed her. Somewhere in the dim recesses of his mind he knew he shouldn't. Not here, not with the door cracked open for decency. Yet should and shouldn't were all mixed up, for what he needed was the sweet taste of her lips under his.

She kissed him back. The curve of her lower lip beguiled him. The touch of her tongue on his devastated.

Which was why the foreign gasp of dismay registered so slowly.

The cry of "Mama," however, cut sharply through the veil of passion.

Oakley pulled away from Maggie with difficulty. He straightened his jacket and faced the two girls.

"Good afternoon," he managed, bowing.

The littler girl dropped an automatic curtsey. Her wide brown eyes, so like Mrs. Coswell's, stared at him with undisguised curiosity. So this was Emma. At six, she was the same age as his youngest sister, but she was a smaller child, clearly made of the same bone structure as her graceful mother.

"Why were you kissing my mother?" she asked. Her older sister put a restraining hand on her arm but the child shrugged it away.

"Are you going to be my new father?"

"Emma!" Both Mrs. Coswell and her stepdaughter chided the little girl. Oakley chuckled, caught between embarrassment and amusement.

"Not quite, Emma," he said, "but I believe your mother's manners are remiss. Please, allow me to introduce myself. I am Lord Oakley. It is a great pleasure to finally meet you."

Maggie shot him a dangerous look and Oakley deemed it a good time to make his exit.

"Are you here to take us for ices, my lord?" Emma asked. "We were supposed to go for ices this afternoon. I thought Mama forgot."

"Unfortunately, my dear, I am otherwise engaged," Oakley said a bit uncomfortably. "Perhaps I may have the honor another day."

"I'll see you to the door," Emma chirped, skipping to keep pace with him. "I'd like to see the menagerie at the Tower, too."

The moment Emma and Oakley had left the room, Olivia turned around.

"You're sleeping with him, aren't you?" she demanded in a furious whisper.

Maggie gaped at her; the truth stuck in her chest.

"You don't deny it!" Olivia threw herself down on the sofa and covered her face in her hands. "I suspected. It's not as if an earl would ever *marry* you but . . ." Olivia came up once more, her face red and furious. "How could you? How could you dishonor my father so? You're ruining my chances of a respectable marriage! What if someone knew?"

Faced with Olivia's anger, Maggie shriveled inside. She had

not been thinking of her stepdaughter, her late husband or her young daughter. For once in her life, she had only been thinking of herself and her desires.

She had thought herself discreet and thought that discretion protection from any scandal or danger. She had thought, perhaps she deserved this little pleasure.

After all, she was only twenty-two.

Chapter Thirty-Three

**Love is swift of foot.
Love's a man of war,
And can shoot,
And can hit from far.**

Sitting on the stairs of his house, fully dressed for the Lords, his wig in his hand, Oakley finally understood what George Herbert had meant.

The morning had started out like any other. He was at liberty until half past one and had intended to spend what was left of the morning at White's.

But halfway down the staircase, the melancholy pull that had tugged at him for days turned into a cannon and bowled him over with resounding force.

All the sighs and stoic moroseness were clear signs of a deeper illness.

He loved Maggie.

The knowledge terrified him. What was he supposed to do with this? The woman no longer wanted anything to do with him. She'd chosen duty to her family over their affair—a choice that Oakley, at the time, could only understand and admire. It was what he would do. *What he should do.*

He didn't want to let her go. It wasn't rational. It wasn't responsible, but she was what his heart most desired.

Therefore, *what would he do?*

He sat there on the steps for the greater part of an hour, ignoring the curious stares of the staff.

Finally, it came to him. He had to wait—wait until the young Miss Coswell was married and safely settled. In fact, he'd ensure she was married as soon as possible to whichever man she fancied.

Then, when Parliament broke, he would whisk Maggie away to one of his lesser country estates where no one would care the least.

All he had to do was convince Maggie to wait for him as well.

"Ho, brother!" Down in the entry, handing his hat to the butler, and looking decidedly worse for a long night out on the town, Charles gawked at him. "Has Parliament taken to sitting in *our* town house? Or is this simply the new fashion?"

Oakley tried to summon a witty, cutting response, but his emotions were all too soft and raw.

His grin fading, Charles bounded up the steps to sit beside him.

"Are you taking ill? Dizzy spells? Shall I call the physician?" The sudden fear in his brother's voice stirred him. Naturally, his brother would be worried. Charles had been the one with their father, hunting in Scotland, when the man shrugged off his bouts of pain and dizziness until one day he just collapsed. Later they learned their father had had a cancer of the stomach, far progressed.

"No, Charlie." Oakley lay a calming hand on his brother's arm. "I'm not sick; at least, it's nothing that time won't cure."

He released his brother and then, elbows on knees, rested his head in his hands.

There was a shuffle of movement downstairs, the butler peering back into the entryway with curiosity and then scurrying away.

Charlie whistled, a long, ringing noise that broke the silence.

"You're in love," Charles said finally, shaking his head, and grinning once more.

Coming from his brother's mouth, the words sounded so ridiculous that Oakley laughed. Then he frowned.

"Have you ever been in love, Charles?" Oakley challenged.

"Only a dozen times a week," his brother said, laughing. "This week it's this little actress over at Sadler's Wells."

Oakley snorted. His brother definitely experienced a different kind of love.

"Who is it then? That Coswell woman that Mum's been so flustered about?"

Maggie, Oakley wanted to counter, not *that Coswell woman.* Instead, he merely nodded his head in assent.

"Here I thought you were a stodgy man, old before your time. You've managed to get yourself involved in one of the more scandalous marriages of the season, procure a membership to the infamous Harridan House, which you did *not* bother to share with your younger brother, I might add, and then you fall in love with a new mistress with whom you've been seen cavorting all over town. What have you done with my oh-so-discreet older brother?"

Harridan House. It had been at least a week since Oakley had thought of Amphitrite. In fact, he couldn't remember the last time he had thought of her. Maggie had replaced her completely in his life. Perhaps he *was* a bit fickle.

Amphitrite. He conjured an image of her in his mind but it was Maggie he saw now—Maggie whose long legs had wrapped around him, whose pink lips quirked in laughter, whose brown eyes were flecked with amber, whose . . .

Wait right there. Oakley gripped the banister to keep his balance. It just couldn't be. But of course it could, and suddenly everything fit into place: why she had broken it off when he'd asked her to be his mistress, why she had flirted with him so brazenly that night at Lady Ashburton's.

Maggie was Amphitrite, one and the same.

He had never been so certain of anything in his life.

Chapter Thirty-Four

Five days after she sent Oakley the note, Maggie believed the world had been leeched of all color. She had not realized just how much she had come to depend upon their time together—how much she cared for him.

Just how much did she care for him? A taunting little voice asked inside her head.

Too much, she answered. So much so that it still brought her joy even while she mourned the loss.

"Darling, this is silly," Diana chided her, running a soothing hand over her back. "The brat is *your* daughter, not the other way around. You've done nothing to endanger her marriage chances. If anything, being seen in the company of an earl is helpful. And poor Oakley!"

Maggie looked up at that. "Poor Oakley?"

"Yes!" Diana cried. "The young man hunted me down two days ago, said you'd returned all his letters unopened and couldn't I change your mind?"

"He came to see *you*?"

"You did have the maid turn him away at the door. Short of waiting outside of your house on the off chance you'd step out, which he did by the way, I suppose he felt he needed to call in the reserves," Diana defended him. "You've made the man so desperate he even returned to Harridan House looking for the long lost Amphitrite!"

"He what?" Maggie gasped. For the first time in five days, she stopped regretting her decision. How dare he? Was one woman so interchangeable for another that he would go to Maggie when he could not have Amphitrite and to Amphitrite when he could not have Maggie?

"He left this for you." Diana pulled out a rectangle of creamy paper that Maggie recognized as his card. The man was bold, so bold that he apparently no longer cared to keep his identity at Harridan House secret. "And Lucy mentioned that he came *only* to find you."

He had scrawled a note on the back of the card: *Amphitrite, forgive me. Grant me just one more night. Your Poseidon.*

"He didn't come to find *me*," Maggie scoffed. "He came to find Amphitrite."

Diana raised an eyebrow derisively. "Please, darling, don't tell me you've forgotten that you're both."

"He doesn't know that!"

Diana sighed wearily. "What are you going to do?"

"I don't know," Maggie said angrily. "But I want him to learn that he can't treat women this way. He can't treat *me* this way."

Chapter Thirty-Five

Harridan House remained unchanged, Madame Rouge's boudoir as well.

With Lucy's skillful help, Maggie dressed up as Amphitrite, adorned her hair with pearls and seashells, tied a blue silk mask around her face.

The mask lay heavy on her skin. It was difficult to breathe.

At every moment, she knew that she was Maggie inside a costume. She didn't have the heart for playacting.

When he entered the room, looking so handsome and vibrant that her eyes stung with a wet heat, she managed to pretend.

She sauntered toward him and pressed her body against his, threaded her arms around his neck.

His arms circled around her, the palms of his hands curving around her buttocks and she nearly forgot her purpose, her desire to teach him a lesson.

"My Lord Oakley," she whispered, "I thought I would never learn who my masked lover was. But now, as you have revealed yourself, you have no need for the mask."

He didn't protest when she pulled on the silk, untying the knot.

Maggie couldn't help herself as she teased him with the cloth, the way he had teased her so many weeks ago, sliding it across his jaw, across the sliver of skin visible above his cravat.

He reached for her mask, but she stopped him and stepped away.

"No, my lord," Maggie chided him, unable to keep the edge from her teasing tone.

"Then I wish for my mask as well," he said, his voice low and more gravelly than usual. "For I must be Poseidon, the *only* man with the right to meet you here."

He said it as if he were so certain of himself, as if she did belong to him. If only she didn't know that he treated all women this way, as interchangeable bodies he wished to own.

"But gods often change their earthly form when they intend to seduce," she managed to say, running the scrap of black silk over her own body now.

"So they do," he growled. He stepped forward and her eyes widened at the coiled strength of his movement. She stood her ground with difficulty.

"I'll need to make certain, my lord," Maggie purred, holding up one hand to stop his progress, "that you have no disguise.

Please, if you would be so kind . . ." She made a little gesture with her hand toward his coat.

He did stop, his head cocked to the side, considering. Then he did as she asked and shrugged out of his coat.

His gaze locked with hers, he continued to undress.

Maggie found herself perspiring. The room was too hot, the air between them tangible with electricity.

Whatever she was doing, she wasn't doing a very good job at teaching him a lesson.

She took a deep breath. It would come. She merely needed patience. And if she was to be perfectly truthful, her actions this night were also for her.

For her pleasure.

Finally he stood naked before her, letting her look her fill. He seemed to know that she was in charge this night and waited for her next command.

"Lie on the bed."

While he did as she said, Maggie bent down to pick up his cravat.

When she rose again, he was on the bed, leaning back on his elbows, watching her. The expression on his face—a funny hiccup in the vicinity of her heart—made her want to burst into tears.

Once again she asked herself what she was doing. Torturing herself? She should run far away from this man. The wild, riotous emotion inside her felt so different from what she'd felt for her husband.

Oakley didn't deserve any of her tender feelings, no matter that look in his eyes.

She took a deep breath and walked around the bed until she stood by his head.

"Your arms, please."

He stretched his arms above his head. She wrapped the cloth securely around his wrists. Then she fastened the loose end around the bedpost.

Her task done, she pushed all other thoughts from her head and studied his body.

"You say you wish to be my only lover," Maggie whispered, "but am I your only one?"

"Yes, and I want only you." The wretch smiled even as he lied. She hadn't really expected him to lie. Not Oakley, not the man she'd come to know these last weeks. The amount his deception hurt surprised her.

She steeled her resolve again and climbed onto the bed.

"Good. A woman wants to know that."

Not a flicker of guilt crossed his face.

"I'll tell you anything you want to know," he offered.

"All right." Maggie leaned over him, letting her hair fall across his chest, teasing his skin, the silk of her dress brushing his groin. "Why did you come to Harridan House?"

She barely touched him but simply the sensation of her hair and the scent of her skin, so near him, was exquisite agony.

Oakley resisted the impulse to pull on the cloth that bound him. He'd play the game the way she wanted. After all, it was clear from what she said that she still thought he didn't know who she was.

But she knew exactly who he was. He was fairly certain she'd known all along, but by sending his card, he'd made certain of it. Apparently, she wasn't particularly happy with him.

As long as she kept touching him, he'd follow her lead.

For now.

Her mouth found one of his nipples and Oakley moved despite himself, trying to get closer to her mouth and to rub himself against any part of her he could reach.

"We had an appointment," he rasped, knowing that he wasn't really answering her question.

Her teeth grazed his skin dangerously, biting down lightly, almost like a warning.

Hell, he knew it was a warning but he wanted whatever punishment she meted out with her body.

"Come now, my lord Poseidon." She used his alias mockingly. "Tell me."

"Oh, you mean the first time?" Oakley tried to keep the laughter out of his voice. She was making her way across his chest, her tongue licking a hot path, and when she found his other nipple all thoughts of laughter fled.

"Exactly," she urged.

He found it difficult to focus on anything but her skillful tongue. Not that he wanted to think about the whole fiasco anyway, but he had promised to tell her whatever she wanted.

"I'd been jilted. I was curious to see the place where it was rumored my erstwhile fiancée had been trysting with her lover. I never expected to stay. I never expected to return. But I fell under your spell."

She seemed satisfied with his answer for she moved again, down his body, the side of his chest, to his hip, finding all the most sensitive places till his skin was alive with the fire and each touch of her tongue was a newly lit flame.

He wanted to run his hands through her hair, to touch her skin, but his movement was aborted by his own cravat and he muttered under his breath.

Her lips touched the hollow where his thigh and groin met, her hot breath tickling his cock, and he nearly leaped off the bed.

Maybe this wasn't a game he wanted to play. Or perhaps he should simply change the rules.

"Why did you turn down my offer?" He knew very well why she'd said no. Maggie Coswell would never agree to be any man's mistress. But Amphitrite . . .

"I ask the questions." She moved again, this time the hard, pointed tip of her tongue met his already straining, fully distended muscle. He pulled again on the cravat.

"If you were my mistress, I would have given you everything," he goaded.

"I told you, Oakley," she began—and for the first time he wondered that he had never recognized her voice— "I don't work here."

Her mouth closed over him, taking him in, and he groaned aloud at the incredible, tight, wet feel of her lips sucking him, her tongue swirling around his cock. He thrust his hips up even as he strained against the cloth that bound him.

He knew he shouldn't say it, but he wanted to see how far he could push her.

"You don't have to work here to work for me."

He tasted so good in her mouth, hard and salty. She could have lost herself in sucking him. She almost didn't hear what he said. Then comprehension dawned.

The man was unbelievable! Why on earth had she spent days moping after him?

As she slid her mouth off of him, she knew at least one reason. She *loved* his body. No matter what he said to her, she wanted to fuck him. She wanted to feel this delicious cock inside of her. She knew she was shameless and right then, already creaming and clenching in anticipation, she simply didn't care.

She straddled his hips and slowly lowered herself over him, savoring the sensation of each steely inch, gasping at the feel of his hard cock spreading the walls of her cunt.

She looked down at his expression, his eyes closed, mouth open, enjoying the feel of her as much as she enjoyed him. The soft skin of his neck beckoned to her and she leaned forward to kiss him there even as she lowered herself another inch.

"For God's sake, Maggie, you're torturing me." Everything within her cried out in alarm and she stilled, but he wasn't having any of that, his hips pushing upward trying to complete the motion she had started.

"Who's Maggie?" she managed to say.

He laughed and kissed her ear. She turned her head in irritation. Then she felt his teeth tugging on the silk of her mask.

And that's when she knew that *he* knew.

He'd managed to pull her mask half off. Irritated, she yanked it off the rest of the way.

"How long have you known?" she demanded, trying to ignore the slow thrust of his hips.

"A couple of days," he admitted, grinning. "I was embarrassed at first that I didn't recognize you."

"You tricked me," she accused. But she didn't move. She stayed where she was, with his cock still filling her. There were too many conflicting emotions for her to decide which impulse to follow: anger or relief.

"Maggie, sweet, if anyone should be furious, it's me. You've known for weeks and kept me in the dark. I simply wanted to see you again."

Just as she had jumped at the opportunity to see him as well, as Amphitrite, without feeling she had to suffer the consequences. Could she really blame him?

"Maybe you'd better untie me, Maggie."

She shook her head. That at least she was clear on: it was better to keep him in her power. Just to prove it, she rose over him and then slid back down.

His pained groan was music to her ears. "All right then. I was thinking we could wait, until after Miss Coswell is married and continue on where we were."

Wait? Maggie considered the idea, her body stilling. Waiting meant being with him, meant allowing herself to love him for just a little bit longer. *Until one of them decided to break off the affair and start the heartbreak all over again.*

"But here with you, Maggie," Oakley was saying. *He really shouldn't move his hips like that, not if he wanted her to concentrate.* "I know that would never do."

Never do? Suddenly Maggie wanted it. She wanted to be with him for even the briefest moment more because, as Diana had said, this was her life.

"I want to be with you now."

"Oakley," she sighed, starting to lift herself off of him, but he bucked his hips against hers and her body answered the call to pleasure. She slid back down, moaning as he filled her again. She wanted now too, but she'd have to tell him it could only be later. Later was something, after all.

"I want to be with you always," he continued.

She might not be the best stepmother in the world but she had to do her duty by the poor girl. After all, both Livvie's mother and father were dead, and she only asked that Maggie not ruin her chances at a marriage.

"Dammit, Maggie, you're not listening to me," Oakley exclaimed. He tugged on the cravat violently, the headboard creaking from the strain.

She blinked and refocused on him.

Finally!

"What I am trying to say is . . ." Oakley stopped, the emotion stuck in his chest. He stilled beneath her, breathing deeply. "What I'm trying to say, Maggie, is that I love you and I don't want to spend another day worrying about whether I'll get to see you or not or whether I'll ever find someone who makes me feel the way you make me feel."

"What did you say?"

Surely she had heard him. She couldn't be asking him to repeat all of that?

"Maggie, I'm asking you to marry me."

She said nothing. She merely stared down at him with those eyes that looked more amber than brown.

"I love you," he repeated, just in case, just to make certain she understood.

"I love you too," she said, but she looked confused and sad, as if she were going to cry.

"You do?" Her look so belied her words that Oakley feared the sharp joy burgeoning in his chest.

She nodded. Then her lips quirked up into a little smile and Oakley wanted to wrap his arms around her.

"Dammit, Maggie, would you *please* untie me?"

She laughed and reached for the knot, sliding off of him, her chest hovering over his face. The soft flesh of her breasts hung above him, beckoning, and he lifted his head to lick one pink nipple.

She sighed, staying where she was despite finishing her task. He reached down to grasp her hips. He savored the feel of her skin under his hands as if he had never touched her before.

Then he rolled her onto her back and covered her with his body.

"Maggie?"

"Yes?" She looked up at him, her smile now lacking any of its previous sadness. The lingering tightness left his chest.

"I love you."

"So you said," she agreed, but she was grinning now.

He settled himself between her thighs and slowly slid back inside her body. She wrapped her thighs around his and pulled him in deeper. He could have come right then, but he held back.

"Maggie?"

"Yes?" Her head arched back; her hips were moving to match his.

"Will you, then?"

"Will I what?" she whispered. He groaned at the feel of her hand on the inside of his thigh. There was no doubt in his mind that she was torturing him.

He pulled out till just the head of his cock touched her drenched folds. He resisted the upward search of her hips, teasing her instead with short, shallow pumps.

"Oakley!" she moaned her complaint.

"Tell me," he demanded, laughing.

"Tell you what?" She gasped, but she was struggling to hold back her own laughter.

He bent his head to lick at the sensitive skin of her neck.

"Oakley!"

He waited, nibbling at the lower lobe of her ear.

"Oakley!" Her hands pulled at his hips and he couldn't stop himself. He followed the movements of her hands and finally thrust in deeply. She met his movements with equal force, her breath coming faster, her body trembling.

"Tell me," he demanded again, grinding himself against her to stimulate her clit. The soft cries grew louder and he retreated, holding back once more, knowing she was on the edge.

"Yes," she cried in frustration, her hands grabbing again at his hips, insistent. Triumphantly, he thrust deeply and gave her what she wanted. "Yes, yes, yes!"

PART III

Roses Are Rouge

Chapter One

Vauxhall Pleasure Gardens

I t was nearly pitch black in the narrow, shrub-lined walk, and as far as Diana could tell, Lord Simon Donavan wasn't anywhere about. He had said this particular walk, had specified the seventh tree from the entrance but there were no trees, per se, in this row, only tall shrubs that continued in a long unbroken line.

As she'd made her way down the dark walk she heard moans, male and female. Worse, she heard the scurrying of rats in those damn hedges.

She should never have agreed. How could she have imagined that making love in a rat-infested garden would be fun? If she even ever found the man.

Of course, she had been bored. She slid damp curls back into place as she lounged in her ridiculously uncomfortable chair. With July almost over, the last pitiful throes of the London season twitched around Mayfair, and only the Lords most dedicated to Parliament remained for the final fortnight.

Despite that, she was surrounded by friends: Maggie and her new husband, Oakley, Earnestina and Lord Ashburton, Lord Simon. Maybe that was the problem. She had grown rather bored of Simon. It wasn't that he wasn't handsome or droll enough. He simply only pleased her in the most superficial of ways.

So when he leaned over and whispered that she should meet him, the flicker of interest at such a novelty guided her answer.

Where was he?

This was ridiculous. Diana turned around and headed back the way she had come, toward the distant lights, toward the rest of her party.

She bumped into the man, not Lord Simon, before she even knew he was there: a shadow that broke away from the hedges and caught her by the waist, swinging her around till she was dizzy.

"What have I here?" The stranger had a thick northern accent and the walloping scent of gin on his breath. His hand came in contact with her chest, with the rather exposed expanse of breast that her stylishly low-cut gown and helpful corset revealed. "A tasty treat."

"Not for you, sir," she returned with a exasperated sigh. She was used to drunken men with wandering hands. She pulled away from his grasp.

His arms didn't budge. If anything, they tightened around her.

"Let me go before you regret it," she warned.

"The only thing I'm thinking I'd regret is letting a piece like you get away." Then his head knocked into hers, his mouth finding her cheek, slobbering on her skin.

This was too much. Even for Diana's high tolerance. She lifted her knee sharply.

And found herself twisted around before she met her target, her back pressed against him and her face pushed into the bushes. Twigs scratched at her forehead and neck. She struggled to move but couldn't.

The man's arms were brawny and thick like a pugilist's.

Trapped.

After five years of marriage and two years of widowhood, Diana Blount knew she could handle anything that came her way. She could defend herself with the ivory-handled pistol from Bunney's that she usually carried or the knife that was often strapped to her leg.

Unusual for a lady perhaps, for the wife of the now dead Sir Roger Blount, but not so unusual for the proprietor of an exclusive club catering to the sexual proclivities of the haute ton.

Not that Diana would ever call herself a madam; she was merely the secret heir to a house of sin, a place of decadent pleasures: Harridan House.

Tonight, the gun was in her reticule left at the supper box and the knife, no matter how her fingers gripped the fabric of her dress, remained firmly out of reach.

Tonight, she had to admit, she may have gotten herself in over her head.

So she resorted to the weapon of heroines in Radcliffe's gothic romances: she screamed.

Chapter Two

"Really, Jas, you should come up to London more often," Elizabeth Throckmorton said.

"We always have a devil of a good time when you're here," her husband, Daniel, agreed.

Jason laughed. It was good to be in London, to see his old friends. How long had it been? One year since the funeral. Funerals. Two years since he'd so unexpectedly inherited the baronetcy and become Sir instead of plain Jason Blount. Solvency was good. Three years since he'd left London abruptly for the country with a new wife and new responsibilities and hardly any finances of which to speak.

Too long. After three hard years of changes, he rather thought he was a new man. A harder man.

Tonight, however, strolling through Vauxhall Gardens in the

company of old and true friends, half drunk on brandy, he felt as if he were thirty again. By the pricking of his thumbs, *something* was going to happen.

Then he heard the scream. High-pitched, desperate. A woman's voice.

He stopped in his tracks and looked around. It was as if he was the only one who had heard it.

The Throckmortons and his other companions, Dick Morrison and Ogden Seymour, stopped a few steps away and looked back at him inquisitively.

"Didn't you hear it? A scream?"

Morrison shook his head. Daniel as well.

"It's probably one of the whores having herself a good time down the dark walks," Seymour suggested.

There were no more screams, but that didn't settle Jason's unease.

"Not a *good* time," he corrected. "I'll meet you back at our box." Unsure what he expected to do but certain he had to do something, he took off down the nearest path, in the direction he thought he'd heard the scream.

The sound of struggle was unmistakable, even though the woman's cries were muffled now. He could just make out the misshapen shadow of their bodies, pressed against the hedge.

He grabbed the large, rounded shoulder of the assailant and pulled hard, his fist swinging around fast to meet the man's face. Or what he assumed to be the man's face. It felt rather like an ear.

With a roar the man lunged at him and Jason dodged the lumbering shadow, his fist making contact with the soft flesh of the stomach.

He knocked the air out of the man and, not waiting for him to recover, grabbed the woman's arm.

"Come, let's get away before he recovers his breath," he urged, guiding her forward, toward the main thoroughfare.

Only when they reached the lighted, crowded path did he stop and turn to look at the woman he'd saved.

And his own breath caught in his chest.

The woman before him, whose face was scratched and red, whose hair was disheveled, whose dress was wrinkled and dirty—whose breasts heaved and pushed against the meager constraints of her bodice as she tried to catch her own breath—was none other than Lady Blount. Diana Blount. Wife of the late baronet, bane of his peace and cynosure of his most carnal dreams.

She recognized him in the same instant and her face flushed. *She was angry at him?*

Which made him reassess the situation, his own ire growing. Only Diana Blount would be involved in the feigning of pain to increase pleasure.

"My apologies, Diana. I thought I was coming to the aid of a woman in need. I didn't intend to ruin an assignation."

He turned abruptly on his heel, furious for more reasons than he could even name.

Her hand on his forearm stopped him. Gloved, yes, but the soft weight burned through all the layers, scorching his mind.

"No! Don't you dare go. Please!" He turned back to look at her, to her wide-eyed expression that now looked very little like anger. "Please Jason, escort me back to my friends?"

Her hand on his arm shook. In fact, when he studied her more closely, he realized she was trembling all over.

It occurred to him that perhaps he had been wrong.

Chapter Three

They walked in silence back to the boxes. She was grateful for his help, grateful he didn't ask why she'd been in the dark walks to begin with or make any other disparaging remarks about her morality and choices.

She simply savored the calming strength that flowed through his arm to her.

Odd that *this* man should be the one to save her from rape, to have the power to soothe her merely by his capable and protective presence.

Diana still remembered the first moment she'd ever seen him—in the lawyer's office at the reading of her late husband's will. He was so very English, the wavy thatch of golden hair coming to a peak on his forehead, his lips full, his eyes the pale grayish blue of the sea on a winter morning. Jason Blount was tall and slender and oh-so-proper in his Sunday-best country clothes.

He'd greeted her kindly and graciously, with the sort of gentlemanly regard that she had felt so infrequently during her married life.

When he bent over her hand, she shivered at his touch and wondered what he would be like in bed. She couldn't help that thought; it was what she'd been trained to think.

Behind him his wife, still plump from a recent pregnancy, looked on rapaciously, until the lawyer requested that she leave the room.

Then, the solicitor revealed the existence of Harridan House and to whom it was bequeathed.

"Impossible!" Jason had cried. "What was he thinking? Lady Blount can hardly run some sort of depraved club. Sell the damn thing as discreetly as you can, or let's simply close it down."

"Quite right," Mr. Jarvis, the solicitor, agreed. "Not a fitting thing for a young woman. I tried to dissuade Sir Roger but he was a man set in his ways."

Diana had listened to the men discuss her for several more minutes as if she weren't there, as if she didn't have a say in the whole matter. The pure arrogance of the man, that he would think in inheriting the baronetcy, he had inherited the right to dictate her actions.

In that one furious moment, Diana made a decision that set the course of her life.

"I'm not selling," she had said, quietly but firmly.

The men kept talking as if she hadn't said a word, discussing the value of the property that Harridan House inhabited.

"Excuse me, Sir Jason, Mr. Jarvis," she interrupted, louder this time. "I have decided not to sell the club. My husband entrusted it to me for some reason, sentimental or other, and I intend to honor his wish."

That's when Jason's benevolent gaze turned to judgment, and in his eyes she was brazen, wanton, sluttish. All words she had been called before, but somehow, seeing it in this man's eyes, made her angry. Furious. Incensed. *Hurt*.

Over the next few days, he tried to convince her, to make her see how dangerous this choice was. He came to her at her London townhouse, which, thankfully, was not entailed. His wife, kept ignorant of all the proceedings, did not accompany him. The townhouse was still draped in black crepe.

He was so very handsome walking in from the snow, his hair windswept and damp.

Under different circumstances, she would have been inclined to make him her lover. Instead, she wanted to shock him, to play with him, taunt him.

He had no power over her.

"Why did you marry him?"

"Why?" Diana turned, surprised at the question. "You were the poor relation till he died, wouldn't you have if our places were switched?"

"I didn't marry for money."

"For love?"

"You can't keep that place," he said derisively, but she noted he didn't answer her question and some little hitch inside her released.

"That club is my livelihood, thanks to Roger. It is also what he made me, fit for nothing else."

"It doesn't have to be," he insisted. "The annuity alone is more than enough to keep you in style, in this house, your entire life. You must sell it."

Jason would never understand. Unless she made him.

"You want to know why I married a seventy-two-year-old man? I was eighteen and asked to read to him at his sickbed. He asked specifically for me after I accompanied my father, his doctor, one day. The book he gave me was *Fanny Hill*. Have you read *Fanny Hill*?" She waited for his affirmative nod and then continued. "He asked me to read it to him. Claimed he was on his deathbed and it was the least I could do. Then he'd ask me questions. Was there any young man I fancied? Wouldn't I like that man to touch me the way Fanny was touched?

"And I'd had many nights where I imagined all those things. Where my hands had stolen to places that before I had barely touched. I'd managed only to inflame passions but not to soothe them. Which is what Roger had wanted."

She watched Jason's face—his reactions to her story—shifting from interest to disgust to . . .

"One day I came to read to him but he was sitting in a chair, looking much improved. He asked me to sit on his lap. I refused. He insisted and started coughing, still quite sick with the influenza. But he was an insatiable old man.

"I sat, innocent as I was. He cupped my breasts through the muslin dress. It didn't matter his age at that moment, they were the first male hands on me, and my nipples came alive. He'd primed me so well for that moment.

"He slid my dress up over my legs. I didn't once say a word to stop him. He held me there then parted the lips, and touched that little rise of flesh within . . . to arousal."

She knew her words had an effect on Jason despite himself, just as her husband had known what he was doing when he seduced her.

"He brought me to ecstasy and despite all that followed, I still thank him for that entry to passion. I might not have survived the marriage otherwise. I might not have married such an old man either, fortune aside."

Jason's mouth opened and closed, a muscle in his jaw pulsed, but he had said nothing.

"You look in need of satisfaction," Diana had remarked, glancing pointedly at his crotch where the hard ridge of his cock now pressed visibly against the fine lawn breeches. "It's the quiet ones who turn out to be the most depraved. How depraved are you, Jason?"

His face had been red with anger.

"Clearly you are a lost cause, so I'll simply ask you to be discreet. If one word of your *business*," he layered that word with contempt, "reaches society's ears and hurts my family—"

"Then what?" she interrupted. "You'll ruin me? Of course, I'll be careful. I care about *my* reputation. But I will not be dictated to. Not by Mr. Jarvis and certainly not by you."

She'd seen him next a year later at the funeral for his wife and the infant son who had lasted one day longer than his mother.

Jason had stared at her, offered her a coldly polite greeting and turned away.

But tonight, as they walked across the raucous grounds of Vauxhall, the coldness was absent. He'd come to her rescue, apologized even for his rash assumption.

"The pavilion is just ahead," Jason murmured.

"Yes, I see."

"Are you certain you're all right?" he asked again. 'You're still shaking. Wouldn't you rather I see you home?"

"No," she said, too abruptly. "I mean, yes. I'd like to go home."

Which was all it took for him to change directions. She let him take care of her, bundle her off in her carriage. She left him to take care of all the little details, like making her excuses. As much as she had rebelled two years ago against his male instinct of taking charge, tonight she welcomed it.

Chapter Four

"We had a bet," Daniel revealed, when Jason appeared again in their box, his commissions done. It had been rather easy to find Lord Oakley and Lord Ashburton and their wives. "Whether you'd met your death due to some scoundrel in the walks or were enjoying another sort of death entirely."

"Clearly, I win," Seymour crowed, pointing.

Jason looked down at his jacket and saw, for the first time, the rip in his sleeve. A chill went through him as he wondered what Diana's friends made of *that*.

"Really, Jas," Lizzie chided him, shaking her head. "Tell me you at least made the most of your gallant rescue and haven't cost me ten quid."

Ruefully, Jason shook his head. He gratefully accepted a glass of wine from the waiter. It was easier to let his friends joke at his expense than to contemplate his turmoiled thoughts. Later. Later he would examine the significance of the evening. Perhaps after a few more drinks. "You're too reckless with your bets, my dear. Men do change."

"Ha!" Lizzie laughed incredulously. "I highly doubt you have."

"Lizzie, love," Daniel began, but his wife ignored him.

"I believe, widower, father, baronet and all, you are still as much a scapegrace as ever and we'll find you embroiled in some scandal or other before the year is out."

"I'll give you double or nothing on that," Seymour said.

"There will be no scandals," Jason said repressively. "At least none of which you'll ever hear."

"Now that's more like it!" Daniel said, raising his glass. "To discreet scandals!"

Chapter Five

D iana was still in bed and nursing her cup of chocolate when Maggie, using her connection as a cousin to excuse the early hour, came calling.

"What happened last night?" Maggie demanded as soon as she entered, dropping Diana's reticule on the bed. "And don't give me the faradiddle about a megrim which Sir Jason gave us. And while I'm on the subject of him, why did you never tell me the newest baronet is so charming? I thought you hardly knew each other."

"Maggie, please sit down before you *do* give me a headache," Diana insisted, pointing to a high-backed chair upholstered in pink-striped silk.

"And speaking of men," Maggie continued, opting to perch on the edge of the bed instead. "Lord Simon returned half an hour later, quite disturbed that you were gone."

"I would rather not talk about it," Diana demurred, placing her cup back on the silver tray that lay heavy and flat on the counterpane.

Maggie gaped at her. "It must have been quite a night for you not to talk about it," she pointed out. "You're the one who's always shocking me to no end."

Diana couldn't help but laugh at that, thinking the Maggie who stood before her now was very unlike the more mousy woman who had arrived in London merely three months earlier.

"Fine, keep your secrets," Maggie sighed, rolling her eyes. "I've assured myself that you are well, so I'll be off."

"Wait," Diana said suddenly, the words tumbling out before thought. "You found Sir Jason charming?" She regretted her question the minute that Maggie, looking like a cat who'd found the cream, settled herself again on the bed.

"Quite." Maggie grinned. "If I didn't have Oakley . . ." She let the words trail off and a slight twinge of irritation struck Diana.

"Regrettably, he's a prudish stick," Diana blurted. "You'd never find him interesting." But even as she said the words, she felt the steel of his arm under hers, the heat of his body. She remembered the fire in his eyes two years ago when she'd described her first orgasm to him.

There was something not quite so prudish brimming under the surface. How hard would it be to bring that to the surface and puncture the man's arrogant disdain?

"Really? How do you know?"

"His eyes," Diana said, before she realized Maggie was asking about Jason's prudishness and not his hidden passion. "I mean"— she coughed— "they're so judgmental. He knows about Harridan House."

Maggie's eyes widened. "And he doesn't approve?" She thought quietly for a moment before she spoke again. "I could imagine, Di, that some men who have no trouble *frequenting* the club might have problems with their female relatives *owning* it."

He's the reason I own it, Diana wanted to say, but there were some admissions that were far too embarrassing to reveal. After all, a woman of reason would never make a decision merely out of spite and pride. But *she* had and it continued to shape her life.

"I think you should invite him there, see if I'm right," Maggie teased.

"He would never go," Diana stated, even as she considered Maggie's suggestion.

"I'd wager he would," Maggie said, one eyebrow raised in challenge.

"I don't intend to see him again."

Maggie stared incredulously.

A scratching at the door distracted them both.

"Come in," Diana called out. Her maid Julia entered, carrying a rather large bouquet of purple irises.

"These came for you, my lady." Julia handed her a card before stepping back and placing the arrangement on the side table.

Under Maggie's curious gaze, Diana ran her finger over the thick, fibrous cream paper on which Jason had sent his regards.

"All right," Diana agreed, reluctantly. "When I win, I'm claiming that lovely green hat at Mrs. Pathenay's."

Chapter Six

Jason sent the flowers early in the morning, knowing it was the gentlemanly, polite thing to do after one rescued a woman. Yet when the afternoon came and with it the hours for social calls, he held back, unsure.

Diana may have been trembling and vulnerable the night before, but that did not change who she was or what she did.

It didn't change that she had been the lynchpin of his most erotic fantasies these last two years, that her husky voice played in his thoughts and her throaty laughter echoed in his dreams.

It was lust, pure and simple. It had been from the first moment he'd seen her in the solicitor's office, the black of her mourning garb setting off the creaminess of her skin, the rich auburn of her hair, the dark fire of her gaze.

His very first thought stunned him: *Why didn't I manage to get myself leg-shackled to a woman like this?* His wife, who entered a step behind him, still pretty in her pale, English rose manner, was a poor light next to Diana's burning flame of beauty.

His anger at his own perfidious thoughts was underscored when Diana proved to be not only a woman who married for money and position, but one who was morally deficient, seeing no problem with owning a "club" that was barely better than a brothel.

Yet here he was two years later, by a twist of fate compelled to call upon her as good manners dictated.

Not just good manners. He wanted to go, to see her again. Rather desperately. That was why he stalled in Lizzie's sitting room, helping her unknot her threads.

"You do realize you're making them worse?" she chided him.

Jason looked down at the pile in his hands. She was right. He'd managed to snarl the red with the white in a dismaying mess. Lizzie lifted it from his lap and deposited the lump into her sewing basket. "Why don't you tell me, Jas, why you're sitting here with me?"

"What have I told you about her?" he asked, finally.

"Lady Blount?" Lizzie's eyes narrowed. "Not much. You inherited from her husband. You rescued her from some sort of attack last night . . . in the dark walks." She smirked at that last. "But I have seen her at the theater. She's always surrounded by men. I've heard she runs through lovers like water."

Jason sighed. Her reputation was exactly what he didn't want to hear, not when he knew it was in truth so much worse than Lizzie knew.

"Really, you should call on her," she said, grinning. "What's the worst that could happen? You end up in the lady's bed?"

The image that leaped into his head at her words caused other parts of him to leap as well and he shifted uncomfortably on the chair.

"Just go to her, Jas," Lizzie pushed. "Unless there is something you aren't telling me. Some dark history between the two of you . . . In fact even then you should go. So I can win my bet with Ogden Seymour."

"You're right," Jason agreed, standing. "But don't count your guineas too soon. There won't be any scandals."

Chapter Seven

After the flowers, Diana knew he would call. But Lord Simon came first, with a jewelry box and apologies, wishing he had been the one able to offer her assistance home.

If she'd been bored of him the night before, now she was completely over the man. She refused the gift unopened and sent him off with as kind words as she could muster.

Then Earnestina called, wondering, as Maggie had, about Sir Jason Blount.

Finally, when it was almost rude, when she was about to change for dinner, Jason arrived.

She'd thought him handsome when she first met him three years ago, drawn to him by some odd pull. She'd thought him strong, tall and kind in the dark shadows of the night before. Today, in the late afternoon light, he looked very much like the kind of man she might have dreamed of marrying when she was fourteen and reading the society pages, thinking London a magical world and her little corner of Devon the remotest country.

"I meant to come earlier," he said, by way of apology, "but the business which brought me to town . . ." He drifted off. His expression revealed what he didn't say: he'd stayed away for other reasons.

"I am truly grateful for your assistance last night. It's good of you to come, to ask after my welfare." Diana offered up her most frivolous smile. "But now, that duty has been discharged."

His lips thinned into a hard line.

"It doesn't have to be this way," he said.

Oh, but it does, Diana thought. *For neither of us has forgotten.*

"You're right, Sir Jason," she agreed instead, "and perhaps as a peacemaking, a truce, I may induce you to stay for dinner?"

Jason joined her at her table, struck by the intimacy of the moment, of a private meal.

Three years ago he would never have imagined being here, at Diana Blount's table.

His wife, Marianne, had been the daughter of a wealthy cit, with the plump beauty and charm of youth. They'd met at a country party and even though he was a man of no wealth and, at that time, no prospects, she was young and willing to ignore the guardian aunt who chaperoned her.

He wasn't so caring about propriety back then. His intentions were not noble. And underneath the shade of a willow tree, with the lapping of water in the pond and the morning birds playing in his ear, he breached the thin barrier of her virginity.

Four months later, when she could no longer hide her growing belly and her father disowned her, she came to Jason and he married her.

Thus his days as a carefree bachelor ended.

Then, a year later, he met Diana. All his calm resignation shattered. Her voluptuous beauty, her bold, lurid words, captured his imagination and magnified clearly what he had given up. By accident he'd settled for a woman who would never really satisfy him, in his bed or in his soul.

He heard Diana describe her husband's planned seduction, and when Jason entered his wife's bedroom that night, he sat Marianne down on his lap, cupped her breasts in his hands and whispered in her ear exactly what he wanted to do to her, all the while knowing it was Diana to whom he wished to do those things. When he thrust into his wife's aroused, welcoming body, it was Diana whom he imagined he fucked.

For twelve more months, it was Diana he imagined every time he came to his wife's bed. Even after his wife's death, it was Diana he imagined each and every time he took his cock into his own hand.

He had never been physically adulterous to Marianne, but he had been unfaithful each time he slipped into her body.

Now here they were, two unattached adults sitting down to dinner as if he didn't desire Diana with every breath in his body.

To honor this truce, he would have to pretend that she didn't own Harridan House, that she didn't have countless lovers, that he should treat her as if she were any society lady accorded all the politeness and respect that good manners demanded.

When all he wanted to do was seduce her into his own bed.

"So how do you like Hertfordshire?" Diana asked. "We spent most of our time here in London, so I never did get to make any improvements to the old place."

Which had made living at the country estate bearable. As it was, Jason frequently imagined Diana in the master suite, in the large carved mahogany bed that was now his.

"It's lovely," he said, truthfully. "A great improvement over my earlier lodgings."

"That couldn't have been hard," Diana said with a laugh.

"No," Jason agreed ruefully. His fifty pounds a year hadn't given much room for luxury. "If one is going to live in the country, it is far better to do it in style. Cassandra is much in love with her new pony."

"Cassandra is your daughter?" He nodded. "I can't quite think of you as a father. But of course, that explains your exceeding domesticity."

He laughed at the way she so neatly insulted him.

"You amaze me, Jason," she continued, her voice silky. As silky as he imagined her skin would be if he could ever touch it. "I am so pleased that you can laugh at yourself. It gives me great hope for this . . . friendship."

"I too, my lady, am hopeful."

Diana couldn't bring herself to do as Maggie had asked. The seeming truce between them was too appealing. She actually liked Jason, and the combination of his newly revealed charm and handsome exterior muddled her senses more completely than four glasses of red wine ever could.

There was that look in his eyes, that simmering desire, and by the time the last course was taken away and Diana invited him into the parlor for a drink, she wondered where the night would lead. Perhaps Maggie was right: perhaps a man who disapproved of her lifestyle might willingly partake in it with her.

They settled in the room. She draped herself across a divan and he lounged on the sofa opposite, swirling the amber liquid in his glass.

"It's good you're here," she said, testing the water. "It's so quiet in town, I'd be beside myself trying to find some entertainment."

"A quiet night at home is never an option for you?"

"A quiet night?" Diana tilted her head and looked at him archly. "Home, yes, but quiet, never."

He didn't respond but she caught the slight tightening of his lips, the lines that showed at the corners of his mouth. Was that disapproval? And if it was, what was she doing?

Testing him? Seeing if she could turn the monk into a satyr?

He took another sip of his brandy. Then he smiled lazily, as if there were no tension between them, as if they were simply old friends, relatives, relaxing in each other's company.

Diana suddenly doubted her ability to read his mood, his thoughts. The subtle, unnamed game bothered her. Despite the one large deception in her life, she was a straightforward woman, honest with herself, with her passions. The game of seduction was the only game she ever chose to play.

She'd wanted to leave all the other manipulation and power play behind, six feet deep with her late husband.

Yet this was the moment. The moment to test him, to see if he really was different from the man she remembered, if his desire for a truce ran deeper than mere words—if his widower status had loosened his iron grip on respectability.

"But in fact, I do have plans this evening. I'm going to Harridan House, to check in, so to speak. Care to join me?"

The genial smile flattened into a thin line and it looked to Diana as if every muscle in his body had gone rigid. Well, almost every muscle.

"Can't you see that you're endangering everyone? Yourself, my daughter. The entire family's reputation?"

There it lay—the shallow worth of his truce. She had known. Why did it hurt?

"We've been here before," she reminded him. "You clearly haven't changed. I certainly haven't."

"I thought perhaps . . ." he broke off, swallowing hard. "Why do you persist?"

"What, Jason?" Diana stood, planting her feet as she demanded, "what would you have me do?"

"I'd have you shut it down."

Diana's laugh was a hollow, mocking imitation of her usual rippling caress.

"Because it offends you? It offends your oh-so-prim and proper morality. What, did you make love to your late wife with all your clothes on, in the dark?" He jumped to his feet, the echo of the drink clattering on the table. "Did she just part her legs and let you do your dirty little work while she thought of taking a bath?"

She'd gone too far. His pale eyes narrowed dangerously and under the finely tailored clothing every muscle of his body clenched with fury.

Diana stepped back, afraid for the first time. She didn't really know this man for all that they were related by marriage. Perhaps he was violent or beat his wife. A man so insulted was an unpredictable animal.

He stalked her and like prey, she wanted to flee. Instead, wide-eyed and frozen, she kept her stance.

"You think because I don't choose to fuck every man, woman and oddity that comes through those doors that I don't know how to fuck you?"

He was nearly on top of her now and she could smell the light fragrance of his musky cologne and the deeper, slightly intoxicating male scent that was uniquely his own.

"Diana, if I wanted, I could have you climaxing right here, right now without laying a finger on you."

It was not what she had expected to hear. Not from him, not

from *Saint* Jason. His words sent a chill over her body. Her nipples puckered to attention, nearly visible over the low neckline of her gown. His eyes were stormy, overwhelmingly intense in their focus on her.

She realized she had misread his intentions. This man did not wish to hit her. He wished something far more violent. For a brief, wildly insane moment, she wanted to know how his cock would feel inside her, thrusting into her, filling her and making her find the violence of her own emotions as well.

She managed to collect herself.

Coolly, she tilted her head back and looked down the length of her nose at him. "Oh Jason, if I had known all you wanted was to fuck me, I might have let you have your small pleasure and then sent you on your way. You don't need to torment me to come into my bed."

"I don't," he bit out slowly, each word staccato and harsh, "wish to fuck you." But he didn't move and the inch of air between their bodies had become a wall of heat and tension.

Deliberately, she turned around and bent over the side table, leaning on her arms, the movement causing her derriere to press against him. The hard ridge of cock pushing against his trousers gave lie to his words.

"Diana," he said her name like a warning.

She didn't stop. She reached back and pulled her dress up till it pooled around her waist and her naked buttocks were only separated from him by the cloth of his pants.

She almost wanted him to call her bluff, to take her up on this. She wanted him with an overwhelming curiosity.

"You can have me Jason, just this once."

He knew he shouldn't. He knew this was a game he should never have agreed to play. He should have kept his distance.

The pale, smooth, rounded flesh of her buttocks against his groin was the stuff of fantasy. Looking down, at this angle, he could just make out a hint of the plump folds of her pussy. He wanted in.

Why not? She was offering, even if it was a taunt. As long as he recognized her move, he was still the one in control. He could take this, take what he wanted and then leave.

He laid his hands on her buttocks, enjoying her small, stifled gasp, and pulled her hard against him, letting her feel his full length, steely and pulsing, desperate to exchange one confinement for another.

He slid his hands down, under her dress, to grasp her where her hips met her thighs. He rolled his hips against her.

He thought of the stories she had told him, of her bent over under his cousin's ancient flesh. Then he thought of all the lovers she had had. All the men who'd used her, all the men she'd used.

He couldn't do this.

He pulled his hands away and stepped back, watching with a keen sense of loss as the silk of her gown fell like a theater curtain over her limbs.

Chapter Eight

Why should one experience have left her feeling so changed? Much later that evening, restless, Diana paced about her house.

Her body was aroused in every which way but she felt completely unfulfilled. She'd given Lord Simon his congé, but even if she hadn't, he would never fulfill this gaping need that Jason had engendered in her.

Why him? Why did that insufferable man have the power to make her feel this way? Was it simply that she was attracted to the challenge of a man who refused her?

Just as well she was going to Harridan House. Perhaps this would be the one night of the year that she took some nameless man to her bed, just to slake the lust, the heated fire, that Jason had stoked within her.

She entered, as usual, through the garden door, a swath of silk obscuring her face and the hood of her cape covering her hair. One short flight of stairs took her to the large private suite where her maid Lucy waited.

She had known about Harridan House long before the solicitor read her late husband's will. Only a year into the marriage, when Roger couldn't always trust his ability to have an erection, he had brought her to this room—his playroom filled with toys she had never even imagined.

That night, the new inspiration had worked for him and with her bent over the curved arm of the velvet-upholstered chaise longue, he'd managed to fuck her. For her there had been no pleasure that night, merely the relief that he'd been satisfied and that she might still have a child.

They'd come many times after that, always to this room. Until that hardly worked, and sometimes he'd substitute a smooth, cool marble phallus for his own cock. She wouldn't have minded those nights, the delicious stretching of the generously sized object, the way the use of it allowed him to put his mouth on her even as he fucked her. She wouldn't have minded if she hadn't seen how it had tormented him. And if in his torment he hadn't taken his anger out on her.

One night, with her hair wrapped up in a turban to hide the telltale reddish curls, she'd gone with him for a tour of the entire house, expanded her education.

He'd prepared her for it, in the dark of night, describing the sorts of scenes she would see, making her wish for the companionship of younger, firmer flesh, so that when she finally witnessed the writhing bodies joined together in every imaginable way, she'd been aroused.

Ironically, that was the last night she'd been able to arouse her own husband.

"Good evening, my lady," Lucy greeted her, helping her with

her cloak, jolting Diana from her thoughts. "It's a lively evening here. In the blue room, Lord Sedgwick has created quite an orgy. Oh, and you'll be interested to know that Lord Simon is here. In the Oriental room, last I saw. I gather you've dropped the man . . ."

"Oh Luce, what would I do without you?" Diana sighed, sitting down on that same chaise longue.

Lucy grinned. "I suppose you'd have to dress up as Madame Rouge a bit more often," she teased.

Madame Rouge . . . although she had visited the club numerous times in disguise, her alias, the mysterious proprietor, was born of the need to freely move about the house once her husband had passed on. She had a man of business who managed the club in her absence, but if she was going to own this place, she felt she should really know it.

And the disguise gave her power and control over men, something she had never had before.

Then she found Lucy. A woman with a past, willing to accept a job in a less-than-reputable situation, a woman who happened to be physically similar to Diana, with the same peaches-and-cream coloring and green eyes that were like enough in shadowy light. While Lucy's hair was more brown than red, it hadn't taken much imagination for Diana to see that in the guise of Madame Rouge, they could easily be twins.

Which was incredibly useful for Diana. So she offered the maid a position . . . with unique benefits.

In many ways, Lucy had been her closest confidante these last two years, the keeper of her secrets. Until Maggie had come to town earlier this season, no other female had known of Diana's double life, her sexual exploits.

"Well, I have dropped him. I should have done it ages ago, or never picked him up." Diana reached her hands over her head and stretched, arching over the curved back of the chair. "The man has no imagination."

"Certainly not enough to please you," Lucy teased.

"What would you know of what pleases me?"

Lucy laughed. "I am your spy, my lady. I would be remiss in my duties if I hadn't ever seen what pleases you best."

Diana blushed, surprised at her own embarrassment. Lucy knew almost everything that went on in Harridan House. The maid acted as Diana's eyes and ears when she was away. Diana had known that Lucy had even seen Maggie and Oakley here in this room, when they had engaged in their affair.

Why had she never imagined that Lucy would also watch her?

"I'll send you to my next lover then," Diana said with her own little laugh, trying to brush away her confusion. "You'll have to instruct him to do just that."

Later, she prowled the hallways, scanning the crowds. Lucy was right. It was a lively crowd here tonight, raucous and entertaining.

Lord Sedgwick's orgy was impressive. He even had Humboldt's new mistress involved, the one the man so jealously guarded.

She'd decided before she arrived that she would take a man back to her boudoir and Lucy's earlier words had heated her memories, but now, faced with actual bodies, her instincts were shying away.

Had Jason managed to poison her with his middle-class morality? Never mind that she, too, came from a less-than-noble family.

She spotted Sir Robert George ascending the staircase, and ducked into a room to avoid him. Generally, she liked the man. His intense pursuit of her amused her. Tonight, however, she wished to avoid it.

From having witnessed his insatiable taste for women, Diana knew exactly what to expect from a night with him. The lack of mystery in and of itself helped her keep her distance. It was something else as well, though. She found his desire to possess her, to have had her simply because he had not yet, off-putting.

As much as she enjoyed men and sex, she had never approached the experience as a cold consumer. Sir Robert clearly did.

Which made her wonder what she was doing here tonight, looking for an anonymous encounter when what she really wanted . . .

What she really wanted was Jason.

Chapter Nine

Earnestina had decided, at the very last minute, that she wanted to throw another little soiree before she moved her household to Brighton for the summer season. She had confided in Diana that she feared she'd have to stretch to fill the rooms. Apparently more people were still in London than other social events suggested, for her rooms had grown stiflingly hot with the press of human bodies and the summer heat lingering in the evening air.

Diana found little enjoyment in the evening. For the first time in years, she had no wish to flirt, no wish to be near any but her closest friends. Even there, pleasure was forestalled. Maggie and Oakley were nauseatingly in love. Watching their little touches and glances when they thought no one noticed made her feel vaguely ill.

Diana escaped to the terrace as soon as she could.

She should be happy for her cousin. Love was rare currency. Diana wasn't even certain she knew what it looked like.

For a week she had been infatuated with her first lover, Patrick, the first man she had slept with who wasn't her husband. But that had paled when she learned that her late husband had hired the man to satisfy her since he no longer could.

The romantic glow had faded quickly.

When she had run into the Irishman, her former lover, a year later, at a benefit for the theater, not even the slightest twinge of desire flittered through her body. He was just a man. She knew now how similar and interchangeable all men were.

Still, these last years she'd courted male attention, basking in the flirtation and sexual undercurrents.

Perhaps all she needed was the change of scene another week would bring.

"There you are!"

Diana shifted slightly to face Lord Ashburton as he joined her by the rail. "Here I am," she agreed, smiling. She considered Ash a friend as much as she considered his wife one.

"I am sent to drag you back inside, to meet my cousin, Colonel Tiptain. He said, 'Introduce me to the fairest woman in London,' and here I am. Although I'm not certain I should."

"And why is that?" Diana asked, knowing he wanted her to. She turned to lean against the rail, her elbows resting on the polished wood.

Ash leaned closer to her, a teasing grin quirking his lips.

"Because I'll be awfully jealous if he manages to snatch up the loveliest, shapeliest woman I know."

"You're too kind." Diana looked away, a smile curving her mouth. She almost couldn't help the intake of breath that pushed her breasts up, enlarging the exposed upper curve of flesh. The flirtation was too much second nature to her.

She laughed and turned back to him, meeting his eyes to let him in on the joke, that it was silly that they should talk this way, two friends who would never in reality choose to mate.

"He was in India, right?"

"Yes, and wounded, too, which is why he's back, but it hasn't taken away his sense of fun. He'll be accompanying us all to fair Brighthelmstone."

Brighton—the sea with its salty air and bucolic delights would wash away the strangeness that had overtaken her ever since Jason had reappeared in her life.

A change of scene was exactly what was needed.

Chapter Ten

"That's a very nice brandy." Jason held up his glass so that the golden liquid caught the light.

"Well-aged calvados," Daniel said, kicking the footstool aside and stretching out in the deep, comfortable chair upholstered in a rich red Moroccan leather. "Seymour procured it."

Jason nodded. The rest was always better unsaid, even in the privacy of Throckmorton's study.

"So does the wealth of my liquor cabinet entice you to join us in Brighton for the rest of the summer? We have rooms hired on Air Street and Lizzie is determined to leave London in time to see the Lewes race."

The idea was an enticing one—instead of returning to the humid heat of Hertfordshire he could spend a few months by the seashore in fine style. Neither Daniel nor he would have considered such a move four years ago when their pockets were to let. Since then, Jason had inherited the baronetcy, and Daniel's wife had received a mysteriously large inheritance after the death of her long-absent brother.

Money had not changed his friends' lifestyle. It had merely lubricated the ease with which they played.

But Jason's lifestyle had changed. Most important, he had become a father, and one could not forget the two-year-old daughter who waited for him at his estate. He may not have loved his wife, having been forced into marrying her, but he did love his child, and while these days in London had been diverting, he didn't mind giving them up.

"Bring Cassandra," Daniel offered offhandedly. "There'll be

more than enough room in the house for the babe and her nanny. I'm certain Lizzie would love to see the little girl. You know how she adores children. Wants one of her own." He said the last in a confiding tone, winking for emphasis.

"I'll think about it," Jason hedged, not entirely certain why he was still hesitant with his one great concern solved so easily.

"Do tell me soon, for I'll invite some other fiend to make good use of the extra space if you don't. August is always packed. While you're thinking about that, perhaps you could tell me about what happened last night."

The image of Diana's plump buttocks overwhelmed him so completely that for a moment Jason forgot where he was. He caught himself just before his hand wandered down to his burgeoning erection.

"I see." Daniel laughed. "Amour unfulfilled." He reached over to refill Jason's glass.

"Like you'd know anything about it," Jason grumbled, wondering for the ten-thousandth time in the last two days why he hadn't simply undone the falls of his breeches and taken the woman like she had wanted.

But had she wanted? Hadn't she merely been teasing him? Taunting him?

No matter what the answer was, Jason knew that as much as he had desired her before, the longing was now tenfold greater.

"I know a bit about it, though I've managed to put it from my mind," Daniel said. "Don't you remember, it wasn't always roses with Lizzie?"

"Right," Jason admitted. "You nearly wasted away pursuing her." His friend now enjoyed the sort of marital bliss only women wrote about.

He wanted to tell Daniel about Diana, but to reveal her double identities, even to his closest friend, would put his name and his daughter's future at risk. Something that might not have bothered him four years ago, but responsibility had taken its due.

Hours later, Jason still couldn't get her out of his mind. It had been too long since he'd been with a woman. Not since before his wife died. It was no wonder that his thoughts kept straying to Diana, to the creamy swell of her buttocks.

She wanted him and he wanted her. Why shouldn't they have an affair? Two independent adults without the need to make excuses to anyone for their actions. Why shouldn't they?

Because she owned Harridan House and God knew what she did when she visited there. What had she done last night? Had some other man thrust between those swollen lips?

He tamped down the jealousy. He didn't own her. He hadn't even fucked her.

Could he blame her for being who she was? Hadn't she even tried to explain, how she'd been seduced, how she'd been molded? Wasn't that sensual fire even part of her very attraction? It was like chiding a tiger for being too fierce.

So he went to find her, to apologize to her, to plan his own seduction.

Chapter Eleven

Earnestina and Lord Ashburton were perched in the race stand, a rather shabby wooden building since the last one burned down five years earlier. Diana couldn't bear the thought of being trapped in the rickety structure. So she sat in her carriage, struggling for any sort of view of the races.

Brighton always seemed to be changing. The old pleasure garden, Promenade Grove, with its breakfasts and picnics had closed in the same year to make way for the Prince of Wales's landscaping. But this year, especially with the death of old Wade, the Master of Ceremonies, everything *felt* different.

"We'll make a party to Rottendean on Thursday, what say

you, Lady Blount?" Arthur Dunbury asked. "Start the season with a proper picnic before the crowds come in earnest."

"As long as your lovely sister comes, how can I refuse?" Diana returned with a smile. She liked the Dunburys. And she liked Arthur too much to take him up on the offer of marriage he had made several months ago.

"Sister, you say?" Colonel Tiptain perked up. "By God, it's good to be back in England. Surrounded by beautiful women, what. Far more diverting than the god-awful heat and the endless mosquitos. I'm awfully glad my cousin knows what fun is." Diana laughed even as she brushed away the vigorous pinch to her thigh that punctuated his words.

Diana had learned quickly what Colonel Tiptain's sense of fun was—a darkened room, with his silver opium kit that went wherever he went. His habit was from his days in India, but his traveling kit was from China. The first night in Brighton, Earnestina had praised the ornate designs and the jade bowl carved in the shape of a dragon, even as she puffed on the silver-handled pipe as if she had been doing so for more than a week.

Ash had teased Diana when she begged off and lounged on the far settee, not touching the apparatus. Not that she hadn't tried the substance. Only, her aversion to it was much stronger, filled with her memories of Roger in his last months, when he'd finally chosen to staunch the pain with something stronger than laudanum.

"She's a young girl, Colonel, not for you," she discouraged him. Lydia Dunbury might have had her first season but she was clearly a late bloomer. She'd hung by the wall through the months, stammering and pale as if she should still have leading strings attached to her dress. If she hadn't sat next to the girl at a musicale, Diana might never have learned about her latent wit and sense of humor.

"I think Lydia might take umbrage at discouraging any suitor so fast," Dunbury quipped, ever ready to make fun of the sister he adored.

Diana's response fled from her mind, for she saw _him_, half a head taller than the crowd, standing with another man and a fashionably dressed woman who hung on his arm, laughing. Which did not bother her. Which had no reason to bother her.

But it did.

Jason was an insufferable prude, who continued to chastise her for her life choices, who'd even rejected her very generous offer. And yet she was jealous.

The long, peaceful dinner they had shared still lingered in her mind, beguiling, as if that was the way it had been meant to be from that first moment she saw him in the lawyer's office, the brief moment before she met his wife.

His fair head of curls, glinting in the sun, turned as if pulled by a magnet until he stared directly at her. He inclined his head the slightest amount, his lips curling into a smile, and Diana found herself returning the greeting, her own lips curving, her chin raising in recognition.

Her breath came a little faster as memory flooded. Suddenly the encounter in her sitting room had been seduction—foreplay—and this moment the continuance. There was the sense of inevitability that soon, very soon, satisfaction would come.

Or maybe that was all in her own mind. Diana pulled her gaze away with effort. She was having ridiculous romantic thoughts. Inevitability, indeed. She was the master of her actions just as he was of his. An affair would only occur if each of them wished.

Did she wish?

Did she have so little pride that she'd sleep with a man who looked down upon her? But pride had been her failing two years ago and had trapped her into her current role. And hadn't pride almost ruined her cousin Maggie's chances at happiness with Oakley?

Pride was overrated. She had to live for this moment, this life.

She looked back but he was no longer there, and a quick scan of the crowd revealed nothing of his whereabouts.

It was like an abrupt cessation in lovemaking—the rising sensations aching until time dissipated them.

Chapter Twelve

The day was hot, the crowds large, noisy and raucous. Jason squinted, surveying the field while Lizzie clutched his arm, laughing and tipsy from the ale they'd drunk.

"C'mon," Throckmorton urged, barely sparing them a glance as he stamped ahead. "Silverthorn will win, I'm certain of it."

"He won't," Lizzie said, giggling. "Daniel never picks the winner."

"Ah, but he picked you," Jason corrected her. "However, I concur. Silverthorn will not win. I've placed my money on Lucinda's Pearl."

"What a terrible name!" Lizzie exclaimed.

"Horrible name, beautiful horse," Jason agreed but his thoughts weren't on the horse anymore, for he'd found his quarry, perched in an open landau, surrounded by men. He tamped down the twinge of jealous irritation. He knew very well what he was planning to get himself into.

Diana's face tilted to the side as she listened to the man sitting next to her. She looked young and innocent with her straw bonnet framing her pale face and auburn curls, but as she moved and laughed it was like watching liquid sensuality.

Jason savored the moment. He had never met a woman like her. She even sat uniquely.

Her head turned, her eyes meeting his. He inclined his head in greeting, the slow smile that curved his lips intended to let her know that he was there for her. From the way she held his gaze just before she looked away, he had no doubt that she had understood that message.

"Oh, look!" Lizzie exclaimed, pulling on his arm. "There's Mrs. Mustlewhaithe. Daniel, don't you see Agathe over there? She's been our neighbor in London all season. Oh, and such a story about her niece! We must say hello."

Jason followed, losing sight of Diana as they moved deeper into the crowds.

It was just as well. Patience was important now. With Brighton small as it was he'd see her soon enough.

Chapter Thirteen

In the early evening, Jason walked up the steps of the Air Street house, a stride ahead of Daniel and Lizzie. Before him stretched the possibility of a very pleasurable evening. A dinner among friends and then the ball to commemorate the final day of the Brighton and Lewes races. Without a doubt, Diana would be there and without a doubt, he wanted to see her.

He wondered what dancing with her would be like, what she would feel like held in his arms. He had an idea, from the few times she'd been close to him—that night at Vauxhall, that afternoon at her London home.

"Sir Jason." The footman who opened the door caught his attention. "Miss Cassandra arrived this afternoon. A nursery has been made on the third floor."

All thoughts of Diana fled as Jason thrust his hat and coat at the young man and then hurried up the stairs. He'd been two weeks away from his daughter.

She was in bed, her nanny, Mrs. Landis, braiding her hair. She was blond, like her mother, tall for her age, sturdy and healthy.

Cassandra squealed when she caught sight of him, pulling

away from the woman. Jason swept her up in his arms and twirled her around till she squealed again, laughing. He had missed that sound, that high-pitched infectious giggling that almost three-year-old girls did so well. He hugged her to him tightly.

"How is my little princess?" he asked.

"Your princess has had a very long day," Mrs. Landis answered for the girl. "But she hasn't stopped chattering once for the last hour about seeing her daddy."

"We saw the water!" Cassie cried. "I want to go in."

"You will, sweetheart," he assured her, putting her back down on the ground and then settling himself on the floor beside her. "But for now, would you like to come downstairs and meet my friends?"

Chapter Fourteen

It was as if Jason had merely been a figment of her imagination, appearing in the crowd. Was it so strange that he should end up in Brighton where half of society had migrated? Yet Diana couldn't shake the idea that he had come for her, for the unfinished business left between them.

The thought perched in the back of her mind throughout the day and into evening, when they attended the last ball of the races at the Castle Tavern, but she ignored it determinedly.

It wasn't too difficult, she found, for as usual she never lacked for dance partners or amusing company.

But then, Earnestina assessed her over the rim of her punch glass.

"Whom are you looking for?"

"I'm not . . ." Diana started to say in the moment before she realized. *She had been looking for him.* During every dance, and every conversation, she continued to sweep the room with her searching gaze. "Well, I suppose I was," she amended. "I thought I saw my cousin earlier this morning. Sir Jason."

"Hmm." Earnestina smiled slightly. "I'm certain if he is in Brighton, he'll call on you. We'll be forced to entertain him then. Ash will be quite put out."

"Put out about what?" Ashburton asked, as he and Dunbury joined them.

"That we'll be entertaining Sir Jason Blount."

"The man we met at Vauxhall?" Ash raised an eyebrow. "I know he's your relative, Di, but it's really too bad old Blount never had a proper heir."

"I think what Ashburton means," Dunbury added quickly, "is that it is unfortunate the late baronet did not find his charming wife when he was still of an age to . . ."

"That's quite enough," Diana interrupted, laughing. "You're only stepping into the muck by trying to save Ashburton. I know he meant no harm."

"Certainly not," Ash said, looking rather affronted. "I'd hardly lay any blame at your feet." Then he flashed his easy, charming smile. "I'd much rather lay myself there."

"What a wicked husband I have," Earnestina exclaimed, hitting him lightly with her fan. "Come, Di, let's take a turn around the room and leave these men. Perhaps we'll spot your Sir Jason."

Diana linked her arm through her friend's, smiling as brightly as usual. She knew Ash meant no harm, but it didn't ease the tight knot in her chest. It was stupid, really, to think about it. It wasn't as if she even liked children.

Chapter Fifteen

Rotterdean was a pleasant little village that had grown up around a duck pond and a pretty church. A windmill added to the town's charm. But what Diana liked best about the outing was the exhilaration of riding over the velvet-green downs, breathing in the fresh country air.

It was a nice change from the sickly sweet scent that seemed to cling to their Brighton rooms, as if they were all invalids convalescing.

The party ended up being a large one, with the Dunburys and Miss Dunbury's companion, the Ashburtons, Colonel Tiptain, and a few of Earnestina's friends. Oakley's younger brother, the Honorable Charles Chistlehurst, and his companion, Mr. Prentiss, joined them as well, impromptu, when they crossed paths in the streets heading out of town.

When Chistlehurst and Prentiss proceeded to monopolize Miss Dunbury's attention, Diana was relieved. The boys might be too young for marriage and far more interested in wine, women and wagers than much of anything else, but they were good-hearted, and ultimately gentlemen, which she was not certain could be said for the colonel.

"Lady Blount," Miss Dunbury called, drawing up next to her. As shy and pale in society as the girl was, she sat her mount well and her usually pale cheeks were flushed with the exhilaration of the ride.

"Tired of the men already?" Diana asked.

Miss Dunbury blushed. "They are quite shameless," the girl

admitted. "But I do like it. Mr. Chistlehurst makes it so easy to converse. It is all laughter."

Whatever respite the girl had been looking for didn't last for long. Prentiss rode up beside them, a grin splitting his ruddy, boyish face.

"Miss Dunbury, Lady Blount, we've started a wager and we need someone to arbitrate."

"A wager?" Miss Dunbury looked toward Diana as if she wished to go with Prentiss but did not wish to be rude.

"Go on, Miss Dunbury, find out what this wager is."

Diana wondered if she'd ever truly been as innocent as Lydia Dunbury. It seemed that as long as she could remember, she'd known far too much: about anatomy, about lust, about what a man could do to a woman . . . and a woman could do to a man.

Away from London, even away from Brighton for the day, in the fresh air and beautiful countryside, Diana felt freer, more relaxed than she could remember being in a long time.

"Yes, go on, Miss Dunbury, I'll keep Lady Blount company," Ash said, moving closer to her.

Mr. Prentiss and Miss Dunbury turned their horses around to ride back toward the others.

"How is your afternoon, Ash?" Diana asked.

"Lovely, now." He grinned. "I must admit, Diana, it's torture having you under our roof, knowing you are sleeping just rooms away. You've done away with Simon; let me be next."

Was he *serious*? Diana stared at him, alarmed. She pulled on the reigns without thinking, guiding the mare toward the left, away from him. She'd always thought their mild flirtation harmless, the normal tension of society, but he was her friend's husband.

She corrected her direction.

"Ash, you know I love you, darling, but what of your beautiful wife?"

"As she's been fucking my cousin these past few days," Ash half leaned out of his saddle to whisper with a grin, "I hardly think she'll care. She knows I fancy you."

Both pieces of information were news to Diana.

"Do you sleep naked, Di?" he asked. "Tell me you do so I can imagine these luscious breasts of yours."

"Ash!" She wasn't embarrassed. She'd heard, and enjoyed, much more vulgar talk, but she needed to discourage his interest, in as politic a way as possible. Unfortunately, she found herself a bit aroused at his words. After all, she'd been on edge ever since Jason . . .

"When we danced last night, I could see the slightest shadow of your nipples. I can't tell you how much willpower it required to not just pluck you out of your dress and suckle you right there in the ballroom."

Diana refocused on Ash, studying him the way she usually assessed men.

He was of average height, average looks really, but he had that way about him that these noblemen often did, a certain attractive arrogance.

For just the slightest moment she was tempted. Then she saw Earnestina, laughing at something Dunbury was saying, and the temptation passed.

"It's just as well you didn't, darling," she murmured. "I would hate to have had to slap you, especially in public."

"But in private?" he pressed. Diana bit the inside of her cheek lightly. She was annoyed with this new face her friend had chosen to present.

"I'll ask your wife," she said, finally, surprised when her words didn't embarrass Ashburton.

"Do, Diana, as soon as you may, then the sooner I can have you."

It wasn't the sort of statement that deserved a response. He could not have her, but as a friend she'd have to let him down gracefully.

When they finally stopped for a picnic, Diana pulled Earnestina away.

"Darling," Diana asked, "are you really having an affair with the colonel?"

"Ash told you that?" Earnestina laughed. "The wicked man, you know he'll do anything to get into your bed."

"What a laugh!"

"No, truly." Earnestina held her gaze. "In London, Ash and I were sharing our secret fantasies, you know, as a way to spice up things in bed."

Diana raised an eyebrow. It wasn't that strange. As far as she knew, the pair had been faithful since their wedding day. After five years it seemed natural for a certain . . . *malaise* to set in.

"Exactly," Tina confided, as if Diana had spoken her thoughts. "And I could hardly blame him for finding you attractive. As succulent as you are, there have been times I've found myself attracted."

Oh, no, Diana thought, her eyes instantly drawn to Earnestina's mouth, to her wide lips which suddenly looked like an erotic toy, which suddenly she could imagine pressed against her own hot flesh—the tongue that even now wet Tina's lips, licking her creaming slit. Diana was no stranger to sapphic love; her husband had enticed her into that as well, until she had no longer minded the strange familiarity of another woman's body in her arms.

Tina flushed and looked away with a nervous laugh.

"I'm flattered," Diana managed, "and what was your fantasy?"

Tina grew even pinker, and after a quick glance at Diana's face she kept her gaze on some object in the distance as she spoke.

"Lydia, you know, Lady Feachem."

Diana nodded with a dawning understanding of where this was leading.

"Well, just last week, after Tiptain arrived, we were all trying his private stash of opium, just that once you know, and she told me that she'd been to that . . . that *club*."

Harridan House, where as far as Diana knew neither of the Ashburtons had ever been. However, Lady Feachem frequently accompanied her husband there.

"She told me that because she thought I might like it," Tina whispered, drawing closer to her ultimate confession. "Because

I'd said I wondered what it would be like to have two men in my bed at once. And she'd said she knew."

Diana took a deep, steadying breath to calm the new wave of warmth spreading through her body, settling between her legs. It was always this way with her—the suggestion of sex, the reminder of past experiences, aroused her immediately.

Two men kissing her breasts, a mouth on each nipple, fingers thrusting into her pussy, hands on her belly, thighs, hips. And in her hands, two hard, velvety cocks, each with their own unique shape and feel, throbbing against her fingers.

That had been a month after Roger died, when she celebrated her freedom, celebrated it by engaging in all the activities he'd taught her—beyond what he'd taught her.

"So that is your desire?" Diana said, her even, silky tone betraying nothing of the swirling sensations memory had ricocheted through her body.

Earnestina nodded, her face ridiculously red against the paleness of her white-blond hair.

"I told Ash," Tina continued with a small smile.

"And what did Ash say?" Although clearly, if Ash was saying that his wife was sleeping with his cousin, he must have not minded so much.

Tina trilled a laugh that sounded strained to Diana's ears. "Why, that as long as we were exchanging confidences, he rather fancied you."

Chapter Sixteen

There was a card assembly at Tilt's, and even though Diana had just been at the Castle Tavern assembly rooms the night before for the last ball of the races, she entered the room with a restless energy.

She had thought she would see Jason at the ball, but if he had been there, he had avoided her. Somehow, Diana felt that he would not have done that.

Unless that was his game—to make her aware of him, to taunt her, to play at seduction.

The rooms were filled with the sounds of glasses and laughter, cards shuffled, skirts rustling and chairs scraping on the wood floor.

She didn't wish to play at cards. She rarely did. She still remembered what it was like to live with much fewer funds and the high stakes of friendly games held no interest for her. Earnestina, on the other hand, had found a table early in the evening and sat there still.

Diana passed from acquaintance to acquaintance, the restlessness making her impatient with conversation. Where was he? When would she see him?

It was when she'd stopped by an open window for a breath of air that he came up behind her.

"Do you know, Diana, that I'm here in Brighton for you, because you were right, because I do want you."

Heat flooded her, and she pressed her thighs tightly together, against the growing damp.

And she was so primed, so ready for him, from all the talk that morning, from all the nights in the last week she'd spent wondering what if . . . what if he had unbuttoned his breeches and thrust into her?

"The offer is closed," Diana said, though she didn't mean it. But it had to be said, so he would understand that in any game they played, she was the one who made the rules.

She heard his intake of breath and waited for what he would say next. Would he make love to her with words, the way he had threatened to last week? She thought briefly of Ash's words that morning, about wanting to lick her nipples in the middle of a crowded ballroom. She had been aroused even though she hadn't wanted Ash, wasn't particularly attracted to the man.

But she wanted Jason. She'd desired him from the first moment she'd seen him, two years ago. Could he really make her come just by speaking?

"I've wanted you since I first saw you in your widow's weeds, looking more lovely in black than any woman should. For two long years I've fantasied about every way in which I'd make love to you if I could. I imagined you undressed. I imagined the shape of your breasts and the curve of your hip. I want to see if my dreams were true. Or if you could possibly be even more perfectly formed than I've imagined."

She didn't doubt his words. It seemed utterly right that he should have been attracted to her as intensely as she had been to him. But where he had let her in to haunt his dreams, she had pushed the thought of him away. He'd rejected her and the life she led, but still he wanted her.

"If there were no one else here I would place my mouth where your neck meets your shoulder. "

She could practically feel his breath on the place he spoke of.

"I would lick your skin, make small circles with my tongue. I would move up, across your neck, slowly, licking my way, sucking my way to that sensitive spot behind your ear. And I'd touch the tip of my tongue to that place."

She felt his tongue, felt the hot trail of sensation even with him three inches away. She felt the echoes of that sensation throughout her body, in the puckering of her nipples and the gooseflesh on her back.

"And then I'd place my left hand on your hip, to draw you close to me, to feel every curve of your body against mine. Do you know when you walk, your hips sway, and I keep seeing the pale gleam of your bare backside when you offered yourself to me? Bent over with your pussy inviting me in, you were as beautiful as you are now, standing in front of me fully clothed."

"You could have had me then," Diana said archly, trying to ignore the seeping warmth between her legs at the image he placed in her mind.

"I should have, I was an idiot," he admitted. "But if I could, while I taste your neck, I'd place my right hand over your breast. I'd stroke you through the cloth, feel the weight of you and anticipate how your bare, round flesh will feel in my hand."

Diana caught herself from leaning back against him, from urging him to do all he said right there in the assembly rooms.

"I'd pull down this silly fabric covering your breasts. Just one tug and I could free them to view, I could touch you." He broke off, his breath a hoarse gasp.

She waited for him to continue, hoped he would continue.

And then he did, veering from the methodical path he'd laid out. "Diana, when I think of the soft mound peeking out between your legs, I want nothing more than to lift your skirts and taste you."

Dear Lord, she wanted that too! Diana thought, as the flesh he spoke of grew heavy with desire.

"I want to know how you smell. I want to know how your juices taste, how they feel on my tongue. I want to thrust my tongue inside you and feel your muscles clench, and know that in time I'll feel those same muscles gripping my cock."

Her pussy clenched involuntarily and Diana breathed in deeply. It was getting hard to stand still, to maintain her posture. She felt weak with need and lust. She wanted his tongue to do all those things he said, to thrust into her like a pointed little cock.

"I want to lick every inch of your pink, wet folds and know that all that is for me."

It was far too hot in the assembly room. Sweat beaded at her temples, under her arms. And it was pointless for her to even think about the hot gush of liquid coating her pussy and even now dripping to the outer folds, to the crevice of her thighs.

She was slick and ready for a man—for Jason.

"I want you wet and yielding, pulsing for me. And then I want to slide my fingers into you, deeper than my tongue can go, while I suck on you. I want you ready for me, I want you on the edge."

She was on the edge. He had exactly what he wanted.

"I've caught your scent, Diana," he said, his voice strained. "Tell me how wet you are."

"You're touching me, Jason," she whispered. "You can feel just how wet I am."

He sucked in his breath. "That's right. You're slick on my fingers. When you're trembling, when you might explode, that's when I'm going to thrust into you as deep as you'll take me. Diana, I can practically feel you right now."

She felt him, she felt his cock inside her, stretching her, pushing her over that edge. Her body jerked suddenly with the force of the orgasm, her pussy clenching again and again at the emptiness where there should have been his cock. Everything tingled, everything in her body vibrated with pleasure.

Jason caught her before she stumbled forward. He swept her up in his arms, settled her against his chest and, carrying her, made for the exit.

"She's fainted, needs some air," he managed to say, aware of the gasps and stares that followed their progress. She seemed to wilt in his arms, playing along with his story.

The hallway outside the ballroom was equally crowded, so Jason continued till he found an alcove with a bench, thankfully deserted, away from prying eyes.

He didn't want to let her down, to release the delicious burden of her body. He looked at her flushed face, desperate to kiss her.

But they weren't that far from the ballroom and at any moment their hideaway could be stumbled upon. He let her down slowly, keeping his arms around her until she was steady on her feet. Then, finally, he dropped his arms.

She didn't move away. Instead she pressed herself more fully against him, so that the hard ridge of his aching cock pressed against the slight curve of her belly. Then she stretched up, on her tiptoes, so that he fit right in the junction of her thighs.

"I am a thousand times impressed," Diana whispered. "I wonder, if you can give me such pleasure without your touch, what else you are capable of?"

Jason groaned at the thought of it, of sliding inside of her. He'd imagined the moment countless times and while he'd described what he wanted to do to her, he'd imagined doing each and every act.

"I'll show you," he suggested. This time he would not walk away. This time he would plow her as thoroughly as he'd fantasized.

"But you won't." Diana laughed and stepped away. The places where her body had pressed against him felt cold and empty. "I told you the offer is closed. My curiosity will have to remain unquenched."

"Why play this game?" he challenged, coming toward her, to close the gap between them, but she stepped back again. And again, until he had her up against the wall. Purposefully he thrust himself against her, grinding his hips against her, letting her feel every inch of him through the layers of fabric.

Then her hands were sliding between them, working at the buttons of his breeches, unfastening the falls.

"I want to see you." Her eyes were glazed over with what he thought was desire and she sounded rather desperate. It made him even harder, but he knew very well that only a dying potted plant and the corner of wall kept them out of sight of anyone else. He started to move away, but when the palm of her hand brushed over him, he stilled. He wouldn't move away if the Prince of Wales and his whole entourage came rounding the corner.

The cloth fell away and his cock sprang free, into the warm touch of her hand.

He moaned at the pleasure of her silken glove caressing his skin. He watched as she touched him.

"Beautiful," she whispered, admiringly, and a drop of fluid pearled at the tip of his cock.

He had never thought of his penis that way, as something aesthetically pleasing. It had always been a tool, a mass of sensation, but the way she regarded the thick, straight rod, fingers tracing the slightly bulging veins, made him feel as if he were a sculpture, a work of art.

As if a man, too, could be beautiful.

She slid down the wall till she knelt on the floor and her lovely lips were in line with his cock.

She was going to take him in her mouth, here in the hallway, with some two hundred people playing cards just yards away.

And he was going to let her.

Her tongue touched him, licking the fluid from his tip, and then retreated.

"Your scent, your taste, is delicious," Diana said, her words floating up to him, "and I'm a wicked woman to tease you so, here in public. So I won't tease you anymore."

Intense disappointment filled him at the thought of her retreat, but then her lips closed over him and she sucked him into the hot, wet cavern of her mouth.

There was no doubt that she knew what she was doing. Her tongue unerringly found every place of heightened sensation. Her lips tensed to create a deliciously tight sheath for him, an incredible friction.

And her hands . . . her hands caressed his inner thighs, the soft skin at his groin, between his legs, the twin heavy sacs between. Each touch drew him closer, higher, spiraling toward orgasm.

He wanted to slow her down, slow this down and savour it. But the passion of the moment was underscored by the illicit nature of their actions, by the idea that any moment they might be caught.

She moaned around his cock, as if merely the act of giving him pleasure brought her an equal erotic pleasure. As if simply having him in her mouth made her wet and yearning with need.

And maybe it did. The thought of licking her moist folds had made him hard nightly these past two years.

He laid his hands gently on the back of her head, wanting to pull all her pins loose and wind his fingers through the curling waves. With effort he kept his touch light. But finally, when his balls tightened and he slipped over the edge, he pressed her to him, pushing deep into her mouth, needing to be completely engulfed while he emptied himself into her.

She took everything he had, her hands cupping his buttocks,

keeping him deep till every last drop of fluid had passed from him to her.

He fell limp from her mouth and she pressed her cheek against the soft, damp flesh. They stood there, silent, listening to the distant sounds of laughter and music echoing down the hall.

Then she leaned back, lifted the flap of fabric and fastened it back into place. He held out his hands to help her stand.

All the heated desire had passed. Diana tried to gather her thoughts, but her mind felt as soft as her jaw, stretched and weak.

"Thank you." Jason moved to her side, leaning against the wall, regarding her under heavy-lidded eyes.

The emptiness of the moment made her feel . . . strange. Cheap, even. As if now that this passion had been spent, there was nothing left between them.

"I was merely returning the pleasure," she said distantly.

"I feel it too."

Diana stared at him in shock. Did he mean the pleasure, or perhaps, just maybe, was he referring to this strange moment, this awkwardness?

He shifted, pushing himself away from the wall, straightening his clothes.

"Sometimes anticipation makes the other side seem . . . less," he stated, holding her gaze with his own. "But it isn't over between us. This was merely the aperitif."

She nodded, not pretending to deny him. And then she watched him bow and walk away.

She did not want it to be over. Not until she'd tasted him again. Not until she'd had him inside her. Not until . . .

She blinked away sudden, appalling tears.

Not until she knew what it was about him that attracted her. That made her feel that sweet sensation in the vicinity of her ephemeral soul whenever he neared.

The attraction had never been just to his physical form. Since the first moment she met him, Jason had called to her like no other man had or did.

But she hardly knew him.

Chapter Seventeen

Jason walked away from her because it was the only thing he could do. Because he needed some air, he needed some space. He needed to compose himself and understand just what had happened.

What happened, numbskull? What happened is that you did exactly what you intended to do and you received more than you imagined.

Jason laughed at himself. The others who stood out on the street in the warm night spared brief looks at him and then went back to their own conversations.

He broke past the crowd and turned toward Air Street. Daniel and Lizzie wouldn't be home yet and his daughter would be fast asleep, and all of that was perfect. What he needed was a quiet place to sit, to think.

Again, what was there to think about? He hadn't felt a woman's touch in a year. No wonder he was so unsettled.

As he'd said to Diana, after intense anticipation there was the inevitable letdown.

Yet that wasn't exactly it. He didn't feel let down. Exactly. He just felt . . .

He wanted more.

He wanted more than just Diana's mouth on his cock, or eventually all of her body under, over or in any way entwined with his. He wanted to know what made her who she was, why she attracted him. Why she fascinated him, even beyond the obvious allure of her delicious flesh.

Chapter Eighteen

She found Earnestina still sitting at the card table, as if the whole episode had never happened, had been just the blink of an eye.

"What a relief," Tina exclaimed, sending only the barest glance in Diana's direction before she refocused on the game. "I'd heard you fainted."

"Nothing to concern yourself over," Diana assured her.

"Yes, that's what I assumed when I heard it was your relative, Sir Jason, who was assisting you." Tina winked. The other three ladies at the table snickered and Diana smiled as the situation demanded.

"He's very handsome," Mrs. Cooke said. "I heard he's a widower."

"And out of mourning," said another lady, who Diana did not recognize.

"Pooh," Earnestina exclaimed, flipping her cards down on the table. "I don't think I wish to lose anymore this evening. Lady Blount? Shall we move on?"

Diana inclined her head in agreement. She followed her friend around the assembly rooms, stopping to chat with acquaintances, to make plans for the following days.

Finally, she realized what she was doing—looking for him, everywhere. It was ridiculous, that was what it was. Ridiculous to fixate on any one man, to crave one man's touch.

And he had touched her. When she'd leaned over that table, he'd grasped her hips. He'd pulled her against him.

Stop! Diana berated herself. *Really, she was too depraved. Per-*

haps Jason was right about that. Could she not think about anything but sex?

"I'm fatigued," Tina complained. She did look tired, shadows beneath her eyes.

They returned home, but neither Tiptain nor Ash was there. Diana rang for sherry.

"Do you mind?" Tina asked, pulling out the colonel's opium kit. "I'm so terribly wound up from the evening."

Diana sighed but waved her hand. It was hardly her place to curtail her friend's choice of dissipation.

"So what did happen with your cousin?" Tina asked, after she'd taken a drag on the pipe.

Two weeks ago, Diana wouldn't have hesitated to tell her friend that she was thinking of sleeping with him. In fact, she would have shared the idea enthusiastically. Now, however, Diana couldn't bring herself to give anything more than a shrug.

Then Ash and Tiptain entered the salon.

"Started without us?" the colonel chided, taking the pipe from Earnestina. "Such wickedness deserves punishment." He settled himself into a chair.

Diana watched the interplay. Perhaps Ash had spoken the truth and he and Tiptain were indulging Tina in her little fantasy.

She couldn't help herself: she imagined the three of them naked, their bodies writhing, limbs intertwined, cocks thrusting. She shook her head. *Really! Earnestina?*

But then Tina and Ash had been indulging in opium for over a fortnight and it had clearly loosened their inhibitions.

Ash sat down, a shade too close to Diana. His wandering hand caressed her forearm.

"I'm thinking of making Sir Jason my lover," Diana finally answered Tina's question casually but deliberately, knowing Ash would hear her. Perhaps it would put him off the scent.

Later though, when the room was filled with smoke and Diana, coughing, stood up to go, Ash grabbed her arm and tugged her back down beside him.

"Don't waste your time on that snail," he urged, sliding one hand up around her ribs, close to the lower curve of her breast. Diana glanced over at Earnestina in alarm but her friend was lying back on the chase, her eyes closed. Colonel Tiptain, however, watched with lazy interest and an amused smile.

"Don't mind me," the colonel drawled. "I love a good show."

I just bet you do, she thought in irritation. Then Ash's hand closed over her breast, and despite herself for a moment she enjoyed the warm weight of his large hand through the layers of cloth.

"I'll do whatever I wish to do, my friend." She brushed his hand away, standing up quickly, before he could pull her back down.

Chapter Nineteen

Jason saw her the next day in the Steine, sitting at a shaded table on the edge of the large park with her friends taking lemonade. She attracted him like a magnet, as if he was the lodestone and she the north. Whichever way he turned, his gaze came back to her. Then when she finally saw him, met his eyes with her own, there was no escaping the pull. Not that he wished for anything as mundane as escape.

Even from twenty paces away, it was obvious that everything had changed. There would be no more fighting, no more scathing comments. Instead an odd sort of comfort existed, a knowledgeable intimacy.

Diana waved to him, so he brought Daniel and Lizzie over and introductions were made.

He recognized Lord and Lady Ashburton from Vauxhall, but there was also a Colonel Tiptain and Lord Bourke. Lord Bourke eyed them lazily through a quizzing glass while Lady Ashburton offered a wan smile. After a few moments of insipid pleasantries, Daniel pulled him aside.

"Lizzie and I are going to take a stroll along the beach."

There was something in Daniel's expression that let Jason know that his friends had grown bored of the company or at the very least uncomfortable.

Not surprising really. None of them had ever spent much time associating with the nobility. And Diana's coterie was not the most friendly bunch.

"It seems your friends have abandoned you," Diana remarked, her voice carrying to him. He turned around to face her, to take in the flirtatious tilt of her head. "But have no fear, I shall make certain you are properly entertained."

He smiled at that. He had no doubt she would. "I was planning to call on you this afternoon," he said, taking the empty seat beside her.

"I fully expect that you still will. In fact, I will be heartbroken if you don't."

"Will you?"

"Of course she won't be," Lord Ashburton interrupted loudly. "Diana, dear, you shouldn't be so cruel to your cousin, you know we won't even be at home this afternoon."

"That's right," Colonel Tiptain agreed. "We're going boating."

"What a delightful idea!" Lady Ashburton agreed.

"It is a lovely idea," Diana agreed, although she didn't look entirely pleased. "I do hope you'll join us."

Jason felt Lord Ashburton's glare boring into him even as he nodded in agreement. If he wasn't mistaken, the man had concocted the whole event in order to get rid of Jason. *Of course he would go.*

That afternoon, sitting with Diana in the little dinghy, he was very glad he was there.

Maybe a dozen yards away, Ashburton and his lady kept apace of them. He could hear the faint sound of their conversation and so he pitched his own voice low.

"Lady Ashburton was my first real friend in London," Diana was saying. "We were of an age and both married. Well, she was newly married and I . . . She's always been fun and light and my husband was willing to let me cultivate the acquaintance."

"Your husband," Jason repeated. "I never did meet him but my cousin sounds like an ass."

She sighed, the amused, flirtatious expression slipping for just a moment and he wished he had said nothing. It really wasn't his business what her married life had been like. In fact he didn't want to think about her past. Far more delightful to think about the very near future, when he would have a chance to do everything he had said he would do. If he only could get her alone.

"He was," Diana said abruptly, interrupting his thoughts. "At times, but he also gave me a life I could never have imagined." She slanted him a pointed glance. "I do like being wealthy."

What about love? He almost asked the question before he remembered that they'd been here before, had this same conversation before. That time, she'd pointed out, very correctly, that he had not married for love either.

So why was he obsessed with the idea?

"Your honesty is admirable," he said instead.

"It's much easier, isn't it?" Diana moved her leg so that the outside of her foot pressed against the inside of his. "I've never seen the point in lying, my one great secret aside." Then, she winked.

Jason laughed despite himself, despite knowing that she referred to Harridan House, to that part of her life that she refused to give up.

"But as one who loves honesty as you do, wouldn't it be easier to forgo a double life?"

For a moment she looked irritated, as she had every right to be. He really shouldn't be inserting serious discussion in the middle of flirtation. They did have a truce after all.

"Yes," she said finally. Then she pinned him with her gaze. "And what about you, Jason? Are you honest?"

He wasn't. He knew it instantly. Oh, he tried to be now. But for so long he'd always done what came easiest, a white lie, a small excuse, to smooth the way to pleasure.

"Touché," he said simply. And because it seemed like the right thing to say, because somewhere inside, he knew it was true, he added, "but I promise you, Diana, I will always be honest with you."

She arched one of those beautifully formed eyebrows, an auburn wing over her creamy skin. "I think we shall get along rather well."

Chapter Twenty

Over the next week, there was not another moment that they were alone together, out of sight of any of their friends. But she was happy to spend time with Jason's friends rather than her own. There were more evenings than not that Earnestina and Ashburton retired to the house with friends to partake of the colonel's pipe.

Diana found that not only was anticipation delicious, but there was so much more to Jason than her visceral attraction to him. He was not nearly as prudish as she had thought before.

But it was the morning he joined her for an early walk on the Steine that she realized that he was a man who knew what love was. At least, one sort of love.

He stopped, not far from the gaggle of nannies and their charges enjoying their morning perambulation.

"See there?" He pointed toward a small child in a white smock and straw bonnet, her fine silky curls falling to her back. "That is my daughter." There was a distinct note of pride in his voice. Pride and tenderness, and it made her think of her own father, of her childhood—of carefree, innocent days.

"A very fine-looking girl," she offered.

"She takes after her mother, of course."

For a moment Diana thought they wouldn't approach, that Jason would strive to keep her away from his daughter. But just then the girl turned and spotted them. She stared, one hand up as if she meant to wave but wasn't quite certain it was her father in the distance. Then Jason bent down and waved, the nanny prodded her, and the girl came running across the paved walk.

"Papa, I touched the doggie!"

He gathered her up in his arms.

"Yes? What kind of doggie is that?"

"White."

Jason turned his daughter to face Diana. She had a rounded little face, with cheeks as rosy as apples. She might look like her late mother, but she stared at Diana with big eyes that looked very much like Jason's.

"So this is the lovely Miss Cassandra," Diana said, reaching out to offer her hand. The little girl placed her own tiny hand in Diana's solemnly, all traces of her early giggling gone.

"Say hello, sweetheart," Jason prodded. "Tell Lady Blount how pleased you are to meet her."

"Please to meet," Cassandra squeaked before she hid her face against her father's chest, wrinkling his cravat with the tight grip of her fists. Then she peeked back at Diana.

"She just started this shyness, and only with ladies, it appears," Jason said, apologetically.

"And with men?" Diana raised a curious eyebrow. She hadn't spent much time around children, certainly not since her days assisting her father with his patients.

"She's taken a liking to Throckmorton."

He put his daughter down, and the nanny grabbed the girl's leading strings.

"Who wouldn't?" Diana laughed. "He's a sardonic fellow. Amusing."

"But Lizzie, she still hasn't quite warmed to yet."

"Well, you know what to expect, then, when she's old enough for a season," Diana quipped.

"I can only expect that by then I will have remarried and her stepmother will guide her."

The cream she had had in her morning coffee must have turned, Diana thought, to explain away the sudden nausea. Only that little brutal voice in her head would not let her pretend she was not disturbed by the thought of Jason married again, to another woman, off-limits to Diana. Not that she was entirely against sleeping with a married man, but she knew clearly, in the way that sometimes certain things were just known, that she would not wish to share Jason. Not now, and certainly not when they became lovers in truth.

As if to underscore her thoughts, the young and fashionably handsome Mr. Travistock greeted them. After he'd passed, Diana smiled ruefully at herself. Only a few scant months ago, she'd been considering taking the man as her lover. Now the entirety of her attention was focused on Jason.

A shout of childish laughter brought her attention back to Cassandra, who ran toward a flock of pigeons even as her nanny tried to pull her back.

Stepmother. It wouldn't be her, of course, but for the briefest, almost infinitesimally small moment, so insignificant as to be negligible, Diana imagined what it would like to fill that role.

After all, whoever Cassie's new stepmama was, she would spend each night in Jason's bed.

Chapter Twenty-One

The following day, they made a party of it to the estate of one of Daniel's old school friends, a Mr. Douglas Randall. Jason invited Diana along. He was happy to have her to himself.

Randall had the largest, flat portion of his lawn set up for a game of cricket, which normally Jason would have been eager to play. He was not the best bowler, but he was a particularly good batsman and runner and had been ever since his school days. Today, however, he wanted only to lounge in the shade at Diana's side and study the hollows of her wrist and the way her nose turned ever so slightly down.

"You don't mind slumming it, do you? Rand being so low in the instep . . ." he asked, once she'd settled herself in one of the wide, cushioned lawn chairs.

She laughed. "Is he? Then what is a baronet doing lowering himself so?"

"I do not keep such august company as earls and viscounts," he returned.

"Don't mind Ash. He thinks very highly of himself but he's a good man."

Jason didn't respond to that. Ashburton did obviously think highly of himself and had, in many small ways, let Jason know his inferiority.

"You won't find a quarrel with me," Diana whispered.

"Is that what I was doing?"

"Yes."

"It's not what I wish to do."

"I know." She met his hot look with one of her own. "I think a stroll around the pond sounds lovely."

"No you don't!" Lizzie cried, who stood looking down at them and blocking their way. "You will not go off on your own to tryst among the trees when there is a cricket match to win!"

"Love, let them be," Danny chided her, as usual a step behind, not really intending to stop his wife from doing whatever she wanted.

"I wish to win, *love*, and therefore Jason must be on our team. Are you any good at cricket, Lady Blount?"

"I don't know," Diana answered. "I've never tried. Do women play?"

"I play!" Lizzie returned with a huff.

Of course, that was that. Jason saw the lazy afternoon alone with Diana disappear. Instead he saw a side of her he never imagined he would see. A side that joined in the fun, swung the wooden bat, and breathlessly ran toward the wicket.

That was after he'd taught her how to swing. A most pleasurable instruction. He'd taken his time, his arms around hers, his body just centimeters away from hers so that he could feel her heat and breathe in the scent of roses as he positioned her hands.

When the bat made contact, and the ball moved several feet away, she looked back at him smiling.

"We make a good team."

"Yes, but now you'd better run, or it will all have been for nothing."

She ran. She looked like the healthy, young country miss she must have been when old Roger Blount found her and plucked her up. Very unlike the polished, sophisticated town flirt that she had become.

"A rather unusual game of cricket," Daniel commented when Jason joined him on the sidelines. "I believe more women would play and more men would be happy to let them play if they witnessed that little display."

"Always happy to forward the game," Jason returned with a satisfied smirk.

"Of flirtation, perhaps, but certainly not cricket."

Chapter Twenty-Two

I t was dark—midnight dark—and he hadn't stripped down to his naked skin and jumped into the sea in God knew how many years. Yet here he was, taking off his clothes, ready to jump in.

As long as the Charlies, holding their lanterns and calling out the hour, didn't come and find him.

Drunk as he'd ever been.

Not because of the amount of cognac he'd downed that evening. Because of her. She made him drunk.

Daniel whooped and then shushed himself, bending down in the water as if he had to hide. Jason could still hear his friend's repressed giggles even though, in the moonless night, he couldn't see the man.

"Keep it down, Danny," he whispered, wincing as even his voiceless breath carried on the wind.

"Hah, that's what *she* said!" Danny cried instead, doubling over with more laughter. Perhaps Danny was here because of the cognac. His company was certainly not because a lack of female companionship at home. In fact, Lizzie would have their heads when they came back, clothes clinging to their damp bodies, clearly engaging in amusements without her.

Jason took a step into the water, grateful that it was cold, grateful that the shivers pushed thoughts of Diana from his mind.

But then the water lapped at his thigh, sweetly, gently, and he remembered her mouth.

His feet went out from under him and it took only a moment to realize what Daniel had done, kicking him at the knees to buckle his legs and dunk him wholly in the water. It was the sort of sport his friend had done when they were schoolboys.

Jason went under, his arms flailing, and for a brief poetic moment he thought, *How apt, this is exactly how she makes me feel.*

Chapter Twenty-Three

Swimming naked?" Diana laughed. Jason was willing to tell her every story of his youthful indiscretions if it would keep her making that rippling sound that sent such sensations over his skin. It was almost as if she had caressed him.

They were taking tea in one of the parlors of the Air Street house. It was not a large room, but Jason thought it well furnished, especially since the sofa he sat on was only just wide enough to accommodate two people. From such a near distance he could catch the faint scent of the rose fragrance Diana favored.

"Daniel didn't want to admit it," Lizzie continued, "but really, when one's husband comes back in the middle of the night, his hair plastered to his skull and stinking of cognac, a wife wonders where he's been."

"I swear, my love," Daniel said, "we'll take you next time. It was impromptu, and of course, my dear, you'd never want to see Blount's scrawny self in his altogether. You'd finally have to admit that I am the finest specimen of manhood to walk this earth."

"That would suggest before now I thought he was. No offense, Jas."

"Am I not?" Jason directed his question to Diana. She laughed. That delightful, throaty sound that sent pleasurable shivers through his body.

"And how would I judge such a thing?" Her head was tilted down and forward and she looked at him sideways. "Perhaps you could take me swimming tonight?"

He heard his friends laughing even as he spoke. "I would but

I've assured Mrs. Throckmorton that if I ever do anything remotely scandalous, she won't hear of it."

"I've a wager on it actually," Lizzie agreed, "so please, make sure it is a full moon when you go."

A while later, Jason saw Diana to her carriage, and after he'd assisted her up, she leaned out and took his hand, stroking his bare palm with her gloved fingers. Ridiculous that such a small touch could make him harden instantly.

"Jason," she said, softly, "I don't need a swimming assignation to know I very much look forward to seeing you . . . altogether."

Then she released his hand and the footman closed the carriage door.

Jason stepped back, clenching his hand into fist. As he watched the carriage roll forward slowly, he wanted to fling open the door and join her inside. Privacy—an hour, an afternoon—alone with her was what he wanted. Not these teasing moments that left him aching and dreaming of her.

But he'd see Diana tonight at the assembly. They would think of something.

When he returned to the sitting room, Lizzie and Daniel were still where he had left them, lounging. Only, they'd broken out a bottle of brandy. Jason accepted a glass readily.

"You know, Jas," Lizzie said, thoughtfully. "I rather like Lady Blount."

"Do you?" He wondered what Lizzie would think if she knew everything about Diana. *She'd probably be amused*, he realized.

"Yes, I do," Lizzie reaffirmed. "She has a bit of a reputation, for lovers and all, and it does seem as though she's now chosen you." Here she stared at Jason expectantly, as if he'd confirm or deny that, or reveal details of his sexual activities. He managed to keep his expression impassive. "Well, in any event, I think she's exactly what you need. And for the record, I don't think she's nearly as fast as her reputation suggests."

Jason almost choked on his wine. *Really, if Lizzie only knew.*

"She's exceedingly polite, and kind. Doesn't put on any airs . . ."

"She's a veritable paragon," Daniel broke in with a teasing

grin. "Come now, love, and leave the poor man alone. He'll think you're trying to sell him a wife."

"I'm not doing *that*," Lizzie protested. "Anyway, you know what they say about love, Jas. In order to be right, it must be wrong."

"Is that what they say, love?" Daniel teased, but Jason was still thinking about the last thing his friend had said.

A paragon? No. Yet as Lizzie had pointed out, despite Diana's *fast reputation*, there was nothing exceptional about her at all. Nothing but all the delightful qualities that made her *her*.

Chapter Twenty-Four

Nothing was negligible, Diana decided later that evening as she entered the Castle Tavern's assembly rooms for the evening's dressed ball. She knew she looked as elegant as she ever did, her brown Italian crepe dress trimmed with gold thread and the circlet of gold and yellow topaz in her artfully arranged hair designed to catch the candlelight. The majority of male eyes were trained on her, observing her progress down into the ballroom with that very delicious sort of masculine approval. But for all those eyes, her own gaze swept the room for one pair of blue. *Nothing was negligible*—for the past two days, try as she might to snuff it, the insidious idea of marriage stuck.

She had hated being married. She had despised having to answer to any man, to do what he wished and please him. Or to please the men Roger had chosen for her, as it had turned out to be.

Of course a marriage to someone like Jason would not be that way. There was something between them, in their relationship, that she valued very much: respect. And that was the truly insidious idea.

Jason was there already, catching her searching gaze immediately from his position near the wall not ten feet from the entrance. He looked splendid, from the top of his golden hair to his impeccable white waistcoat, the gold buttons on his neat dark blue coat to his nankin breeches and blue dancing slippers.

Diana didn't bother to dissemble, to make any sort of circuit of the room before seeking him out. Clearly, he had the same idea, because he met her halfway, or what should have been halfway, as his long strides ate up far more of the ten feet than her own.

"You like to arrive late," he murmured, tucking her arm into his.

"I'm not even fashionably late," Diana countered. "I was far too eager for this night to come." She shot him a sidelong glance. And was met with his own, with the wintry gray-blue of his eyes. Her breath hitched and she wet her lips quickly. She found it difficult to remember there was an orchestra playing and a ballroom full of people around them.

"I confess to the same," Jason admitted. "Lizzie and Throckmorton refused to come as early as I wished."

Diana laughed. It wasn't her usual throaty sound, it was far more giddy. *How embarrassing*, she thought, just before she caught his expression, staring at her as if he liked the novelty.

"You're blushing," he observed, as if it were some sort of wondrous, rare thing. Perhaps it was.

They danced together, and when they didn't dance, they strolled about the room, or lingered by a window. When Earnestina came by to say that she, Ash and Tiptain were leaving, Jason offered to take Diana home in his carriage.

"Now, I'll finally have you to myself," Jason whispered, leaning close to her when Earnestina had departed.

"What, are you planning to kidnap me?" she returned, half hoping he'd give her some enticing reason why she shouldn't simply return to the Ashburtons' house.

But when they finally climbed into his carriage, a two-seat

open phaeton, there was no privacy and Diana shot Jason a mocking look.

"So much for alone."

"Poor planning, I admit," he said with chagrin. "But tomorrow, tomorrow you're mine, all day. I'll show you just how well I can plan."

"I think I can arrange that," she agreed.

They weren't going very far; if they had walked they could have traversed the distance in far less time, but the east sea frontage road didn't connect to the west and they had to take a longer, more circuitous route.

"Do you know," Jason said abruptly, "I never would have imagined, two years ago, standing in the solicitor's office, that we would be here together like this. I may have wished it, but I never would have imagined."

Diana laughed at that, because she knew exactly what he meant. Only, it was his disapproval that had kept them apart so long after his wife's death. She sighed then, remembering: *his disapproval stemmed from her own stupid pride.*

"Do you know, Jason," Diana said, wanting him to know everything, to absolve her of anything ugly, to help her start anew, "that I kept Harridan House because of you?"

"You're blaming me for that?" he stared at her disbelieving.

"Jason, please, I'm not trying to blame you, I'm trying to confide, to explain . . . Not because of you, that isn't really fair, but because of my own stupid pride. Finally, I was independent, able to make my own choices, and then you and Mr. Jarvis were there, trying to make them for me."

"You would have sold the place?" Jason stared at her.

"Yes, I believe I would have, but we'll never really know."

"And now?"

"I'm, I'm rather tired of the life, Jas. I'm still young, I could still have a family, be a mother . . . Maybe there is something more to all of this than just sex?"

"Why are you telling me this?"

She looked away, uncertain, embarrassed, she had made an

assumption. Oh, not that they would marry, hardly that, but that . . . but that this affair might be a longer one, might eventually hold some more emotion than simply the scalding brand of desire.

He kissed her, softly, tenderly, sweetly, ignoring that they were exposed to the view of anyone they might pass by. It was completely unlike the hard passion they'd shared in the past. *As if he cherished her.*

Which was a laughable thought, so she thrust it away to concentrate on the taste of him, on the light touch of his lips on hers.

Then it deepened. The fire came coursing through her veins and blanketing her skin, everything in her rising to meet him.

The kiss was everything all at once, the desperate and the tender, the sweet and the relentless. Every experience in her life up until that moment bound itself into that kiss until she felt that he knew her, he knew her from every little corner of her being.

When he finally pulled away, he looked as unsteady as she felt.

"Perhaps," he began, "perhaps we both misjudged each other. Perhaps, we've been given another chance here, for a different life, for new choices."

"That's what I want," Diana said, intently. "I'm ready for a new beginning."

Diana allowed Jason to assist her down from the carriage. The feel of his hands on her body was the slightest pressure and then it was gone and the earth stood solid beneath her feet. In silence he escorted her the few short steps to the already open door where the butler stood, illuminated by candlelight. Her pulse still ran like a thoroughbred making for the finish line; her mouth still tingled from the pressure of his lips. And then he lifted her gloved hand and brushed it with the barest kiss. Then, that too was over. She took a step toward the house, then paused on the threshold. She couldn't stop herself from looking back, from wanting one more glimpse of him.

From the darkness of the night she could make out the white

of his eyes, meeting hers. There was a promise there, a promise for tomorrow. Feeling like the young girl she hadn't been for years, she yearned for what tomorrow would bring.

She entered the house when the stamping of the impatient horses and the cough of the impatient butler were too insistent.

Inside, the sickly sweet smell assaulted her almost immediately, wafting down the staircase. So they were smoking opium again.

When she reached the first floor, she paused at the open doorway of the sitting room. Inside, as usual, her friends lounged, with hardly a care for elegant positioning of limbs, the proper way to sit in a chair, or that the floor was not a fashionable place to lie down. She wondered briefly what the staff thought of their little group, of the dissipated evenings.

Tiptain spied her and lifted a hand in greeting. "Finally the lady has returned. Let the festivities begin."

"You must be in great pain, Colonel," Diana murmured ironically.

"I may have started it for the pain, Lady Blount, but I continue for the visions. Such a lovely life it is." Tiptain's glazed eyes didn't focus on her, but he leaned heavily toward Earnestina, passing her the pipe. Tina took it, sucking deeply.

"Join us, Di," Ash pleaded, half rising from the sofa to reach for her.

"Another time," she murmured, backing up into the cold marble hall.

Chapter Twenty-Five

Despite the long day, despite the hours of dancing, sleep eluded Diana. She lay in bed, her eyes open, studying the furniture that loomed in the dark as large shapes, just barely differentiated from the other shadows.

She was too wound up with thoughts of Jason. Maybe, maybe if she just spent some of this excess energy . . .

Diana pulled off her nightgown and tossed it away. She lay back on the bed, closed her eyes and ran her hands down over her body. What had Jason said? He'd place his hand over her breast, enjoy the weight of it? Diana cupped herself in her hands, kneading the flesh, imagining it was him.

She circled her nipples with her index finger slowly, letting the sensations awaken and then she tugged on the hard peaks till she could feel the touch in the growing heat of her pussy.

She ran her right hand down to her hip, the palm firm on her flesh, grasping at the curves of her body.

How would he feel inside her? She'd know soon. Perhaps tomorrow or the day after; when the time was right, she would know.

She moved her hand between her thighs, skimming over the tight curls, holding herself, enjoying the pressure of her hand. Then she slipped her third finger between the plump lips, into the slick moisture within.

She gasped at the feel of it, at the sharp sympathetic pang in her nipples. She wanted to be filled, but this wasn't Harridan House, she didn't have any of her usual toys, she couldn't simulate the feeling of a man.

So she settled for a release of the tight knot of tension. She caught her clit between her fingers, massaging the little muscular nub, imagining it was Jason licking her, Jason's hand still kneading her breast.

She played, keeping herself from orgasm, the speed of her fingers slowing every time she neared the peak.

What was he doing in the bathing machine when this one was just for women? What was he doing naked and his cock jutting out so hard, so appealing she just wanted to take it in her mouth? Diana could hear the gasp of all the other women as she fell to her knees and hungrily sucked on him.

He was so delicious, so firm in her mouth, she couldn't get enough. But he pushed her away, down to her back, lifting up her skirts. Yes, she wanted this too. She wanted him to fuck her, finally. Finally.

His cock slid into her and she pushed back against him, wanting him to come in deep, but she couldn't get what she wanted, she could hardly feel his body in her hands. It kept moving, almost as if he were just his cock, pumping into her.

But then he sucked on her ear and it brought her so close that she moaned and wrapped her legs around his hips.

It was so good. Too good. Finally.

She'd known it would be this way with Jason. She'd known from the first moment she'd seen him.

He kissed her, his mouth over hers, and there was a faint scent in the air that she couldn't identify as they lay outside in the field, the red flowers everywhere pulling at her memory, tugging at her.

She clawed her way awake.

It wasn't a dream. There was a man, here, laboring above her, his breath hot against her ear, his cock thrusting hard and rhythmically between her legs, into her. God it felt good to have a man again.

But this wasn't Jason. It was Ash.

She moved to push him away but her body was too far gone, she was reaching the crest, the sensations peaking, and she cried out with the pleasure of it.

"I knew it would be this way with you, Di," he moaned against her, pushing, thrusting until he stiffened and she felt the flood of his seed within her, the softening of his cock, the easing of his breath.

"Ash?" she whispered, disgust and fear growing in her belly, rising up toward her throat.

He kissed her neck, moving his hips against her.

"Ash," she said again. "Please get off of me."

But he was hard inside her again, grunting, and as his lips moved to her chin she could smell the opium on his breath.

She might have expected this sort of thing in her life at Harridan House, but not as Lady Blount. Not under the man's own roof.

She pushed harder.

"That's it, Di," he said, thickly, "move with me."

"Stop it, Ash!" When pushing at his shoulders and kicking the heels of her feet against his shin achieved nothing, she raked her nails across his skin.

"My tigress," he murmured.

It was useless. In this position, sprawled beneath him, he was immovable.

And why should she bother? It wasn't as if she had never had sex, was some sort of missish girl. He'd be over soon enough.

Soon enough wasn't good enough, not with him pushing into her again and again as if she were just her cunt, just there for his cock, taking away any control she had ever had over her body, over her life.

This was her friend. Her friend's husband.

Ash stilled over her, his body pressing heavily down on her, deep into the bed, making breath difficult.

It took Diana a moment to realize that he hadn't climaxed—he'd fallen asleep. Right there, on top of her, still hard inside her.

Asleep, he was heavier but unresistant. It was difficult at first, with his cock still keeping them joined together, but she managed finally to push him aside and wriggle out from under him.

She slid off the bed, sweaty, sticky, shuddering at the feel of his juices sliding down her thighs. So often in the aftermath of sex she had enjoyed the messiness, the feel of a man all over her body. Now she wanted it gone. She reached for her nightgown where it lay crumpled on the floor and wiped the wetness away as best she could.

She glanced back at the bed where Ash slept.

Just a few hours earlier she had been looking forward with anticipation to the next day, to a new life, to Jason . . .

The thought of him made her body clench with pain and she doubled over, gasping, trying not to cry aloud, trying not to wake Ash.

Ruined. Everything ruined.

The one thing she did know, she couldn't stay there anymore, not under the same roof, not in the same company.

From all Earnestina had said, her friend would likely have cheered him on.

As quietly as she could, Diana dressed herself. Out of necessity, she chose the simplest morning dress, the one she could fasten herself, and then packed her valise with the few things she wanted to take with her immediately. Everything else, she would have her maid bring later.

Her primary, urgent need was to be as far from this house and Brighton as possible when morning came.

She made her way out of the room and down the stairs, thinking to disturb only the footman who would need to get her carriage and driver.

But the door to the parlor on the first floor, where Earnestina, Ash, Tiptain and the others had all lounged, was open, light pouring out.

Diana drew closer and peered into the quiet room.

And found that Ash had spoken the truth. Her dress bunched around her waist, Earnestina lay sprawled across the insensate Tiptain, whose breeches were in an equal state of disarray.

It was as if Diana had woken up back at Harridan House rather than Brighton, and the strange confluence of her two lives overwhelmed and dizzied her.

She stumbled from the door and continued down till she reached the entry hall and pulled the rope for the footman.

"Di, is that you?"

She looked to the landing, one floor up, where Earnestina, her dress messily reassembled, peered down at her.

"Yes, darling," Diana managed to drawl, calling on her years of playacting, of wearing the most elegant facade, to face her friend.

"Whatever are you doing?" Earnestina started down the stairs, making her way slowly, carefully, leaning heavily on the banister. She was clearly still under the effects of the drug.

"I'm going back to London. Do send Julia after me with my luggage in the morning."

"But at this hour, Di?" Earnestina stared at her. "Whatever for?"

"I'm sorry, Tina," Diana said. "But I really must go."

"Did Ash embarrass you too much?" Earnestina sighed. "I told him you weren't interested."

Embarrass her? There were hardly words for what Ash had done. The worst of it being that Diana had enjoyed it all, had physically enjoyed it. But she wouldn't say any of that to her friend.

"Yes, that's it," Di agreed, as the footman entered the room. He, too, had obviously just woken up.

"Fetch my carriage, will you? I'm returning to London immediately."

The sleepy young man barely blinked as he turned around and headed to do her bidding.

"But we're having so much fun." Tina came close, tugging on her sleeve. "And really, why shouldn't you sleep with Ash, I promise I won't be jealous if you do."

"You're too kind," Diana bit out. She hoped the footman would hurry. She wasn't certain how much longer she could stand there, knowing that Earnestina didn't care, had fallen into her own delirious sexual journey.

Chapter Twenty-Six

Jason could not forget the image of Diana standing on the stone steps, her artful curls blown by the ever-present Brighton breeze, her skin glowing in the moonlight, her expression so sweet and innocent, as if she were not the same woman who had tortured his dreams for years with her sensuality, who had offered him the chance to fuck her just to get it out of his system and leave her alone.

He didn't want to get this Diana out of his mind. It was an intriguing new side of her. He'd seen her powerful and taunting, vulnerable, flirtatious, serious, amusing, worldly and coy. But he had never before seen that anticipatory look, that hopeful innocence.

As if he were everything in her eyes. As if he were her suitor.

And what was he? He supposed he was a suitor of sorts. There was no doubt where this "friendship" was going, not after that kiss this evening, that embrace. And there was no reason they shouldn't have an affair. It was why he had followed her to Brighton after all.

He'd just never thought he'd come to admire her as much as he lusted after her.

He arrived at the Ashburtons' house at nine in the morning. The stoic butler allowed him into the hallway, took his card and then stood there, staring at Jason as if he had spoken in Greek rather than English.

"I said, I am here to see Lady Blount."

"Lady Blount is not at home, sir."

Ashburton, still in his robe, appeared at the stairs.

"What's this, Travis? Morning, Blount."

"I was explaining to Sir Jason that Lady Blount is not at home."

"This early?" Jason said doubtfully. "But she was expecting me. Perhaps she is still abed?"

"I know she's not in her bed, man, I was just there." Jason's attention swiveled back to Ashburton as he tried to imagine how he had misheard the man's words.

"Her bed?"

"Never mind." Ashburton ran a hand over his face. "I suppose you'll have to wait for your ride, Blount, as we've obviously misplaced Diana."

Just then Lady Ashburton, looking very dour, joined her husband at the rail.

"She left this morning, Ash," she said soberly, "but she didn't say . . . My apologies, Sir Jason, to find our household in such disarray. Diana returned to London. An emergency, she said."

Jason could not remember the last time he had felt this way, if ever. A cold panic settled in his bones, in his head. And beneath that, an anger he tamped down, because he didn't know, he didn't know yet what had happened.

But if it was true . . .

"If I had known, Ash—" He only dimly heard Lady Ashburton berate her husband, her ire giving weight to the nagging image that filled Jason's mind. Dear Lord, if Ashburton had shared her bed last night! How could he have thought her changed? How could he have thought her willing to be constant to just one man? To be his?

"Tina, dearest, you know I left you in good hands."

His? Who was he fooling? Clearly, Diana would never belong to any man, could not be faithful even to a lover.

Perhaps it was a mistake, a misunderstanding? Why would Diana leave so furtively, in the middle of the night, without even a word to him?

"To London, you said?" Jason repeated. Two pair of startled eyes refocused on him. Good God, they'd even forgotten he was there, so focused were they on their argument. And what would they have to argue about if it were not that Ashburton had shared Diana's bed?

Whatever he had thought of Diana, he had not thought she would betray her friend in such a way.

"I'll leave you then," he murmured and stumbled his way out of the house, aware that the servants were watching the drama play out.

He walked back to the house on Air Street. Slowly, circuitously, by way of the beaches where he and Daniel had swum just a few nights earlier. By way of the Steine, where nannies were playing with their charges before the green was taken over by the afternoon promenades of society. He spied Cassandra there, toddling after Mrs. Landis, but he didn't try to catch their attention.

Just then, he didn't want to have to be a father; he didn't want to have to be responsible for anyone other than himself, for anything other than the disappointment sloshing around inside him.

He took a last look at his daughter, just shy of three, her fine hair ending in blond ringlets down her back, and continued on.

Perhaps Diana would return and the mystery would clear itself. But from the scene he had left at the Ashburtons', Jason suspected that would not be the case.

There were Daniel and Lizzie, just sitting down to breakfast, very casually wearing their nightclothes and wrappers as if it were a family home, as if he were one of the family.

He sat across from them, folded his arms on the table, and lay his head down upon them.

He was asking for help, because dear God, he didn't know what to do. Did he go after her? And be proven the biggest fool?

His friends said nothing. He could hear the slide of their utensils across the plates as they continued to eat.

Finally, he looked up and found them watching him, waiting.

"I need to go to London briefly. But I intend to return. I'd hate to move Cassie for such a short jaunt," Jason said. "Do you mind if she stays in my absence?"

"Of course not," Daniel said quickly, though he was usually the sarcastic one.

Lizzie's mouth opened and closed but she said nothing. He'd never seen the woman display such forbearance. Clearly, he looked how he felt.

Chapter Twenty-Seven

When the maid brought her the card bearing his name, the fine print wavered before Diana's eyes. So he'd come after her, to find out why she'd fled, to call her coward. And she was a coward, but not for any of the reasons he could imagine. She hadn't simply changed her mind about their affair, she'd realized it was no longer possible.

How cruel could life be?

What would she tell him? What could she possibly say?

"I'm not at home," she said finally, unable to stop the nervous shudder that racked her body.

She couldn't stop herself from running to the window that overlooked the street. From three stories up she watched as he stepped out onto the stairs, his hat still in his hand. He turned then, as if he knew she was watching, his eyes looking up.

She didn't step back, even when she knew he'd probably seen her, even though clearly she was at home. She stayed exactly where she was, arrested by his expression.

He looked . . . hurt. No, now he looked angry. So, which was he, hurt or angry? Or both?

Her head hurt. She felt hot, feverish.

He pivoted again, slapping on his hat as he descended the stairs.

Finally, Diana stepped away from the window. So that was over. He knew clearly now that she did not want to see him. *And though she hadn't prayed in years, she prayed to God that he would never know why.*

Chapter Twenty-Eight

L ater that evening, hours later, when the house felt stifling and small, when she'd looked into each and every room and found it as empty and unsatisfying as her thoughts were full and unsatisfying, she decided to go out. To Harridan House.

After all, it was where she belonged. It was the life given to her, and that she had accepted, and she might as well embrace it fully for the few pleasures it could offer.

How melodramatic, she chided herself as she dressed. It was more difficult to tie all the fastenings with her lady's maid still in Brighton, but she managed. Really, it wasn't as if anything had changed. It was simply an aborted affair. Her next lover would easily make her forget.

Forget what? That for the briefest moment she had been able to taste possibilities she had never before considered?

It was the cruelest interruption to her thoughts that when she stepped out the front door to enter her coach, there was Jason, leaning against the wall.

He was at her side in a moment, his mouth open to speak. Quickly, she struck, to forestall whatever he wanted to say.

"What, have you been waiting here for me? Like some sort of perverted fiend?" Diana accused. She flinched inwardly at her rising tone. She sounded like a veritable harpy.

"What emergency brought you back to London?"

"No greeting for me?" Diana forced a laugh. "You're very cold, Jason."

"My apologies," he agreed. "I'm not myself. I'm confused, frustrated. You see, I thought, I thought we had reached an understanding—"

She cut him off. "An understanding? All I understood, Jason, was that we were close to bedding, finally, after all these years."

His jaw clenched, she could see it in the movement of his skin, the thin line of his lips.

She stepped up into the carriage, only slightly taken aback when he slipped in after her, shutting the door behind him.

"Ah, well. How fortuitous though, that you should insist on joining me," she said, forcing her voice to be light despite its steely edge. The carriage seemed far smaller than it was. Could he not keep his knees to his side of the vehicle? "I am on my way to Harridan House. Perhaps I may give you your tour."

"Why do you do this?" Jason demanded. He sounded like he was pleading and it caught her attention. It nearly made her close her eyes, lean back against the seat and give in to her sadness. But she couldn't do that. This was a farce she now needed to play out. Until he finally left. Until she was alone again, left to her old life—the life she could never escape. "Diana, if I didn't know about your actions in Brighton, with Ashburton of all people, the husband of your friend . . ." he trailed off, shaking his head, but he'd lost her moments ago.

He knew. She could actually feel the blood leaching away from her face. What a creeping sensation, and yet she could do absolutely nothing about it. Here it was, her pride at her feet. No, beneath his, beneath Ash's, beneath all men's. Her prayers weren't answered, had never been answered in the last seven years of her life. Unless one counted her husband's death. She had wished for that many times.

Now, she wished for hers. And then that brief, dark, suicidal moment was past.

So she could no longer pretend that she had merely jilted him.

He knew why, thought that she was no better than she should be, no better than he had thought her for two long years.

The carriage came to a slow stop, the wheels rocking back and forth before finally settling. *Harridan House.*

Diana laughed and pulled her red mask out of her reticule.

"So you know." She shrugged, tying the silk around her head, obscuring the upper half of her face.

"Diana," he pressed on, his voice low, painfully urgent.

"No, Jason, here I am merely Rouge. Remember, I have a reputation to uphold." She punctuated that statement with another throaty derisive laugh, the effect only somewhat lessened by the need to maneuver around his long legs as she flung open the door of the coach.

She let the footman help her down, into the unbelievably sultry August night. Unreal. This could not be her, stepping onto the stone-paved ground, pretending that nothing had meant anything to her, that she hadn't wanted everything Jason represented, everything he had tantalizingly offered.

Yet he had never actually offered anything, she realized. He'd only hinted at the possibilities.

Diana fortified herself with that thought and glanced over her shoulder to look back at him, still sitting inside the coach.

"Are you coming?"

She turned back and entered the house. He was just a step behind her, then closer, his breath almost against her neck as they ascended the stairs.

He said nothing more and she wondered what he was thinking, what he was feeling. She wondered why he stayed. If he knew about Ash, what more could he possibly want from her?

The back stairs were plain, like any other well-to-do home in London, but when they entered her suite, he gasped at the sight and for the first time in the last half hour, her laugh was not faked.

The poor man's sensibilities had clearly been attacked.

Lucy met them there, in her plain gray dress, staring curiously at Jason, as curiously as Jason looked at his surroundings—the draperies, upholstery and bedding, all done in various shades of red and deep, dark purple.

"Don't gape, Luce," Diana admonished. "It isn't as if I haven't had a man in here before."

The room was ludicrous, Jason thought. Ridiculously vulgar, almost a parody of lust. If it weren't for the circumstances in which he found himself there, he would have laughed. Even more amusing was the very prim and proper maid, dressed in gray, who helped Diana off with her cloak as if they were back at the Mayfair townhouse, as if there weren't a collection of marble phalluses standing tall on the mantel.

What was he doing here?

Movement brought his attention back to Diana, whose dress had just slipped from her shoulders and was making its way down her body, toward the floor.

Of course, he thought, studying her body, encased only in her undergarments. *She* was why.

In the candlelight, her petticoats were a thin barrier to the long shadow of her limbs. Despite everything, he was captivated, wanting to see more. Fascinated, he watched the maid undo the laces of the short stays, his breath caught in his chest as more soft curves were unbound.

Then he realized she was watching him, even as he watched her. Her left cheek shimmered as if stardust had fallen on her skin. The stardust moved, crept downward, till he realized it was a tear.

He swallowed hard.

"Why did you do it, Diana?"

She stiffened, looking away, her hand coming up to wipe her face, and when she looked back, a smirk curved her lips so that he cursed himself for his weakness, for believing a trick of the light had meant she cared more than she said.

The maid stared at him sharply, but continued her work, taking off layers of petticoats till Diana stood only in her shift, the fine fabric hardly hiding anything.

She was utterly magnificent, the cloth molded to her breasts, revealing the large rosy shadows of her nipples; then it fell straight till it clung to her hips, her thighs, revealing so many curves, but hiding just enough that his fingers itched to remove the offensive fabric.

"Why do we do anything?" Diana returned, looking away, lifting her arms above her head—dear God what that did for her breasts!—to let the maid place a red silk dress over her head.

When the gown slipped into place, bereft of corset and extra petticoats, but yet revealing much of the creamy upper swell of her breasts and clinging indecently to her curves, he remembered that here she was not Diana. She was Rouge.

"Rouge," he tried out the name. Diana's gaze flew back to his immediately, her mouth parted. He thought she looked rather . . . shocked. It reminded him of that tear, of that trick of the light. He shook his head. "I don't think it fits you, Diana."

She looked away again, and sat down on a plush stool. The maid began working on Diana's hair, pinning the auburn strands up.

It was odd, watching this little ritual, clearly one that had transpired countless times in the past. The maid worked quickly, until all the hair was firmly where she wanted it. Then she took a length of gold tissue and began wrapping it around Diana's head.

A turban. A shimmering gold turban that would completely cover her hair. So that was how she kept her identity secret.

In but a moment she was completely transformed. With a silk mask in place, all that was visible were her lips and chin, the long column of her neck—and every luscious curve of her body.

How did she ever fool anyone? Jason would know her anywhere, had the lines of her face memorized, the way her jaw curved toward her ear, the shape of the hollow between her shoulder blades.

"Would you like a mask, Jason?" Her husky voice cut into his thoughts and he realized she now stood, holding out a black strip of silk toward him. "I know how you care for your name. Our name."

He stepped forward to take the cloth and in the motion, his

hand brushed hers. The sensation was too intense and too brief. Grief welled up in him for what could have been.

But only in his own mind, he reminded himself.

Diana led him into the hall, where the sounds of laughter and passion rang noisily in contrast to the quiet of her private rooms.

They entered the drawing room, or what should have been the drawing room. Instead he had entered some Grecian god's orgy atop Mount Olympus—nymphs, satyrs, grapes, ambrosia and all. There were beds where stately carpets and couches should have been. Jason had had his fair share of youthful indiscretions, but never before had he seen so many naked limbs entwined at once in one space.

She stepped back next to him, her hand coming to rest on his arm, her body pressing up next to his. He could smell her, every intoxicating scent that made up Diana. Her touch undid him, made him forget everything, everything but the feel of her body against his. Later, he thought he must have been possessed, that the devil had addled his brain, his wit, his soul, any part of him that might make sense. Then, in that moment, he grabbed her, turned her into his arms so that her body pressed up fully against him, so that her head was at just the right angle, so that he could just bend down.

Chapter Twenty-Nine

Jason was kissing her. Diana knew it intellectually, although she could hardly feel it. From the moment he had pulled her into his arms, she had begun trembling. It was too much. Too much and too soon and yet everything she had wanted only two days earlier.

Then the warmth of his body permeated her skin, eased her fear, reminded her who this was. She ran into the kiss then, holding him, begging for everything with her lips, her tongue. She could almost taste her own desperation.

Then there was nothing. He was ripped out of her arms as if he had tasted that desperation himself. She stumbled back, refocusing, searching for him.

He was staggering now, twice his size, and she realized there was another man attached to him, wrestling him to the ground.

The most unbelievable thing—Sir Robert George attacking Jason, as if he held some grudge against the man, as if he wanted to tear him limb from limb.

"Stop it!" she cried out, stepping forward uselessly. There were others watching now. One of her Grecian boys grabbed Jason by the shoulders, but that just let Sir Robert take another free swing, striking him in the jaw.

"Sir Robert!" Diana shouted. This time she grabbed the man's arm. He swiveled his head toward her. In all the times she had met Sir Robert he was lascivious, yes, but worldly, gentlemanly and polite. She had never seen him so out of control, such utter rage on his face.

But then he focused on her, his expression easing from rage to confusion. As his hands fell to his sides, the fists unclenching, that expression gave way to something else.

Diana didn't wait to understand his sudden sanity.

"Charles, Douglas," she called to the two footman who hovered nearby. "Escort Sir Robert off the premises." She focused her steely gaze on him. "You are no longer welcome at Harridan House, sir. Please remove yourself."

Sir Robert didn't speak. He merely bowed, ever so slightly, and then brushing off the footmen, pivoted on his heel and left.

She looked back at Jason. His mask was long gone, his clothes completely disordered and his jaw a purpling mess.

"Sir," she held out her hand, very aware of the large audience. "I apologize for the baronet. Come, let me tend to your wounds, and we'll call a doctor."

Chapter Thirty

The brawl had happened rather fast and now that it was over, with Diana towering over him, her hand stretched out, Jason wondered how it had even started. He knew Sir Robert by sight but he'd never so much as exchanged a greeting with the man.

With difficulty, Jason stood, clutching at his right side, where the other man had managed to land a particularly powerful punch. The room spun dizzily and while he steadied himself, dozens of faces crossed his view.

"Lucy," Diana snapped when they entered her suite, "we need ice if there is any left, and bandages perhaps."

"What happened?" the maid asked. Jason collapsed onto the chaise longue, resting his head on the rolled velvet back, hardly listening to Diana's brief explanation.

Then the door shut and the room was silent but for Diana's soft sigh and his own labored breath.

"I'm so very sorry, Jason."

"I can't imagine what you have to apologize for," Jason said, groaning as pain stabbed through his chin at the movement. George had managed to connect a right hook to his face rather successfully. Jason wondered if he'd managed to hurt the other man at all in return. Barely parting his lips, he continued. "What would make a man act that way?"

"Jealousy, I suppose," Diana mused. "I can't think of any other reason. But it's so odd. I know he's always wished to bed me but he never had any right, any hint that I would ever let him touch me."

The reminder that Diana had other men, that just two nights

ago she had slept with Ashburton, hurt worse than his wounds. What was he still doing here? He should have left already. He should have never come.

"Is it always this way for you, Diana?" he asked, ignoring the pain. "Is it always one man or another?"

Then he wished he could take the words back, because she looked so stricken, so hurt. He was as bad as George, using his words to hit instead of fists.

"In many ways it was," Diana admitted finally. "Before that night at Vauxhall. Indeed, even that night."

Damn it to hell, he was a fool! Brazenly she even admitted it, and he was worried he had hurt her feelings.

"But I thought," Diana continued, "I thought perhaps things could be different. When we were in Brighton."

"You just couldn't help yourself," Jason said, bitterly, closing his eyes.

"No! That's not it!"

Arrested, Jason lifted his head and looked at her again.

"How can I explain to you?" She started pacing, her arms wrapped around herself. "I didn't want it."

"He raped you?"

"No. Yes. I don't know," Diana said finally, resting against the edge of the bed. She seemed to have gotten smaller, curled into herself.

"Which one is it?" Jason pressed.

"I was dreaming. I was dreaming of you and us and then when I woke up he was inside me." Diana pressed the back of her hand to her mouth, looking toward the wall. "I couldn't help it, Jason, my body responded, but I had no choice. He just . . . kept going until finally he fell asleep on top of me. I think it was the opium."

Then Jason felt pinned by her gaze, by her wide green eyes, so dark yet so light, pleading with him to understand.

Finally, Jason thought he did.

"So you left Brighton," he filled in for her, "because you couldn't stay there after that."

"I knew," Diana blinked rapidly. "I knew it was over between us, between you and me. I thought you'd never know, I'd never have to admit what had happened."

"Oh, Diana."

"I was right, wasn't I?" she asked. "It's over?"

For a moment he just stared at her, wondering if it could be any other way.

"You said you'd always tell me the truth," she stated flatly, prodding him.

He nodded slowly and met her gaze. *It was over between them.*

"It's not that I think you did anything wrong." Jason struggled to find the words. "Indeed, I'm sorry. I'm very sorry for you—"

"Oh, don't be that!" she interrupted. "I don't need any pity."

"I just . . . this life," he shrugged helplessly, and then winced again at the pain in his, well, all the pains in his bruised body. "It isn't for me. I can't . . ."

He stood up. Crossed the room till he was next to her.

Somehow he found the presence to lift her hand and press his lips to it.

"I'm sorry, Diana, I'd better go."

Chapter Thirty-One

I'm sorry, Diana."

How many times had he apologized? Apologized because of what he was going to do: walk away.

He was gone. She'd watched him leave, let him leave, and then she'd fallen asleep at Harridan House as if staying there could keep reality from settling in. But the following day, when Lucy, in clearing up the mystery of Sir Robert's episode abruptly gave her leave, Diana began to feel completely abandoned.

She had few true, close friends. In fact, she had even less than she had thought. She could hardly turn to Earnestina, although she often had when life with her late husband had been too dark. In those last months of his life, Tina had been the dearest of friends and endlessly supportive.

Now, Diana yearned for Maggie but was loath to interrupt the newly wedded bliss that her cousin was sharing with her husband at Oakley's country estate.

Diana's footman announced that Lord Ashburton was there to see her. He'd come all the way from Brighton to offer assistance in her "emergency."

"I'm not at home," Diana insisted, not even trying to keep her voice down, though Ashburton waited in the foyer beyond.

She'd have to see him eventually. If she ever wished to mix in society again; that was. Just not yet, not now.

She didn't wait to hear him complain that he knew she was here. She left the parlor through the servants' door, surprising her staff as she traversed the narrow hallway to the back stairs so she could reach her room undetected and in peace.

She could not remain in London. She could not stay always wondering whom she would run into, or who would call upon her.

Where could she go?

Chapter Thirty-Two

Jason returned to Brighton. He was no longer angry. How could he be, after what Diana had revealed? He could hardly feel, actually.

He wanted to see his daughter. The one bright, innocent thing in his world.

But when he arrived back at the Air Street rooms, the first person he saw was Lizzie.

"What happened, Jas?" she asked. "Your jaw is purple!"

He simply looked at her. Wasn't the story there on his face for anyone to read? Apparently, some version of it was, because Daniel pulled his wife away.

"He's only just arrived, my love, give the man some space."

Yet, the following afternoon, it was Daniel who clapped him on the arm.

"What's this I just heard of a brawl with Sir Robert George? In Harridan House of all places! Whatever were you doing there? Well, never mind the last, but what do you have against the man?"

"That's the tattle today, is it?" Jason shrugged. "It's rather what does he have against me? He came at me out of nowhere and for no apparent reason. Come, Throck," he used the old schoolboy nickname, "in all the years we've been friends, have you ever known me to pick a fight?"

Much later that evening, after allowing his friends to drag him out to the theater, Jason realized he shouldn't have spoken quite so quickly.

In the lobby of the year-old building, he saw Lord Ashburton with Lord Bourke at his side.

For the first time in days, a different emotion struck Jason. Fury boiled in his veins and he crossed the room before his mind caught up to his actions.

"You damn bastard," Jason bit out. He grabbed the other man by his cravat and slammed a fist into his cheek before Ashburton had a chance to register anything other than surprise on his face. Ashburton stumbled back, amid the gasping crowd of onlookers who parted ranks to let him fall.

"What the hell, Blount?" Lord Bourke cried, taking a step toward Ashburton, but Jason was already on top of the viscount, his fist drawn back.

Ashburton blocked the coming blow with his forearm, and Jason felt the following thrust of the man's fist into his side.

"Jealousy, is that what this is about?" Ashburton drawled, his bruised face a twisted sneer.

"You're a pig, Ashburton." Jason punctuated his words by driving his palm into the man's chin, forcing his head down against the wooden parquet floor.

"Get off of him!" He heard the cries of onlookers but ignored them. It only barely entered his consciousness that someone was calling his name.

Then Ashburton surged against him, his legs entangling with Jason's until Jason found himself on his back looking up at the son of a bitch.

"You must not take rejection well," Ashburton sneered. A drop of blood hung off of his chin for a long moment before it finally fell onto Jason's coat.

"She didn't want you," Jason growled, despite the fact that Ashburton was choking him now and it was getting increasingly difficult to put voice to the words. "And I'm going to teach you that when a lady says no, she means it."

There was a ringing in Jason's ears and a fog shadowing the corners of his vision, but he thought he could just make out the sentence formed on Ashburton's cracked lips.

"She did not say no."

Then Ashburton was off of him, stumbling back as he stood, shrugging off the help of others.

Jason lunged up from the ground, focusing on his object despite the creeping blackness and threw himself at Ashburton with all the fury and despair he felt, for himself, for Diana, for everything the man's casual violence had destroyed.

Jason never made his target. He found his arms held back and looking to his right he saw Throckmorton.

"Let me go, Daniel," Jason warned.

"No." Throckmorton held his right arm firmly, even after Jason managed to free his left from the other man who had restrained him. "We're at the *theater*, my friend. This isn't done. We're going home. *Now*."

Jason looked back toward Ashburton, but the man had moved on. Instead he saw Lizzie, staring at him in shock.

The fight left Jason as quickly as it had entered. His shoulders slumped.

"All right," he said to Daniel. "All right."

The three of them sat tensely in the carriage for the ride home. The silence so thick, Jason could almost taste it. That and the nauseating metallic of his own blood.

"Well, if the brawl at that club didn't cause a scandal, this certainly will," Lizzie said finally. "I suppose I'll have to collect on that wager I've won. Where is Ogden Seymour now, do you know?"

Chapter Thirty-Three

Out of the not particularly companionable silence, Mary finally spoke.

"You've done quite well for yourself, Diana."

Diana winced as her needle slipped and stabbed her index finger. She glanced at her stepmother, who sat in the rocker, creating neat seams as if she were a machine designed to do so.

"I suppose I have," Diana muttered. She knew what was coming next. Mary seemed capable of conversing on only a few subjects.

"I suppose you must think us very poor society here."

"Not really," Diana answered, knowing by now that her response was useless. "I did spend my first seventeen years here. It's hard to ever forget the tranquility of life."

What Diana didn't add was that she had not found that tranquility in fleeing to Devon, to the modest cottage near Exeter where her father still lived.

It had been two months and in that time, Diana had come to understand that trying to run away to her childhood, to a time *before*, was impossible. After all, her father's life had not stood still. He was remarried to a young wife, with a babe and another on the way. Although he no longer practiced medicine, between his arthritic hands he held his young son and bounced the child on his knee.

Perhaps if Mary weren't here . . . but she was, and the older woman appeared to feel threatened by Diana's presence, as if Diana were challenging Mary's place as woman of the house.

"If I weren't so near my confinement," Mary complained, "we could go into Exeter. Perhaps to one of the assemblies at The Hotel, but you know how it is for a woman when she is in my condition." Her dark eyes flittered toward Diana as if sharing a secret. "Oh, but perhaps you'll marry again and then know. You are still young after all."

"Perhaps," Diana admitted, unwilling to let the woman goad her. For the sake of her father she would be polite. For the sake of her little brother and whatever new sibling would be born in three months' time.

"I'm sure you'll be such a help when there are two babes," Mary continued. "If you'll condescend to stay so long. To be sure, you'll be wishing for a more lively place."

Diana sighed. Mary wanted her gone. She rather thought her father did as well. Although he was perfectly happy to accept the money she had sent over the years. Even Diana wanted to leave. The only reason she dawdled was that she hadn't the faintest idea *where* to go.

Last year this time, in the middle of October, she had left Brighton to return to London. Then she had spent all of December at the Ashburtons' annual house party at their country seat in Sussex. Most definitely she would not attend *this* year and she was equally loath to return to London.

So where? Sighing again, Diana tried to focus her mind back on the line of stitches before her. She'd go wherever she didn't need to think.

Chapter Thirty-Four

Diana accepted Maggie's invitation to join her and Oakley for the season in Bath. Within minutes of arriving at the spacious house at the top of the hill, she knew it had been the right decision. For three months, she had been running from place to place searching for comfort, for solace, and here it was, in the company of friends. Of family, really, even if Maggie was a second cousin.

Now, in late October, the house was not so full with just Maggie, Oakley, Maggie's daughter, Emma, and her stepdaughter, Olivia, in residence. In another month, the rest of Oakley's family would arrive.

"Finally," Maggie exclaimed, closing the parlor door firmly behind them. "I have so much to tell you, and I'm nearly certain that you have much to tell me." She underscored her pointed look with a raised eyebrow.

"Marriage definitely agrees with you, Maggie-doll," Diana said with a laugh as she took a seat in one of the green brocade chairs.

"Yes, it does," Maggie smirked. "I'm pregnant."

"How wonderful!" Diana exclaimed.

"I've started to show already, but with the extra petticoat I think the bump is rather obscured." Maggie pulled the fabric taut across her belly to show off the nascent curve. Then, abruptly, she let the dress fall back and turned the full force of her intent stare on Diana.

"Your turn, now."

"I don't have any news, Mags," Diana returned, fidgeting despite her usual poise. "I've been moldering in Devon, with my father, and the only thing I've heard is that our men are going to Spain."

"Then you didn't hear all the scandal about Sir Jason? You never mentioned anything in your letters, but I thought . . . I thought perhaps . . . well, after that brawl that happened between him and Sir Robert in Harridan House. *Your* Harridan House, I thought for sure . . ."

"I'm thinking of getting rid of it," Diana interjected, putting voice to the idea for the first time. Maggie's eyebrows flew upward, her mouth in a comical *O* of surprise.

"What happened?" she demanded. "Whyever are you going to? Is this because Sir Jason disapproves of it?"

"There's nothing between me and Sir Jason," Diana answered truthfully. There wasn't nor would there ever be. But there had been. For the briefest time there had been something so tantalizing growing between them. Diana didn't think she could be the person she had been before, the person who hadn't understood such a possibility existed.

"Well, at the very least, you owe me a hat."

Diana laughed. "I'd forgotten! But of course, you're right."

"In any event," Maggie continued, "I heard Sir Jason nearly killed Lord Ashburton. Quite a mess it was in Brighton. You wouldn't know anything about that, would you?" Maggie looked at her suspiciously.

What? The new information sat heavily in Diana's head. Jason had . . . had fought for her honor? Was that what had happened? "I didn't hear about Ashburton," Diana said slowly.

"Earnestina didn't write you?" Maggie said incredulously. Diana understood her cousin's disbelief. After all, she and Tina had been inseparable for years.

"We're on a bit of the outs," Diana admitted.

"You *do* know something." Maggie's eyes narrowed. "What happened, Diana? I've never seen you like this before."

"Please." Diana held up one hand in entreaty. She didn't have it in her to protest ignorance, she simply couldn't talk about it. Not yet. It may have been three months since everything had fallen apart, but she still felt raw.

"At some point you'll have to talk, Di," Maggie insisted.

Diana simply nodded. Perhaps she would someday, but just not quite yet.

Chapter Thirty-Five

"Perhaps we should take advantage of this and enjoy a cup of chocolate?" Olivia asked. They'd been walking back up the hill to the house when the skies had opened up and let loose torrents of rain. Maggie, Diana and Olivia had ducked into a confectionary shop for cover while Oakley went to procure umbrellas.

Diana enjoyed the rhythm of life in Bath. There was a calming routine to the mornings at the pump room and the evening concerts. Most of her usual set never came to the town and Diana was grateful for that.

Maggie and Oakley were gracious and entertaining hosts and Diana even found Olivia's company diverting. Six months earlier, Diana had found Olivia insufferable and a bore. She was one of those girls raised to think highly of themselves because of the slightest connection to a title. However, it seemed as though the last half year had mellowed the girl, had made her deeply appreciative of the new opportunities offered by Maggie's marriage to Oakley.

And Olivia was now making the most of the kind of situation the girl would have complained about only months earlier.

"Lovely idea," Maggie agreed with alacrity. As far as Diana could tell in the past two weeks since she'd been in Bath, she hadn't seen Maggie refuse any offer of food.

"It's gotten rather stuffy in here," Diana said, finding it difficult to breathe in the crush of people seeking shelter from the sudden storm. "I think I'll wait outside under the awning."

She made her way through the crowd of people and through the doorway and finally found a small section of relatively dry pavement just outside.

She avoided, as she usually did these days, looking at any one person. Her gaze swept over the crowd, focusing on the ornate iron knocker of the house across the street.

The sky lit with a blinding flash of lightning, spooking the horses of the waiting carriages and one reared up in front of her, obscuring the intricate ironwork.

So she looked down instead.

And saw the little girl just as the horse's legs started to come down. Diana didn't think, didn't question, but ran forward into the rain and scooped the child up and out of the way, just as the horse's hoofs touched stone once more.

She held the girl to her tightly, looking around for who was responsible for the child. Then a woman ran toward her, a terrified expression across her vaguely familiar face.

"Thank you, ma'am," the woman said, reaching for the girl.

Diana peeled the child off of her pelisse, finally sparing the girl a look. A shiver ran down Diana's spine that had absolutely nothing to do with the freezing rain.

Shocked, she thrust the child toward the nanny. Looking up, looking away, looking at anything but this child.

"The carriage is just around the corner . . ."

Looking at him.

Oh, my God! Diana thought, staring at Jason, wet from the rain, holding an open umbrella that he was positioning over the nanny and his daughter.

He stopped and stared, just as she stared at him.

It was laughable really. She *wanted* to laugh.

"The lady stopped Miss Cassandra from running in front of the horses," the nanny explained, taking the child in her arms.

With his free arm, Jason took the girl quickly from the nanny, trying to protect her from the danger that had already passed. That was when the little girl started bawling, as if suddenly realizing the peril she had faced.

Diana stood there silently, pulling her sodden hat from her head and wiping her wet, bedraggled hair out of her eyes.

It was too much.

"You have my deepest gratitude," Jason said, staring at her as if he'd never seen her before.

She blinked back the tears that seemed ever ready these days and nodded, not trusting herself to speak.

"May I . . . may I convey you somewhere?"

"I . . . I . . ." she started.

"Diana, there you are!" Maggie came flying toward her. "Oakley's procured us umbrellas. He's waiting with Olivia. But look at you, it hardly matters now." She stopped suddenly, seeing Jason. "Sir Jason, how pleasant to see you, I didn't realize you were in Bath."

"We've only just arrived, Lady Oakley, yesterday," he said. "Excuse me . . . my daughter."

Then he was gone.

"Oh, Di!" Maggie exclaimed, taking her arm. "How uncomfortable that was! Come, let's go home."

Diana followed her through the throng of people waiting under the awning till they found Oakley.

In the warmth of the cozy sitting room, with a dry dress, India shawl and a hot cup of tea, Diana knew what was coming next. There were questions that had to be answered. She could hardly deflect her friend when so much of the story had been laid out before her in the rain.

"Please, tell me what happened between the two of you in

Brighton," Maggie urged. "You don't have to have so many secrets. You don't have to always be so strong."

"Strong, Maggie?" Diana stared at her incredulously. "You think of me as strong? Now, when I can't interest myself in any of the things I used to do? I'm hardly strong. I'm barely even me anymore."

"What happened, Di?"

"I've made such a mess of things. But I never knew, I never thought . . . Maggie, it was all I knew how to be, how Roger made me!"

Diana poured out the whole story, the seduction and marriage, the lovers and the inheritance. And how Jason fit into all of it.

"In Brighton, I came to know him, not just as a potential lover but . . . for the first time I thought I might actually wish to be married again, to have a normal life, to give up Harridan House."

Maggie giggled, covering her mouth apologetically and ruefully, Diana smiled with her.

"I know, it's hard to imagine, but truly, Maggie, he made me feel it was possible."

"It is possible, Di," Maggie said with no trace of humor, leaning forward intently. "If that is what you wish. It's all up to you."

"And so I thought." Bitterness laced Diana's words. "But then I learned that it's not really possible. Fate seems to conspire to keep me in my place."

Finally, choking through the words, she told Maggie about Ashburton.

Her friend looked horrified but said nothing, and in those painful moments of waiting for Maggie to say something, she knew the last thing she could handle right then would be pity.

"Well, that explains Brighton," Maggie said, at last, a wry little smile twisting her lips. "Good for Blount."

Diana let out her pent-up breath with a long, shuddering sigh.

Chapter Thirty-Six

Jason was in Bath because his mother was in Bath and she wanted her son and granddaughter to spend Christmas with her. Madeline Blount was a simple woman who'd married a younger son of a younger son and had never imagined her own son might inherit any sort of title, lands or wealth. She was grateful that he had, and grateful that he took care of her, buying her a pleasant home in Bath and giving her countenance which she lorded over her friends frequently but without rancor.

Bath was hardly quiet at this time of year. Society tended to move north from Brighton around Michaelmas. But somehow, Jason had never imagined . . . Well, he had imagined seeing her again—on some London street, at some London rout, in a dark walk in Vauxhall. The last thought brought a reminiscing smile, which ended in a scowl when he remembered just why he had come across her that night.

Here, in the stone-cobbled streets of Bath, in the middle of a storm, he had seen her.

Cassie chattered the entire way back to the house but Jason didn't hear a word she said. He was still shaking. He nodded and smiled but his thoughts were still out in the rainy street, Diana's face imprinted over everything.

He had thought himself over her, had put the whole affair behind him, and . . .

But . . .

No. He would not think about it. He may have said he would be honest with her, but he did not have to be honest with himself.

Jason laughed aloud at his own thoughts. Cassie laughed with him, not knowing what he thought was funny but clearly thinking that seeing her father laugh was reason enough to laugh.

It was stupid, irrational and true. Three months had done nothing but push his emotions down to lie dormant, only to rear up again, fully formed and shocking.

Three months had done nothing. How was it possible that, bedraggled by the rain, the woman had looked even more beautiful than he had remembered?

Chapter Thirty-Seven

Diana slept poorly and then lay in bed late in the morning till finally she asked Julia to draw her a bath. She lingered in the tub until the last warmth had seeped from the water.

Three months. At the close of any of her other relationships, she would not have waited a week before moving on. Certainly seeing a former lover three months later should register only the briefest smile of memory.

This hadn't been the usual relationship and she could no longer deny that.

More than that, Diana had changed.

Early in the afternoon, when Maggie was at work on a new reticule and Diana perused the latest fashion plates, Jason called. She had half expected him to come. After all, it was the only polite thing to do and Diana knew that Jason was unfailingly polite.

The sun-dappled parlor with its cream silk-lined walls and its green-striped chairs felt far too small when Jason entered. Yesterday it had been like seeing a ghost. Today he was all too real, all too male and all too *him*.

She struggled to acknowledge him but couldn't find the easy turns of phrase that should have come effortlessly to her lips.

"Good afternoon, Sir Jason," Maggie greeted him. "Such a pleasure to see you again."

"The pleasure is mine, Lady Oakley," he returned.

"Won't you have a seat?" She gestured to one of the chairs, the one closest to Diana, and he hesitated for just a moment before he finally sat.

"I wished to convey my . . ." He turned toward Diana. His eyes were still blue. Not that they would have had any reason to change, but somehow that constant surprised her, foolish as she knew it was. "My gratitude for your actions yesterday."

"It was . . . of course," Diana said, lamely.

"It is terrifying to have one's child in mortal danger, is it not, Sir Jason?"

Diana looked at Maggie gratefully.

"I have a daughter myself. She is six now, which only means she can get into that much more trouble."

"Exactly so," Jason agreed, but he didn't look away from Diana. She knew this because she felt his gaze on every inch of her body.

Coward, she chided herself. *Look at him*.

So she did.

"It is an unexpected pleasure to find you in Bath," he said, as if he meant it, as if three months earlier he hadn't simply walked away from her.

"Are you here to take the water?" she managed to say finally.

He shook his head, smiling, and she found the expression infectious. "No, you couldn't torture me to drink that foul stuff. My mother lives here and she wished to see her granddaughter."

They sat there for a moment, smiling at each other, until they both seemed to realize at the same time what they were doing.

"I should be off," he said, not quite meeting her eyes.

"Yes, well, thank you for calling."

He stood, and bowed to her, then turned to Maggie.

"Lady Oakley."

"Sir Jason, I do hope you'll join us for dinner tonight," Maggie said suddenly, smiling at Jason warmly. "I know Oakley would love to have another male at the table."

Jason looked uncomfortable. Diana knew without a doubt he would say no. There would be some excuse . . . a prior invitation, his daughter, a letter he had to write. Perhaps not a letter, Diana allowed.

And Maggie, what was she thinking, inviting him to dinner?

"I could hardly refuse such an invitation," Jason agreed, returning the smile at last.

Chapter Thirty-Eight

That evening, lounging in Oakley's study after dinner, Jason wished he had refused. He wasn't quite certain what he was doing. It had been torture to be so close to Diana, just across the table, hearing her voice, seeing her lips, her hair, the dark gaze of her eyes. He'd fidgeted in his chair throughout the meal, wanting her desperately but knowing that he'd given up that opportunity three months ago. Now, closeted with Oakley, he was beginning to feel as though he'd been corralled.

Jason had nearly a decade on Oakley, but the younger man had a manner that commanded respect, taking his position in life seriously, not as an entitlement but as a privilege and as a duty.

"I have a fondness for Lady Blount. It was due to her influence that I met my wife." There was a glint in Oakley's eye that let Jason know there was a story there, but that was not what the earl intended to communicate.

Jason waited, taking a slow sip of his brandy to fill the space until Oakley continued, revealed whatever it was he wished to say.

"It's not really my place to speak of this . . ."

"No, likely it's not," Jason agreed, because anything he might say about Diana and Jason was certainly no one's business but their own.

"Right." Oakley sighed and then took a swallow of his own drink, as if he were mustering up the strength. *To do what?* "Suffice to say then, Blount, that there are stories circulating about you and from the few things I do know, it's not hard to put two and two together and reason that you're why Diana came to us looking like a shadow of herself."

Jason filed that last bit aside, to think on in a moment, but his curiosity was piqued.

"What do you know of her, Oakley?" he asked. Did either Oakley or his lady know about Harridan House? He doubted it, if only because Oakley was known as being a straight-arrow sort of fellow.

"She's Maggie's cousin," Oakley returned, a bit of steel in his voice. "As her relative, I know quite a bit more that most."

So he did know. And if he'd heard the story about the brawl in Harridan House, then he knew Jason knew.

"And you don't care?" Jason asked.

"I care about her character." Oakley placed his glass on the mahogany desk he'd been leaning against.

Jason stared at him. *Her character?*

"My wife invited you to dinner because she had some idea from your visit yesterday that even if you were the cause of the shadows, you might also be the cure."

Jason forced himself to laugh.

Oakley's lips thinned and he leaned forward intently until Jason had to meet his gaze.

"Take it from a man who almost lost the woman he loved, Blount. There is such a thing as too much pride." There was something in Oakley's face when he made that admission, something that Jason recognized in himself.

The silence thickened, and Jason turned the glass in his hands around and around, watching the amber liquid swirl as he came to a decision.

"I don't care about the club."

"Then what?" Oakley pushed. "Because clearly, you care for her or you wouldn't be sitting here still, talking to me."

"I'm just . . . I'm not certain . . . I don't want to lead that sort of life."

Oakley studied him for a long moment before he finally spoke.

"Does she?"

Chapter Thirty-Nine

He needed to speak to her, to get her alone, but with Maggie and Oakley guarding their interactions there wasn't an opening and he returned home frustrated. He spent a long night reliving the past, remembering every second they had shared, every look, every word.

He finally found his moment late the following morning when chance allowed him to escort Diana home from the pump room without any other company.

In the bright light of day he finally saw the slight changes to which Oakley had alluded. She was thinner than before, the slight hollow of her cheeks more pronounced, and there was a tentativeness to her conversation that he'd never before witnessed in her.

Was he the cause of those changes? The thought disturbed him greatly and he looked away from her, hardly aware of their quickened pace and the silence in which they walked.

"I wanted to thank you," Diana said softly, breaking into his thoughts. "I heard, I couldn't help but hear about what you did to Lord Ashburton."

"I did not do it for your gratitude." Jason clipped his words, his jaw tight, lips thinned and pressed together. He did not want to think about Ashburton. He didn't want to think about that man or any of the other lovers Diana had had over the years.

"Of course not," Diana said quickly and even her alacrity frustrated him.

Had he done this to her? Broken her so that her throaty laugh had disappeared?

She stopped suddenly and he looked at her in surprise, practically in expectation.

"Thank you for escorting me." She gestured vaguely with her hand and he realized they stood at the foot of the stairs to Oakley's house. "Would you . . . would you care to come in? Have some tea perhaps?"

"Yes," he said curtly, although tea was the last thing on his mind. He followed her inside, up a flight of stairs to the cozy parlor he had found her in the day before when he'd made his call.

She walked to the fireplace, rested her hand on the mantel. The room was quiet. The house was quiet.

"I believe everyone is out," Diana spoke into the silence, not quite looking at him.

Alone. At last. Only just then, Jason didn't know where to begin.

"Diana," he said, finally. "I . . . I owe you an apology."

Her gaze flew to meet his, her eyes wide and surprised. And light. The light, clear green of her irises catching the sunlight.

"I should never have left you as I did."

She laughed then, that deep throaty sound he remembered so well, and the sound of it relieved him. *Aroused him.*

"Are you saying, Jason, that you shouldn't have left in the manner in which you did? Or are you saying you wish you had stayed?"

"What I am saying," Jason answered slowly, taking a step toward her, and then another one. "Is that I don't want to talk about the past. I want only to think about the future."

It was a beguiling idea. *Forget the past and look to the future.* Diana thought she could revel in such a concept, embrace it as her motto.

Could she, though? Could he really? He had once, she knew, back in Brighton, when they began their affair. But then everything had twisted.

Did she want him enough that she was willing to forget or to chance him rejecting her again?

He was close to her now, so close that if she took just one step forward she'd be in his arms.

She heard the words fill the air as if it weren't her voice that had sounded then.

"What is the future, Jason?"

His mouth closed over hers and for a moment Diana remained rigid, untouched. Such a yearning filled her that it was hard to accept that here he was now, doing exactly what she wished. Then, the tender heat of his kiss began its slow burn through her body.

She swayed against him, leaning into his embrace, the support of his arms—the world falling away at the touch of his tongue on her lower lip.

Then he traced a path from her mouth, across the line of her jaw, to her neck. And with each inch of skin, she felt her heart expanding, stretching beyond its earthly bounds.

She gave herself over to him, to his touch, his exploration of her body. She could hardly do anything but that when his kisses made her feel boneless, a mass of quivering sensation. Vulnerable, all her usual defenses stripped away entirely.

"Diana." There was an edge to his tone, to the steady cadence of his voice. She struggled to open her eyes, but her lashes fluttered weakly and instead she merely turned her face to rest her cheek in the palm of his hand. "Diana."

She didn't want to open her eyes. She didn't want anything else but the feel of him touching her, the beautiful fantasy that in the gentleness of his embrace lay a deeper regard. The ridiculous dream that there was anything more than lust in his eyes.

"I'm going to make love to you, Diana."

Which she wanted . . . desperately.

"Here, in this parlor."

"Yes," she managed to whisper, the words more of a sigh against his wrist than anything audible.

He must have heard her, or taken her movement for assent, because he turned her face back and plundered her mouth once more with his.

He let go of her only briefly, to turn the key in the lock of the door, and then he was back, holding her in his arms.

It was only when a cool flutter of air touched her bare skin that she realized he'd managed to successfully unfasten her dress, her stays, and her chemise, all of which gaped, freeing her breasts to his gaze . . .

. . . to the heated suckling of his mouth . . .

. . . oh, Lord—to his tongue!

Energy coursed through her and she stirred in his arms, needing now to be an active partner in this, to touch and taste him as he now tasted her.

Her eyes flew open. The scalding look on his face was the succor she needed—the tinder to feed her flaming desire.

She tugged at his jacket, but he wouldn't release her. Finally, one arm at a time, she managed to get the bloody thing off of him. While his hands ran down her dress and cupped her buttocks through the many layers of cloth, she did away with the perfection of his cravat and the restriction of his waistcoat.

Then the floor was beneath her, and she could smell the earthy wool of the rug. He knelt between her legs, his hands resting on her ankles, stroking the skin through her thick winter stockings.

His shirt hung loosely around him, gaping, and she could see the soft hair of his chest. She wanted to sit up, push him down and lick the bare skin, follow the contours of his muscles. But she didn't, she lay there where he had placed her, her arms above her head, her breasts as bare as his chest, and met his eyes once more.

What she saw there shook her more than even his touch. She'd never seen such a thing in any other man's eyes, not to her. Still, she recognized it.

The idea of a man caring for her was so new, so frightening, that it colored everything. When his hands inched up her legs, it felt just as frightening, new and beguiling as the first time anyone had ever touched her. As he skimmed over the woolen stockings, her dress pushed higher and higher, she held her breath, anticipating his touch on the bare skin of her thigh.

The touch came and finally he broke their locked gaze. He bent down to kiss the exposed flesh just above her garter. There were so many sensations, the roughness of his cheek, the soft touch of his lips, his breath hot and moist on her skin, and then his tongue drew lines of fire.

When his mouth closed over the small pink hill of her clitoris, sucking, drawing her hips up toward him, she nearly jumped off the floor with the intensity of the sensation.

It was too much . . . but not nearly enough. Her hands found purchase in the waves of his hair and she found her fingers making little swirling motions, echoing the ministrations of his tongue.

The shuddering peak came over her before she even knew she was rising, so sudden and sharp that she nearly pushed him away. His hands clutched at her hips and his lips kept their position, till the climax grew fuller, rounder.

Finally he released her, eased himself up her body till his lips met hers and she tasted the earthiness of her own juices on his mouth.

His hips were solidly between her thighs, the heat of his cock nearing her cunt and then she felt the hard, thick length of him part her wet folds, sliding in easily, smoothly.

He filled her as if he had always been meant to be there, a part of her, his warm, male body joined completely with hers. In the long moment before he began to withdraw, began to make love to her with deep, rhythmic strokes, she knew a complete and utter peace.

So this is what it is like to make love to a man one loves.

"No, I can't do this," Diana whispered, twisting to push at his shoulders.

Jason stopped moving. He was struggling, she could see, to bring himself back, to gather himself.

"What," he said softly, each word measured and separated, "do you want me to do?"

"Please move. I need air."

For a long moment he didn't move. Then he pulled back, rolled himself to the side. She was vaguely aware of him lifting his arm up, covering his face, even as she curled up into herself.

Stupid. She was inexcusably stupid and foolish. As the cooler air blanketed her body, she knew she had panicked and in the silence, long after she understood why, she shivered from embarrassment.

Then he placed his hand on her hip, just that one touch, not stroking, not doing anything but letting his warmth seep into her.

"Jason?"

He took his hand away and at the absence, Diana pulled into a tighter ball, her knees pushing the bunched up fabric of her dress toward her chin.

"I'm sorry," she whispered.

She knew he moved. She heard the rustling, felt the vibrations through the floor, felt the heat grow as he neared. He curled himself around her, nestling her against his body.

Diana felt safe there, safe and protected in his arms. She was grateful as well that it was he who was there, holding her, waiting, making her feel as though the future was more wondrous than her childhood self had ever imagined. Making her feel strong, beloved.

"You don't need to . . ."

"I love you," Diana interrupted, turning her head back up toward him.

His face darkened, tightened and expanded—that was the only way she could describe the transformation.

She didn't know if it was the guidance of his arms or her own volition, but she turned to face him, her mouth meeting his.

"I love you," she said again, urgently, her lips tugging on his. The words freed her. The panic had fled and what was left was a bouyancy that she poured into the kiss.

He moved over her, positioning himself between her legs again. She welcomed him in, as if she could simply wrap all this newly embraced love around him as she wrapped her legs around his hips and her arms around his chest.

Then his hips bucked against hers, driving her down into the rug. His lips moved against hers but she didn't hear anything until he buried his face into her neck with a growl.

With his mouth, open and hot on the sensitive skin under her ear and his cock pounding into her, the wave of sensation built.

He grew within her, impossibly hard, impossibly large, touching every inch of her inside, stretching her. He was close, she knew. His lips moved against her neck, mouthing words that pushed her to her limit. When he finally came within her, hugging her tight within his arms as he convulsed, kneading the muscles of her back with his hands, she exploded again, pulsing around him, shuddering in the strong circle of his arms.

When his movements eased, her shaking continued, joined by the hot sting of tears and an involuntary gasping sob, till suddenly she was weeping in his arms like a child.

"Did I hurt you?" he whispered, holding her tight. "God, Diana, I'm sorry, I'm so sorry, I don't want to . . ."

"No," she gasped through the tears, "No, you didn't, I'm fine."

He moved back so he could look at her, so he could see her face.

"But you're crying." The knowledge of it felt like a hammer to his chest, to his heart.

"I can't help it," she said, wiping at her eyes. "I don't know why, I just can't help it."

He held her close again, silently, feeling her shuddering against him.

Jason didn't understand why she was crying. He was afraid that, despite her protestations, he had somehow hurt her. She was so much more fragile, so much more precious to him than he had ever imagined and he couldn't bear her tears.

She was laughing then, even as she cried, until finally the weeping ceased.

He didn't stop touching her as they dressed. Then, after he finally unlocked the door, when they sat, he pulled his chair close to her, finding little ways to stay in contact, his hand on her knee, on her wrist, his thigh touching hers.

They didn't speak, but they were giddy with the freedom to enjoy each other's body. Even when they rang for tea and the maid came in, he didn't move his hand from hers.

He heard the chime of the church bells in the distance strike the hour.

"They'll be back soon," Diana said, lifting his wrist to her mouth, kissing his palm, his fingers.

"Then perhaps you shouldn't be doing that," he murmured, "or they'll find a shocking scene."

"I don't think anything would shock Maggie anymore, or Oakley for that matter. But I suppose I mustn't forget that Miss Coswell is with them."

"We wouldn't want to shock Miss Coswell."

"Or perhaps we would," Diana teased.

Jason thought of that moment in the rain when he'd seen her there, holding his daughter as if it were the most natural idea in the world. In that one instant, seeing her again, he'd known. Just as if Cupid had shot his arrow and struck unerringly.

"Marry me," he said abruptly.

She stopped kissing his hand and moved it down to her lap but didn't let go. He was glad for that.

"What about Harridan House? What about everything else and your daughter?" They were reasonable questions, he knew, for Diana hadn't had the luxury of being in his head, of knowing that though what she said was true, he had had all those concerns and in truth still did; he just didn't care as much because now he cared about Diana just as much.

"But I'm teasing you, Jason. I'll find some way to dispose of it," Diana laughed, squeezing his hand.

"You mean that?" Jason asked, stunned. Stunned, pleased and happy. Diana nodded with a tentative smile.

"I don't need it anymore. It isn't my future. You are."

He didn't trust himself to speak just yet, to say the right thing to let her know how much he understood what this meant. That he didn't take her decision lightly.

"I'm not going to be stupid now." She lifted his wrist to her lips again. The touch of her mouth was exquisite, and watching her kissing him—it took his breath away, how beautiful she was. "This isn't about pride, or proving that I am free and can take care of myself, that I don't need to answer to anyone."

"You can," Jason said quickly.

Again she dropped his wrist to her lap but this time she let go. She let go, rose from her chair and stood in front of him, stopping him before he could rise too, as a man should do in a lady's presence.

"Do you love me, Jason?"

"Of course, haven't I said?" he asked before he realized that perhaps he hadn't. "Yes, I do."

That wasn't enough, of course. He dragged her down into his lap, and brought his lips to her ear.

"I love you, Diana, and I intend to spend the rest of our lives letting you know just how much I do."

It was Oakley who finally found them, half an hour later. In the midst of nibbling on Diana's neck, Jason only vaguely registered that the man kindly closed the door and let them continue taking their tea.

PART IV

A Maid for the Taking

Chapter One

She was watching him again. The woman said she didn't want him, rebuffed all his advances, but then she watched him. Robert caught her gaze, not letting go of her even as he fucked little Ella. It was Rouge he wanted to fuck and he let her know as he narrowed his eyes, that every thrust into this woman was a thrust he wanted to make into her.

With the barrier of her red silk mask it was difficult to decipher Rouge's expression, but her lips softened and parted and the swell of her breasts rose over her scarlet gown.

She licked her lips. Slowly. As if she wanted to taste him. Right then, Robbie would have wagered his fortune on it. She knew just how to make a man feel like he was the only one, that there had only ever been him. Then again, she was a professional, so he couldn't be sure, certainly not with this game of hot and cold she liked to play.

Rouge reached up to stroke her own neck and the movement made him jerk inside Ella. After all, she was wearing gloves again.

Safely inside Madame Rouge's suite of rooms at the rear of the first floor, Lucy pulled off her gloves. Then she unwrapped the gold turban from her head and drew the pins from her reddish-brown hair until it fell free down her back. She slipped off the silk gown and draped it over the velvet-upholstered chaise longue.

She stood for a moment, naked, in the center of the room. Then she turned her head so that she caught her reflection in the large mirror that hung on the far wall.

Her breasts were full and high, the pink nipples puckered and tight. Lucy lifted her hand to stroke her left breast, cupping it, feeling the weight overflowing her palm. She liked the way her body looked, as if she were one of the paintings that hung in the hallways of the club. She liked the way her breast looked covered by a hand.

What would it feel like if it were his hand instead of hers— Sir Robert George's warm skin touching hers? Another rush of heat gathered between Lucy's legs and she reached her other hand down to touch the moisture, the slickness of her cleft.

She shifted, stretching her arms out and bending from the waist, so that her palms rested on the bed, her back arched like a cat and her buttocks lifted. It was the position the lovely, sultry Ella had been in while Sir Robert thrust himself into her.

Lucy slid her fingers back down to her slit, to the little muscular curve that was begging to be touched.

She sighed at the light pressure, the circular movement. But she wanted more. Her inner muscles were grasping at air. She needed to be filled, she needed to be fucked.

She'd waited this long. She could wait a little longer.

After all, a woman only undoes her virginity once and therefore it would have to be a truly momentous occasion. In the sultry halls and rooms of Harridan House, Lucy had seen that sex could be both beautiful and cheap. She'd spied on any number of encounters, either in the guise of Madame Rouge or unnoticed in her usual drab maid attire, which signified her as off-limits and simply staff.

The women in the flimsy Grecian costumes were the ones who experienced all the sensual pleasures the house offered— they, their male counterparts, and the members of Quality, male and female, who chose to visit the private club.

Lucy was a plain, no-nonsense woman. She knew well enough that a country girl from the Cornish wilds shouldn't expect anything more than the generous salary Madame Rouge paid her. Perhaps in a few years she would have saved up enough money to buy that tavern and a respectable husband for herself. But this was now. At eight and twenty years of age, having, despite the bawdiness of her current employment, walked the straight and narrow path all of her years, Lucy desired something more.

She wanted what she saw in the eyes of so many of the House's members, the orgasmic rapture and the shuddering sensation she could only imagine. She wanted it all now.

Lucy knew the man for the job: Sir Robert George.

From details her employer had dropped, she knew he was on the far side of forty. She wouldn't have thought. He looked nothing like what a man on the far side of forty should look like. Surely a man that old shouldn't smolder with sensuality, shouldn't be an Olympian when it came to lovemaking, tirelessly and endlessly inventive. He'd been frequenting Harridan House as long as Lucy had worked there, and from a discreet peek at the membership book when the house manager wasn't looking, she knew he had been a member for longer than that.

But for his fair coloring, he looked the way she imagined an ancient Greek athlete might, like the statues scattered throughout Harridan House. Straight nose, full lips—he was of average height, his body compact and well defined.

Not an inch of his flesh had started to soften with age. Lucy had seen almost every inch of his body.

And every time, those eight hard protruding inches had thrust into someone other than her.

She groaned, thinking about his lovely cock. She wanted it, she wanted him. But there were two rules that Lady Blount had given Lucy when she hired her two years earlier. One, that she must never reveal Lady Blount's identity; and two, that when she dressed as Madame Rouge she could take no one to her bed. Diana did not wish to deal with the consequences of those actions and wished to maintain the aloof reputation of the mysterious proprietor.

So Lucy settled for her fingers and the fantasies that flickered through her head like reflections on still water.

Chapter Two

"George!" Robert didn't need to look to know it was Raoul Molineaux who called him. The Frenchman's accent made him stand out like a sore thumb on Pall Mall.

"Afternoon, my friend," Robert greeted him warmly. He did consider the man to be a friend as well as business partner. It was a partnership that had seen both of them through difficult times. At first, Robert had sponsored the refugee in British society, and then, when Robert inherited the surprisingly bankrupt baronetcy from his older brother, Molineaux had helped him rebuild the family fortune.

More than rebuild.

Robbie was now rich because he'd never given a damn about what anyone else thought. If he wanted to dabble in trade, he dabbled in trade and his coffers were all the better for it. He was sinfully rich. Perhaps no amount of wealth could ever be sinful, but nonetheless he was wealthy. Perhaps the sinful part came from his other actions—his disinterest in monogamy.

That, however, was where he and Molineaux parted ways. The Frenchman had married fourteen years earlier and claimed to never regret a day in his life.

"It's fortuitous we meet. Madame has requested your presence at a dinner tomorrow evening. She's taken up a protégé and thinks this might be the very one you are looking for."

A wife, of course. Molineaux knew that Robert was looking and having difficulty in the search. Though rich he was considered a rake and not fit for young, impressionable girls. Hargreaves might have been eager to sell off his daughter to pay off his gambling debts, but most of society didn't quite see it that way. Robert would likely *not* be marrying up.

At forty-two years of age, Robert could not count on all the years to come. His own father had died at forty-four, his older brother at thirty-five. Death could come at any time, and before that he still had two things to do: leave a legitimate heir and live life to the fullest.

The second he was succeeding remarkably at. The first . . . well, the Hargreaves slut had slipped through his fingers.

Robbie needed an heir and now was the time. Not later, when his cock had withered and his seed gone impotent.

"Who is she?"

"Miss Emmaline Clarke. Lovely young lady."

Robert now understood why Clarissa Molineaux thought the girl might suit him, for if he would not be *fortunate enough*, her words, to fall in love, he might as well make a profit off of the marriage. "Clarke, her father's the silk importer?"

"Yes, that's the one," Molineaux affirmed.

"Interesting. I've been meaning to speak with him."

"Now you may, tomorrow evening."

Chapter Three

ood evening, my lady," Lucy greeted Diana, Lady Blount, as the woman entered the bedroom. She quickly stepped forward to help her employer with her cloak. As she always did, Lucy rattled off the status of the house and the goings-on that she thought would most interest the lady. "It's a lively evening here.

In the blue room, Lord Sedgwick has created quite an orgy. Oh, and you'll be interested to know that Lord Simon is here. In the Oriental room, last I saw. I gather you've dropped the man . . ."

"Oh, Luce, what would I do without you?" Lady Blount sighed, sitting down on the chaise longue. Now, in their own distinct attire, the differences between their appearances were quite marked. While they shared the same peaches-and-cream coloring, in a well-lit room Lucy's eyes were a lighter, clearer green and her hair was more brown than the shocking red of Lady Blount's.

Lucy took great pleasure in knowing she had made herself indispensable to her employer. She valued the trust and freedom Lady Blount gave her, as well as the myriad little confidences the woman had let drop over the years.

From everything the younger woman had said, she had had a barren, unhappy marriage to a much older man whose sexual abilities had floundered in the latter years of his life. When he had taken the unusual step of bequeathing to his wife the sex-oriented club that Harridan House was, Lady Blount had embraced the opportunity for the freedom it gave her.

The open confidences didn't go both ways. As much as she liked her employer, the woman was still that—her employer—and thus there were some matters Lucy preferred to keep private.

She grinned. "I suppose you'd have to dress up as Madame Rouge a bit more often," she teased.

Of course, dressing up as Madame Rouge was one of Lucy's favorite parts of the job. She had an expansive choice of clothing, each indecently cut dress made out of the most sumptuous materials. There was nothing plain or rough in that wardrobe. For the hours she pretended to be her employer, Lucy reveled in the luxury.

But there were things she had to do to maintain the disguise: wear gloves to cover her work-calloused hands, change her accent to ape Lady Blount's well-modulated tones. That wasn't particularly hard as she had been working for years already to mask the Cornish cadence of her childhood.

"Well, I have dropped him. I should have done it ages ago, or never picked him up." Lady Blount reached her hands over her head and stretched, her back arching over the curved rear of the chair. "The man has no imagination."

"Certainly not enough to please you," Lucy teased. Over the last two years she'd had opportunity to see Diana in action. The very infrequency of the encounters at Harridan House had intrigued Lucy enough to watch.

"What would you know of what pleases me?"

Lucy laughed. This she was not embarrassed to admit. She knew that Lady Blount liked when Lucy was outspoken and a little bit brash. So even though that demeanor was one that came from artful practice rather than nature, she used it to effect. "I am your spy, my lady, I would be remiss in my duties if I hadn't ever seen what pleases you best."

Lady Blount blushed.

"I'll send you to my next lover then," Lady Blount said with her own little laugh. "You'll have to instruct him to do just that."

Lucy giggled, imagining such a conversation. She'd had any number of odd conversations since coming to work at the club. Whether it was one of the "nymphs" sharing a sordid tale or conversations between the "members" of the club, she had gained a wealth of knowledge that would surely rival what young men studied at university.

"Of course it may be a while before I choose my next," Lady Blount continued, sighing again. "Oh, and I did tell you, did I not, that I will be staying in Brighton for the season?"

Lucy had not been told. Of course, she had expected Lady Blount would travel, but the entire season?

Why did the image of Sir Robert George, the muscles of his back flexing with every movement, fill her mind?

No—Lucy pushed the insidious thought away.

But after Lady Blount left, a sense of freedom beguiled Lucy. Why not? Why not, after all this time, have a little affair?

Lady Blount would be in Brighton and intended to stay there

for the season or at the very least through August. For the first time in the two years she had worked for the lady, Lucy considered breaking her trust.

She wanted Sir Robert. She knew Sir Robert wanted Madame Rouge. Therefore, she would give him Madame Rouge.

Chapter Four

Robert left Molineaux's house late in the evening, slightly drunk on the rich Bordeaux wine the man continued to stock despite England's war with France.

Late perhaps for the Molineauxes, who, after shepherding away most of their guests, wished to retire. Not that Robert could blame them. He, too, felt the amorous effects of the wine.

Not quite yet ready for the evening to end, he directed his coach to Harridan House.

The club was slow, the majority of its members having vacated London in the previous weeks. He climbed the stairs to the first-floor drawing room, his evening's desires not yet formulated. Only one of the three large canopied beds was occupied.

Then he saw her, Madame Rouge, a glass of champagne in her hand, lounging in one of the club chairs at the center of the room, chatting with young Lord Percy.

Chatting but not flirting. It was obvious to him in every line of her body that she was neither interested in the boy nor interested in giving Percy the impression that she wanted him.

Just then she looked up and met Robert's gaze. Lifting one elegantly gloved hand, she offered him a toast with her half-full flute and what he had come in the last months to term *that look*.

That look was certainly not the one she had trained on Lord

Percy. No, it was Robert she chose to torture with that "come hither" expression.

It was an invitation he could never resist, even though he should know by now that she preferred to tease him rather than to satisfy him.

"Sir Robert," Rouge murmured in greeting with a pleased smile.

"Evening, George." Percy nodded in acknowledgment, unfolding his tall, loose-limbed frame to reach a hand out.

"Evening, Percy." Robert shook the boy's hand. He had known Percy's father well, even seen the boy grow up to some extent. "I thought you had left for Brighton already."

Percy smiled sheepishly. "I intended to, but then I, um, as I was just telling Madame Rouge, I have an assignation . . ."

Robert raised a curious eyebrow. "And where is this mysterious . . . lady?"

Percy flushed then. "I'm not quite sure."

Rouge laughed, giggled almost. It was a sound that fascinated Robert. He'd only recently started to notice the interesting dichotomy of her personality. Sometimes she appeared completely refined and sophisticated, aware of every aspect of her movements. Then sometimes there were these moments when she didn't seem quite as in control.

Which was fine, since what he wanted was to be in complete control of her body. Just one night, perhaps even just one time, but he wanted to know how she felt, how she tasted.

He knew very well that half of his interest was the challenge, the game of hard-to-get that she'd been playing with him for the last two years.

"Well, Percy, let me advise you. There is only so long you let a lady keep you waiting."

"Is that so, Sir Robert?" Rouge tilted her chin up toward him, one side of her mouth curved up just slightly.

"Well, it does depend on the lady."

"I am so *pleased* to hear you say so."

Percy coughed and Robert gave him his attention.

"Hmm, I suppose I'd best be going." Percy laid his palms flat on the arms of the chair and pushed himself up.

Rouge stood as well. As usual, her silk gown clung to her body, revealing the obvious absence of petticoats.

"Don't forget, my lord," she said, as Percy kissed her out-stretched hand, "we have many women here more than willing to ease any heartache you might suffer."

"Yes, yes of course," the boy said, flustered, taking a step back. "Good evening."

Robert didn't wait to watch him leave. Instead he moved closer to Rouge, till she was trapped between him and the chair.

If she wished to step aside she could. If she wished to step forward, well then, there were only a few inches to traverse to be in his arms.

"And how much longer do you intend to make me wait?"

She stepped to the side, her thigh just grazing his as she turned.

"I believe, Sir Robert, you have never had a proper tour of Harridan House." She slid her arm under his and peered up at him through the slits in her red silk mask. She propelled him forward, slowly, across the drawing room until they entered the hall.

"I'd much prefer an improper tour."

"Yes, yes," Rouge said, brushing his words aside with a little laugh, "that's what I meant of course. Some of the most interest-ing artwork is just across the hall."

She gestured to the large, carved doors that led to what he as-sumed were her private rooms.

He knew then. Half in disbelief, he closed his hand around hers.

"I believe it is long overdue." He couldn't keep the depth of his desire from his voice and the deep huskiness surprised even him.

He followed her across the threshold and kicked the door shut.

Chapter Five

It was not Lucy's first kiss, but when upon entering the private rooms, Robert pulled her into his arms and lowered his lips to hers, she thought it may as well have been. This was nothing like the mildly pleasant contact of skin all those previous encounters had been. The sensations were sharp and fierce. He didn't start slow or gentle: he used his lips, his tongue, his teeth even, to pull everything out of her until she was kissing back, following his motions, running her own tongue along his lower lip.

The room spun around her, wildly dark, but his arms held her up. His hips pressed against hers and through the thin layers of her dress, she could feel his cock, warm and hard.

He was moving fast, as if she would stop him if he gave her too much space. Despite everything, she nearly laughed at the thought. She would *not* stop him.

She sank into the embrace.

When he tugged at her turban, unravelling the gold fabric, she didn't protest, but when he started to touch her mask, she did.

"There are rules, Sir Robert," Lucy reminded him. The foremost rule of Harridan House was that if someone wished to keep their identity anonymous through the use of a mask, their wish must be respected.

"I wouldn't dream of breaking them," he responded and moved his hand away—down to her hip, then sliding further to her buttocks as he pulled her tighter against him. He bent his head again. She tilted her head up to meet his lips but found only air and then the hot, dizzying press of his mouth against her neck.

She cried out at the sensation. His tongue moved and Lucy

knew she would simply die if he licked so exquisitely even another inch. Which of course he did and she wrenched her head away. It was *too* much.

He let her break away. She found him staring at her as if she were a puzzle he had to solve.

"You have limits then, as well as rules."

She struggled for something witty and sophisticated to say, something Lady Blount would have said in such a situation, but her mind was not working this evening. Clearly, her rational thoughts had fled the moment his lips touched hers.

"Do you always talk this much, Sir Robert? I'd rather thought you were a man of action."

From the curving of his lips and the intensity of his gaze, she knew he recognized the challenge.

He lifted her swiftly, before she knew what he was about, one arm around her back, one catching her below her knees, and he carried her the five steps to the bed where he laid her down.

Then he grasped her hips and dragged her to the edge of the bed so that he stood between her legs. He leaned against her, hips pressing against hers once more, but in this position, with him so intimately nestled, everything was different.

He reached forward to play with one of the long strands of her hair.

"I wondered why you are named Rouge, but I think one theory has been disproved." He let go of the curl and took the fabric of her dress in his hand instead. "Almost."

He lifted her dress so that it no longer fell between her legs but pooled around her waist.

She gazed down at herself, at what he too studied: her naked belly, flat and pale between her hips, her naked legs, and in between the darker thatch of curls more brown than red.

It surprised her how natural it felt, to be undressed before him, her most private area exposed.

Lucy watched him place his bare hands on her bare hips. His thumbs began a slow, circling massage, drawing a "v" down. They both watched his progress, till his fingers met, closing in on her clitoris.

Lucy gasped and her head fell back against the bed.

His right hand stayed, caressing her there, but his left hand continued down, moving between the folds, where she knew she was hot and wet. He thrust his fingers into her.

"How delightfully tight you are," he murmured. Then his hands were gone, leaving her gasping with dismay until, raising her head again, she saw that he was unfastening the falls of his breeches.

It was one thing to see his cock when she was several feet away, to view it as a voyeur. It was another thing entirely to know that the long, thick rod was about to go inside of her.

It was all rather sudden, too fast almost. She wanted him, she wanted this and him inside her, but a fear she hadn't anticipated made her stare at him in shock.

She could speak now, she could tell him to wait, to stop. But what would she say?

Then she felt him hot against her and she marveled at the sensation of the round head of his cock spreading her lips.

She knew that sometimes there was pain the first time and sometimes there was blood, but not always. From the easy way he slid between her slick folds, she had the distinct feeling that if there was any pain it would be minimal.

He pushed in further, slowly, so slowly that it made the rest of her, the part he didn't yet fill, clench in anticipation.

She heard him groan and her gaze flew to his face. His eyes were closed and he had the smile of a man enjoying a good wine, savoring it.

Then he opened his eyes, those lovely striated eyes that reminded her of glass marbles, and caught her watching him.

"I'm glad you made us wait, Rouge, the anticipation has made it all the sweeter."

"You find me sweet?" she asked, feeling him move ever so slightly deeper, tantalizingly deeper. She could feel just how big he was now, stretching her. There was a pressure, too, that had started to build, a tension that was not entirely pleasurable.

"I find you . . ." He moved his hips just a bit more—the pressure almost painful now—and then he stopped, his expression changing.

He eased back ever so slightly and the tension in her body subsided.

"Is this some trick?" Sir Robert demanded.

"Trick?" Lucy stammered. Clearly, he had figured out that she was a virgin, though she hadn't been entirely certain a man could tell such a thing. After all, she hadn't met any other virgins during her time at Harridan House.

He still throbbed within her but he didn't move, either forward or backward. She could see the beading of perspiration at his hairline.

"*Madame* Rouge?" His voice was low and even, dangerously even. "Either I've just butted up against a rather unexpected hymen or there is some other explanation for how incredibly tight and incredibly virginal you feel."

Lucy could not believe they were having this discussion now, with him partway within her body. She'd imagined at the very most, after the deed was done, there might be some small question.

"I expect, Sir Robert," Lucy answered with as arch and confident a tone as she could summon, trying to hide her embarrassment, "that no other explanation is necessary. But will we really talk all night?"

He didn't answer and he still didn't move. She could see that he was conflicted, that he was deciding what to do. But this was Sir Robert, the man whose virility was legendary in Harridan House. She offered him a welcoming smile.

She gave him *that look*. As if he should ignore the most surprising fact of her virginity, the myriad questions it raised. As if he should fuck her like he had intended to. Well, he still intended to fuck her. Simply *not* as he had intended. If he pressed forward now, he would be doing both of them a disservice.

He pulled out of her, consoling his aching flesh with the knowledge that he would bury himself back inside her in good time.

She was surprised. He could see it in her expression, just before she twisted her body away from him and sat up on the bed. Now, she was angry.

"Sir Robert, I've invited you here to *my* rooms with the understanding that we had a shared desire. If you are unwilling to . . . perform, then I must ask you to leave."

Robert laughed. *Perform, indeed.* As if he were a stud to her mare. Not that he would mind that so much, come to think of it.

"I'm not leaving, my dear, I'm simply reassessing the field." Now she looked confused and angry at the same time, as if she weren't quite certain which direction to go.

Sitting there, with her legs tucked under her in that red silk dress pooling around her, her long hair falling to her waist and that silly strip of silk obscuring her face, she looked utterly irresistible. For the first time in two years he didn't *have* to resist her.

"Even if we leave the question of how such an interesting condition has impossibly occurred, I would never consider deflowering a lady so roughly. It's been quite a few years, but I do believe I know that a woman's first time is something that must be breached gently."

"I'm not entirely certain I want *you* anymore," she said, pointedly, almost petulantly.

He didn't laugh at that, although he wanted to. Instead, he joined her on the bed and took her face in his hands.

"Don't say that, Rouge," he murmured, his thumb running over the soft skin of her lips.

She met his gaze. There were only inches between them. He watched the muscles of her neck work as she swallowed.

"Lucy," she said, abruptly, her voice the merest breath. "That's my name."

"Lucy," he repeated, trying it out and finding that he liked the way it felt on his tongue.

All this time, these two years, she'd been the mysterious, seductive, experienced Rouge. Now she was the mysterious, seductive, knowledgeable yet virginal Lucy. She was not what he had expected. She was infinitely more interesting.

He closed the distance between them, buried his hands in the silken fall of her hair and kissed her.

This kiss was different. It feathered across her mouth and melted through her body like warm honey. With his hands cradling her head, and his lips on hers, she felt as if she were floating in a world that was only Sir Robert's mouth and Sir Robert's touch.

He moved slowly and gently across her skin, awakening every inch to sensation her imagination had never equaled.

She stared at his head, at the sandy blond waves of his hair, as he lowered his lips to her bosom, to the flesh revealed by the indecently cut dress. This strange moment differed from her daydreams. This was a *man* at her breast—who'd been *inside* of her only moments before.

Perhaps she'd gone too far. She could stop here, send him away, walk away. This moment did not need to happen.

As if he could read her thoughts, Robert lifted his head.

"Come back to me." His deep voice made her feel like chocolate melting atop the stove. But for his voice, the room was silent.

What was she doing?

He was watching her. She met his gaze and something else loosened within her, something she hadn't known was there.

The mood unfurled within her, bubbling out as a smile, a slanted look, a realization that this was her moment. He was hers.

Lucy lifted her hand to his neck, to the sliver of flesh visible above his cravat. She dragged her finger along that line, not looking away.

She traced the line of his jaw, ran the pad of her finger over his lips.

He caught her finger between his teeth, tugging on the silken glove, stroking her with his tongue and she felt it all the way down her body. She wasn't melting, she was being born into acute sensation.

There was the slightest hint of a smile on his lips as he caught her wrist in his own so that she could not withdraw her hand.

She had him off guard and he was trying to regain control. She wouldn't let him, not so fast. Tonight, he was hers.

She leaned forward, letting her weight fall upon him as she pressed her lips to the place just below his ear. He let go of her hand then, moving his to catch her at the waist, to shift them both so that she lay atop him.

Triumphantly, Lucy straddled his body, pressing herself against the still hard ridge of his cock that strained at his breeches.

"Now I have you exactly where I want you," she teased him, deftly unraveling his cravat, unbuttoning his coat. "Aren't you hot, Sir Robert? I do believe this is the most I've seen you wear during your trysts here."

"Yes," he agreed, studying her.

The night was nothing the way he had imagined it would be. Robert raised himself up on his elbows, letting her pull off his coat, one arm at a time. Then she pushed him back gently with her palm and he relaxed into the soft mattress. He forced himself to stay there, to let her have her way.

Her gloved hands caressed his shoulders. Something about the mixture of fabrics, the heavy silk of her gloves over the fine lawn of his shirt, intrigued him.

He lifted his hips slightly, nestling himself more fully between her legs. Her sharp inhalation pleased him.

She kneaded the muscles of his arms, working her way down to his forearms, to his wrists. Then she took one hand in both of her own and gave it her complete attention.

Well, perhaps one thing was the way he had imagined it would be: Rouge . . . *Lucy* was worth the wait.

She was finding parts of him that in all his forty-two years, Robert had never consciously noticed—the space between his fingers, the hollow at his ankle. He relaxed into her touch. He no longer had to force himself to let her have her way. He just wanted her to never stop.

Sometime later, when he lay naked and utterly relaxed upon

the bed, the sexual intensity a mere hum in the background, she began to use her mouth in all the places she had touched him.

His body came alive instantly and he pulled his mind out of a waking dream to watch her run her tongue from the base of his cock to the tip.

Then her mouth closed around his cock-head. Robert groaned at the exquisite sensation and at the delicious sight.

He reached an arm out toward her, needing to touch her, taking whatever limb of hers was closest. He found her calf under his fingers and he caressed her flesh the way she had caressed his.

She was moving so slowly upon him, watching him, as if she were listening to his every reaction to decide what to do next.

It made him feel like a viol being worked by a master. The thought did not settle well with him.

"You're a virgin," he said aloud, reminding himself, reminding her. Because where in the world was there another virgin who could work this kind of magic on a man? Perhaps in India, he'd heard, or among the Ottomans and their harems, but not here in England or anywhere on the continent.

She kept sucking him, but he felt her smile around him more than he saw it. It made him want to turn her over and thrust himself into her. He wanted her now.

He reached for her shoulders and gently pushed her away. She looked slightly confused as she raised up onto her forearm, her lips pink and swollen from their work.

She was an erotic fantasy come to life. His erotic fantasy.

"I like the way you taste, Sir Robert."

"Do you?" Robert asked, reaching around her to unfasten her dress. She shifted to give him better access.

"Exactly the way a man should taste to make a woman wish to have him in her mouth always."

He pushed the gaping dress off of her shoulder. She wiggled to pull it off of her and then tossed it on the floor.

Her pale naked body gleamed in the candlelight, and wrapping his arms around her, he lifted her breasts in his hands. He pressed his chest to her back, his mouth to her neck and watched his hands play.

"And do you taste exactly the way a woman should to make a man wish to lick her honey pot till she clenches at his tongue?"

He moved his right hand down, caressing the tight curls between her thighs, stroking the hot folds. He massaged her little pink button, enjoying her gasps and sighs. Remembering what she had felt like around him, wet and ready, he pushed his third finger into her.

When he withdrew his fingers, he held them up for both of them to see, slick with her cream.

"I think it's time to find out."

He brought his hand to his mouth, just beside her cheek. With the musky scent of her arousal heavy in the air, he licked his fingers.

"The verdict, Sir Robert?" she asked, her voice a shaky, breathy thing.

He moved so that he could give her his answer, pushing her down into the mattress, spreading her legs with his hands and burying his face in her cunt.

Her first gasp filled his ears even as the taste of her filled his mouth. He lapped at her folds, worked her, buried his fingers once more in the tight muscles of her pussy.

The feel of his tongue on her, his mouth sucking her clitoris, his fingers—all the things he did down there between her thighs—was beyond anything she could have imagined. The room swirled when his tongue swirled, and when he nibbled, his teeth grazing at the sensitive flesh, her body jerked up toward him. The heat rolled through her body, gathering in waves, each rising and then ebbing until suddenly her climax surged through her. Her knees came up of their own accord, her thighs pressing against his shoulders. Her hips bucked toward his greedy mouth, which still suckled on her, drew everything out of her.

Finally, he let go, his fingers retreated and her body still trembled, grasping at air. Robert loomed over her then, settling his hips between her thighs and she felt the blunted point of his cock touch her, part her.

He covered her with his body, took her mouth with his own, which tasted of her in a way she found both strange and arousing.

Then he thrust into her and all the pleasure stopped. She struggled to relax as he pushed against her, short powerful jabs that tore her inside each time he moved. She clenched at his arms, her fingers digging in. She knew she was probably hurting him but she couldn't let go.

She simply hadn't imagined it would hurt this much.

Then he was fully inside her, every part of him touching every part of her, and he stayed there, his hips stilled.

He kissed her cheek, moving toward her neck again—small little touches—until finally she began to feel the sweetness of them.

He was so big inside her. She was stretched and full of him.

He lifted himself up on his forearms and looked down into her face. She met his gaze.

This was Sir Robert George inside her. Absolutely nothing separated their bodies. It was odd, looking into his eyes, to be so aware of him, to be so joined with him.

Experimentally she squeezed him inside of her. She heard the sharp intake of his breath as he pulsed within her, as if he could grow any larger.

He moved his hips back, his cock retreating. She winced at the slight discomfort, but it was more like a pinch now, rather than any real pain.

He slid back inside of her again, till she felt his balls slap against her and she gasped at the feel of it.

He started a slow pattern of retreat and thrust. She marveled at each new sensation as he picked up both speed and force.

Finally, she held on, for he was grabbing her thighs in his arms, her buttocks in his hands, sucking at her neck, as he pounded into her.

He was fucking her, finding his own pleasure now, and she

wrapped herself around him, moving her hips to meet his, to aid him in his goal.

When she felt his body tighten, felt the acute pleasure of his cock readying for release, she felt an answering rise in her own body. His embrace tightened and his body jerked against hers, again and again.

Giddy, almost victorious with him climaxing in her arms, inside her body, Lucy hugged him tightly until he quieted and stilled.

Chapter Six

Robert stayed within her until he hardened and grew. That time, when he moved, there was hardly any discomfort and what there was, the pleasure quickly overshadowed.

Finally, after they'd both found their release, he lay beside her, pulled her tired, sweaty, sticky body against him, curving himself around her.

In the distance, church bells rang out the hour. All too soon, the sun would rise. He was expected in Richmond in the afternoon, but there was still time yet, time to lie here and contemplate the utterly unexpected events of the night.

He wasn't a man who went looking to sleep with virgins. In fact, it had been nearly thirty years since he had last and the experience hadn't been exactly pleasurable for either the girl or for him. He had assumed, of course, that his future wife would be one, but he wasn't particularly looking forward to it.

Tonight, however, had been a revelation. He understood suddenly, in the most primal way, why men prized virginity: he had been the first.

Robert knew quite clearly that if the night had been as he had expected, he would be able to walk away come morning and continue his life as always. But there had been that little thread of skin and all the mystery it suggested.

This was not a one-night affair. He would not let it be. Perhaps it would take a week, perhaps a month, but he wanted more.

He would have more.

Lucy didn't realize that she had fallen asleep until his wandering hand stirred her.

His voice cleaved the silence.

"May I?" he asked, touching the silk mask that still obscured her face.

She shook her head.

"You wish to keep your secrets," he said softly, "but there's one secret you gave up tonight. I thought I knew, without a doubt, that men had joined you here and left satisfied."

"There are many ways to satisfy a man." Lucy smirked, unwilling to reveal more than she wished. She wriggled against him to punctuate her words. His cock stiffened against her. "Just as there are many ways to satisfy a woman."

"True," Robert conceded. "But then why me? Why now?" He traced the circle of her nipple with his finger.

That one Lucy could answer honestly. "I was tired of anticipation. I knew I would be in good hands."

He lifted her leg, moving his knee beneath and then she felt his erection pressing against her. He grasped her hip and slid in.

It was very different from this angle, in this position, with them lying on their sides and him behind her. His thrusts were slower, more languid.

"I want to know all your secrets," he whispered in her ear.

She looked down at his right hand splayed over her breast.

Secrets.

"Perhaps I'll stay here, keep you in this bed, until you reveal them."

Which made her remember exactly where she had to be later that day: in the other end of London, where she did her duty every other week. However, morning was hours away and Lucy relaxed her attention back to the sinuous movement of Robert's hips, which made the two of them move together as if they were the ocean, swirling off the Cornish shore.

"You'll leave after breakfast," Lucy gasped, making certain he understood that here in Harridan House she was just as powerful as he. "But I'll welcome you back, Sir Robert, when you return."

"Tonight," he agreed, his mouth hot and open against her shoulder.

Chapter Seven

With Sir Robert gone, Lucy once more put on her gray dress and tidied the room. While it was the chambermaid's work to replace the sheets every day, the small bloodstains on the counterpane horrified Lucy. She stripped the bed quickly and remade it with fresh linens.

Lucy bundled the counterpane with the other laundry and hurried downstairs.

"Morning, Sara, Felicia," she greeted the two laundresses. Unlike most homes, the linens in each of Harridan House's rooms were changed daily and sometimes more frequently than that. There was constant work in the hot basement room.

"Morning, Lucy," Sara said, turning her head to offer a smile, but her hands never stopped moving and she quickly turned back to her work. Felicity, however, put down the cloth she was about to feed through the wringer.

"What gossip do you have for us, miss?"

Lucy laughed, depositing the sheets in the basket for Madame

Rouge's personal items and then taking a bar of lye soap to the stains on the counterpane to treat them before they soaked. She ran through the few details she remembered from the previous night, before Sir Robert had appeared.

It was not unusual to see Lucy with the laundresses for she often cleaned Madame Rouge's clothes herself. However, she was keenly aware how odd it felt to be washing off the last remnants of her virginity while chatting with the other women.

When finally she could retire to her own little room on the fourth floor of Harridan House, Lucy freshened up as best as she could, promising herself an indulgent bath when she returned in the evening.

She was late as it was, for it was Thursday again, her afternoon off, and at half past one she was due at Mary's.

The boardinghouse was in the east end of London, in the older warrens of the city. The proprietress, Mrs. Jones—although she'd never been married—mostly rented the rooms out to prostitutes.

Mary Penneck's room was on the third floor. Lucy knocked on the door and waited until she heard the plaintive cry.

"Is that you, Lucy? Well you'd better come in . . ."

Lucy opened the door and stepped into the cramped space. The room was at the rear of the house, and a narrow, dirty window, the wood frame splintered, was cracked open to let in the weak breeze off the river. Lucy fought the urge to close the window, for she found the summer stench of the Thames far worse than a stifling room.

". . . as I know you are late and if you had any consideration . . ."

Mary looked well, better than usual, lying in her bed, a blanket draped around her body.

". . . for a working woman . . ." Suddenly the tirade stopped and she sat up in her bed and scooted so she could rest her back against the wall. "You've fucked!"

Lucy blushed furiously despite herself.

"Don't deny it, Lucinda Leigh Penneck! You have that look

about you. Who was it? Was it that lusty baronet you keep blabbering on about?"

Lucy gaped at her sister. Had she really revealed so much that Mary could guess in but seconds all the wondrous news of the night? A bit deflated, Lucy sat herself down in the single frayed chair.

"And you gave it up for nothing too, didn't you? You'd have to go waste your virginity like that. I've told you time and again, sis, that when you're ready to do it, you tell me. There's many a man who'd pay a pretty price to pluck a flower."

"I didn't want just any man," Lucy mumbled stubbornly, half wishing she hadn't come. But she had a duty to her older sister that she couldn't simply forget or dispatch. After all, despite their youth, when Lucy had shown up on her doorstep, Mary had taken her in, at least until the fortuitous encounter with Lady Blount.

"What's done is done is what I always say," Mary said with a heavy sigh and a shake of her head that let Lucy know just how little the matter was done. For months now she'd hear complaints that Lucy could have made their fortune if only she'd sold her "flower" to the highest bidder. "So, do you have a taste for it now? You giving up all your lady's maiding to whore out?"

Lucy rolled her eyes at her sister's vulgarity. Mary was only two years older than Lucy but she had been living in London since her fourteenth year, when she'd run away from home. She'd turned to prostituting almost immediately, and for all Mary's advice, she had once in a drunken haze admitted to Lucy that she'd lost her virginity at the age of eleven to their cousin.

Lucy's experiences had given her different opportunities. She'd left home six months earlier than Mary to work as a maid in the manor house. Then, when the daughter of the house, Brigit, married, Lucy went with her to her new home. Then finally, when Brigit's new sister-in-law married and moved to London, Lucy became part of that household. She'd had ample opportunity to see the way the rich folk lived, to study their manner and speech.

The first time she had visited Mary, in a room even worse than this, Lucy had been horrified.

"I'm having what is termed an *affair*," Lucy returned evenly. "And for the record, I do believe I have a taste for it."

Mary laughed, clapping her hands.

"Well, you're my sister, of course you do. It's only surprising that it took you this long with all those months of watching others do the fucking. At least when we do buy that pub, there'll be two of us to service all the men."

No, Lucy thought decisively, *it would never come to that.*

Chapter Eight

Could he have achieved a greater contrast if he had tried? Robert thought as he entered the modest Tudor cottage in Richmond, his grandmother's house, where his mother now lived as well. Had it really been only that morning that he had left Lucy's decadent boudoir?

The elder Lady George sat in her Bath chair, her head drooping forward with sleep. His mother took her cup before it spilled and placed it back on the table.

"Forgive her, darling. She couldn't sleep last night, so worried she was about your cousin."

Robert winced. He never liked hearing about Archibald, his uncle's youngest child, much spoiled after two daughters, who at twenty-four had just been let go from his position as a land steward for Lord Cheltham.

"I offered him a position and he rejected the idea," Robert reminded her, dismissing the subject. He was not close with any of his cousins, which didn't stop the lot of them from asking for funds intermittently. When it had been his female cousin's sudden widowhood, his cousin Philip's new crop experiment, or his uncle's ill health, he had given freely. Archie, however, was a man of no discipline and his recent dismissal was due to his own extreme negligence.

There were many faults Robert could excuse in a man but that was not one of them. As dissipated as much of Robert's life was, his moral code was clear. Which was why this last year he had finally decided to marry and have a legitimate heir. With his uncle likely to die before him, and his cousin Archie next in line to inherit all the entailed property, it was clear to Robert that he needed a responsible successor.

"He's not my blood relative," —his mother excused herself— "any nephew of mine would recognize that working as a clerk, no matter how ignoble the job, breeds discipline." But there was something in her tone that suggested she thought Robert too particular, that he should demand his cousin work at such a demeaning effort as clerk.

"Naturally," Robert agreed, with a cynical twist of his lips.

"Of course, it does raise the question, when I may expect a grandchild," she continued. "And don't give me that uncouth answer that I have three already. I do not wish to hear of them again. It's really not fit for polite society."

"I said not a word, madam." Out of years of training, Robert forced himself not to fidget. He should be used to this by now, the snide little ways she made her disapproval known.

His mother sniffed.

"Well, I've found you a lovely girl," she whispered, "but your grandmother is adamant that you should keep Archie your heir. Regardless, she's a distant relative of mine, from Yorkshire. Uncle Clive has been caring for her since she was orphaned. He writes that she is everything one could wish for: young, attractive, properly modest, which you know is hard to find these days."

And clearly someone who would be properly grateful for his mother's interference and amenable to her influence.

"I will not be traveling to Yorkshire."

"I would never put you to such an inconvenience, Robert. I've invited Miss Ambrose to visit here."

Chapter Nine

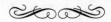

As far as Lucy knew, Sir Robert did not have a fixed schedule. He came as he pleased, in the afternoon or late in the evenings, three, four times in a week or not at all. She supposed his desires fluctuated with the day, as did hers.

However, this night, she knew he would come. He had said he would. She waited for him on the first floor at the top of the stairs. As she watched him ascend, she admired the way he walked, as if he were molten sensuality poured into his trousers. And his cheekbones—the man was blessed with the sort of hawkish features that only perfected with age.

She'd appreciated his physique on numerous occasions, but it was far different to observe that same body having known its power intimately.

"I've thought of you all day," Robert growled, moving to take her in his arms. She stopped him and took his arm instead. She might chance her dismissal by having an affair with Sir Robert, but she would not do so in the public rooms where anyone could see them.

"I thought of you too," Lucy admitted. "Actually I felt you, the memory of you inside me, with every step I took."

He looked pleased, which of course he should be, Lucy thought. She'd given him a rather large compliment.

He followed her into Madame Rouge's rooms, reaching for her again the instant the door closed behind him.

"Why only in private?" he asked just before his head dipped down and his lips met the sensitive skin of her neck.

Lucy let her head drop back against the door, let his arms be what kept her upright.

"You watch others," he continued, his kisses continuing as well, across her neck to her other shoulder.

"Hmmm," Lucy murmured, "do you *wish* to watch me?"

Robert's answer was to grab her buttocks and urge her up against him till she lost her balance completely and had to wrap her arms around him to keep upright. He lifted her up and his hot mouth closed over her nipple through the silk of her dress.

"You don't like answering questions, do you?" he said finally, letting her body slide back down his.

Shakily, she stepped away.

"This is Harridan House, Sir Robert," she reminded him, reaching to undress him. "The only question relevant is *how much pleasure.*"

When later she carefully lowered herself down on top of him, the fullness of his cock inside of her brought both pleasure and pain, reminding her of the newness of the activity.

There was no pain the next night nor any night after, and Lucy reveled in it, in her new lover. He pressed several times for explanations, for she was what he termed "an enigma." Lucy found herself wanting to answer him, wanting to give him any-thing he desired. She held back and teased him instead, invoking the throaty laugh she had learned from Lady Blount—a laugh she knew she had perfected in recent days as if the loss of her virginity had been the necessary payment.

Yet Sir Robert found different ways to question her and there was the night, some two weeks into the affair that she couldn't quite maintain the shield.

"Do you never take these off?" Robert asked, reaching over her to where her arms rested on the back of the chaise longue. He stroked her wrist through the silk gloves, feeling the pulse of her blood under his fingers. He vaguely remembered, even as he asked, having seen the pale curve of a forearm, jewels sparkling off of fingers. But everything in the past had melded into one indistinct dream. What was real was the present—this woman who had managed to surprise him when so few things did these days.

He slowly slid his hands down over her shoulders, the smooth skin of her back. Then he grasped the swell of her hips, and pulled her back against him to thrust deeper.

Lucy moaned, tossing her head, and he watched the long brown wave brush across her skin.

"A woman always removes her gloves before a meal and at many other times," she gasped.

"But do you?" he pressed, not really expecting her to answer. It had almost become a game between them, for him to ask questions and her to avoid answering them.

And then there was her disguise. Even naked beneath him, she still wore her mask and her gloves. At first he had found the secrecy intriguing, but with each day that passed, the strip of silk that covered her face infuriated him more.

He increased his pace, pumping into her, till her arms bent and she shuddered her climax, collapsing against the chaise, her cheek pressed against the velvet. He pulled back on her hips, to lift her up again. Her little moan was music and she tossed her hair again, moving the heavy mass away from her face—

Her bare face—for the red silk mask lay puddled beneath them.

His hips stilled. He studied her, barely breathing. Her face was still turned down, he could see nothing but the pale gleam of her ear.

He watched her shift her weight. One gloved arm reached down to pick up the mask.

Robert swiveled his hips against her so that she had to brace herself to keep her balance. He caught a fistful of her hair in his right hand and gently tugged. She resisted at first but then turned her face, slowly, the bare curve of her cheek illuminated by the candlelight.

He slid out of her. She pushed herself away from the chaise to stand as well.

There was nothing earthshaking about seeing Lucy this way, unmasked. She looked much as he had imagined she would. Yet somehow, bare and vulnerable, she was even more lovely.

She watched him as if waiting for him to say something, to do something.

He stepped closer and reached out, cradling her face in his hands. Her eyelashes fluttered down to rest against her cheeks.

"Lucy," he whispered. "Don't close your eyes now."

Finally, she opened her eyes, the clear green irises meeting his gaze.

He let go of her face and caught her up in his arms—taking her to the bed. He wanted to be inside her. He wanted to see her naked face when he climaxed inside her.

He covered her with his body, sliding in easily, his hands cradling her face once more.

In the aftermath of his release, Lucy nestled against him, finding all the hollows where her body fit perfectly, her face in the space between his shoulder and neck, her legs hooked just below his buttocks.

She'd let him see her. See almost all of her . . . her hair, her face . . .

There was a tension to the quiet of their embrace, an inevitability, as if having started the motion, there was nothing Lucy could do to prevent the consequences of her actions.

Nothing to do but face them when they came, *whatever they may be.*

Chapter Ten

Walking through Mr. Clarke's warehouse, viewing the bolts of silk, the rich fabrics, all of it made him think of Lucy, of the silk of her mask, her gloves—her body laid upon silken sheets.

He found himself at Harridan House hours before he had said he would come, not quite certain how he had gotten himself there. He caught a glimpse of red from the bottom of the stairs. A surge of fierce pleasure filled him. She was here, there would be no waiting. He ascended the stairs quickly, two at a time.

And then froze, one foot still paused in the air.

There, in a torrid embrace with a gentleman he had neither the time nor the inclination to recognize, was Lucy.

It was instinct that propelled Robert forward, pulling the man off her and connecting his fist to the man's shoulder even as he wrestled him to the ground.

When the man pushed him away, stumbling back, Robert followed.

"Stop it!" He heard the feminine cry but he didn't heed it. No one touched Lucy but him. *No one.*

He swung again, the pain of fist striking jaw barely registering.

"Sir Robert!" He felt the desperate tug on his arm and heard the strange timbre of Lucy's voice even as he turned, ready to let her know . . .

His gaze focused on her face—pale beneath the red silk. Pale and strange. Pale and strange and *not her*.

His hands dropped to his sides. His fists unclenched. The anger that had filled him so quickly dissipated in an instant.

And then he saw the pieces of the puzzle fitting together—*she wore no gloves*.

"Charles, Douglas," the woman said, this other Madame Rouge who was not Lucy, "Escort Sir Robert off the premises." She focused her steely gaze on him. "You are no longer welcome at Harridan House, sir. Please remove yourself."

He didn't speak, he couldn't. What on earth could he say that would make any sense? He bowed, ever so slightly, shrugging off the footmen who reached to restrain him. Then Robert, a more simmering anger building inside him, pivoted on his heel and walked out of Harridan House for the last time.

Chapter Eleven

L ucy was in Madame Rouge's dressing room, mending a small tear in the dress Lady Blount had been wearing before changing, when she heard Diana call for her. She dropped the dress onto the chair and quickly answered the summons.

"We need ice if there is any left, and bandages perhaps," Lady Blount snapped uncharacteristically.

One look at Sir Jason Blount's bruised face and hobbled stance and Lucy understood the tone. Violence was not frequent at Harridan House, but on occasion, men brought their enmities with them to the club.

"What happened?"

"Sir Robert George has gone mad." Diana barely looked at her, so intent was she on her new lover. "He's been barred from Harridan House. Remember that."

Lucy nodded, not trusting herself to speak, her mind racing even as her feet flew down the back stairs.

Robert had attacked Sir Jason Blount. *Why?*

It was all too clear—he must have seen Madame Rouge and Sir Jason together and thought Lady Blount was Lucy.

She'd never pegged Sir Robert for the jealous type. Then again, they had been exclusive lovers for the last two weeks. As far as she knew, he'd been with no one else and he knew intimately that he had been her first.

Which explained his possessiveness. Men had a thing about virginity—it was why it was so highly prized, why she'd even intended to wait until marriage.

The kitchen was oppressively hot. Almost blindly, Lucy looked around the busy room.

She had to go. She had to tell him it wasn't her so that he understood.

"Eleanor." Lucy grabbed the nearest girl. "Madame Rouge needs ice, if we have some, right away."

Lucy didn't wait to see if the girl obeyed her. She let herself out into the kitchen garden, tearing off her apron as she went.

She had to see him.

The footman didn't want to let her in, until she explained she was Lucy from Sir Robert's club and most certainly he would wish to see her. The footman clearly knew about his employer's reputation and he let her into the hall to wait.

Other than the clicking of her heels on the floor while she paced, she had only the vaguest impression of her surroundings.

Hardly a minute later she followed the footman down the hall toward the rear. *His study,* she thought, *or the library.*

Sir Robert was standing by the fireplace when she entered the room, in the act of pouring a glass of liquor. From the way he focused on his movement, she knew it was not his first.

He put the decanter down and faced her. He looked worse for the evening, his blond hair unruly and flopping over his brow, his shirt torn.

"Here you are," he said softly. *Dangerously,* she thought, as if everything had changed between them.

He held the glass in his hand precariously, gesturing with it, as if he didn't notice that the liquid within was near to sloshing over the sides and staining the fine wool carpet beneath their feet.

"I need to explain," Lucy rushed her words, desperate to convince him. "It wasn't me."

"I know."

"My lady, she came back and . . ." Suddenly Lucy stopped and stared at him. "You know?"

"I'm too old to be running around in a jealous rage, but that's what I did." He walked toward her, his gaze boring into hers. The corner of his right eyebrow twitched. "I've been stripped of my membership, but I don't think I can let you go that easily."

He still held his glass, but he laid his free hand on her cheek, his fingers tangling in her hair. His palm burned her skin where he touched but she didn't move.

"I want you."

She knew that and she wanted him too, but somehow, hearing those words, stark and potent, left her struggling for breath, struggling for clarity of mind.

"In my bed and my bed alone," he continued, "as my mistress." It wasn't a question and he didn't wait for an answer. He lowered his head and took her mouth with his own. She could taste the brandy on his breath and opened up to him, drunk with the kiss, with the night, with his demand.

His mistress. A vision of that life flashed through her mind—a life devoted solely to his pleasure.

She could feel the cool glass of brandy pressed against her back as he pulled her closer to him. She wanted to wrap her legs around him and hold him against her, against the need and heat building up inside.

Then he moved away, just enough that she opened her eyes and saw him looking down at her.

"I will take care of you, Lucy. You will want for nothing."

She pulled out of his grasp, pressing her palms to the sides of her head, turning so that she did not see his face. She needed to think and she simply could not do so in his presence. Even turned from him, she felt him. He filled every room he was in, permeated every one of her senses. She had never before met a man who made her forget everything so that even her name sounded by his deep voice was foreign and strange.

"How I didn't realize there were two of you playing one role, I will never understand," he said with a chagrined laugh. "The only similarity is the way you both fill the bodice of that red dress."

She turned back to him, stunned.

"She is softer than you, more curvy and round like a ripe peach. You are like my mare, Dancing Girl, well-developed, voluptuous in all the right places, but sleekly muscled and strong."

Never in her life had Lucy heard herself described that way. Indeed if any man had ever compared her to a horse, she might have slapped him. Somehow, the way Sir Robert said those words, the appreciative gleam in his eyes, she knew it was a compliment.

"Indeed, I'll give you Dancing Girl as a gift. Yes, it's fitting."

"I don't ride," Lucy admitted, for want of anything else to say.

"I'll teach you," Robert growled, reaching for her again. "I've found you to be a fast learner."

She hadn't said yes, Lucy reminded herself, even as she gave herself over to his embrace. She could think about it all later. Later, when he'd quenched this fire within her.

Contained it at least—if she waited for it to be quenched, she might as well say yes now.

Chapter Twelve

Sleepily, Lucy peered at him. The morning light peeked through the crack in the heavy draperies. Heavy, masculine draperies.

Morning. Oh, dear. With morning came decisions, consequences, confessions. Lucy wanted to close her eyes again and sink back into the erotic dream of his bed.

He moved, catching one of her wrists in his hand, running the pad of his thumb over the rough skin of her bare hand. They were the hands of a woman who worked, she thought unashamedly. She had covered them as Rouge only to conceal her identity.

But this morning her identity was a shiftless thing, unmotivated to commit to any one possibility, to choose any one way.

"So explain to me everything." Even as he spoke, he brought her palm to his lips.

Lucy did. She told him some of it, much of it. That she was lady's maid to Madame Rouge and that her duties had required the disguise.

"And who is Madame Rouge?" His tongue worked its way down to her wrist, distracting her.

"I can't tell you," Lucy said, hesitantly. "I *did* promise." When his mouth paused in its ministrations, she rushed on: "She has been exceedingly generous and good to me."

He held her wrist several inches away from him and stared at her, his eyebrows knitting together.

"You are now in *my* employ," he reminded her. She didn't correct him, didn't remind him that she hadn't yet agreed. It was all too clear to both of them that last night she had chosen. Lucy wondered briefly if he was disappointed with her, if he wished it had been the other Madame Rouge with whom he had engaged.

"Her secret is her own," Lucy said firmly, drawing her hand back. He didn't let go. "I cannot tell you."

Robert moved swiftly, rolling over till she was beneath him, bracing himself with his hands on either side of her shoulders.

"Then tell me," he pressed, the intensity of his gaze pinning her in place even if his hips were not pressed against hers, "who is Lucy? Besides being an impressively loyal woman?"

She let her breath out in a shaky laugh.

"I am exactly what you see, Sir Robert. Your new mistress who is quite distracted by . . ." She didn't bother finishing her sentence.

He was sliding inside her, thick and hard, and he knew exactly what was distracting her.

She would be loyal to him, she promised herself, even if she had betrayed Lady Blount, even if she had no idea what she was doing other than following the inevitable path of her desires.

She reached up to thread her fingers through his and he lowered himself atop her, his hips thrusting against hers. She wrapped her legs around him, echoing his movements, meeting his hips with her own, his cock with the tight squeeze of her cunt.

They writhed together, each focused on their own pleasure, on the sensations emanating from the place where they joined. He came before her, his cock pulsing and throbbing and just when she thought she would leave this encounter unfulfilled, her own climax overtook her.

He collapsed over her and she ran her hands over his body, until finally, she simply hugged him tightly.

She envisioned him as a starfish spread out above her and she clung to him in every way possible, thighs gripping him, ankles linked, hands clutching around his back, kneading his muscles.

This was some dreamlike world, where all that mattered was his body entwined with hers.

"I'll be back soon," he whispered into her ear. "Don't move. I want to come back to you here, exactly as you are."

He disengaged his body from hers, returning her to reality. Despite his words, she sat up quickly.

"I must though, Sir Robert. I have to tell La . . . give my resignation. I can't just disappear." There were choices and then there were consequences. Returning to face Lady Blount was the very least she could do.

Robert stared at her for a moment, as if frozen. Then he moved again, ringing for his valet.

"Naturally. And you wish to do so in person?"

Lucy nodded, clutching the sheets to her body as the valet entered the room. The man, somewhere in his thirties, was dressed impeccably in the height of fashion.

"Peters, this is Miss . . ." Robert shot her a quick look, his left eyebrow quirked in question.

"Miss Leigh," Lucy offered, biting her lower lip. It was the same name she'd given to Lady Blount two years ago. She did not wish to be the other Lucy, the one who still had a family in Cornwall, a family that might very well be as ashamed of her as they had been of Mary.

"Right. Miss Leigh. She'll be staying with us for a few days."

"Very good, sir," Peters said mildly. Of course, he looked to be a man who did everything mildly—as valets often were.

"Lucy," Robert turned his attention back to her just before he followed his valet into the dressing room. "Hurry back then, will you?"

"And you as well," she agreed. The thin paneled door closed between the rooms and she looked about his bedroom for the first time since she had arrived the day before, noticing the elegant, masculine decor. Everything in the room breathed of Robert.

Even her body, she thought with a laugh.

She was cutting off the life she had known, moving on yet again, but she didn't have to do this, she reminded herself. Even if Lady Blount would not keep her on after she learned of Lucy's actions, there were other jobs she could take. Other respectable jobs . . .

She pushed the thoughts out of her head as she swung her legs over the side of the bed. She wanted Robert, so the consequences be damned.

Chapter Thirteen

The bedroom was dim—dimmer than usual. Lucy hardly expected Lady Blount to be there, but there she was, lying on the bed, staring at the wall. Or in the direction of the wall.

"Where have you been?"

Lucy strained to hear the soft, plaintive words. Her employer didn't even turn to look at her.

"I . . . I had to attend to . . . Lady Blount, I am very sorry, but I can no longer work here."

That seemed to rouse the lady out of her malaise. She turned her head and peered at Lucy.

"You have found a better position?" The doubt in the lady's voice was obvious.

"No, I mean, well, it's a different position and it starts immediately."

Lucy hadn't intended to say more but there was that heavy silence, and Lady Blount stared at her.

"I . . . I will be Sir Robert George's mistress."

Again silence. Then Lady Blount began to laugh.

"You slept with him, as Madame Rouge, in my absence?"

Lucy nodded, embarrassed, guilty. She had known this would be difficult but knowing was no preparation.

"And thus it was jealousy, only, not for me."

Lucy bit her lip, nodding again.

"Go on Lucy, leave me then. It's all too ridiculous for words. Sir Robert George, indeed." Diana pressed her face back down in the pillow as she laughed again.

The laugh sounded rather close to tears. Lucy had never seen her employer cry. She did not wish to now.

It was cowardly, Lucy knew, but she fled.

Lucy didn't have many belongings to retrieve from Harridan House, and with the one small, worn leather valise that she had brought with her to London eight years earlier, she began the long walk back to Sir Robert's home.

A new beginning. Two years earlier, she had made a similar walk, one that had landed her in Harridan House. Now she was to be a mistress. Clearly, hers was a path of sin.

Walking in her sturdy black half boots and her plain gray dress, Lucy didn't feel in any way the temptress she had played at these past weeks. She felt like a maid. Like the servant she had been her whole life.

Sir Robert was not at home when she arrived, but the butler expressionlessly let her in, handed her belongings to the footman and asked if she would care for some tea while she waited or if she would prefer to be shown to the room that had been prepared for her.

There were too many people here in the hall watching her. She could feel the stares of all the servants, even though they blended in very well to the background, as she had done just days before.

The man snapped his fingers and a young maid stepped forward.

"Corrine, please show Miss Leigh to her room."

Lucy followed the girl up the stairs. Just like his bedroom, the hallway was elegant and tasteful, exceedingly masculine, as had been the entry hall. Of course, Sir Robert had lived here alone for over a decade, so naturally the decor would reflect his own tastes.

"It's a very nice room," Corrine said, "but no one has used it for years. Sir Robert's rooms are next door."

Then the maid opened up the door and inside Lucy found a space that was completely opposite to everything else she had seen.

Above the wainscoting, the walls were papered with a delicate pink rose pattern that made her feel as if she had entered a spring garden.

The high canopy bed with its freshly ironed sheets and hangings was done in ivory and green damask. Spring green, of course. For the first time in years, Lucy longed for home, for the lush fields of St. Keverne, for open space and fresh air.

"Sir Robert purchased this house from the late Lady Aubrey, and the whole place was supposedly like this. It must have been just beautiful," the maid informed her with a dreamy sigh. "He left this room, two of the guest rooms, and the small parlor with the original decor."

"It's lovely," Lucy agreed.

Corrine hurried over to the fireplace to nudge the flaming wood with the wrought-iron poker.

It was very uncomfortable. She was just a guest here, and as his mistress no less, but despite the slightly doubtful look in her eyes, the maid deferred to Lucy.

"Would you like anything else, miss?"

She could ask for anything. How decadent. In all her twenty-eight years, Lucy had never had the luxury of being attended to. She had assisted Lady Blount in every way, and before her there had been other employers, to each of whom such an action was commonplace rather than a novelty.

From now on, or at least as long as she was Sir Robert's mistress, it would be commonplace for her as well. If she was wise, and continued to save funds the way she had the last two years, when she moved on from here, she could continue such little indulgences.

"Yes, Corrine," Lucy said finally, straightening her spine. "I'd love a cup of chocolate and a bath."

Chapter Fourteen

Maneuvering his curricle through the busy streets on his way back from the solicitor's office, Robert enjoyed the tight handling of the new vehicle as he turned a corner. The construction was remarkable. He wasn't a man who took foolhardy risks with his life, but he was itching to take the carriage out to the open road and give it a good test. His horses would like that too, he thought, admiring the matched bays—their sloping shoulders and strong limbs.

Right. He'd have to send to his estate for Dancing Girl. He'd send a note as soon as he arrived home.

All in all, Robert was pleased. Perhaps he'd made a bit of a fool of himself the day before, and likely he'd hear about it from his friends when the gossip made the rounds, but he didn't think he'd miss Harridan House.

He'd been a member of the club for just over ten years. Ten good years during which he'd enjoyed the sexual freedom, the mutually pleasurable encounters with the women who either visited or were employed by the club.

Now he had a mistress—a delightful, unexpected, and fascinating mistress. As soon as she signed the papers that Mr. Burke was drafting, she was his by contract.

He knew very little about her. Mr. Burke's numerous questions had made that abundantly clear, but somehow, for a man who triple-checked his business agreements, it didn't seem to matter. He knew almost everything he needed to know about her: she was loyal, clever, wickedly skilled, and above all, *she had chosen him*.

His new mistress—who awaited him at home. Having a woman in his bachelor house was in and of itself a novelty. He felt like a young child with a new toy.

Giving in to all his desires, Robert urged the bays into a canter.

He found her in the bath, the soapy water concealing little of her body, her hair piled atop her head, a few stray tendrils damp and curling around her face.

A most well-developed toy.

She was alone, her head resting on the lip of the tub, her eyes closed.

He took a step forward into the bathing room. The air was moist and hot, beads of condensation clung to the blue Italian tiles that lined the walls and he could still see the faint curl of steam rising from the water.

"Robert," she sighed, not opening her eyes, but arching her back so that her breasts broke the surface of the water and her nipples puckered instantly in the cooler air. "I was thinking of you and here you are."

A perfect, erotic toy, as if it were Christmas already and not merely the middle of August.

He adjusted his suddenly uncomfortable trousers.

"Where is the maid to help you?" he asked.

Lucy opened her eyes finally, her gaze unerringly finding him. "I've been a lady's maid much of my life," she reminded him. "I asked Corrine to leave."

Robert pulled a stool away from the wall and after shrugging out of his coat, sat down.

"You were a lady's maid before Harridan House?"

"Yes, since my twelfth year," she informed him with a little smile, as if she knew just what question he would ask next.

Robert began the slow process of unfastening his hessians instead.

"I've never had anyone to wait on me," Lucy said abruptly, filling the silence.

Of course Madame Rouge would have servants to wait on her, but Lucy had not truly been Madame Rouge.

Robert pulled off one heavy boot, and moved to the next. There was an art to taking off one's own boots with elegance.

"You'll have to get used to it then," he said finally, placing his boots to the side and moving on to his cravat. He noticed that she looked away from him.

"I must warn you that if you are intending to join me in this bath, it will never do."

His cravat fluttered to the ground. It was only a matter of the wrist, a shrug of the shoulders, to undo and remove his waistcoat.

"An interesting idea," he murmured, "but the tub is far too small."

"And the water is losing its heat," Lucy agreed.

Robert stood and crossed the room to retrieve the large, soft bath towel that lay folded on a bench. As he walked back to the tub, he shook it out and held it up in invitation.

Lucy stood and the water poured off of her body as if she were Aphrodite rising from the half shell.

Like his mare, he had said only a day ago, and he still thought the description apt. As she raised her leg to step over the edge of the tub, her sleek muscles worked and flexed, her movements fluid and graceful yet utterly economical. In that way she was like his matched bays, a perfect mix of rare beauty and practicality.

And rare spirit?

Both feet flat on the tile floor, she stepped into the waiting towel, which he wrapped around her, folding her in his arms. He knew vaguely, as he kissed her, that his clothes were growing damp and uncomfortable.

Which was just as well. They were clearly getting in the way.

Chapter Fifteen

He kept her in his house for two days. They hardly left the bedroom. He canceled his business meetings, everything, until there was an appointment that he could not refuse.

"But I'll be back soon. Perhaps after, we'll go to Vauxhall." His gaze fell on her gray dress, crumpled on the floor where they had left it days ago. She looked as well. She should have done something with it, asked Corrine to launder it, anything but leave it there.

"Don't you have anything else?"

She shook her head. "Nothing that's any better."

"Then we'll take care of that this afternoon."

Lucy watched him leave. She pulled the bed cord for Corrine and flopped back under the covers, snuggling up in the place that was still warm from his body.

She liked this dreamworld into which she had awakened. New dresses, all for her. Any new dresses she had ever had had been made by her own hand or her mother's. Her best dresses had always been hand-me-downs from her employers that she had gratefully accepted and altered.

Visions of fashionable gowns filled her head, material she had hemmed, or mended, spot cleaned or ironed. *Silk stockings, velvet bonnets, lace trimmings and ivory fans . . .*

When Robert returned a few hours later, he took her up in the landau with the roof closed despite the fine weather.

"Do you have a dressmaker you prefer?" Sir Robert asked, as he handed her up into the carriage. "Peters recommended Madame Ferrars, Mrs. Baswick or Mrs. Abernathy."

"I've only heard of Mrs. Baswick," Lucy said with a shrug. "Her work was lovely but that was years ago."

"We'll try her then." Robert gave his coachman the direction and then followed her inside.

The small shop was situated on Oxford Street beside a millinery shop whose front window displayed a compelling array of bonnets. Tearing her gaze away and into Mrs. Baswick's shop, she could see that it was empty of other customers. That was a bit of luck, for even the dress she wore, her best rose muslin dress, was several years old and much mended.

Lucy recognized the thin, angular dressmaker immediately, despite the spectacles that now perched upon the bridge of her nose. The woman wore her gray curls under an embroidered mobcap that looked similar to one of the designs Lucy had seen in the window of the store next door.

"Good afternoon, Sir . . ." Mrs. Baswick greeted Sir Robert, even as she eyed Lucy speculatively. Lucy hadn't expected to be recognized, as lady's maids were rarely noticed, but the slightly disapproving look in the woman's gaze startled her. Was it that obvious she was now one of the *fashionably impure*? Or was it simply that Lucy's dress was so appalling the woman couldn't keep her distaste from showing?

"Sir Robert George," he filled in for her, handing her his card. "Good afternoon to you, ma'am." Lucy pasted a polite little smile on her face, waiting to be acknowledged.

"I am Mrs. Baswick. I am honored you've found my shop. How may I help you, Sir Robert?"

"This is Miss Leigh," he introduced her. "I believe she needs everything."

It was a fairy tale and she was Cinderella. For the next hour, Lucy was measured and prodded, draped with fabrics and plied with designs.

Robert watched her, commenting infrequently.

Then Mrs. Baswick ushered Lucy into the dressing room and had her try on one of the few dresses she had readymade, almost finished.

The hem was unfinished and fell long on the floor, in case a taller lady should wish it. It was an evening gown, and the neckline was low, though not scandalously so, for having worked at Harridan House, Lucy had seen dresses that revealed far more of the breasts. In fact, it was almost too respectable.

It was blue. A fine sky blue with a trim of Belgian lace about the sleeves. Staring in the mirror, Lucy hardly recognized herself. All the fine gowns she had worn as Madame Rouge had been utterly indecent.

"And we'll have a petticoat made for you, miss, with the same lace."

"Should we make the neckline lower?" Lucy asked. Wasn't she supposed to be more on display? Wasn't that what a courtesan did? She knew nothing about what was expected of her.

"Lower?" the woman gasped, as if she didn't know that Lucy was Sir Robert's mistress. "Hush now. Go on out, Miss Leigh, and show Sir Robert the dress."

As Lucy stepped around the door she could hear the woman huffing, "lower," but all her attention was focused on Robert, who lounged on the sofa, his legs stretched out before him as if he were at home or at his club rather than the shop.

He looked up. She felt his gaze run over her but his expression didn't change. Although his right eyebrow flickered in that funny way it sometimes did. She hadn't deciphered the mannerism yet.

"She looks lovely, doesn't she?" Mrs. Baswick asked, bustling around Lucy to speak to Sir Robert. "As if the dress were made for her. And by tomorrow, I promise, it will look exactly as if it had been!"

Robert nodded. "Tonight you say?"

"Absolutely!" the dressmaker assured him.

"Good." Robert stood, slapping his gloves, which hung loosely from his right hand, on his thigh as if it was a whip he held instead and he intended to ride. "Well, then, you'd better change, Lucy."

His gaze found hers and her own eyes widened in sudden understanding. They couldn't. Surely not here!

Not a hint of levity expressed itself on Robert's face. She knew that look well. He wanted her and he would have her.

So this was what it was like to be a mistress. A mistress could do as she wished, be as outrageous as she wanted, in public or in private. A sudden giddy happiness inspired a conspiratorial smile as she turned around again toward the dressing room.

"Sir!" Mrs. Baswick gasped when Robert followed her. "I must insist you await Miss Leigh out here."

"But Mrs. Baswick," Lucy protested quickly, struggling not to laugh. "I need Sir Robert's assistance."

"I believe that I can assist you," Mrs. Baswick returned, her voice icy. "As I have all afternoon."

"Ah, but you haven't my touch, Mrs. Baswick," Robert interjected, as if it were completely proper to say such a thing. "And I should hate to have to take my business elsewhere."

Lucy had never seen anyone's face turn quite so red as the dressmaker's.

It was shameless, that's what it was, Lucy thought when Robert shut the door behind him and rested his hands on her bare shoulders. He turned her around so that she faced away from him and deftly undid the buttons at her back.

"Arms up," he urged, his voice low.

She followed his directions. "You've done this before, have you?"

He pulled the dress up over her head and then draped it across the chair. She still wore her plain cotton chemise and unadorned petticoat. Without the lovely blue dress, she felt equally plain.

But then his mouth was on her neck, where the curve met her shoulder and his hands covered her breasts, lifting their weight through the worn fabric. She sighed, her own hands reaching back, caressing his thighs.

He turned her in his arms and pushed her against the wall.

"Hold on to me."

She draped her arms around his neck, leaning against the wall for support when the touch of his hands on her thighs as he lifted her skirts sent a bolt of pure heat to her core.

"Wrap your legs around me." Again, she did as he said, and he shifted her weight in his arms. She could feel his hand between them, unfastening his breeches.

Then he pulled his hips ever so slightly back and the round tip of his cock pressed against her.

He slid inside smoothly and the movement thrust her against the wall.

She leaned her head forward and kissed him, tugging on his lip. His hips pounded against her and she held on. He wasn't gentle and she reveled in the pure maleness of him, the joy of it all.

Lucy was surprised when she came, crying aloud into the warm air that smelled of them. Her head fell back, bumping against the hard wall, but she hardly noticed. His hips kept pumping against her as he moved toward his own release. His mouth fastened on her neck, licking her hungrily.

She felt his cock grow inside her, that moment just before, and then he pushed in deep, clutching her buttocks and holding her tight against him as his body shuddered and rocked.

He lifted his head and kissed her—a long, deep, searching kiss.

Finally he broke away and slowly, one leg at a time, let her stand.

Her petticoats fell, covering her, but the dampness between her legs made her feel naked.

He fastened his breeches and then helped her into her dress. Standing behind her once more he kissed her nape.

"I haven't actually."

"Haven't what?"

Lucy could feel his breath hot against her ear, his lips so close to her skin but not touching.

"Fucked at the dressmaker." Then he caught her earlobe between his teeth and tugged lightly.

It was wicked of them, utterly wicked, but Lucy didn't avoid the dressmaker's eyes when they entered the main room. After all, if she was to embrace this new life, this freedom was one of the consequences. And Lucy always faced the consequences.

Chapter Sixteen

The following day, Robert's secretary informed him that rooms had been obtained for Miss Leigh and a temporary staff had been hired. He took Lucy to the large apartment, which the landlord, a Frenchman, referred to as a *maisonette*. Lucy didn't know French but she did know that two stories of the stately stone building were now her new abode.

Sir Robert had seen to everything, or rather, had instructed his secretary, Joshua Pale, to see to everything. From the lovely, airy apartment of rooms to the name of the bank in which he'd deposited funds for her disposal, to the small staff, footman, cook and maid, to wait upon her.

Lucy was quite certain she had never been more pampered in her entire life. There was nothing, absolutely nothing she was expected to do but decorate the apartment as she liked, shop for whatever clothing she desired and attend to every wish Robert had when he came to visit her.

The last could hardly be too difficult, as she seemed to share his every desire.

Tonight would be the first night he came to her—a man visiting his mistress.

Robert left her at the apartment and went back to his house to change for dinner. She had only been there three days, but his room still smelled of her, still felt like she should be there.

Perhaps he should have kept her here, he mused, but even a man with a reputation like Robert's could hardly go that far. Certainly not if he intended to marry.

Peters handed him a freshly starched cravat. Robert tied it simply, ignoring the small moue of disapproval from his valet. Peters had been in his employ for three years now, and every day threatened to leave him for a more fashionable man.

"If I might say . . ."

"No, Peters, you may not," Robert interrupted. "I am not courting this evening. I am merely observing the young lady."

"And at what point, sir, does observation become courting?"

Robert sighed. That was the trouble with Peters—he had opinions.

"When I invite the lady out for a drive or call on her, or any other activity that takes me out of my way."

"If I might be permitted, sir," Peters began again, "with Miss Hargreaves you were much clearer in your intentions."

True, of course, but then Lady Stanton, née Carolina Hargreaves, had held far more appeal. The same way Lucy appealed to him.

No, not the same. Lucy was far more appealing.

"Listen, Peters, I shall let you know when I am courting," Robert said finally, as the valet helped him on with his jacket. "Then you may have your chance at my cravat."

"Well, Robert?" Clarissa Molineaux caught his arm with her own plump one as soon as they entered the drawing room after dinner and pulled him into a corner. "Miss Clarke was your partner for dinner, *again*. You do realize that if you don't call on her tomorrow or send her flowers at the very least, you will have *no chance* with her?"

He sighed, following Clarissa's gaze to where Emmaline Clarke now sat, chatting with Mrs. Hodgkiss, whose husband, Geoffrey, worked at Robert's bank.

She was a lovely girl. She had the sort of pale blond beauty that seemed to come with a life spent indoors. Her breasts were small, though she apparently wore one of those devices that gave a little more heft to a woman's bosom. The lace fichu she wore regrettably obscured the resulting upper curve. The rest of her body was fine; she was the sort of woman who was small on top but well-rounded in the hips and thighs.

"And I might add, my friend, that taking a mistress . . ."

Robert's gaze shot back to Clarissa.

". . . when you are thinking of taking a wife is not the most intelligent move."

"How in God's name did you hear of that?"

"News does travel," Clarissa said, rolling her brown eyes. "Let us hope that Mrs. Hodgkiss is not revealing that information to Miss Clarke."

Robert's lips thinned as he contemplated the idea. But he'd be damned if he'd make any excuses for his life to anyone, especially not to some miss out of the schoolroom.

"It's just as well she knows now," Robert said. "For I won't be giving Lucy up simply because I've taken a wife."

"Lucy," Clarissa repeated. "Somehow I expected her name to be something far more sinful, like . . . like Esmerelda, or Deirdre, or . . ."

"Stop!" Robert laughed, holding up his hand. But there was just the slightest edge to his laugh. He didn't want to talk about Lucy with anyone, to share her even in words. Really, couldn't a man have anything private anymore?

Midnight came and went and finally the guests began to leave.

This was the sort of evening on which, just five days ago, he would have taken himself to Harridan House. And two weeks ago, he would have lusted after Madame Rouge but pleasured himself with one or more of the other lovely whores.

Tonight, sleeping in a bed he had paid for, in an apartment he had rented, lay Lucy.

It had been twelve years since he'd last kept a mistress and then he had tired of the woman quickly, visiting other women's beds more frequently than hers. He wondered how long it would take him to tire of Lucy.

Perhaps he wouldn't.

He wanted to dismiss all the thoughts of the future, as he had managed to do for the last twenty years, living for each moment.

When he arrived back at his house, the emptiness of his bedroom struck him anew. Then he wondered why he was there when his mistress was halfway across the city.

It was only a matter of minutes before he had his coat on again. With luck, his groom hadn't even finished unhitching the carriage.

Chapter Seventeen

R obert felt like a thief letting himself in to the *maisonette*. A candle still burned in the entryway, but clearly, the maid had gone to sleep and the footman as well. He walked upstairs as quietly as possible, wincing when the wood creaked beneath his boots.

As he crossed the hallway, he saw that the soft glow of candlelight flickered beneath the door of Lucy's room.

The door opened as he neared and suddenly he was filled with the fragrant, lacy armful of Lucy in her new night rail, her lips on his neck.

He held her, savoring the feel of her lush body under his hands and her exquisite tongue on his skin.

"I thought perhaps you'd be asleep, and I'd have to wake you," he managed to say, the words a half groan as she pressed herself against him, her thigh nudging itself between his legs.

"I've always kept late hours," Lucy explained in a rush between kisses, "and of course, I hoped that you'd come."

Then she broke away and pulled him after her. He followed almost helplessly, deliriously.

So, this was the joy of having a mistress.

With the bedroom door closed behind them, she reached for

him, undressing him as carefully as his valet had attempted to dress him only hours earlier.

When he was naked and hard in her hands, he finally took control, lifting her and placing her gently on the bed.

The fine, thin snowy-white nightgown hardly concealed anything.

"Do you like it here?" he asked, running his hands down her body, molding the fabric to her curves.

"It's a lovely place," Lucy answered on a sharp intake of breath. She fidgeted under his hands, reaching for him with her legs, running one soft foot down his calf. "But more lovely with you here, touching me."

It was the answer that was more than right, that was perfect, and he wondered at how such simple words could make his desire grow more fervent.

Her toes trailed over his thigh and then found his cock, running up and down the length.

Robert pushed her leg away, spreading her open, and leaned forward over her body till he touched her, touched the greedy suction of her wet heat.

He thrust in smoothly, pulling her hips up toward him and she extended the motion by wrapping her legs around him and holding him tight. Her soft, pleased sigh filled his ears as they matched their rhythm, each urging the other on.

His mouth opened hot, ravenously on her neck until she twisted her head away, panting.

There was no way in hell he would be giving Lucy up, not for any woman, any wife.

"You're mine, Lucy," he grunted, punctuating his words with the forward thrust of his cock.

Her hands reaching under his thighs to urge him on echoed her soft "yes." "As long as you wish," she added breathlessly.

Which didn't sit right with him, though he didn't know why. Robert pushed his thoughts away and concentrated on the feel of her wet cunt gripping him. There would be time enough for thinking later. Now was the time for pleasure.

Chapter Eighteen

Lucy dreaded seeing her sister. She paid a boy on the street to take Mary a note saying she was unable to come that Thursday.

Mary sent back a note by the boy that clearly something was havey-cavy and if Lucy did not visit immediately, she would come to Harridan House to find her.

Although Lucy hadn't seen her sister outside of that room in three months, she wouldn't put it past Mary to finally rouse herself to action.

"Lord! Who turned into the bloody duchess?" Mary gaped at her when she walked in. Lucy had worn one of her old dresses for the visit, but she couldn't help pairing it with one of her new bonnets, her new half boots and a lovely new pale blue pelisse.

"I've left Harridan House," Lucy announced, knowing she may as well get this part over with. "I'm Sir Robert's mistress now."

Mary gaped at her, and then her stare cracked into a grin and a full-bodied laugh.

"You're more like me than you thought, aren't you, sis? Blood will tell, they always say. You thought you could keep yourself high and mighty, so pure in the middle of a house of sin. Untouched. But here you are, turning to whoring just like me."

Lucy took a deep breath and stared determinedly out the window. She could see, between two other buildings, a sliver of gray sky.

Perhaps she could simply give her sister a good portion of her savings and have done with it, never see her again.

"Well it's a bit of luck, anyway." Mary nodded. "He'll pay for that virginity now one way or another. Has he given you any baubles yet? Any tiny little diamonds?" She laughed again.

"It's not like that, Mary." Lucy sighed. "I have everything I could want, a new wardrobe, an apartment, a maid and a cook! And of course, him."

"Him," Mary scoffed. "And what's with the rag of a dress you're wearing if he treats you so well? You've got a few fripperies I see, but where are the goods?"

Lucy sighed heavily, not trying to hide her displeasure.

"Will you be inviting me over for tea?" Mary goaded her, mimicking Lucy's more modulated tones, the manner of speaking she had worked hard at perfecting. "I'd like to see what a fancy place you have before he tires of you."

"The plan, Mary, has always been to save up until we can buy that tavern. And that's *your* dream, not mine, so *let me be.*"

"I hear St. Keverne in your voice," Mary snapped.

Lucy unclenched her fists. If Mary wished to have the last word she was welcome to it. All Lucy wanted was to leave.

Although, as she made her way back down the creaking stairs, she knew it was the truth she wanted to leave.

Chapter Nineteen

Robert sent flowers to Miss Clarke. As Clarissa had said, it was the least he could do if he wished to keep her open to his suit. But somehow it felt like too great a step in the lady's direction.

Then he set out on the hour journey to Richmond to pay his duty call on his mother.

The instant he stepped into his mother's sitting room a few

minutes before lunch, he wished he hadn't gone. There sat his
mother; his grandmother, who was wide awake and staring at him
through her quizzing glass as if she had forgotten who he was; and
a young, bland, fresh-faced girl in country togs who stared at him
with an expression of the utmost hopeful expectation.

He had forgotten about the poor orphaned relation whom his
mother had invited down for his perusal.

"Robert, dear, come and have a seat," his mother directed,
pointing toward the chair closest to where the girl sat. "You
haven't met Miss Ambrose yet. She's Uncle Clive's ward, whom
I've invited for a visit."

His lips twisted into a rueful smile at being forced to play at
the charade of not knowing exactly why Miss Ambrose was here.

Forced? Who had ever forced him to do anything?

He sat through the next two hours with the utmost tolerance. In fact the luncheon was almost bearable because, as his
mother and grandmother were putting on their best behavior for
Miss Ambrose, there wasn't any discussion of his nephew Archie's
antics.

Nothing spoiled a meal like hearing about Archibald. The boy
was the very reason Robert was considering marriage in the first
place.

One thing was certain, if he intended to pursue this whole mat-
rimony thing, he should get about it as soon as possible. It wasn't
like him to dawdle about decisions, and as far as Miss Clarke was
concerned, he had been dawdling for almost a month.

As for Miss Ambrose, Robert had not the slightest twinge of
indecision. He had known from the first moment he saw the girl,
who did seem to be lovely in temperament if not in form, that he
would not marry her. At the very least, Miss Clarke, who held no
particular attraction for him either, came with her father's good-
will and business contracts.

Miss Ambrose held little attraction for him and his mother's
approbation took away what small amount there was.

Chapter Twenty

It took Lucy a good portion of the morning to cleanse her mind and spirit of her visit to Mary, but determinedly, she pushed away any doubt and self-incriminations and threw herself back into her new life.

She was in the parlor, fresh from the bath and lounging in her dressing gown with the latest issue of *La Belle Assemblee,* when Robert arrived.

"Get up, you lazy girl," he urged, stroking the underside of her bare foot. "It's time for your first riding lesson."

Lucy snatched her foot away as his caress turned ticklish.

"I believe I've already had that lesson," Lucy returned, scrambling to her knees on the sofa and reaching for him, "but I'll take my fortieth, or fiftieth . . ."

"Unfortunately," Robert murmured as she pressed herself against him, her face resting against his waistcoat, her fingers caressing the insides of his thighs through his leather breeches, "today will be sidesaddle. If we were in the country I'd teach you astride." His hands caught her around her waist and pulled her up so that her feet dragged off the sofa and dangled in the air for a long moment before she slid down his body to stand, her legs caught between his.

Lucy stared at his mouth, almost even with hers now. He had such a lovely mouth, the lips so well defined and expressive.

"You're right, I don't know sidesaddle. Show me?" Lucy leaned forward and pressed her lips to his. She caught his lower lip between her teeth.

He tasted good, like an early-afternoon brandy, and he smelled good too.

Then he pulled away.

"I think, rather," he said, "you'll have to show me what you've learned later. For now, I assume there's a riding habit in your new wardrobe?"

Lucy nodded. In fact there was a lovely russet habit, but while she was excited to wear it, she wasn't particularly excited about the horse part. The last time she'd ridden a horse was when she was six and her father pulled her up in front of him on the ancient pony that pulled the cart.

"It's in the bedroom." She started for the door and then paused, flashing Robert a flirtatious smile. "I'll need a little assistance. I sent Charlotte out to buy some pins."

He followed her and she was ridiculously pleased that he did. He even helped her dress, although he made an abominable lady's maid. Of course, Lucy had to admit, that was really her fault, since she was spending much more time trying to convince him to take his clothes off than to dress her.

It was his fault too, Lucy amended, when, her hands above her head, fastening her hair into some semblance of a fashionable knot onto which to perch the adorable hat that matched the dress, he pressed his mouth to the back of her neck. Her hands stilled, her arms shaking as she relaxed back into the kiss.

"You're wicked, Robert."

"Am I?" He moved away, not enough that she couldn't feel his heat so close to her body. She struggled valiantly to finish her hair.

"Yes, and you're torturing me." She caught his eyes in the mirror and held the gaze. "We could always put off the lesson till tomorrow?"

She watched him place his hands on either side of her hips, watched their progress up her body to cup her breasts. His hands were so hot she felt as if there were almost nothing between them and her skin. Despite the cloth, his thumbs found her nipples and rubbed circles around them till she strained against the fabric.

"Are you afraid, Lucy?"

"No," she whispered. His eyebrow arched upward and Lucy laughed ruefully, dropping her hands to cover his. "Perhaps I am a bit."

"It will be all right. I'm a good teacher."

His smile was wicked, the sort of smile that gave her every confidence that here in the bedroom he could teach her all manners of things.

"Well, I suppose if we are to do this before it gets dark, we may as well do it." Lucy sighed.

His groom had kept the horses walking outside back and forth on the street and now they were just a few yards away. There was a gray stallion, which she recognized as Robert's new highly prized Arabian, and then there was the mare.

She was an exquisite animal, sleekly curved and muscled, her mane glossy and flowing down her neck. And those legs—so delicate it was hard to believe that even four of them could keep the animal upright—prancing really, almost as if she were showing off for them.

Dancing Girl. The name fit and the horse was hers. *Hers.*

Suddenly Lucy was more excited than afraid.

"So what do we do?"

"For now," Robert said, "we'll just seat you, and Harry will lead your horse as we walk the horses to the park slowly."

Lucy did not feel particularly graceful when Robert helped her up and she settled into the saddle. It was difficult to keep her balance even with the horse standing still. But of course, the horse was never truly standing still, she was always moving in some way, dancing.

Once Lucy was seated and holding on tightly, keeping her left foot carefully still, Robert mounted his own horse.

"Did you have a nice day?" Lucy asked

"It was well enough," Robert answered, noncommittal. She knew he had gone to visit his mother, who lived with his grandmother. She thought of her own parents, much farther away than an hour's ride. "My mother invited a Miss Ambrose to stay with her."

There was something about the way he said the woman's name that made Lucy shiver.

"*A Miss Ambrose?*" Lucy repeated. "That sounds rather matrimonial." He looked at her in surprise and Lucy knew that her instinct had been correct. "Do you plan to marry? Oh, but of course you will, how silly of me!" She waved her hand in the air as she laughed.

"Don't let it worry you about us, Lucy," Robert assured her. "It will have no bearing on the situation."

She shot him a sidelong look, the only sort of look she could really do without shifting her posture. Studying his profile, she saw the small line at the corner of his mouth that belied his unconcern. Perhaps it was his age, that she thought him a bachelor set in his ways, but somehow she hadn't expected that he might marry. Which was a foolish assumption to have made, one she couldn't afford. She opened her mouth and then shut it again.

If he wished to pretend, then that is what she would do. For now.

They arrived, after what had seemed an eternity, at Hyde Park. Lucy's legs and backside were already sore from the unusual motion, but Robert insisted on teaching her the basics of mounting and dismounting, proper use of the reins, the whip and her left leg. Every time Dancing Girl responded to one of her commands, Lucy felt as though she had achieved a great victory.

Of course, Dancing Girl had known all this for quite a while; it was Lucy who was learning.

There were too many people around. Not as many as during the season, she remembered from having escorted her former employer, Mrs. Marrack, on occasion, but there were still a great many, and of those, a few who were obviously birds of paradise. *Like her.* Which was probably why they were attracting so many curious stares. That or her abysmal attempts at riding.

It was only on the way back, when Harry once again took the reins and all that Lucy had to concentrate on was keeping her balance and staying in the saddle, that her mind turned once more to the idea of Robert marrying.

The circumstance would change if he took a wife. Clearly, he was looking, so change was even closer than she had imagined. She had just been settling into this new role in life. He might be away much of the day when he had business or social engagements, but he had spent every night with her. That, of course, would change. She'd have to share him with some nameless woman. Some other woman who lived in that beautiful house with him, who slept in that rose bedroom and took one of the parlors for her own.

Nearly a month before, when Lucy had first taken him to her bed, she hadn't thought beyond that night. Having watched him with so many women over the years, she had never imagined that one day she would have his undivided attention. *Or that she'd wish to guard it jealously.*

Chapter Twenty-One

For two weeks Lucy had been his mistress. Two very quiet weeks, for after a few days the excitement of shopping with his carte blanche paled.

The day after he'd taught her to ride, he'd had to leave town for Portsmouth to check on a ship that was due to arrive. That night with him gone was pure torture.

However, Lucy hadn't realized she was lonely for female companionship until the day Charlotte handed her a cream-colored card and said it had just been delivered by a handsome footman who wondered if the lady of the house was at home.

Lucy enjoyed the way the crisp card felt between her fingers. The lotion she'd been using had softened the calluses and she was delighting in the more heightened sensation of touch.

The name on the card was vaguely familiar and she tugged at the faint wisps of memory.

Miss Penelope Partridge.

Suddenly she knew.

"Yes, Charlotte, I am at home."

Of course she would be at home to this woman. Who would not be interested in meeting the infamous Miss Partridge, who, according to the gossip of Harridan House, had taken both the London stage and the beds of the aristocracy by storm when she'd arrived on the scene more than two decades ago?

Tall and voluptuous, with black hair and striking eyes. The woman might be in her late thirties, but age had only refined and sculpted her beauty.

"Do you know who I am?"

"Miss Partridge, your reputation precedes you."

The woman's satisfied smile slid quickly back into haughtiness.

"I've come to meet you, of course," the lady said, studying Lucy carefully. "It would be utterly remiss of me, upon hearing that the infamous Sir Robert George has finally taken himself a mistress, to not find out just what new competition has entered the field."

"Competition?"

"I suppose you could hardly be called that. You're much older than I imagined. What are you? Twenty-six?"

"Eight and twenty," Lucy returned, despite herself, too many years of servitude ingrained in her.

"Eight and twenty," the woman repeated, shaking her head. "And Sir Robert just plucked you up from obscurity, from some remote Cornish village if I trust my ear, and made you his mistress."

"I'm not intending to be a mistress professionally," Lucy protested. "Just Sir Robert's. When he's tired of me, I'll marry some other man."

"I've heard that story more times than I can count," the woman derided. "Turned to a whore by love. How utterly boring. I can see there is no point introducing you to anyone else in our society, for you shall be on the street in months, spreading your legs for the ha'pence of sailors."

Suddenly Lucy felt the need to prove herself and she grasped at the woman's unanswered question.

"I was a maid at Harridan House, you know," Lucy drawled in her best imitation of Lady Blount, pleased when the woman's eyebrows arched upward in surprise. "Not a nymph, you see, but a lady's maid, in service to Madame Rouge."

"Then you know her identity." The woman's eyebrows swept back down as her gaze narrowed, her interest quickened. "Who is she?"

Lucy laughed, again drawing on the throaty tumbling sound she had practiced well. "I would never betray the lady so."

Miss Partridge invited her to a small gathering of a select few—an afternoon tea for her inner circle of the demimonde.

"You'll need friends, my dear," the woman purred, "for London is a dangerous town for courtesans."

Friends. Somehow Lucy doubted that she would find friends at this gathering if they were all like Miss Partridge—"Penny" as she wished to be called—but one could not sit around the house in wait of a man. Lucy was used to Harridan House, where there was always activity or someone with whom to chat. Here, there were too many hours of the day when he was not with her, and Lucy was terribly bored and terribly lonely.

She accepted.

Hours later, Robert arrived. He let himself in and found her in the parlor, lounging on the sofa in a new green silk dress, perusing the latest copy of *The Philosophical Magazine*, which he had forgotten a week earlier.

Which in itself was arousing, but then one leg was draped over the back of the sofa so that the dress gathered around her thigh and the long expanse of creamy flesh was laid out for him to see.

She saw him and smiled, tossing the magazine aside, and started to rise off the pillows to greet him.

"No, don't move," he ordered, coming closer. He laid his hand on her bare ankle even as he knelt down on the cushions between her legs.

Her smile grew as she relaxed, arching her back so that her breasts swelled over the very low neckline of her dress.

He ran his hand along her calf, up her thigh, pushing the cloth as he did till it bunched at her hips. Then he undid the falls of his trousers and settled himself over her, thrusting into her tight, heated flesh.

He groaned into her hair and then lifted himself back up to look at her.

"I've missed you," he said, circling his hips slowly, enjoying the way her eyes glazed over as he moved. She was so responsive, so open to him. He enjoyed learning everything about her, each reaction, each sensitive inch of her flesh.

"I missed you, too," she whispered. She reached up to caress his chest. He could feel the pressure of her touch through the many layers of cloth. Too many layers, he now realized, but the moment he'd seen her, legs parted so invitingly, he'd wanted only to seat himself within her as quickly as possible.

He moved slowly inside her, testing out each subtle movement. "How was Portsmouth?

"The shipment arrived and all is well."

She thrust her hips up toward him, grasping for more, but he stilled her with a firm hand at her hips.

"There's no rush, love," he said. "We have all night."

"Mmmmm." But she stilled her urgency and opened her eyes. Such a pretty, clear green. Like fresh grass. "Well, that's a relief for you then," she said, finally.

That was one of the many things he liked about the woman, she understood the value of hard work. It wasn't like the rest of society that branded trade vulgar even as their coffers dwindled.

"Yes, and I visited with Mr. Davy today."

"The man you said plays with that electricity?"

"He might take exception to the word 'play,'" Robert chided with a short laugh, "but he's working on a new invention I might invest in." It was a beguiling idea really. He'd never imagined such a thing possible, but it was a new world these days. First light from the coal-derived gas, now from electricity.

Odd, whoever had hung the painting in the far corner had done an abysmal job, for it was crooked and tilting to the right.

He groaned as she tightened around him, squeezing him. He didn't chastise her, for he could feel the fluttering motion of her body, the involuntary clenching. She was close, too close, and he had to decide if he was going to let her come just yet or if he wanted her to wait.

"I had a visitor as well," she gasped, and he could hear the tension in her voice, trying desperately to hold back the orgasm. "Miss Partridge came to welcome me."

"Penny?" He stopped moving and stared at Lucy. She forced her gaze on him again, but her eyes closed quickly again as she took a deep breath and swallowed hard.

"Robert," she pleaded, her voice high and breathy. "Please. Please."

He had to admit, he liked to hear her beg. To hear his name in that passionate voice of hers.

He laid his right palm flat on her lower belly and pushed himself deeper inside her. Then he arched back, to give space so that he could move his hand down and massage her flesh between his thumb and third finger.

She jerked under him, crying out and shaking. Her whole body moved with the force of the climax and he marveled at how she embraced it all, as if she'd been electrified. Each orgasm was different and each time she reacted slightly differently.

He pumped into her, short, hard strokes to pull more tremors from her body, to lengthen the ride. Finally, when she'd calmed to mere shivers, he stilled again.

"Do you think that's really possible, Robbie? To make light out of copper and zinc?"

"I don't know but it's exciting." Just thinking about the possibility intensified the pleasure he was feeling simply being encased in her heat. It had been hard enough to resist taking his own pleasure after being squeezed so vigorously by her cunt.

"How exciting!" Lucy flashed him one of her sly smiles, complete with *that look*.

He groaned again and, laying himself down over her, sucking her lower lip between his teeth, he took up a new rhythm: slow, long, deep strokes.

He knew his revival time was slower than it had been in his youth. If he went with this now . . .

"Robbie," she sighed, wrapping her legs around him, her thighs squeezing his hips. He slid his hand down, to hold the firm curve of her buttock.

Really, he didn't have much of a choice, he thought briefly before his climax hit. It came the way his movements had been, a long, deep shuddering that traveled all over his body till he felt it everywhere, even in his toes. He wrapped his arms around her and held her to him tightly, burying his head in the curve of her neck.

Could a man be more sated?

Chapter Twenty-Two

There was something distasteful about leaving Lucy's bed in order to call on Miss Clarke. Yet he was expected and the fact that he had changed his mind upon returning from Portsmouth, and had spent the night in his mistress's bed, should not upset his plans.

It did. He struggled to hide his irritable mood. He felt like a veritable codger, but even being aware didn't lesson the effect.

He found her in the sitting room, her mother close by. A bit of cloth peeked out of a work basket, which itself peeked out from behind her mother's chair. One small forgotten bead glittered on the floor beside it.

"It's so good of you to call," Mrs. Clarke gushed. "Mr. Clarke is not at home, but perhaps my daughter and I can entertain you?"

Robert spared a smile for Miss Clarke, who was much more reserved than her mother, eyeing him under pale lowered lashes. *Entertain* was such an unfortunate word. He could hardly imagine either of these women—the young girl fresh out of the schoolroom or her mother, who was closer to his age—knowing how to properly entertain a man.

Miss Clarke said softly, "You mentioned your estate is in Kent. Do you go there often?"

"No, hardly ever," Robert answered. "My brother's widow lives there now. I much prefer London, or my smaller estate in Sussex."

"The dowager house must be lovely," Mrs. Clarke said.

"Actually it's quite small, which is one of the many reasons my mother prefers her childhood home in Richmond. As I said, my brother's widow, Lady George, lives in the main house." Robert saw the next question in Mrs. Clarke's eyes. "I don't intend to inconvenience her."

"You're such a kind man," Miss Clarke said in that soft, dulcet voice. He wondered if that was how she spoke to her mother when there was no marriageable man around.

"Hardly," Robert returned with a laugh. "I simply enjoy London."

Miss Clarke didn't like that and Robert wondered what it was she didn't like: life in London, or that he'd somehow rejected her compliment?

"At Monsieur Molineaux's," Miss Clarke continued, pronouncing the French word abominably, her voice still soft but not quite as dulcet, "you mentioned your new stallion. Is he very large? Wonderfully powerful?"

It wasn't his horse that filled his mind at Miss Clarke's words, it was the image of Lucy after he'd taught her to ride, naked and sweaty astride him, urging him on. *You're so large inside me. This is much, much nicer than sidesaddle.*

Robert shifted uncomfortably in his seat. He couldn't do this, try to sit here and do the pretty when all he wanted to do was get back to Lucy.

"The horse performs admirably," Robert managed to say, and then steered the conversation to a safer topic.

The next twenty minutes passed interminably, and when politeness allowed, he gratefully took his leave.

There was something mildly attractive about Miss Clarke, but she was everything he had avoided since he knew what to avoid: fresh out of the schoolroom with more understanding of notions and beads than of any conversation that would matter to a man. Comely as she was, she was a virgin in a way that Lucy had never been. And last of all—perhaps most important of all—she didn't want him. She didn't say as much, or let on in any of the obvious ways, for she did, after all, want his money.

And that realization was far more dampening than any attraction he found in her soft, submissive voice.

Chapter Twenty-Three

Penny Partridge's sitting room was pink and white with lace and floral chintz everywhere. The women who filled the space were pink and white underneath their jewel-colored afternoon gowns.

These were what proper mistresses looked like. Lucy found herself studying her own new pale yellow muslin dress critically.

It was daytime and the dress that Mrs. Baswick had created for her was stylish but reserved, the fine muslin making her look every inch the proper lady. In front of her mirror at home, Lucy had been pleased with the way she looked. Here, among these women, she realized she was sadly outshone.

She would definitely need to lower her necklines.

They were like birds, their plumage out for effect, competing quite obviously with each other in their own little game. It might be midday, but there was no modesty here.

"What little mouse have you brought us, Penny?" One very rouged woman asked. "Don't tell me this is Sir Robert's mistress?"

Lucy laughed, drawing on all her best Madame Rouge affectations.

"A little Cornish mouse, Bess, that somehow found her way into Harridan House. Miss Leigh, allow me to present to you the ladies: Bess Nightingale, Regina Smitten, Calliope Andrews and Flora Pheasant."

After a round of "how do you do," the women settled back into gossip.

"Did you hear?" Calliope leaned forward, her voice in a theatrically hushed whisper. "Nan Lunt had enough of Jenny Smollett tempting her lover and has thrown the slut out."

Lucy smiled politely though she hadn't the faintest clue who either of the women were.

"Let this be a lesson to you, Miss Leigh." Penny Partridge wagged her finger toward her. "As fast as one rises, so does one fall."

"It's one thing to cuckold your protector discreetly, but to do so publicly?" Regina Smitten added.

"And when her contract specifically said she would forfeit everything Humboldt had ever given her if she did!"

"But you worked at Harridan House, Miss Leigh. Did you see the orgy?" Flora Pheasant asked. All the women leaned forward attentively for Lucy's answer.

"There are many orgies at the club," Lucy said with a shrug, "and so many are masked, I couldn't say."

The women grumbled and relaxed back into their lounging postures.

"Ah well, keep it as a caution, Miss Leigh: the life of a courtesan is not easy."

"Thank you for the advice," Lucy murmured, thinking this little gathering held much more in common with the frustrating battles she had with her sister than she would have imagined. She was not *this* bored. She would find ways to occupy herself.

"And for your dresses, Miss Leigh: really, Madame Fifi is much more fashionable. She dresses a woman as she should be dressed, not as some virginal little girl. Perhaps Sir Robert likes that though? Does he make you wear leading strings?"

Outraged, Lucy stared at Miss Partridge. She could accept the warnings and the pointed gossip, but suggesting anything about Robert she would not tolerate.

"Really, Penny," the one named Calliope chided, "whatever will Miss Leigh think of us if you say such things? Sir Robert is truly all that a noble protector should be."

Lucy drew on her gloves, noting with satisfaction that that simple action had made all of the women shut up.

"I'd better be going. Thank you very much for the invitation, Miss Partridge. It has been an edifying afternoon."

Edifying? Lucy inwardly laughed at herself as she left the room. Funny, the same word that had been so useful today had cost her the position with Mrs. Marrack three years ago when her employer took offense at the idea of a maid having an opinion.

Chapter Twenty-Four

D ammit!" Lucy cried out, as she stuck her scalp with a hairpin. She was too nervous, too excited to focus on the intricate style that really required another set of hands to do properly. She removed the pin, took a deep breath and let it out in three slow counts.

Just because tonight she was going to the theater for the first time since she'd come to London, would be sitting in a box, wearing an exquisite amber velvet dress with its newly lowered bodice, did not mean she couldn't do this. She *had* to do this. If her hair looked insipid, it wouldn't be fair to the dress.

"Miss, if you don't mind, you could let me do your hair for you," Charlotte offered hesitantly.

Lucy stared in surprise at Charlotte's reflection in the mirror.

"Can you?" At Charlotte's nod and hopeful eyes, Lucy lowered her hands. The girl was very young, just fourteen, had been hired more as a maid-of-all-work than as a lady's maid since Lucy mostly liked attending to herself. "Well, let's see what you can do."

Charlotte seemed to bounce with as much excitement as Lucy felt about the play, but her hands as they unpinned her hair were steady and sure. She brushed Lucy's hair thoroughly and then began separating the long waves into parts. Within a few minutes, Lucy could see a promising shape taking hold.

"You are quite good," Lucy said, admiring Charlotte's progress.

"Thank you, miss. I used to practice on my younger sisters. I want to be a lady's maid someday."

"I'll keep that in mind," Lucy said. "We'll see how you do."

Lucy watched Charlotte as she worked, her young thin face, her girlish body that hadn't even begun developing yet. Just fourteen and trying so hard to please. Lucy rarely thought of her early years in service, but right then, Charlotte reminded her so much of her younger self that it hurt.

What would she have said to a young Lucy if she could go back now? You're going to be a mistress someday, give up any shred of morality and respectability. *Run away?*

But then Lucy caught her own reflection in the mirror, her hair exquisitely coifed, the slightest bit of paint setting off her eyes and highlighting her cheekbones. She knew Robert would be pleased with how she looked tonight, maybe so pleased she wouldn't quite make it through the carriage ride looking so completely perfect.

Enjoy it, Lucy thought with a satisfied smile. That's what she'd tell herself.

"By God, that's the best money ever spent on a dress!" Robert exclaimed when she finally joined him in the front parlor, where he'd been waiting the last ten minutes. She looked magnificent, as if she'd been poured into that dress. If it weren't the opening night of Sarah Siddons playing Lady Macbeth, after all the rumors of the actress quitting the theater for good, he'd march Lucy straight back upstairs.

But it was Siddons, and Lucy had said she'd never been to Covent Garden, let alone any other theater in London.

He stalked toward her, thinking he'd have to walk half behind her skirts all evening for decency's sake.

"Do you think so?" Lucy frowned, drawing her gloved hand across the pale upper curve of her breasts. Actually, the luscious expanse of flesh was quite a bit more than the upper curve. He was certain if he looked just so . . . "I was worried you wouldn't like it."

Robert laughed, snatching her hand away and replacing it with his mouth. He found the nipple he'd been looking for and tugged it out of its meager confines with his teeth. He heard her moan, felt her soften against him.

"Oh, no you don't!" Lucy exclaimed, suddenly pushing him away. "We'll have to save that for later." She threw him one of her looks and he shifted his cock in his breeches, looking for some sort of relief. "I rather think the waiting will heighten the fulfillment."

"If I get any fuller, Lucy, you won't be making it out of this room." He reached for her again, but instead of kissing her, he tucked the errant nipple back beneath the fabric of her dress. "Shall we?"

She loved the theater. It was big and gaudy and completely like Harridan House, although everyone was wearing quite a bit more.

And the play was wonderful. The only Shakespeare she'd ever

seen was when she was eight and a touring theater company had put on a production of *A Midsummer Night's Dream*, full of fairies and people getting lost, and though her father had laughed and slapped his thigh—she'd been scared of the big donkey head. Tonight was different. She was very glad Mrs. Siddons had not retired.

When the intermission came, she hardly wanted to get up from her seat. Even though the first act was over, there was so much to look at in all the boxes and down below in the pit, but Robert insisted and she found herself in the shadows of the box, her back against the wall as Robert kissed her.

"I have been wanting to do that since we first sat down," Robert whispered as he moved to her cheek, to her ear, her neck.

"Mr. Kemble and Mrs. Siddons didn't keep you enthralled?" Lucy asked, even though Robert had found the one thing that could distract her from their surroundings.

"Siddons yes, but her brother leaves much to be desired. You, however, leave nothing."

Just as Lady Macbeth plotted and pushed her husband to greater heights, each time the scenery changed, Robert teased Lucy, tormenting her with her own words that *anticipation would only sweeten the fulfillment.*

It was during the second intermission that a slender Gallic man parted the blue curtains and popped his head in.

"Forgive my intrusion," the man said with a wink. "But as I am charged with obtaining refreshments for my wife and she is still in her seat, I thought I'd say hello and meet the woman who has so obviously bewitched you."

"Ah, Molineaux. Lucy, may I present my friend, Raoul Molineaux? Molineaux, this is Miss Leigh."

Molineaux's gaze raked over her appreciatively. "A pleasure, Mademoiselle Leigh," he said, lifting her hand to his lips.

"I've heard so much about you, monsieur," Lucy returned, retrieving her hand. It was strange, at Harridan House, in the guise of Madame Rouge, she'd had any number of men kiss her hand in greeting, but somehow, it felt far more personal now that she was merely Lucy. "And your wife, naturally," she added, "which one is she?" She surveyed the boxes for a woman who looked like she would match Molineaux.

Instead she saw Mrs. Marrack with her husband. The woman's gaze flittered over Lucy but didn't linger. Which was exactly what Lucy had expected, because she looked nothing like she had three years ago.

Molineaux coughed and Lucy flushed, realizing then what she should have known already: she could hardly force the man to stand at the edge of the box with her and point out his wife. She was a mistress and men didn't introduce mistresses to their wives.

Molineaux turned his attention to Robert. "A pity, mon amie, that I cannot stay with you longer, but Madame Molineaux . . ." He shrugged.

"Naturally," Robert agreed.

"I'm so sorry, Robert, I didn't mean to embarrass you," Lucy whispered after Molineaux had left, conscious that she had committed a faux pas. "Do you think he'll forgive me? Do *you* forgive me?"

"It was nothing, Lucy," Robert said, laughing, gesturing to a box across the way where Molineaux was joining a lovely woman with inky black curls that bobbed around her face as she laughed. "And it made him leave all the sooner. Now I have you to myself again."

It wasn't his laugh or his words that relieved Lucy, it was his hand running across her thigh as if he'd burn the fabric right off of her body.

But Lucy would not forget, for it was just as the women in Miss Partridge's living room had said: everything, her situation, her stability, depended on Robert. Which was why it was even more important that Lucy prepare for her life after—for the tavern she didn't really want.

Chapter Twenty-Five

The weeks flew by, lulling Lucy into a sense of security and contentment. London was a different town for her. There were the plays and the pantomimes, the excitement of horse races or the occasional outing to the country. But surprisingly to Lucy, what she liked best were evenings at home with Robert.

She admired him. Not just his body, but the way he lived his life, unapologetic and following his own desires and interests. And when he talked about business, or politics, or science or any of a number of topics that had captured his attention, she hung on his every word. He was curious about everything and it made her equally curious.

Although Lucy never pretended to herself that this time of her life could last forever, the dreams of a respectable future that she had nurtured while working at Harridan House no longer held any appeal. This life of sin was not perfect, but it was better than anything else she could imagine.

It was early November when Lucy realized she was with child. Dr. Berry, the physician who lived on the other side of the street, confirmed her suspicion.

She had known it was possible, that a child was always a danger of sex, but Lucy had no idea how Robert would react. Would he support her and the child? Would he tire of her as soon as her body was swollen and ugly? She thought of all those courtesans she had met and their talks of contracts.

She should have paid far more attention that day at the lawyer's. Certainly the man had said *something* about children, but Lucy hadn't really listened to that part.

How could she tell him?

She went to Mary because she was her sister—family—and right then, Lucy needed family.

For the first time since she left Harridan House, Mary didn't insult her. Her expression was deadly earnest when she stood up out of bed and took Lucy's hand.

"You can't have it, Lucinda," Mary warned her. "I know a doctor . . . He's the one who fixed me when I needed it."

The shock was not so much from the idea of the abortion but from the fact that Mary actually seemed to have Lucy's best interests in mind. Not that Lucy agreed with the option. She lived a different life; Mary didn't understand. Even if Robert put Lucy aside for it, she didn't think she could do what Mary suggested.

Lucy nodded slowly, until her sister released her hand.

"All right, then, we'll go now," Mary said. She started toward her dresser energetically.

"Mary, I have to think," Lucy hedged. She didn't want to wholly reject the first real sign of compassion Mary had shown in two years.

"You're keeping it, aren't you?" Mary dropped her hands from the wood cabinet and shook her head with a bitter laugh.

Again, Lucy nodded.

"What about our pub, Lucy, our dreams? You're giving it all away, keeping this child. He'll tire of you and then you'll have lost your employment."

"I have to, Mary."

"Then what are you doing here, sister?" Mary goaded scornfully. "You'd better hurry home and start your packing."

Chapter Twenty-Six

Lucy put the conversation off for three days, but when Robert arrived at the apartment before dinner on the third day and found her pacing the sitting room as if she'd walk a trench into the wooden floor, she could barely put it off a moment longer.

But she did. She waited through dinner, waited until they were back in the sitting room having a digestif of Armagnac, his free hand lazily wandering over her legs, which were draped across his thighs in the most inelegant but utterly enjoyable way.

"Robert," Lucy began, as if it were a topic of the least concern possible, "what should happen if we should have a child?"

"A child?" he repeated, his hand never stilling. "Surely you've learned something about prevention of conception in your years at Harridan House?"

"Yes, but what if there were an accident? It isn't as though the sponges are as good as those sheaths you hate."

"I would make provisions for the child as I have done for the others."

"Others?"

He looked rather amused at that, and Lucy almost pushed his hands away. The one thing she hadn't imagined was that he might laugh at her.

"A man doesn't get to be my age and not have a few by-blows. There are three that I know of. A boy and two girls. Well, four if Lady Greenaway is to be believed, but as that young man is officially a Greenaway, it would do little good for me to acknowledge him."

"Three?"

"Yes, two are in London. Meg, the oldest, is married now. I see my son fairly regularly. The other girl, Alissa—when her mother died, I sent her to school."

It was both a shock and a relief to hear about his children and how he cared for them.

"I may not be the most attentive father," Robert admitted, "but I do look after them."

Which was more than many fathers did for their own legitimate children, Lucy acknowledged. Her father had been one of those.

"So you wouldn't be angry then, if I did. I mean, because it would create difficulties, in our relations I mean."

He gave her the force of his full attention then.

"Lucy?"

She nodded, biting her lower lip, struggling not to look away and hide. "Because, truly, Robert, I'd understand . . ."

"Lucy." His tone was much more warm, kind, melting her really. He pulled her toward him, wrapping her in his arms. "My dearest girl."

She settled against his chest, listening to the steady beating of his heart, willing hers to match his pace.

"You have nothing to fear."

Which was the moment that Lucy learned that her passionate, rough, ofttimes crude and demanding lover could be utterly and embarrassingly sweet.

And when she understood that the expansive tugging in her chest was love.

Love.

Lucy wasn't a romantic. She hadn't been for over a decade and she certainly wasn't one now. She had entered her latest employment with eyes wide open. She had given up respectability and virtue for the fleeting passion and contracted generosity of a life of gallantry.

She had thought she understood the situation, knew the pitfalls and had taken steps, though not extensive, to forestall pregnancy. However, she had taken no pains to protect her heart.

Now Lucy knew that was a grave mistake. It was one thing to walk away from an affair financially improved and emotionally independent. It was quite another to know she would pine for Robert even after he had tossed her aside.

There would always be the child to link them, even after many years. She would mother his child and watch him with woman after woman, perhaps even a wife. Perhaps even that Miss Ambrose he claimed to dislike.

Her heart her own she could bear anything. Her heart his . . .

Lucy shook her head to disperse the thoughts. There was no use for that sort of maudlin self-pity. Thinking about the future was only borrowing trouble, and trouble Lucy did not want.

Chapter Twenty-Seven

The necklace was exquisite. Lucy had seen jewels glittering off the bodies of the ladies who frequented Harridan House incognito and in the collections of her former employers, but often as not they were paste. There was no doubt in her mind that these were the genuine article. The cut, the purity, the way the stones caught the light, were all magnificent. It was far beyond the little baubles he'd given her thus far.

She turned away from the window and looked back at him, to where he still lay on the bed.

"So this is what you were doing this morning," she said, undoing the clasp. He was by her side in a moment, taking the necklace from her and draping it across her chest.

"I wish to give you a gift, Lucy," he murmured. "Lift your hair a bit."

She reached back and gathered her hair up above her head

while he fastened the clasp. When he was done, she let her hair down and walked over to the mirror.

"They're so lovely."

Emeralds and diamonds winked back at her, cascading down her neck to dip almost into the hollow between her breasts.

"Thank you very much, Robert, really it's too generous."

Robert laughed. "I'm quite certain your Miss Partridge never said such a thing in her life."

"Oh," Lucy said, quietly. Then she laughed as well. "As it's only what I deserve, what else do you have for me?" she teased. She turned back to face him, her hand up in the air as if he should place another black velvet case in it.

"Exactly so," Robert approved, "because I do wish to give you a gift, but it's not one I can simply present to you fait accompli. It requires your participation."

"Oh?" This time Lucy said the word with a flirtatious inflection of her voice and tilt of her head. "I think the gift you would give me has already taken root."

"A house, my dear, deeded to you," he persisted. "But I thought perhaps you might wish a country house rather than one in the city. Of course, in that instance, we will keep your rooms here as they are."

A house. Her house! Then the initial shocked wonder turned. Was this her congé? Did he wish to "put her out to pasture," so to speak?

For the briefest moment she wanted to reject the house, yell at him that the only gift she really wanted was for him to let her stay, to love her the way she loved him.

Which was an appalling thought and Lucy pushed it away immediately.

"Because I'm carrying your child?"

The pleased smile he'd been wearing fell.

"Is it not natural?" Robert demanded. "I wish to ease any fears you may have about the future." He grabbed her shoulders, forcing her to look at him, pleading with her to understand.

Ease her fears? Of course he wished to. He was Sir Robert

George, whom she loved, who was both fiercely passionate and surprisingly tender.

Just as his lips touching hers now carried that intoxicating mix—passionately tender.

It never failed to amaze Lucy how each time they joined, it was utterly different. Even when it was simply him covering her with his body, her legs wrapped around his, there were different shades, different qualities to the lovemaking.

Lovemaking. For her that was what it had become, a far cry from the first days back in Harridan House. Sometimes when they were joined, she even forgot which limbs were his and which were hers.

But right then, sitting on the edge of the bed with his cock sliding into her, she knew exactly what belonged to him.

And she welcomed it. She welcomed him home.

Chapter Twenty-Eight

By the end of February, Lucy knew it was time to order new clothes. Even with the current style conveniently falling straight below the bosom, she could no longer hide the swollen curve of her belly.

But it was Robert one night, as they lay in bed, who made it very clear that if she didn't go to the dressmaker and get clothes that actually fit her, he'd send her off to that cottage he'd purchased for her and keep her in confinement till the baby was born.

"I can't help it, Robert, my breasts are fuller now."

"I know and I like it, but they're mine, not for the whole world to see."

Lucy laughed at that.

"Robert, first of all, it isn't as if a woman expecting is of any attraction to a man." The look on his face let her know that argument was completely useless and reminded her of the time that Lord Dobson at Harridan House had specifically requested . . . She pushed her thoughts back to the matter at hand. "Second of all, I love you. I have no need for anyone else, in my heart or in my bed. Our bed."

"It's other people's thoughts that bother me," he muttered, but let the subject drop, let her fall asleep.

Our bed. Simple words but they conjured up such an exceeding domesticity. It made him realize just how much this rented maisonette had become his home more than the house in Mayfair. All because she lived here and thus this was where he wanted to be.

Her declaration of love didn't surprise him. He'd known, somehow he'd known, understood it in the way she looked at him, in the way her face seemed to glow whenever he returned, even when she'd been having that morning sickness.

Furthermore, it was not uncommon for a woman to "love" the man who protected her. Indeed, it was practically part of the bargain. But still . . .

She was five months along, not quite ready for her confinement. He hadn't been there for the birth of his other children. He had known the women were expecting and then had come to visit after.

He stroked his hand over the curve of her hip. Pregnancy had changed her body. She was rounded now all over. He enjoyed watching her body change, knowing that it was his seed that caused it.

He hadn't seen the other pregnancies of his children's mothers.

He moved his hand to her stomach, caressing the distended skin, smooth and fragrant from the vanilla-scented creme Lucy massaged in every day to keep supple.

He hadn't slept with Lucy in over a fortnight. She'd seemed too ill and fragile for such a thing. He had not slept with anyone in that time actually, nor anyone but Lucy since the day at Harridan House when she'd drawn him through those doors.

If that constancy wasn't some sort of love, what was it?

Here he was, about to be a father again. He could give this child his name. And he liked Lucy. How difficult would it be to live with her as his wife? He slept in her bed most nights as it was.

Wife?

Robert couldn't breathe. The tightness in his chest alarmed him. Then he let out his pent-up breath and turned onto his back.

What was he thinking?

He peeked over at her. She lay exactly as she had been and he studied the beauty marks that dotted the pale skin of her back. How many times had he kissed those marks in these past months, one at the base of her neck, one under her right shoulder blade, working his way down her body, to the one on the upper curve of her left buttock?

He didn't need a rich wife, or a titled one. Perhaps he needed a respectable wife, but then why should he ask more of the woman than he asked of himself? Could he imagine his life, every morning and every day, with this woman?

With Lucy?

Of course, he could do as he had planned earlier, keep her as his mistress for as long as he wished and marry another woman. But the idea of two households, two women in his life, a woman other than Lucy that he had to please, did not appeal. Not in the slightest.

He sighed. So this was how far he'd come, from wanting every woman to just wanting one.

As if she knew he thought of her, Lucy stirred, turning over and reaching for him. Even with her eyes closed, she found him unerringly, nestling her body against his. It was awkward, and her belly rested on his hip, but she burrowed her face against his chest and he could feel the even intake and exhalation of her breath across his skin.

He shifted her slightly so that he could wrap his arm around her, rest his hand on that part of her hip that seemed made for him.

"Lucy?" He felt her eyelids flutter against his chest and she moved infinitesimally, but then stilled again. "Lucy?" he prodded, slightly louder.

"Mmmm?" Lucy managed to vocalize as she held on to the last warm blanket of sleep.

"I was thinking, love . . ."

"I like when you think," Lucy murmured, running her hand sleepily down his chest. They hadn't had sex in far too long and suddenly it seemed like the very thing she craved. Her fingers closed over his cock, which was surprisingly soft at first and then started to fill her hand.

"Lucy." His rested his hand on hers, stopping her movement.

She finally opened her eyes, hearing the strain in his voice, the hesitancy. He sounded so very unlike himself.

"I'm feeling better, I promise," she assured him, rubbing her breasts against his arm—those ridiculously large breasts that had absorbed all his attention earlier that night.

He pushed her hand away, off of him, and Lucy's smile disappeared.

This was it. The moment her sister had warned about. Hell, the moment Penny Partridge had warned her of. It was over. He'd even hinted at it before she'd fallen asleep with talk of the cottage he'd bought her.

She rolled away from him, onto her back, and flung her arm over her face, hiding her eyes.

She would not cry. She'd told herself again and again that she would not, that when this time came she would plan for the future, think of the tavern, think of her baby and the cottage and all the wonderful memories she had saved up.

Memories. Despite herself, her arm grew wet against her eyes.

The bed shook and then he loomed over her, torturing her with his heat, his scent.

"I'm glad you're feeling better, I really am; it's just, first I wanted to discuss something with you."

He sounded slightly more like himself, and Lucy dragged her arm away from her face, trying to discreetly wipe away the tears as she did. Whatever he had to say, she would have to face it at some point.

"You're crying?" He stared down at her in wonder. "By God, I don't think I've ever seen you cry. Not even when you were puking your dinner, your lunch *and* your breakfast into the chamber pot."

"What did you want to discuss?" Lucy managed, trying to keep calm, but it was so difficult with his body half over her, his hand resting so possessively on her belly.

Robert laughed. "You'd think as I've waited forty-two years for this moment, I'd manage to do it somewhat romantically, but here we are, having a discussion and you're crying."

"Romantically?" Lucy stared at him, wondering how someone she knew and loved so well could look so much like a stranger.

"Right." He let himself down till he rested on his side, his head propped up on his hand. "I'm asking you to marry me."

Lucy did cry then, more from shock than from anything else. Those words were the last thing in the world she had ever expected from him. This was not real. This was some fairy tale into which she'd awoken. It was hard to believe but he was looking at her, expecting her to say something, expecting an answer.

Yes, yes, of course yes!

But she was too full of all the confusing emotions to speak, so she didn't. She turned onto her side, ungainly from the pregnancy, and kissed him. From the way his hands roamed her body, she was absolutely certain that he understood.

Chapter Twenty-Nine

Lucy went the next day to tell Mary. But even as she made the long journey across town, this time giving in to the exhaustion of pregnancy by hiring a hack, she knew it wasn't a good idea. She wasn't entirely certain of the reason she kept torturing herself with these visits.

Mary huddled under her blankets and Lucy could understand why, for a cold draft snuck through the poorly sealed window. The hard, thin line of her sister's mouth was another matter entirely.

"Come Mary, for once can you not simply be happy for me?"

"Happy for you? The little princess? It doesn't matter what poor choices you make in life, there's always someone to save you, help you out, whether it's me, that Madame Rouge, or now your baronet."

Lucy's hands fell to her belly, as if she had to protect the unborn child when it was really her own heart that ached.

"You're my only family, Mary," Lucy said, as evenly as she could. "It's you and me in this world. That's what you said to me when Mrs. Marrack fired me and I came to you."

"Wrong, sister, it's you and your baronet. I only have myself to look after. Only me."

They stayed there in silence, their gazes locked.

Then Mary broke away. "I'm not too proud to take the money though," she admitted. "I want that pub. I'll need an income after I can't give a good tup anymore."

Chapter Thirty

It was ridiculous how unburdened he felt. No more searching for a wife, no more worrying about an heir, at least if the child was a male. Even if not, there would likely be more. He could have everything he wanted in one package: mistress, wife, mother of his children. *Lucy.*

And having made the decision, everything changed.

The afternoon that he went to tell Molineaux, even Clarissa remarked on it.

"Many men marry their mistresses, Robert," she informed him, explaining her pleasure at the match. "And we'd be very honored if you'd let us host your wedding breakfast."

Robert cocked an eyebrow toward Molineaux, but his friend merely shrugged with a small smile.

"You wanted me to marry Miss Clarke," Robert reminded her.

"That was months ago, and I thought you would never fall in love. But you have, utterly. It's quite remarkable." Clarissa clapped her hands together in satisfaction.

Robert coughed, embarrassed despite himself. Of course he loved Lucy, but it wasn't at all the sort of relationship Molineaux had with his wife. Robert knew clearly he didn't need Lucy the way she needed him. He could walk away, find another woman, many other women, satisfy himself in all the old ways he used to satisfy himself. He might not wish to, but he could.

"I appreciate and accept your generous offer," Robert said, finally.

"Excellent!" Clarissa said. "Of course, we really should ask Lucy, and of course, I'll need a list . . ."

Robert listened to her ramble on about all the things that would need to be done, even as she left the room. He was lucky in his friends; his mother hadn't been remotely as accepting.

"She's a good woman, your wife," he said, raising his glass to his friend.

Molineaux smiled, raising his glass as well. "I know."

Chapter Thirty-One

She had nothing to wear. She was getting married in three weeks. To Robert. To Sir Robert George, baronet, and here she was, fat with child, making her best dress look like the casing for a sausage.

"It's not that bad, miss," Charlotte said, holding Lucy's hair back so that they could better see the neckline. "I'll let it out a bit."

But there wasn't enough extra fabric in the seams to cover her belly, and then, when she let out her breath, they both heard the tearing sound of stitches bursting.

"Get it off, now," Lucy ordered, her eyes damp despite knowing how silly it was to cry over this. She was happy, ridiculously so, but she wanted to make sure Robert was happy too. He might be marrying a common woman but she didn't have to look like one.

The sound of the heavy knocker falling on the front door briefly stilled Charlotte's hands. They both heard the familiar sound of the footman and then the less-familiar muffled sound of a woman's voice.

Mary.

"Shall I go see who it is, miss?" Charlotte asked.

"It's all right, I will go down and see." Lucy reached for a shawl, a large paisley wrap that didn't go with her dress but covered her up well enough.

As she walked carefully down the stairs, Lucy's heart seemed to pound in her chest. She hadn't realized how much she wanted or needed this. How much she wanted somebody standing by her, somebody with whom she could share her joy and fear.

She met the footman at the base of the stairs.

"Where is she?" Lucy asked, already walking past him.

"I put her in the front parlor," he answered. "I have her card, miss."

It was only when she had already stepped across the threshold of the parlor and spotted the petite, fashionably plump woman with ink-black curls that the footman's words registered with her. Mary didn't have calling cards.

And naturally, this well-dressed woman was not Mary.

It was Madame Molineaux.

Lucy was uncomfortably aware of how she looked, her hair hanging down her back like she was a schoolchild, nearly bursting the seams of her dress. Before Lucy could apologize, the woman was striding across the room to her, hands reached out to take hers.

"Pardon the intrusion, Miss Leigh, but Sir Robert visited us today and told us the happy news."

Lucy let the woman take her hands, even though her shawl slipped to her elbows and revealed far more of her dress than she wished.

"I don't know if you realize, but Robert and my husband, well, they were friends for years before I married, and to hear Raoul say it, everything we have today is because of Robert's generosity."

Although it was Lucy's parlor and Madame Molineaux was only a few years older, the other woman had a motherly way about her and Lucy found herself being settled onto the sofa as if she'd been invited over for a little coze.

"Robert, I believe, sees it the other way," Lucy said hesitantly, not wanting to insult the other woman by challenging her words.

"Of course he would." Madame Molineaux smiled happily. "They're such good men, your fiancé and my husband."

It was ridiculous how easily they fell into friendship. Within minutes they had dropped any formality and Lucy found herself telling Clarissa about her dress.

"This dress?" Clarissa studied it carefully. "You're absolutely right, this won't do. Let's get you a new one."

As easy as that, Lucy thought, feeling something inside her snap—the last threads that tied her to her past. There was no turning back now. She was giving up the loneliness of her life in service and stepping fully into Robert's life.

She would not—could not—look back.

Chapter Thirty-Two

The three weeks that passed played tricks with Lucy's sense of time, at once feeling both far too short and far too long. Shopping with Clarissa had been wonderful. For the first time she had fully enjoyed the activity. Everything was different when done with a friend, and as the days passed, Lucy realized it was a relationship she hadn't had since she was a child.

Clarissa had been the one to suggest the pale blue silk that now draped her body in flattering folds, and had handed Charlotte the page from *La Belle Assemblee* that showed the hairstyle she thought Lucy should wear. And now she was the one who stood by Lucy's side in Clarissa's parlor while they waited for the reverend to arrive. It was a far cry from the day, so many months before, when Raoul hadn't even wanted to point out his wife to Lucy.

Lucy had suspected it would be a small wedding. She had

no one to invite on such short notice, and even on longer notice she wasn't entirely certain she would have invited her parents. Most of Robert's family had refused to attend, all except his widowed cousin, who surprised them all when she arrived the night before.

But Lucy was completely happy. For somewhere, out in Clarissa's drawing room, was Robert. Robert, who had spent every last night in her bed, who had left that morning with the greatest reluctance, wondering why they couldn't simply arrive together. Robert, with whom she seemed to fall in love more every day.

Robert . . .

Molineaux's drawing room was stuffy and hot, although no one else seemed to be complaining. Maybe it was simply the ridiculously complicated arrangement of his cravat that Peters had insisted upon.

Robert found it difficult to breathe, difficult to think. Then Lucy walked in and for a moment, his breath left him entirely.

There were times that Robert looked into Lucy's face and saw that she loved him. Really, truly, beyond a shadow of a doubt loved him. But it was so easy to forget, until one of those moments happened, and he would meet her gaze, actually see the human she was, and know that she loved him.

Standing there, in Molineaux's drawing room, with the reverend asking them to gather before him to bind themselves to each other for life, was one of those moments.

Forty-two years of age seemed rather late for a man to have an epiphany.

He loved her. It wasn't simply that he would never choose to walk away: there was no way in the world that he could.

Robert took Lucy's hands in his own, the smoothness of her white silk gloves startling him. Then he laughed, suddenly calmer and more sure than he had been of anything in his life. Lucy met his gaze with her own, her expression shifting from curiosity to understanding to a promise of the hours to come.

Of course she understood. She always did. And if he paused

the ceremony, urged her out of the room for a few moments, he rather suspected she'd lead the way.

Robert sighed happily, stroking her palm through the silk. Perhaps it was improper for a man to be visibly aroused at his own wedding, but then again, when had they ever been proper?

PART V

Epilogue

February 1809

*D*amn the snow, Jenny thought as she trudged across the inn
yard toward the stables, trying to see through the flurry that
clung damply to her cloak, her cheeks, her messily reconstituted
knot of straw-blond hair. A round blob entered her field of view,
bringing with it the sharp sensation of ice. Yes, there was even a
snowflake on her nose.

If the storm would just let up, she could leave this godforsaken
place where she'd been reduced to sleeping with the stable hands
for pence. How far she'd lowered herself in seven months! She'd
been at the pinnacle of life, given every lovely dress and bauble
she could desire, and all she'd had to do was give it up to old Lord
Humboldt. Make the poor man think she was quivering at his
every touch and only had eyes for him.

It should have been easy.

But dammit, she'd never once come at the old man's hands!
Quite frankly, when the athletic and young Lord Sedgwick cor-
nered her in the hallway at Miss Partridge's masquerade and whispered all the naughty things they could do, his finger running up
her thigh, she'd felt more pleasure than she had in all the time
she'd been with Humboldt.

Only four weeks in, she'd let Sedgwick lift her skirts and fuck
her behind the screen in the ladies' retiring room. She should have

been satisfied with that stolen moment, but no, once she'd had a taste of what she could get away with, she'd met Sedgwick again and again, until the night she'd followed him to Harridan House, in disguise of course, and participated in his spontaneous orgy.

And what an orgy! Her knees went weak and her cunt grew heavy and moist just thinking about the night.

Jenny's progress across the yard was stopped by the arrival of a carriage. A stately, expensively rigged carriage at which even Jenny stopped to look, despite the weather. After all, with the two grooms coming out to meet the carriage, it wasn't as if she'd have any work, for a few minutes yet, anyway.

A uniformed footman opened the door and out stepped a gentleman whose greatcoat billowed about him in such a way that she didn't get much of an impression other than tall and blond.

The gentleman helped down a lady, and despite the woman's own heavy cloak, Jenny couldn't help but notice the auburn curls that peeked out beneath her bonnet.

When the wind swept the cape open just enough, Jenny sighed, admiring the woman's fashionable clothing. She sighed again and turned her attention back to the man. His back was to her but she could tell that his boots were well made, hugging his shapely calves.

Then Jenny realized the woman was looking at her strangely, as if she knew her, but Jenny didn't know any ladies. Her friends in the demimonde could hardly be termed ladies. Yet the woman did look slightly familiar. One would think Jenny would recognize a lady with hair that strikingly red.

Irritated, Jenny brushed at the skirt of her dress. Unless the woman and her husband were planning on a threesome this evening, she wished they would bugger off and leave her to earn a few bob so she could make her way back to London.

With all those soldiers back from the Peninsula, surely there'd be a few wounded gents in the city needing a bit of comfort.

The woman seemed to make a decision and let her husband lead her away. But then Jenny decided to have some fun. She sauntered up to the pair.

"Evening, sir," she addressed the gentleman. He was handsome now that she looked at him, all that blond hair and those icy blue eyes. He looked like he'd be good in bed. His lady had that well-pleasured look about her. He did too, as a matter of fact.

The man seemed like he was about to wave her away, but his lady stopped him, murmuring something low that Jenny didn't catch.

"M'lady." Jenny finally bobbed a saucy curtsey toward the woman, throwing in one of her seductive looks, which had won her Humboldt.

The lady's eyes widened and that was when Jenny knew that the woman was no stranger to having a fuck with another woman.

Maybe she would make a bit of money out of this.

"It's an awfully cold night, perhaps you might be needing another body to help warm your bed?"

"Excuse me?" The gentleman gaped at her, but the lady laughed and slanted a teasing look up at her man. Then the gentleman's tense stance eased.

Jenny smiled at them hopefully.

"Miss Smollett."

Jenny jerked from her thoughts in surprise at hearing her name.

"How on earth did you come to this?"

"Do I know you, my lady?" Jenny asked, staring at the woman warily now.

"No, I suppose you don't." The lady seemed a bit bemused.

"Well then, how do you know me?" Jenny glanced at the man who was with her, but he merely shrugged.

"Weren't you Lord Humboldt's mistress?"

Suddenly Jenny saw her mistake. This lady, for all her finery, was this man's mistress.

"What of it?" Jenny placed her hands on her hips. "Who the hell are you to ask?"

"The lady . . ." the man began, clearly angered and reaching for the woman's arm. But his mistress shrugged him off.

"It's just a surprise, really," the woman interrupted. "I suppose he didn't take the cuckolding too well?"

"As if that were news," Jenny returned scornfully. Her stupidity was likely the new byword in the demimonde. After all, not every woman was naive enough to sign a contract she hadn't read all the way through.

"And Sedgwick didn't provide for you at all?"

"Who are you?"

"Come, Miss Smollett, why don't you join us by the fire in the inn and we can discuss this further.

The gentleman seemed about to protest, but the lady turned to him, said something, and a moment later he sighed resignedly.

Jenny followed them inside, still somewhat hopeful to see a profit. After all, they were inviting her to join them.

An hour later, after the best meal Jenny had had in three weeks, she'd managed to reveal everything that had happened to her over the past seven months to Sir Jason and Lady Blount.

"We are going back to London," Lady Blount remarked, glancing toward her husband. They shared one of those long looks that Jenny had begun to realize communicated much more than a look should. "It would be no trouble at all to take you up with us in our carriage."

No trouble? Of course it would be trouble, but if these Blount folks were do-gooders, Jenny wouldn't quarrel with them. Whatever got her back to London.

Or perhaps they merely wanted a bit of entertainment on the road. Jenny was rather skilled at maneuvering around a moving carriage.

"Please, Miss Smollett" —Sir Jason held up his hand as if he knew exactly what she had been about to say— "no *show of gratitude* is necessary."

"As you wish." Jenny shrugged. She bet if the lady were alone she might be more interested in the idea.

The storm passed. Much later that evening, as the well-sprung carriage rolled as evenly as it could on the rough London road and Jenny Smollett lay sleeping in the far corner from Diana,

Jason caught Diana's hand in his own, thoughtfully tracing his index finger over the seams of her glove.

From the moment he had heard Miss Smollett describe the infamous orgy that had cost her her position, the idea had been brewing in his head. The girl had unabashedly reveled in the decadence. She genuinely loved sex, was perfectly suited to the world of the demimonde, except that a man wanted fidelity in a mistress and fidelity clearly bored her.

He squeezed Diana's hand. Very unlike Diana, though even now, four months after that day in Bath, three and a half months after their wedding, he still felt an instinctive twinge of jealousy. Roughly, he forced the thoughts away.

Back to Miss Smollett. She had clearly learned her lesson about impetuosity. If she could be believed, and he was inclined to believe her, her experiences since losing Humboldt, to being dropped so far from London with no way to get back, had hardened her, made her wiser and more worldly.

"I was thinking, love," he said quietly. "As you were planning to sell the place anyway . . . ?"

Diana looked at him sharply. "She might do very well for one of the nymphs or Grecian girls but . . . to run the place?"

"You said yourself if you didn't want to, with your manager as conscientious as he is, you never really had to look at the books or handle any of the business."

"But . . ." Diana looked away, biting her lip.

"You don't really want to get rid of it, do you?"

She turned back quickly, wrapping her hand around his and drawing him closer.

"I do, truly I do, but it's so hard, you must understand, to actually let go." Her gaze locked with his as she pleaded with him to understand. "It was a part of me, defining me, for so long. My past, you know. But I don't *want* it."

He sighed. He did understand. Funny, he'd thought being married would mean the end of any heartache, minor or otherwise, but somehow there were always little things that made him need to be reassured.

Her gaze flittered away for a moment, to where Jenny was still sleeping. Then a small, mischievous smile crossed Diana's face—a smile he recognized and his body recognized.

"Do I have to show you just how much I love you?" Diana whispered, letting go of his hand to caress his thigh, inching her way up.

He sighed, closing his eyes as her hand covered his cock, which was now hard and straining against his trousers.

"I'm not quite sure *this* is love," he returned, unbuttoning his falls to allow her better access. He hardly cared if Miss Smollett did wake up and see them amorously engaged. He wasn't the one who had invited her to ride with them, and anyway, if she was shocked by such a thing, it would be better to know now.

Diana brought her lips closer to his face and just before her mouth touched his, he heard her words, barely even a whisper: "But I *do* love you, Jason, more than anything in this world."

Then she kissed him and showed him just how much.

When Jenny woke next, the brick beneath her feet had lost all its warmth and her neck ached from leaning against her own shoulder. It took a moment, with the rocking of the moving carriage and the haziness of her mind, to remember where she was: on her way to London courtesy of Sir Jason Blount and his wife. She opened her eyes gingerly. The carriage was still dark, the curtains drawn, but from the thin sliver of light that peeked across the seat, she knew it was day.

They slept still, curled up in each other's arms in a way that made Jenny uneasy and vaguely nauseous. She wanted to open the curtains and see where they were, see if she could recognize the landscape, ask them how much longer, how much farther to London, but instead she shifted her weight, closed her eyes again and slept.

She woke up next to the bright glare of the midday sun and a hasty apology from Lady Blount.

"But we're here, Miss Smollett, in London," Lady Blount announced. The carriage was slowing down.

Jenny peered out at the street. It looked familiar, somewhat.

Then she saw the building they were passing. *Harridan House.* She wondered if Sir Jason and Lady Blount even knew what that place was. Sir Jason perhaps, as most men seemed to know.

The carriage turned down the street and then into the mews. Jenny stared at Sir Jason in surprise.

"Again, I must apologize, Miss Smollett," Lady Blount said with a throaty laugh that made Jenny distinctly nervous, "but as we didn't know where to drop you off and I have a proposition for you . . ."

For one brief moment, Jenny was angry. Was this some sort of ridiculous joke, that they would bring her to the scene of her greatest folly, where she had thrown away her chance at a career as a mistress?

"Please, Miss Smollett, let me explain." Lady Blount laughed again and then Jenny tilted her head in shock, staring at the woman in wonder.

Jenny heard the woman speak, but it was difficult to concentrate with this new revelation. They said Madame Rouge always wore a turban, but one imagined her hair to be red to suit the name and now with Lady Blount acting so strangely . . .

"Have you ever considered running an erotic club catering to the diverse sexual whims of the ton?"

Lady Blount pulled a wad of silk out of her reticule and then dangled the red mask in the air.

Jenny watched the silk wave hypnotically.

She? Madame Rouge?

SABRINA DARBY has been reading romance since the age of seven and learned her best vocabulary (dulcet, diaphanous, and turgid) from them. She started writing romance the day after her wedding when she woke up with an idea for a Regency; she's been back in the early nineteenth century ever since. Sabrina graduated from MIT and received her MFA from USC. She currently resides in California with her husband and their Cavalier King Charles spaniel.

Sabrina Darby